THE
SECRET KEEPER

**Center Point
Large Print**

Also by Sandra Byrd and available from
Center Point Large Print:

Ladies in Waiting series
  To Die For

**This Large Print Book carries the
Seal of Approval of N.A.V.H.**

THE SECRET KEEPER

A NOVEL OF KATERYN PARR

SANDRA BYRD

CENTER POINT LARGE PRINT
THORNDIKE, MAINE

This Center Point Large Print edition
is published in the year 2012 by arrangement with
Howard Books, a division of Simon & Schuster, Inc.

All Old Testament Scripture quotations are taken from the
King James Version. Public domain. All New Testament
Scripture quotations are taken from *Tyndale's New
Testament*, a modern-spelling edition of the 1534 translation
with an introduction by David Daniell.
Translated by William Tyndale. Copyright © 1989 by
Yale University Press. Used by permission.

This book is a work of fiction. Names, characters, places,
and incidents either are products of the author's imagination
or are used fictitiously. Any resemblance to actual events or
locales or persons, living or dead, is entirely coincidental.
The text of this Large Print edition is unabridged.
In other aspects, this book may vary from the original
edition. Printed in the United States of America on
permanent paper. Set in 16-point Times New Roman type.

ISBN: 978-1-61173-467-6

Library of Congress Cataloging-in-Publication Data

Byrd, Sandra.
The secret keeper : a novel of Kateryn Parr / Sandra Byrd.
pages ; cm.
ISBN 978-1-61173-467-6 (library binding : alk. paper)
1. Large type books. I. Title.
PS3552.Y678S43 2012b
813'.54—dc23

2012006872

You women who are so complacent,
rise up and listen to me;
you daughters who feel secure,
hear what I have to say!
In little more than a year
you who feel secure will tremble.

—The Book of the Prophet Isaiah

Henry VIII Family Tree

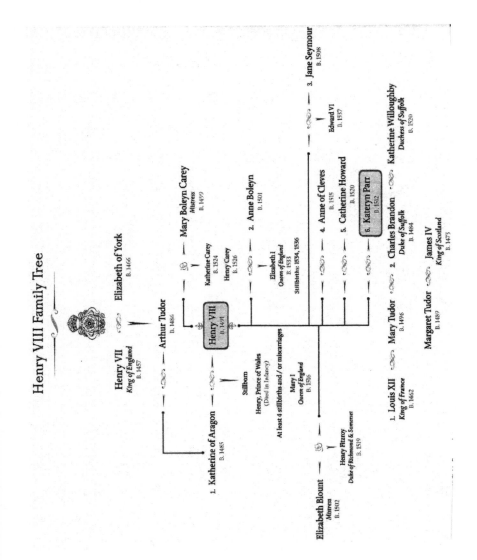

Henry VII
King of England
B. 1457

⚭

Elizabeth of York
B. 1466

Arthur Tudor
B. 1486

⚭

Henry VIII
B. 1491

1. Katherine of Aragon
B. 1485

Stillborn

Henry, Prince of Wales
(Died in Infancy)

Mary I
Queen of England
B. 1516

At least 4 stillbirths and/or miscarriages

— Mary Boleyn Carey
Mistress
B. 1499

Katherine Carey
B. 1524

Henry Carey
B. 1526

2. Anne Boleyn
B. 1501

Elizabeth I
Queen of England
B. 1533

Stillbirths: 1534, 1536

3. Jane Seymour
B. 1508

Edward VI
B. 1537

4. Anne of Cleves
B. 1515

5. Catherine Howard
B. 1520

6. Kateryn Parr
B. 1512

Katherine Willoughby
Duchess of Suffolk
B. 1520

Elizabeth Blount
Mistress
B. 1502

Henry Fitzroy
Duke of Richmond & Somerset
B. 1519

1. Louis XII
King of France
B. 1462

Mary Tudor
B. 1496

2. Charles Brandon
Duke of Suffolk
B. 1484

Margaret Tudor
B. 1489

James IV
King of Scotland
B. 1473

Parr Family Tree

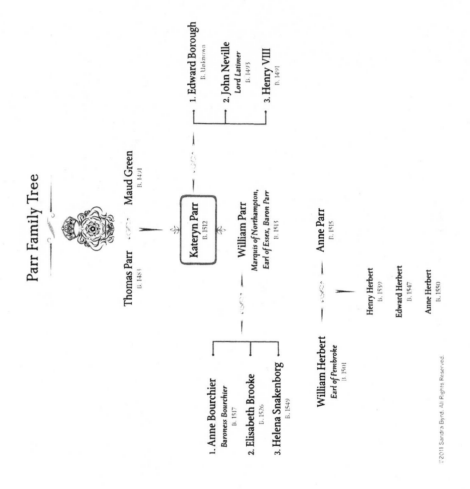

Thomas Parr
B. 1483

Maud Green
B. 1492

Kateryn Parr
B. 1512

1. Edward Borough
B. Unknown

2. John Neville
Lord Latimer
B. 1493

3. Henry VIII
B. 1491

William Parr
Marquis of Northampton,
Earl of Essex, Baron Parr
B. 1513

1. Anne Bourchier
Baroness Bourchier
B. 1517

2. Elisabeth Brooke
B. 1526

3. Helena Snakenborg
B. 1549

Anne Parr
B. 1515

William Herbert
Earl of Pembroke
B. 1501

Henry Herbert
B. 1539

Edward Herbert
B. 1547

Anne Herbert
B. 1550

Seymour Family Tree

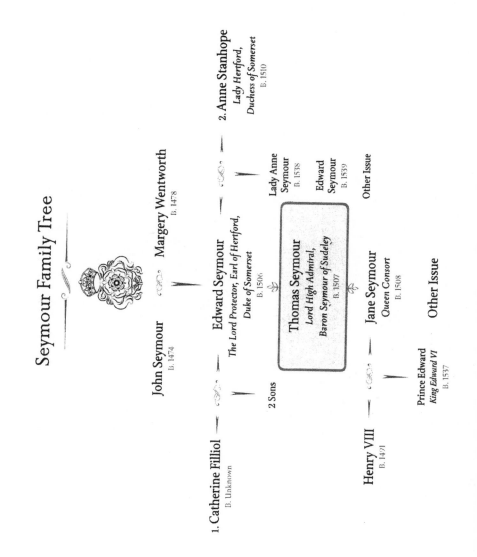

John Seymour
B. 1474

Margery Wentworth
B. 1478

1. Catherine Filliol
B. Unknown

Edward Seymour
The Lord Protector, Earl of Hertford,
Duke of Somerset
B. 1506

2. Anne Stanhope
Lady Hertford,
Duchess of Somerset
B. 1510

2 Sons

Lady Anne
Seymour
B. 1538

Edward
Seymour
B. 1539

Other Issue

Thomas Seymour
Lord High Admiral,
Baron Seymour of Sudeley
B. 1507

Henry VIII
B. 1491

Jane Seymour
Queen Consort
B. 1508

Other Issue

Prince Edward
King Edward VI
B. 1537

St. John Family Tree

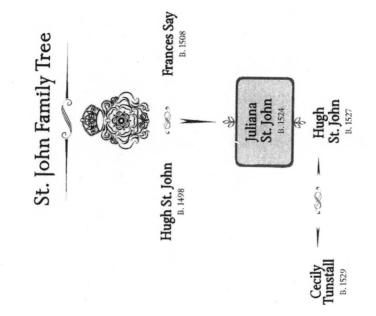

Hugh St. John
B. 1498

Frances Say
B. 1508

Juliana
St. John
B. 1524

Hugh
St. John
B. 1527

Cecily
Tunstall
B. 1529

Hart Family Tree

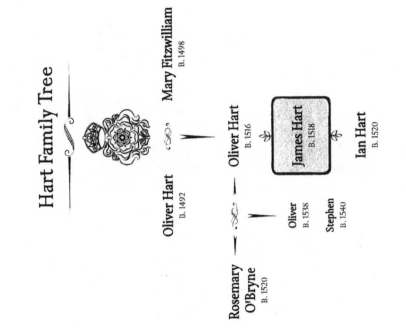

Oliver Hart
B. 1492

Mary Fitzwilliam
B. 1498

Rosemary O'Bryne
B. 1520

Oliver Hart
B. 1516

Oliver
B. 1538

Stephen
B. 1540

James Hart
B. 1518

Ian Hart
B. 1520

Ogilvy Family Tree

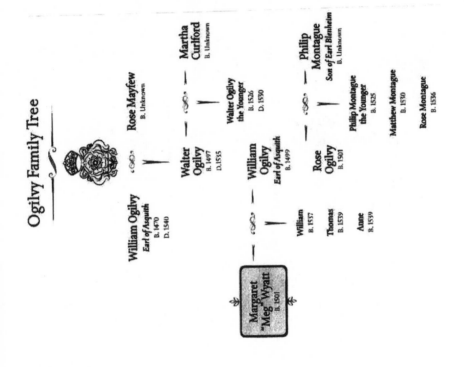

William Ogilvy
Earl of Asquith
B. 1470
D. 1540

Rose Mayfew
B. Unknown

Walter Ogilvy
B. 1497
D. 1535

Martha Curlford
B. Unknown

Walter Ogilvy the Younger
B. 1526
D. 1550

William Ogilvy
Earl of Asquith
B. 1499

Margaret "Meg" Wyatt
B. 1501

William
B. 1557

Thomas
B. 1539

Anne
B. 1539

Rose Ogilvy
B. 1501

Philip Montague
Son of Earl Blenheim
B. Unknown

Philip Montague the Younger
B. 1525

Matthew Montague
B. 1530

Rose Montague
B. 1536

THE
SECRET KEEPER

PROLOGUE

Her voice sounded by turns pleased and then pleading, her laughter scaled from bass enjoyment to treble fear. A highborn woman held fast the girl's arms while the rougher hands of a man ran over the young woman's jawline, her hairline, her hemline. I could not see his face, but on his left small finger he bore a costly gold and black onyx signet ring. With the other hand he took his dagger and began to slash.

Pieces of her black gown fell to the ground, one by one, like the locks of a condemned woman shorn before execution, though he stayed himself from touching her bright red hair before sheathing his dagger again. Her woeful face betrayed that she knew this would be her utter undoing. The gown was ruined and the black clumps, which had plummeted to the ground, received the breath of life of a sudden and became a flock of beady-eyed ravens that took wing toward the Tower of London, whilst we watched in horror and dread.

ONE

Spring: Year of Our Lord 1542
St. Peter's Church, Marlborough
Hungerford House, Marlborough
Brighton Manor, Marlborough

I entered the church on a May morn and allowed my eyes to adjust to the dim light and my body to the chill of the stone-cooled air. I sought Father Gregory, who caught my glance and smiled. I tried to return it in kind but my lips quivered. I waited in the back till he finished lighting the candles before the morning service.

Once he joined me, he immediately asked, "Daughter, what ails you?"

My face had betrayed my qualms. No others were around us so I answered him frankly as was my habit. "My mother believes I am a witch. And I fear that she is right."

Father Gregory reflexively drew back a little and for the first time I tasted dread. If this man, who knew me well and trusted me to read aloud in his church, might consider the possibility that I was a sorceress, all was lost. All would be lost, whether it were true or not, if my mother had whispered her accusation to any but myself.

" 'Tis not so," he said soothingly, and then as he was about to say more the rough townsfolk began

16

to pool in the church's nave like motes on a ray of light. Father Gregory's face registered surprise, and then humility, and then perhaps a tint of fear. I turned toward the door to look upon whom he'd fixed his gaze: a well-dressed man, the most finely dressed man I had ever seen. The man nodded and approached us.

Who was he? Was I to curtsey? Cast down my gaze? Take my leave? Before I could decide, the man was upon us and introductions begun.

Father Gregory bowed. "Sir Thomas Seymour, please allow me to present Mistress Juliana St. John."

I decided, quickly, on a short curtsey and a brief, modest dip of the head. This pleased Seymour, who held out his right hand toward me. I took it and he did not wait afore softly kissing my slightly bent knuckles before speaking.

"I am well pleased to meet you, Mistress Juliana." His deep brown eyes held my gaze with immoderate affection and I turned away from it. All knew that the Seymour family was the highest, richest, and most powerful family perhaps in the entire realm. Prince Edward, the long-awaited heir to King Henry, was also the son of their sister Jane, the lamented queen who had not lived long enough to enjoy the rewards of her greatest achievement. They flew high and we dared not offend.

"Mistress Juliana is one of our lectors. Her

father, Sir Hugh St. John, God rest his soul, was a great benefactor of the church and also ensured that his children were well educated." Father Gregory turned toward me. "Sir Thomas was an occasional associate and, er, friend, of your father." He pointed toward the front of the church. "You'd best prepare for this morning's reading, Mistress Juliana."

I nodded toward Sir Thomas. "I am greatly pleased to make your acquaintance, Sir Thomas."

"As am I," he said, and then bowed toward me, a maiden not yet eighteen, who was well beneath his standing. I gathered my skirts and my courage and made my way to the front, where the chained Great Bible, which had been secured to the altar to forestall its being stolen, was already open.

Once I began to read out the Acts of the Apostles, I quit, for the moment, of my fears and lost myself in the resonant words of Saint Paul and the upturned faces of the crofters, the millers, and the goodwives, breathing heavily in their mean woolen garb. Sir Thomas remained for the reading but left before the townsfolk did. Afterward, Father Gregory called me back to a quiet closet shut off from hungry eyes and thirsty ears.

"And now, Juliana. Unburden yourself."

I spoke immediately. "You know of my dream."

He nodded. "I know a little. Would you like to share its entirety?"

"About a year ago, shortly after my father died, I began to have a dream. 'Twas not an ordinary dream, but it was powerful and left me in a sweat and fever with my senses vexed," I said. "My maid, Lucy, would calm me afterward, though she was frightened too." I forced my hands from twisting ropes of my fine skirts and continued.

"I saw a barn, a large barn, filled with wheat and livestock of all kinds. And of course the husbandmen and others who tended the flocks and fields. At night, something kindled within the barn and within minutes it was aflame. The livestock and grains were all burnt and the building was too."

"Yes?" His voice was gentle but prodded me to continue.

"At first I had the dream only once, and then six months later it came back. Then after a month, and then a week. Each time the dream would grow more fervent. The heat peeled my skin like parchment and my ears could not refuse the desperate bleating of the animals and the screams of men. One night, I noticed that the doors to the barn looked exactly like the doors to my father's warehouses. And then, 'twas pressed upon my heart, *For this reason you have been shown the fire.* After some nights I knew I must tell my mother. It was not a choice but a compulsion."

He grimaced, as though swallowing bitter ale. "And she . . ."

"Disbelieved me at first. But I was insistent. As you know I am wont to be."

We smiled together at that.

"At some point she said she would approach Sir Matthias about having the warehouses cleaned and sorted and the goods removed to temporary holdings for inventory. She did so. And then I came and told you that was her plan. Within weeks the goods in my father's warehouses had been moved, and shortly thereafter those warehouses burnt down but the goods were saved." I met his gaze. "She has had little to say to me since."

"She had little to say to you before," Father Gregory pointed out kindly, but bluntly. "The townsfolk said the inventory came at the right time because your blessed father had been a good man and this was our Lord's way of taking care of his family." He cleared his throat. "Sir Matthias said what of it?"

"He said nothing at all, which was disturbing. My lady mother has said no more. But lately, I . . . dreamt. And I know she heard me call out, though my maid sought to wake and still me as soon as she heard my unrest."

"Is this another of the same kind of dream?"

"Yes."

"Have you told your mother?"

"I have told no one." My voice made it clear that I would not be forthcoming, even to him, with the contents of *this* dream. "But she came to my chamber and saw my countenance. After my maid had left us she declared me a witch." I swallowed roughly. "Is it true? Am I a witch?"

I looked at my hands, not wanting to see his face, nor how he might now view me, afore I heard his answer. I desperately wanted to keep his good opinion of me.

"No," he said gently. "You are not a witch. Do not let that trouble you again."

I sighed with relief, perhaps too soon, and looked up as he spoke. "But others could claim that you are one if they hear of your dreams or do not like the content of them. The penalty for witchcraft is death and forfeiture of all material wealth, no matter how highly born. Wait here." He rose and left the room, his long black clerical robes sweeping the fine dust beneath them whilst I tried to quiet the worries that beset me.

When he returned, he handed me a book. "Tyndale," I said, tracing my finger over the lettering.

He nodded. "'Twas in the warehouse afore it burnt. Your father was a good, honest man, importing cloth and rugs and tapestries from the Orient and transporting them to England. He also smuggled books."

I looked agog at Father Gregory, as though he had suddenly started speaking a strange tongue. "My father? A smuggler?"

"Not for earthly profit, mistress; he had plenty of that. And he had friends in high places to protect him."

My mind went to Thomas Seymour.

Father Gregory nodded toward the book he'd just handed me. "I knew these were hidden in the warehouses, and after you shared your dream with me I had them removed to the church. A new law will soon make them illegal. It will also make it illegal for women to teach or read Scripture publicly."

I shook my head. "So the king reverses himself again?"

Father Gregory nodded. "Alas, yes. 'Tis never safe to act on what he says today, for that may be heresy tomorrow. I have already distributed the rest of these. A few I've held back, and this one seems intended for you."

He took the book from me and opened it up to the Acts of the Apostles, just a few pages on from that morning's reading. "It shall be in the last days, saith God: I will pour out my spirit upon all flesh: and your sons and daughters shall prophesy, and your young men shall see visions, and your old men shall dream dreams. And on my servants, and on my handmaidens I will pour out my spirit in those days and they shall prophesy."

We sat there, time marked by a hundred quiet breaths. Then he took the book from me and slipped threads that he pulled from his vestments between various of the pages before handing it back to me.

"My dreams . . . they are prophecy?" I whispered, suddenly understanding why he'd chosen that passage.

" 'Tis your gift." His drawn face showed me that he knew it to be a heavy burden.

I stood up. "An unsolicited gift! An unwarranted trouble!" I pushed my hair back from my head and when I took my hand away it was wet with the evidence of fear and despair.

"Woe to the pot who tells the potter how she should be fashioned," he rebuked me.

I sat down again, shamed. "I know it well. I am afraid."

"God has specially chosen you, and He will be with you, Juliana."

"And you, too? You will advise me?" I asked.

"I am returning to Ireland. 'Tis not difficult to disappear back into the fens, where we are free to minister as we like, well out of the reach and even the sight of His Majesty, whom I cannot refer to as Defender of the Faith. God loves no false oath. I shall serve the simple people I've come from and serve in the manner I long have."

"What of me?" Cold seeped from the church walls and into my bones, which now felt very like those buried in the plot outside must feel.

"You must take care. There are laws against prophecies, too, if those who are in power or are noble or highborn are not pleased with the predicted outcome. The prophet or prophetess may be thrown into the Tower for such—and worse."

He took my hand in his own again and I readily yielded it. "God Himself has opened your eyes. Many of the things you foresee shall be difficult and unwelcome, and the temptation will be to remain silent or run away. Some you must act upon in faith but may not learn the reason why during this lifetime. I shall pray for you," he said gravely, "that you may be able to resist in the evil days that will surely come. And to stand."

My servant waited for me outside of St. Peter's, horses ready to transport us to Sir Matthias's home to sup. Our estate was at one end of the town, and Sir Matthias, who had been my father's business partner, lived at the other. On the way I grieved over the forthcoming departure of Father Gregory, who had been a comfort and guide to me all of my life. I then ruminated in fear over my gift. *When shall it next appear? To whom will I be compelled to speak, and of what?* I'd drawn near to our Lord as I'd read from the Great Bible and had felt that naught could come between Him and me. Now I rather shamefully felt as if, given the right circumstance, I could easily imitate Saint Peter and deny Him thrice if it meant saving my life.

I urged my horse on, as I did not want Matthias's family to delay the meal on my behalf. Lady Hurworth was always quick to find fault with me, though why she was I knew not, as I was always overly solicitous to her. I suspected she took her cues from my mother.

I urged my horse through the town, trying to ignore the stench and slick and muck, the smooth bits of bladder and spleen that had spilled into the roadway outside of the butcher's as we passed. Children and adults alike stood aside as we rode through. "Godspeed, mistress," they called out. We were not lords, but my father had been knighted and gentrified, and in our town that counted for much. His business employed many folk and they then had a bit more coin to spend on better bread and cloth because of his generosity. I smiled with true affection at those who caught my eye, knowing their goodwill was not based only on position but upon genuine fondness.

We arrived at Hungerford House, and while the horses were stabled I made my way up the set of smoothly polished stone steps toward the doors. My father had been the merchant traveler, sailing to foreign lands to barter for and buy tapestries, rugs, and other Eastern treasures coveted in the West. Sir Matthias had stayed in England and taken care of financial matters. As the great wooden doors opened up toward a grand and fine hall, paneled with oak and floored with marble, I wondered not for the first time if the accounts had been balanced in Sir Matthias's favor.

"Juliana." Sir Matthias's son, also named Matthias, came into the hall to greet me. He was a fine man, soft as a cushion, but mostly kindly. He took my hand and placed it in the crook of his arm before leading me into the dining chamber. "You look lovely," he said. "As you always do."

I ducked my head to hide a grin as a picture came, unbidden, from a story my father had told me before his untimely death. The franklin, a good man who ate well and constantly, was a lavish host who berated his cooks if the sauces were not fine enough or the fowl not fat enough. This franklin was a rich landowner who was well thought of in his town but had little desire to venture beyond it. Perhaps this franklin had been named Matthias?

"You are amused?" Matthias asked with a smile, but behind the smile, a sheathed demand that an answer should be forthcoming.

"Nay," I said. "I am glad of your company." Which was partially true. I took his arm and smiled sweetly, which allowed me to conceal my amusement and please him at the same time.

That appeased him and we sat at a table laden with everything that the franklin could have imagined and some foodstuffs I was certain he could not, like eels baked in pies and custard dishes spiced four or five ways. We then discussed the town.

"Sir Thomas Seymour is in Marlborough," I stated. "He was at church this morning whilst I read as lector."

All set down their knives. Matthias looked at me disapprovingly and his father cleared his throat before glaring. I sighed deeply. I should have waited for Sir Matthias to bring up important news, after which I could comment approvingly.

Matthias grunted and threw another greasy bone under the table upon one of the fine carpets my father had conveyed back from Constantinople. "'Tis not proper for a woman to read aloud in church."

"Father Gregory told me that the king will be changing the law soon. Mayhap next time Parliament sits. Women will no longer be allowed to lector nor teach Scripture even to their servants."

"Good King Harry." Sir Matthias tucked some partridge roasted with herbs into his mouth. "That is how it should have been all along." He was either unaware that he had reprimanded me or had meant to. Young Matthias said nothing, but sat with a self-satisfied smile. He had oft voiced to me that he did not like my reading, or overeducating my mind, or speaking it. Poor qualities in a mother, he'd said. *Mother of his children,* he'd meant, though we'd never spoken of it, but that had softened me some because I loved children. My own mother would like as not begin negotiations soon, as Sir Matthias was now aware of the great dowry my father had left for me. My father had wanted different for me and had resisted that arrangement whilst he lived, but there were no other matches of consequence in our town and my mother rarely ventured out from Marlborough.

"Sir Thomas has already been to see me to check on our mutual accounts," Sir Matthias said with a superior look in my direction. "We established some business together this year with his shipping interests now that, well . . ."

Now that my father was dead, he meant. I lost my hunger. I'd not yet recovered completely from the loss.

Lady Martha stopped chewing and spoke up with unexpected and unnerving news. "I too knew that Sir Thomas was about. Your lady mother sent a servant earlier, for fruit, which she knows my confectioner prepares to perfection. She will be entertaining Sir Thomas and his retinue at Brighton Manor tonight upon his request."

"Here, then, mistress. Some of the kohl tha' your father had brought back from the far lands," Lucy said, and brought to me a stick of kohl from a cupboard on the far side of my chamber.

I took it and then edged the tiniest amount of it

28

round the frame of my eyes and at the base of my lashes. I had not worn kohl before, being young, and also because I knew Matthias would not approve. In any case, we rarely entertained.

Lucy helped me into a gown of deep green that set off my dark hair and eyes. She laced up the back and helped me into my slippers afore assisting with my hair. She had not been trained to be a lady maid but she had learned as I'd grown; her own mother had served my mother for many years—and my mother's standards were exacting. At the last minute, Lucy fastened a small gold bracelet with an emerald around my wrist. It had been a New Year's gift the year before my father died.

"You look beautiful," Lucy said.

I grinned at her faithfulness in spite of the fact that my mother had made it very clear that I was nothing special to look upon. "I shall not have a maid who speaks untruths. Even one who is well regarded."

She grinned with me, curtseyed, and left my chambers. A few minutes later I arrived at the sitting hall that was ablaze with beeswax candles—no stench of tallow in this household. My younger brother, Hugh, sat, uneasy in his finery, in an overstuffed chair covered with damask, driving his boots into the floor to avoid slipping off of it. "I'd rather be jousting or hunting or even cleaning stables," he muttered. "Rather

29

than be sitting here trussed up like a partridge." A beard of the finest blond hairs was beginning to poke through his cleft chin, which was losing its padding.

"What are those?" I asked, gently running my finger along his chin.

"*Those* are my beard! Have you not seen a beard before, mistress?" he blustered.

"I have indeed, young sir, but not upon your face." I squeezed his shoulders and he warmed beneath my touch. Our mother was not given to physical affection, though Hugh and I had both thirsted for it since our father's demise.

"I'm sure we can arrange for some stable cleaning," I teased. "If that's your pleasure." We continued talking for a moment and then walked over to where my mother stood conversing with Sir Thomas and several of his men. I was shocked to find her face in high pink and her manner almost flirtatious. "Sir Thomas, my daughter, Juliana," she said. She looked worried. Had my mother finally found someone who daunted even her?

"We are acquainted." Sir Thomas took my hand in his again and explained to all how he'd listened to me read in church that morning. He introduced me to the other courtiers around him, all finely garbed, and I had the opportunity to show, by my manners, my learning, and my use of language, that my mother had brought me up well. One or two gazed upon me admiringly and that pleased my mother not at all, but it made me feel young and desirable and hopeful for the first time in many years. Within a few minutes the musicians stopped playing and my mother's chamberlain led us into the dining hall.

After a fine meal of roast chicken with honey and almonds, several of Sir Thomas's retinue begged their leave, and we four—my mother; Sir Thomas; my brother, Hugh; and myself—were left at table. I kept waiting for my mother to dismiss my brother and me but she did not. And then, Sir Thomas made an announcement.

"Mistress Juliana," he said, looking at me. "I have a proposal for Lady Frances's consideration."

I felt a flush up the back of my neck and my mother looked alarmingly from Sir Thomas to me and back again. 'Twas clear she had not anticipated this.

"Indeed, Sir Thomas?" I asked demurely.

"My friend Lord Latimer's lady, Kateryn Parr, is a fine woman who loves reading, and Scripture, and cultivating young women of good birth in her household. It is seemly for every maiden to spend some time in a good household, besides her own, of course, to further her education and polish."

I could sense that my mother was about to object when he said, "You were a companion to my sister Jane, were you not, Lady Frances?"

"I was indeed," my mother admitted. "Afore I married Sir Hugh." There were familiar shards in the tone of her voice at his rebuke, so I did not voice my incredulity that my mother had once known a queen. The servants, recognizing her tone, too, melted into the background. "But, Sir Thomas, it had been my husband's understanding that you were going to take our son, Hugh, and place him with a household, so that he may learn better the ways of the world. And make connections that will help him when he assumes his father's business."

"All in good time, lady," Sir Thomas said. "He is young." I looked at Hugh, who seemed crestfallen that he would not be leaving Marlborough immediately. "After hearing Mistress Juliana read today, I knew that Lady Latimer would immediately take her to heart and it is now my wish to see her placed there. Unless you object?"

His voice was a challenge and the room grew quiet. I thought it bold that Sir Thomas could speak so confidently about placing me in another man's household and wondered exactly what his ties were with Lord and Lady Latimer.

My mother did not answer directly. She preferred Hugh above all others, and I suspected she was unwilling to let him leave yet anyway.

"Not at all . . . if Juliana wishes it," my mother said, forfeiting.

"Good!" Sir Thomas grew jovial again. "I have

reason to believe that soon enough there will be a place for Master Hugh in one or another fine household. And now, young Hugh, whilst I get my horses from your stable, shall I teach you a sea song that we sailors sing when no ladies are present?"

Hugh broke out in delighted laughter and Sir Thomas thanked my mother profusely for her hospitality.

I had noticed something alarming about Sir Thomas, though, and I knew I had to ask my mother one question before I could consider Sir Thomas's offer. I knocked gently on her chamber door.

"Yes?" she called out as she sat at her dressing table while Lucy's mother unwound my mother's hair. I went in and stood next to her.

"If I leave with Sir Thomas, will I be safe? I mean, is he safe? With me?"

My mother barked out a laugh. "Even Sir Thomas would not stoop that low," she said, waving me away with nary a glance in my direction. "He has the pick of the realm."

"Thank you, lady," I said as I withdrew, crushed, but keeping a steady look upon my face so she wouldn't realize my pain, if she looked up to glance at me, that was. If I hadn't suspected already that she found me unlovely, I knew it now.

Late that night, I visited Hugh in his chamber. "Will you go to London with Sir Thomas?" he asked.

"Yes I will. I will miss you greatly, Hugh, and home. Truth be told, I am a bit afraid of what I may find in London, especially as I shall be alone but for Lucy in a household that is mighty and grand and well beyond what we've ever experienced." I thought back upon my vision, and the timing of my discussion with Father Gregory, who had urged me to be faithful to my gift, and Sir Thomas's appearance in Marlborough. "But I believe that going is the right thing to do." I smoothed the coverlet at the foot of his bed. "And so I must."

"Sir Thomas liked our wolfhounds," Hugh said approvingly. Then he asked, "Will you come back to marry Matthias? You do not wish it, do you?"

"Nay," I said, my heart and voice resigned. "But I believe that is what our lady mother wants and therefore that is what I shall do. But there is time." *Time for our Lord to fulfill this prophecy and bring no more,* I thought hopefully.

"I shall miss you," Hugh said. "We've not ever been apart."

"God forbid that we be apart for long," I quietly replied. Hugh was all I had. "Shall I tell you about the knight Saint George?" He was really too old for such fooleries. But he nodded and I began to recount a story our father had oft told us when we

34

were children because it comforted us both, then and now.

"Now this knight was heroic, and chivalrous; he lived by truth and honor and justice, having won great esteem in his lord's wars, and was well liked in both Christian and heathen lands," I began.

"Like our father," Hugh said sleepily, half-man, half-boy. I agreed and continued the story.

Later, I returned to my chambers in darkness, after Lucy had also retired to her own room nearby. I lay in bed stark awake. It was not in fear of another dream but of something yet more dreadful in the present reality, the knowledge of which I wrestled with.

At dinner I had noted, with apprehension, that Sir Thomas wore a gold and black onyx signet ring on his left small finger. He was, without a doubt, the man with the dagger, slashing the maiden's black dress, in my prophetic dream.

TWO

Summer, Autumn, and Winter:
Year of Our Lord 1542
Charterhouse

My father had settled us in Marlborough because it was between Bath and London, which made it convenient for shipping and selling. He'd brought our family to London once and we'd seen the Thames and the fearsome Tower perched upon it. Some of his seafaring friends had taken us in a rich skiff to view the royal palaces of Greenwich and Whitehall; from the water Hugh and I had marveled at them while my mother was a guest at the London home of a friend. So it was not as if I had never been to London.

But I had never been to London to stay. My thrill near spilled beyond containment.

Several months after his visit to our home, Sir Thomas had sent a fine litter and several of his men from Wulf Hall, his family seat nearby, to convey my belongings, myself, and Lucy to Lady Latimer's home in London. 'Twas near fifty miles along the Great Road, so by leaving early in the morn we would arrive while there was still light. I rolled up the rug at my feet along with several boxes of gifts for Lady Latimer. Lucy sat behind me. She chattered and I chattered back, though my mother had warned me not to mix with her overmuch.

"You are a knight's daughter, and Lucy is your maid, not your friend," she'd said.

"Yes, my lady," I'd answered. "I will obey you and bring you honor while in the Latimers' household." But I knew, too, that my mother confided in Lucy's mother as much as any other so there was some margin to the rule.

If one were to put Hungerford House and

Brighton Manor side by side and then copy them by three, one would not end up with a building as large or magnificent as the Charterhouse in Charterhouse Square. When the litter finally stopped, Lucy gasped, and I remembered just in time not to do so myself. The heart of the building was both stout and high, with turrets and towers and long arms that stretched to either side. I was awestruck and delighted to be in such fine surroundings and on such a delectable adventure! The stable was as big as my home. One of Lord Latimer's servants was there to greet us as we arrived. He showed us to a chamber with a small servant's room on the left arm of the building.

Lucy set about pouring a bowl of water for me to wash with and then putting my gowns and personal items in the lacquered cupboards before hanging my tapestries. She then brought her own bag to her quarters, connected by a door to mine. I washed the dust from my face and then a young woman who appeared to be of an age with me arrived at my door.

"Mistress St. John," she said, a fine and honest smile upon her face. "I am Lady Margaret Neville, daughter of Lord Latimer. I bid you welcome to Charterhouse."

"Thank you, Lady Neville." I smiled back and curtseyed slightly. "I am honored to be a guest at your home."

"You shall be expected to attend a large supper

tomorrow," she continued after nodding. "Sir Thomas had alerted us to your arrival, and Lady Latimer and her entire household are pleased that you should stay with us. If you should need anything at all, I hope you will not hesitate to seek me out."

I opened my mouth to ask several of the most pressing questions that were on my mind, but as I did she smiled once more and took her leave, several ladies trailing behind her. I was bewildered. Was I truly to ask questions or was that a polite trifle offered all guests? She'd had an honest look about her.

I had not much time to think upon the matter because another young woman, also of an age with me, appeared in the hallway just outside of my chamber. She was about to enter the chamber directly across the hall from mine when she saw me. She stopped and came to my rooms instead.

"You must be Mistress Juliana St. John." Her hair was the color of young ale and her bright blue eyes held my own without wavering.

I was pleased that she knew and had remembered my name, and hoped I might have found a friend. I was about to say as much when she started speaking again.

"I am Mistress Dorothy Skipwith. I've been in Lady Latimer's household for some time. How do you do?"

I could not answer before she pressed on.

"Since you have, unusually, brought your own maid, 'twill be easy to send her to the laundress to bleach the country dust from your sleeves." She smiled at me so authentically, so beautifully but for one small hooked tooth, that I was left not knowing whether she meant me good or ill.

"Thank you," I said, and she turned and took her leave, her faded pink gown swirling about her as she left. I now understood that not all arrived at Lady Latimer's with their own maids. I carefully inspected my sleeves for dust again and again, but found little.

Had I already misstepped?

Lucy and I looked at one another and I set about trying to decide which of my gowns would be most appropriate for the following day's event.

The next day after church Lady Latimer sent word to call upon her within the hour. Lucy helped dress me in one of my finest gowns and I navigated my way through the maze of hallways toward the heart of the manor, whence came the sound of laughter. In my experience, laughter was a strange sound coming from the suite of a lady's quarters, but I was to find that it was a common grace in this household and I drew toward its welcoming sound. I approached the hall tentatively but Lady Latimer, at the center of things, waved me forward, dismissing her ladies, who dispersed into various closets and chambers adjoining the hall.

"Mistress St. John," she said to me. "I am pleased to have you join my household. Sir Thomas holds you in high esteem, and upon his word I believe you'll make a fine addition to my household."

"If you please, my lady, I should prefer you to call me Juliana," I said, curtseying awkwardly as I nearly lost my balance. As I did, I heard the titter of laughter from a far corner and watched Lady Latimer suppress a smile.

"Very well then, Juliana. And I shall permit you to call me Kate, as my friends do. But only when we are close quartered with the ladies."

The rolling tide of murmurs at the edges of the hall indicated that I had misstepped again. I wished to repent of it but was not sure if that should worsen matters. "I shall certainly endeavor to, madam. Rather, Kate."

"Lady Neville, Lord Latimer's daughter, will inform you of your duties and the expectations of my household. I hold discussions in my chambers often, and my ladies ride and hunt with me. We engage in dancing and dine and provide pleasant conversation for Lord Latimer's guests, with whom we sup. And of course, we attend church daily."

"Yes, lady," I said, sticking with the formal for now. Then I rushed on with enthusiasm. "I am most interested in your discussions. I was a lector in Marlborough."

She broke out in a true smile and reached out and brushed my shoulder with her hand. It felt like soft butter whispered across a slice of manchet; this was what I suspected others knew as maternal love, though Kate was only a dozen years older than I. "So I have heard. You shall make a lively addition. We will be entertaining Sir Thomas and some of his household today and he shall join the hunt tomorrow. As Lord Latimer is in Scotland, fighting for His Majesty, our gowns are somewhat subdued." She glanced at my current choice with a motherly concern, then smiled encouragingly, and I understood. Something betwixt dusty sleeves and fine damask would do. She wanted me to be at ease.

"Thank you, my lady," I said, already wanting to please her, desiring that affection to be visited upon me again and again.

"You may take your leave, Juliana. I will look forward to speaking together often."

That evening Lady Margaret Neville, a year or two younger than I but already an accomplished hostess, took care to seat me near to her and introduced me to not only those in Lady Latimer's household but some of the gentlemen who had arrived with Thomas Seymour. I'd kept a distance from Sir Thomas, after thanking him for bringing me to Charterhouse, not sure whether to trust the friendliness he portrayed or the wickedness I saw of him in my vision. Sir

41

Thomas did have a kind word and a friendly wink for me early on in the evening, but it was clear that he was blindingly attached to Lady Latimer. She behaved with the utmost grace and fidelity, but though I may have been young, I knew the look of women and she was not indifferent to his attentions.

I spoke mainly with Dorothy, who seemed pleased to introduce me to the others. I noticed that one of the locks of her hair had escaped its netting. "May I tuck this strand of hair back into your net?" I whispered to her.

Her eyes opened widely and she nodded, but she seemed rather put out by the gesture I had intended to be friendly. After I attended to it for her, she turned to speak with another of the maids. I stood, alone and awkward for a moment, looking about the crowded room for anyone that I might join in pleasant conversation.

"Mistress St. John?" A hand touched my sleeve, and I turned to face Lady Margaret Neville as she spoke to me. "Have you been acquainted with James Hart from Ireland?"

James Hart.

His black hair charmingly tipped up at the ends like ravens' wings; blue eyes were set in a sun-bronzed face that boasted a scruff that was undecided between a close beard and clean shaven. I must have stared a bit too long.

Lady Margaret Neville disappeared to other

hostessing duties and as she did, James said, "Is there something amiss?"

I blushed deeply but could not confess that I found him uncommonly attractive, so afore I could stop myself I said, "I've not seen many men who were near clean shaven before I arrived in London."

He looked shocked and then he laughed aloud. "Well, mistress, do speak your mind."

"I meant no offense," I said.

"Nay, offense not taken, especially from such a charming girl," he said. He smiled in a manner that obliged a like response, willing or not, and I smiled back. A woman several years older than I with the fragrance of good manners swept up behind him and without a word of introduction presented herself for conversation. I took it by her familiar manner that she knew James well, and bowed my head a bit to take my leave. He caught my arm and held it, not tightly enough to hurt but enough that I knew he meant to have my attention. "May I enquire after your name?"

"Mistress St. John," I reminded him.

He shook his head. "I should like to know your given name."

"Juliana," I answered to the impatience of the lady, who now placed her hand on his arm.

"Juliana," he repeated. "I shall remember it." Then he bowed and left with his companion.

Later that night, after Lucy had brushed out my

hair, I considered, with dismay, that he had called me a charming girl. I did not wish to be looked upon as a girl whilst in Lady Latimer's elegant household, but rather as a woman.

We rose early the next morn to hunt after Lady Latimer sent fresh horses ahead with some of her stable boys. I was thankful that my father had been fond of finery and that when he procured cloth for his trading he'd also made sure that my mother, my brother, and myself were properly attired, as befitting our station. My mother had lost a babe betwixt me and Hugh and had none after him so my father doted inordinately upon us two. Lucy helped me into a riding suit of wheat-colored velvet that set off my dark hair, combed to a lustrous sheen. "Canna have Mistress Dorothy looking finer than you, m'lady, if'n 'twere possible. Which it aren't."

I grinned at her and she continued to glide the brush through my hair.

Lady Margaret Neville instructed a stable boy to give me a fine horse and then I set off with the others. *I shall remember to thank her later,* I thought, *and find a way to repay her for these small kindnesses.* Dorothy rode beside me and we made pleasant but wary conversation about our reading and our homes. "You are a fine rider," I told her, complimenting her gladly, as it was true.

"Thank you," she said. "As are you. Your riding outfit is perfectly suited to your coloring."

I then looked at her riding outfit, which was slightly threadbare, and saw that some of her jewels were chipped. Though I knew her family to be more highly placed than my own, I wondered if they had fallen upon difficult times. Mayhap that was the source of her barbs. She saw me looking at her outfit and then spurred on her horse without another word.

I was confused. I hadn't drawn my gaze to Dorothy's clothing till she'd noted mine, and then only so I might offer a compliment in return. I was left riding by myself, till one of Lady Latimer's ladies rode alongside me and made pleasant conversation. I slowed my horse to meet hers and smiled at her gratefully. She smiled back knowingly.

The greyhounds ran ahead of us. Some men of Lady Latimer's household returned to Charterhouse with the morning's kill whilst we spread out among the tables and cushions set up for the day's dinner. 'Twas a generous spread and I was about to indulge myself in a second serving of strawberries, unheard of at my home, when I felt someone come alongside me.

"Ah, strawberries. My favorite fruit. Yours too, I presume, Mistress Juliana?" I turned to face the teasing blue eyes of James Hart. He held his hand out to me, I held out my own in return, and he brushed his lips against my knuckles before letting go.

I had nearly forgotten the question but recovered myself enough to answer. "I had not tasted them before today, Sir James, but yes, I do believe they are a particular favorite now."

He grinned. "I admire that you do not pretend to have eaten of them often when you have not. And thank you for the honor, but I am simply James, no 'sir.' I am not knighted. Yet."

"James. 'Tis not a particularly Irish name," I said more to myself.

"Ah, then. You think mayhap my name should be Patrick or Seamus and my sister's name Siobhan? Would that be Irish enough for you, mistress?" His eyes were still alight but I sensed hurt behind them. I, however, was not to be cowed by one not yet a knight, especially as I had meant no harm.

"I think your name should be Incorrigible and your sister's name must surely be Patience!"

He threw his head back and laughed, and all caution fled his eyes. "I have no sister, only brothers. And it would please me if you'd call me Jamie. My friends do. And before you tell me that Jamie is not a particularly Irish nickname, 'twas given me by my Scots nurse."

"Jamie, then," I said, and smiled without caution in return.

"Would you care to walk with me?" He

indicated the large clearing in which the hunting party reposed.

I nodded. As long as I stayed within eyesight, surely there was no harm. I glanced at Lady Latimer, sitting with her sister, Lady Herbert. Lady Herbert had been in charge of Queen Catherine Howard's jewels afore the king dispatched that young queen heavenward rather sooner than she'd envisioned her departure. Sir Thomas and several of his men, as honored guests, sat with those highest-born ladies too.

I placed my hand in the crook of James's arm. "I've heard that Sir Thomas will be leaving soon for battle in Austria. Will you go with him? I know that he will shortly take his leave and represent the king, joining forces while the emperor fights the Turks."

"I shall, for the time being. I hope to win some battles. And my knighthood," James said.

"Shall you be afraid of sailing, or of battle?"

He smiled. "Nay, Juliana. I am eager for battle, to prove myself. And I am comfortable at sea. My family is a shipping family, and we do business with the Seymours, which is how I came to be attached to his household. My brother Oliver spoke with Sir Thomas's older brother. They became great friends. But Sir Thomas, as an oft-overlooked younger brother himself, had an eye to helping me make a name and enjoy the fruit"—he looked down upon his strawberry-stained fingers—"of the world outside Ireland. He's brought me to London, with my brother's full approval, and I work both for his interests and for my family's, in a partnership. My father was English, God rest his soul." He paused afore continuing.

"My mother is Irish, and whilst she sees no reason for the Irish to need English training nor anything else English, she knows that King Henry has reaffirmed himself as king of Ireland and it behooves us to see how the wind blows. She's also raised enough boys to know a man needs to make his own way."

I wondered if Lady Hurworth understood that a man needed to make his own way, or if Matthias even had a care to find that way for himself. A thought came to mind. I knew it was faintly saucy, but I said it anyway. "I have a particular fondness for a certain Irishman." 'Twas the sort of thing women said. Not girls.

Jamie raised his eyebrows in pretended shock.

"I'm fond of a kindly Irish priest who took me under his wing when my father passed on," I admitted with a grin.

James laughed, and I talked about my own home and family, and how my father had considered many Turks his friends, though they be infidels.

He drew near to me—it was both discomfiting and welcome. It was nothing akin to being near Matthias; instead, I was overwarmed, breathless, and pink, as though I'd drunk deeply of wine that had not first been watered. I could grow fond of the Irish scruff rather than a full beard and looked upon with favor the manner in which it highlighted his jaw and lips.

Alas, he moved away and put more space between us; I recalled to mind the woman he had kept company with the night before and wondered if there was an agreement between them.

"I admire that you are young and life has not leached the mettle out of you nor tempered your free speech. But you must have a care, mistress, to whom you speak your mind. London is a merry town, a glittering city, a place to enjoy oneself, and I intend to do just that." He paused. "A ship, as you know, is great in size, but is turned by a small helm. In the same way, the tiny tongue can bring great damage to the whole body if not controlled."

"Saint James." I recognized the passage. "Have you read it for yourself?"

He smiled. "I confess I have not. But what kind of man would I be if I did not read the words of him for whom my father named me? And all sailors know the sailing analogies in holy writ."

He stood up then, as the rest of our hunting party rallied to begin the hunt back to Charterhouse. "I admit to being grieved that our time together is over, mistress," he said.

"Juliana," I reminded him.

"Juliana," he said softly. "We'll be taking our leave tomorrow to war."

"I shall pray for you," I said. "That you meet with success."

He held out his hand so I might steady myself afore mounting my horse. After I did he pressed my hand to his lips for much longer than was strictly necessary and yet not nearly long enough.

Later that night Lucy and I heard a knock on my door whilst I was in my chamber, dressing. I slipped into her room whilst she opened the door. 'Twas Jamie's voice! I hurriedly dressed myself but by the time I had finished and opened the door he had taken his leave.

"'E's gone," Lucy said. "But he left this for ye."

She handed over a small basket in which were ten perfect strawberries and a note. "Thank you for a charming afternoon, beautiful Juliana, and for your prayers."

"Who was tha'?" Lucy asked.

"A boy I was introduced to last night."

"Tha' is no boy, mistress," Lucy said. "Pardon my correcting your sore eyesight, but tha' is a man."

"That is not talk befitting a servant!" I chided her, but she ducked and grinned and I grinned back at her as she left to mend my kirtle.

He found me beautiful.

Was the note an indication of his feelings? Or

naught more than courtly manners? It did prod me toward some courtly manners of my own, though. I sent a finely wrought hairnet to one of my especial favorites, Lady Margaret Neville, along with a note thanking her for her many kindnesses. I also sent a ribbon to Mistress Dorothy, because I knew she read, and I enclosed a note indicating that I hoped that it might be of some help for her to save her place.

Dorothy sent back a small posy. We had found a common ground, and mayhap a truce, which delighted me.

The next day, I watched from my window as Sir Thomas and his men gathered on the green before setting out. I spied Jamie near the middle and could not withdraw my gaze from him, glad that he could not see me staring in such an unseemly manner.

That is a man.

Mayhap that is why I'd felt so different with Jamie, why he wound through my thoughts in a quiet moment. He was the full man, whereas Matthias was half-watered.

The fair tidings that autumn were that Lord Latimer returned from Scotland, having proven himself in the service of the realm. After the Pilgrimage of Grace, in which Lord Latimer, a staunch Catholic at heart, unwittingly took sides against the king, Lord Latimer must have felt the need to prove himself and his loyalty. The poor tidings were that he returned home in very bad health. Most often he kept to his chambers and illness whittled him week to week from a virile man into the thin shape to be angled inside a shroud.

Occasionally he dined with us, or Lady Latimer had some of us join them in his chambers so that our youth and frivolity might lift his spirits. One night near Christmastime, she invited me along.

I mostly made small talk with Margaret, his daughter, attempting to distract her from the forthcoming inevitable, but I was well acquainted with the Angel of Death; he had become a familiar during my own father's ill health and I thus recognized him when he made himself comfortable at Charterhouse.

"The king is completing the renovations on the Lady Mary's apartments," Lord Latimer said. "I hear that they are fine and on the river. It seems he has forgiven her and has reinstated her in his affections."

"I am glad of it," Lady Latimer said. Her mother had served the Lady Mary's mother, Katherine of Aragon, as a lady in waiting and indeed, she had been named for that very queen.

"I am glad of it too," Lord Latimer said. "The king has extended an invitation to us to visit the court after New Year's, and for you to call upon the Lady Mary."

We grew quiet, no one wanting to give voice to the obvious.

"I shan't be well enough to go." Lord Latimer said it for us. "But you, my dear, you must go. It would not do us well to have him think we shy away from the honor. I've agreed on your behalf."

At that, he succumbed to a fit of coughing from which he was not able to quickly recover. All of us save Lady Margaret Neville and Lady Latimer left the room. That night I wrote a note to Lady Latimer telling her that I was praying for her lord and for herself. I sealed it with wax and handed it to Lucy.

"Please deliver this to one of Lady Latimer's maids. They shall know when to hand it to her."

"Are ye certain, mistress? I do na hear of tha other mistresses writing to the lady."

I nodded and kept my hand, and the note, firmly held in her direction. Reluctantly, she took it.

Two weeks after New Year's, Lady Margaret Neville came to tell me that Lady Latimer had requested that I come to court with her and a small group of attendants. It was a singular honor and Dorothy was invited too. We would room together.

"I am glad we shall share a chamber," I said to her.

She grinned. "I too. We can perhaps share our combs and slippers. I've noticed that our feet are of a size." She stuck her right foot out from under her gown and I came alongside her and put my left right next to it.

"Nearly a perfect match!" I said, and then laughed, happy to have a true friend come along on this most unusual adventure. We would depart immediately.

THREE

Winter and Early Spring:
Year of Our Lord 1543
The Palace of Whitehall
Charterhouse
Hampton Court Palace

W hitehall was a magnificent square palace of stone with slate roofs the color of ash. Its huge windows drank in the view of not only the tidal Thames but the city tops of London. The splendidly dressed were so many in number that they paid me no mind as I gaped at them. Lady Latimer had fine chambers near where the Lady Mary, the king's daughter, resided, and we settled in quickly.

One day soon after we arrived, I came to Kate's reception chamber to find that I was the only one in attendance aside from her lady maid.

"B-beg your pardon, Lady Latimer, did I mistake the time for your reading?" I stammered.

"I leave for the Lady Mary's in one hour. I've

canceled my reading today because the king especially invited me to assist the Lady Mary with ordering fabric for dresses and with her jewelry. We have that in common, you know," she continued with a smile. "She and I both like finery and dancing."

"I'm sorry to disturb you, then," I said, and began backing away.

"Stay yourself for a moment," Kate requested. "I do feel as if I could use a reading before meeting with the Lady Mary and I know you to be an excellent reader, mistress lector." She waved toward a large oak cupboard in the corner of the expansive chamber. "My books are in there. Turn the key to unlock it and then choose one and you can read aloud whilst my hair is being done."

Her lady maid went back to brushing her hair into an elaborate twist that would be tucked under a gold and ruby net. I opened the cupboard she'd indicated.

"Oh, my lady, 'tis truly more valuable a treasure chest than that which holds your jewels," I said aloud. Then I looked up in alarm, hoping I hadn't offended, especially since she'd just indicated her affection for jewels. I needn't have worried. She laughed aloud as she was wont to do. I felt myself uncoil.

"You are right. Now choose well, as I haven't much time."

I looked them over. There was *Roman de la*

Rose—a fable of romance! A bound copy of *The Canterbury Tales*. I felt compelled to reach for one of them but somehow I knew that my selection was a test. There was Tyndale's translation of holy writ. Too simple of a choice. *The Institutes of the Christian Religion*, by John Calvin, was tempting because it was banned. I wondered if Lord Latimer knew it was there. Or if the king knew it was in Whitehall. I finally settled upon *The Paraphrase on the Epistle of Paul the Apostle to the Romans*, by Erasmus of Rotterdam. I brought it to my lady and she smiled warmly.

"Excellent selection, Juliana. I should like to see it translated into English someday. Please read to me."

I had read for about fifteen minutes when a page appeared at her door. I recognized him from Sir Thomas Seymour's retinue. The boy handed a note to her.

"Sir Thomas is back at court?" she said.

I smiled when the manservant indicated that he was. Not only was Sir Thomas my patron in the lady's household, he also traveled with Jamie. Kate saw my pleasure and nodded affirmingly.

"Er, m'lady." The man looked about the room with caution. There was only myself and Kate's lady maid.

"'Tis fine to speak freely," Kate told him. Which meant I had earned her trust.

The man pulled a small box out of his pocket. "Sir Thomas asked me to deliver this to you too." Kate opened it up, looked inside, smiled quickly, and then snapped it shut, a look of indecision on her face. She kept it in her hand and took on a slightly cooler tone.

"Thank you. Tell Sir Thomas I shall respond presently."

The serving man withdrew and Kate took the small black box to the locked cupboard where she kept her forbidden books and then returned to the closet to finish dressing herself. I stood there, not sure what to do till she called out to me. "Please return Erasmus, Juliana, and then bring me the key. If you've no other commitments, you may accompany me to the Lady Mary's apartments."

If I had no other commitments! My heart soared. I was to meet a princess. Well, not a princess in title any longer. But we all knew that she was a princess of royal blood. 'Twas a singular display of affection for Kate to invite me, and Dorothy would never forgive me for it, but I would remember all the details to tell her, every word spoken, every gown chosen, so I could relay all when we stayed up, as usual, past dark, gossiping about the day.

I picked up Erasmus and lifted the cupboard lid. As I did, it tipped over Kate's new little black box. Inside was a miniature portrait, the traditional gift to a beloved from sailors hoping to remain in their lady's remembrance whilst they were away.

'Twas Thomas Seymour, of course, looking as dashing as ever with a feather in his cap, and appearing a bit arrogant. It unsettled me. I had not forgotten my vision, though it had blessedly not reappeared since I'd left home.

It was a short walk down a long hall to the Lady Mary's. One of the men in her household opened up the door to her suite of chambers, and as he did, we entered upon a great center hall. The windows were tall and wide and let in the gray winter light. I watched rare snowflakes float like feathers to the ground. The Lady Mary stepped off the tailor's stool and exclaimed in delight, "Kate!" She gathered her kirtle and went to greet Lady Latimer with a warm embrace.

I kept my eyes downcast, but through my lashes I took her in. She was twenty-seven years old, only a few years younger than Lady Latimer. Her hair was red, tempered with brown, and whilst she didn't have Kate's thin waist she was clearly not overfond of rich foods, either. You felt the circle of personal power around her; it moved as she moved. Mayhap that was royalty. She looked up at me and then asked in a rather stern voice, "And who is this?"

Kate's voice was lightly submissive. "One of my maidens, my lady. She is come with me to court. I pray you have no objection to her accompanying me today. She can assist with the fabric draping."

Kate threw a look to cue me. I curtseyed deeply and said, "Mistress Juliana St. John, my lady."

Lady Mary looked at me as though she couldn't decide whether I could help or she should dismiss me.

"My mother was a companion to Queen Jane," I added, trying to gain her favor, wanting not to shame Kate for bringing me along. "In their youth."

At that, Kate looked at me with surprise. Had I misspoken?

"Ah." The Lady Mary broke out in a smile. "Queen Jane was a truly pious and good woman. Unlike the concubine she followed. Yes, yes, Mistress St. John. You may stay." She clapped her hands in delight. "Let's begin!"

The tailor opened up his cases and unwound roll after roll of fine fabric across the spectrum in color and texture. The Lady Mary and Lady Latimer spent several hours choosing fabric for hoods, pleats, and sleeves; I held the fabric along with the tailor as they draped it in the glass. A babe in his nurse's arms could not have been better contented than I. The Lady Mary brought out her jewel cases so that they might choose which of her finer pieces would be set best against certain fabrics. Kate had an unerring eye and the Lady Mary showered her with affection for her friendship and her help.

The next week, a manservant presented a bill to Lady Latimer for the fabric and work in process. Lady Herbert took it to Kate and Kate scribbled, "For your daughter," on it and had it sent to the king.

I thought that overbold at the time, and even more so the next week when we returned to the Lady Mary's chambers.

The women were playing cards and Dorothy had just waved to me to join her at a table with some of the Lady Mary's maidens when all talk and play came to an abrupt halt.

The Lady Mary stood and curtseyed. "Your Majesty."

King Henry strode into the room and as he did, every knee bowed and every head tilted down till he passed. He greeted his daughter with kisses and then the air swirled around us as he passed by and stood in front of Lady Latimer.

"Your Majesty," she said. Her voice was soft and pliant but not subservient, and after she curtseyed she brought herself up to her full height, which was not inconsiderable, and smiled at the king.

"So we have you to thank for this?" The king held out the tailor's bill of sale.

"Yes, sire. The bill was mistakenly sent to me, as the tailor's assistant had somehow believed that the gowns were being commissioned for me. I have helped to array your daughter in the manner that will bring honor to her father," Lady Latimer said with a grin. "At your command, of course. And thus sent the expenses on to you."

At that, the king broke out in a loud laugh. "Yes, dear Lady Latimer. It was perfectly right to do so." The rest of us finally exhaled. He drew Kate aside and they sat in front of one of the large windows. We returned to cards, but because the room echoed well we could hear their conversation.

"How does Lord Latimer?" the king asked. He stretched his bad leg out in front of him; the Lady Mary had told us that it was causing him continual pain now as the ulcer upon it rarely closed and often oozed pus. Although he was extremely large, one could see a faint echo of the handsome man he used to be, a man who both drew and repelled, like a magnet turned this way then that.

"Not well, I fear," Lady Latimer responded quietly. "He shall . . . recall me soon, I expect."

I was not surprised. Margaret Neville had returned to Charterhouse the week before but Lady Latimer was not given leave to return yet.

"You must return to him," Henry said. "And then, perhaps afterward, you shall grace our court again?"

"As you wish, Your Majesty," Kate said. They spoke together for another fifteen minutes, in muted voices, so I knew not what they said. But you'd have had to be a fool, or blind—I was neither—to not see that the king was besotted with Kate.

The next day the Lady Mary's tailor came by Lady Latimer's chamber once more. Kate talked to him quietly and then closed the chamber door behind him. We all looked at her expectantly.

"The king has kindly ordered half a dozen gowns of the highest quality for me, as well, in light of the tailor's error."

My breath suspended for a moment, and none of us dared to look at one another for fear we'd disclose our dismay.

Later that night as we reposed I heard her sister, Lady Herbert, speak to her about it in a hushed voice in the next room as she changed into a bed gown.

"They say the king is looking for a new wife," she began. "It has been nigh on a year since Queen Catherine Howard's unfortunate death."

"What is that to me?" Lady Latimer asked.

"Come now, Kate. You are young, but not too young to make folly. You are beautiful—yes, you are! Your husband is unto death and the king is ordering very expensive gifts for you."

Lady Latimer snorted, mayhap willing herself blind to what she did not want to see. But when Kate returned to the chamber the merry look she had entered the closet with had hardened into one of disquiet and fear.

· · ·

Lord Latimer died on March 2, 1543, after having been shriven, according to his desire. His lady did not hold with such practices any longer but she honored her husband. Within a week, Henry recalled Kate to court. To my sorrow, I was required to send Lucy home to Marlborough, to the young man she'd intended to marry and to assist her mother at Brighton Manor. Whilst at court, we maidens had to avail ourselves of the king's servants.

"Who will assist ya if one of them dreams comes?" Lucy asked while packing her things.

I shook my head. "I shan't need anyone," I said with confidence. "I haven't had any since we've been here. Mayhap it was Marlborough that troubled me, and once I departed, the dreams departed too."

She looked doubtful but said nothing, hoping for my sake, I knew, that it was true.

I hoped so too.

To celebrate the arrival of spring His Majesty held a series of festivities at Hampton Court Palace. First was to be a pageant and then a dinner followed two evenings later by a masked ball. I hoped beyond anything that Jamie would be present, and spent much of my prayer time, I was shamed to admit, to that end.

Lord Latimer had left his wife a rich widow and

she supplied each of us in her household with coins so we could purchase a new mask. I had made the acquaintance of one of the seamstresses through Kate and the Lady Mary and I knew where to find her. "I shall have a mask made to exactly match my dress," I whispered to Dorothy. "Should you like to come along and have one too?"

"Oh yes," she said. She showed me the lovely blue gown she planned to wear. The color set off her fair skin and eyes but I could tell that the fabric had been turned. I knew the others would notice it, too, at the event.

" 'Tis a beautiful gown and color," I said. "I have one of a similar hue, a gift from my mother. Alas, it goes poorly with my complexion and I do not wear it." I fixed a look of surprise upon my face as though something had suddenly occurred to me. "Mayhap you would like it? It would be an honor to have it worn since it is my misfortune that I do not look well in it."

The expression upon Dorothy's face resembled that of a fish who had been stunned with a quick slap to a table, which troubled me greatly, but then she recovered. I had meant the offer to be a pleasure and not cause pain. "If it shan't unsettle you, I should like to," she said. "Thank you."

" 'Tis my pleasure," I said, and took the expensive gown from my wardrobe. "I am glad that it will get some use, and your lovely coloring suits it admirably." Afterward, we walked arm in arm to the seamstress's and bid her to make masks for us.

"I believe we shall be the only ladies in Lady Latimer's household with masks to match our gowns," Dorothy said with excitement. Mayhap it was the gift of the gown, but she grew friendlier on the walk back to our chamber, even speaking of how she came to be in Lady Latimer's household, which she had not told me of in detail before. Her mother was a distant cousin and her family had thirteen children; they could not afford to keep all of them in their own household.

I shared that my mother was of a higher-born family, too, which had fallen upon difficult circumstances many years back. "You and I are not so very different," I said.

"How did you come to stay with Lady Latimer?" she asked.

"Sir Thomas Seymour was an associate of my father. When my father became ill, Sir Thomas had, apparently, agreed to advance my brother on my father's behalf. And then, I suppose, me as well."

"I haven't seen Sir Thomas seek to advance others without also advancing himself in some way." Her tone was sharp and disdainful.

Dorothy was my friend, but I was not likely to let my benefactor go undefended, regardless of my niggling misgivings. Sir Thomas had helped Jamie, too, after all. "He seems right kind to me and likely to keep a promise," I replied promptly.

"He's right kind to all the ladies," Dorothy said, seemingly taken aback by my tone. "But he keeps an especial eye out for what will please Lady Latimer. Now that I know Sir Thomas placed you with Kate, 'tis easy to understand why you are becoming her favorite. She prefers all things connected to Sir Thomas."

I was uncertain if she had insulted me with the insinuation that Kate could not prefer me on my own merits, or if she was being honest, which I normally preferred but did not just now. I did not know what to believe about Sir Thomas, nor about most anyone at court. At least in Marlborough I knew where the wolves denned.

I said nothing more for a moment as our slippers tapped down the long stone hall. She spoke up again, pressing her point. "It was said that one of the women executed for robbery last year accused Sir Thomas of debauching her some years back, which left her little recourse but a sinful life and poor company thereafter."

I rolled my eyes in exasperation. I had been going to let the matter rest but now she had forced me to respond yet again. "I don't listen to servants' tittle-tattle."

" 'Twasn't servants passing that along." We soon reached our chamber and I handed over my linens to one of the court laundresses and then retired to bed early.

That night we lay quietly in our beds, which were mere feet from one another, not chatting as we usually did. My vision of Sir Thomas chopping the young maiden's dress into pieces while she looked on in agony joined neatly with Dorothy's tale of Sir Thomas's careless treatment of another woman. But both of those images collided with the friendly face and demeanor Sir Thomas had at court, and with his generosity in looking out for me and for Jamie, and with his affections for Kate. I did not know what to make of any of it.

And yet, I did not want to leave things unsettled between Dorothy and myself. I finally spoke into the dark silence. "I think your new mask will look quite becoming on you. It sets off your hair color just so."

"It shall," she said softly. "With the beautiful gown you've given me. You shall look becoming too."

I turned over then, able to relax, and wanting to sleep so I could be well rested for the next day's masque.

This was one occasion when I had been given leave to wear one of my finest gowns and I was again thankful of my father's pride in attire. My gown was claret colored, overstitched with gold thread, and had matching slippers. I arranged my hair in an elaborate knot with pearl pins embedded within. Mistress Dorothy and I walked to Lady Latimer's rooms together, whence we all left for the great hall.

We arrived at the dining table and one of the king's men showed us where we were to be seated. Kate was notably placed at the table in front of the king and the Lady Mary. After the supper there was a grand dance with a dozen musicians. The hall was ablaze with light and rich with the alchemy of sweat and perfume and ambition and lust, and the acrid wisps of burnt candle wicks.

I looked for Jamie but I did not see him. I had depended upon his being there because I knew Sir Thomas was. I was therefore sorely disappointed, but I heard another's voice behind me. "My lady, a dance?" A fine young man with a tousled head of long blond hair came to where I sat with Dorothy and several of the other ladies.

"Yes, of course, sir . . ."

"Tristram Tyrwhitt," he said. He took my hand and led me to the dance floor. His friend, mayhap not quite as finely wrought as this Tristram, followed behind with Dorothy. I was glad she'd been invited to dance as well but her eyes were not on her partner; rather, she fixed her gaze on Sir Tristram.

"I've not seen you here before," Sir Tristram said.

"No, I have only been in Lady Latimer's household for nigh on six months."

He nodded approvingly. "My aunt Lady Tyrwhitt is a good friend of Lady Latimer's."

"I have met her!" I exclaimed. "She is a most devout woman."

Sir Tristram rewarded me with a smile. "She is. And I suspect you are, too, mistress. Lady Latimer would not have her household be otherwise."

We made pleasant conversation about court and he danced with me thrice that evening, though keeping me at an arm's length. I did not have time to decide whether that was respectful modesty or an indication of his dislike of dancing before another young man approached.

"My lady, might I be so bold as to ask you to dance?" he asked. I looked up into the face of a tall and broad man a few years older than I. His green eyes gleamed in an unsettling but compelling manner. "Sir John Temple," he said. "Of Gardiner's household."

He wore the badge of his association and it did not sit well with me because I was not overfond of braggarts. He swept me out to dance and I had to admit that he was a fine dancer and kept good conversation. He drew me much closer than Sir Tristram had and while the sensation wasn't entirely unwelcome, it wasn't wholly welcome, either.

"Are you new to court?" he asked.

"I am, sir," I replied. He smiled with approval at my seeming subservience. "From Marlborough."

"You must watch your company then, my lady. Mayhap you do not know that the Tyrwhitts are reformers. A lady's reputation is made—and lost—quickly here."

"I thank you for your warning," was all I said, though a half dozen tart retorts begged for liberty.

"I would that our king would rid us of their pestilence. His Grace Stephen Gardiner makes continued efforts in that direction. *Ad maiorem dei gloriam.*"

I restrained a smile and translated. "'For the greater glory of God.' I suspect the reformers feel likewise."

Sir John held me at arm's length as the song ended. "You must have had good tutors. You speak Latin well," he said approvingly, but looked befuddled at my response, perhaps wondering if I was a reformer.

I curtseyed slightly and gave him a demure, ladylike smile. "Thank you for the dance, Sir John." I ended our time together.

He bowed in a courtly manner and moved on. "My pleasure, mistress."

While we watched the other dancers I had occasion to notice that His Majesty, a great bear of a man who completely dominated the room and still, somehow, exuded charm, danced with Lady Latimer as often as his demanding leg would allow. He did not unfasten his eyes from her whilst she was partnered by another. The other she was most often partnered with was Thomas Seymour. Her high color, her steady gaze into his eyes as they danced, and the frequent warm laughter they shared indicated that she was as besotted with Sir Thomas as he was with her. I grudged her not. Lord Latimer had long been ill and they had oft been separated by time and chance afore then. But now she was free.

I was nearby when the king stepped in. "May we intrude?" he asked Sir Thomas, as though there could be any answer but yes.

Before Sir Thomas could answer, the king made a point to ask Lady Latimer, "Is that one of the gowns we bought for you, Kate?"

She indicated that it was and he said, "We shall have to make for you a fine girdle of rubies and garnets for when you next wear it."

As I was next to Sir Thomas he looked at me and, though clearly discomfited by the discourse between Kate and the king, let a smile waggle his beard.

"Mistress St. John?"

" 'Twould be my distinct honor, Sir Thomas."

"How do you like your stay in Lady Latimer's household?"

"I am very happy, thank you, Sir Thomas. I have oft written to my mother to tell her about the kindness you've bestowed upon me."

Sir Thomas smiled, and apparently noticing that I continued to look about me, he asked, "Whom do you seek?"

"One of your men, sir," I said. I had no choice but to divulge my intent if I wanted an answer. "James Hart. Has he accompanied you this evening?"

Sir Thomas laughed. "He has. I expect if you look for a circle of ladies you shall find him at the center." He pulled away from me. "You're taking on the sheen of the court, Juliana."

'Twas the first time he'd spoken to me in such a familiar manner, but it was brotherly and seemed to hold no ill intent so I warmed to it. "I hope that is a compliment, Sir Thomas."

" 'Tis," he said, "and a warning." He bowed and I curtseyed and our dance was done. He took time to kiss my hand and as he did, I spied the gold and black onyx signet ring he always wore. It gave me pause, as it always brought my prophecy back to me.

I noticed that he next chose another young woman to dance with. She looked delighted, perhaps enchanted, to have been chosen to dance with him and her enthusiasm radiated outward from her countenance. Sir Thomas, like a man who'd long tarried in a gray season, absorbed that bright enthusiasm with apparent pleasure and repaid it in kind. He glanced at Kate, I assumed, to see if she took note of him with the pretty maiden. By her glance and grimace, she had.

I took a seat and a cup of watered wine and watched Dorothy on the dance floor, in the arms of Sir Tristram, who appeared slightly wearied in contrast to her rapt attention to his every word. I closed my eyes for a moment and rested. I'd have returned to my rooms but I'd agreed to help the Countess of Sussex assist Lady Latimer after the masque. Her sister, Lady Herbert, normally assisted but had left early because her mercurial husband had stalked out in anger at a perceived slight.

"I thought I'd never get my chance," said a voice from my side. I looked up. It was James. "May I keep you company, Juliana?"

"Of course," I said softly. His eyes were deeper than I recalled; I turned away from the intensity of them for a moment. If I had any doubts about his being a man afore he went to war, there were none present who could question it now.

"You look tired. And 'tis no surprise. Thrice I have sought to partner you at dance only to find you firmly in the arms of another."

I could hardly tell him that I had sought him as well. "The king's minstrels have played countless songs, so mayhap you did not try hard enough. Or mayhap you were already absorbed in the company of others."

He grinned and grew faintly red and I knew I had found the truth. He owed me no dance nor anything else, so I did not press the tease again. "How were your travels?"

"Unsettling. Daunting. Wondrous. Marvelous. But I have not yet earned my knighthood nor my fortune, so I shall have to return."

"To Austria? I had understood that the campaign was over."

He shook his head. "To war. But that is not talk for this night. If you have strength for one more dance, I should very much like to partner you."

I stayed myself from thinking of the many ways I could interpret that statement and simply said, "It would be my pleasure."

He took my hand and led me out to dance; the musicians had struck up a melody of the king's own composing so all danced for fear of giving insult by remaining seated. I noticed little else but the feel of Jamie's hand on the small of my back, his eyes holding mine, and the unforced rhythm of both our steps and our conversation.

"Lady Latimer is much in demand at court these days," he said.

" 'Tis true," I noted as I looked toward the king, who partnered her again. Sir Thomas was firmly in the arms of another lady but did not look happy. "Lady Herbert believes the king is eager for another wife. His Majesty visits Lady Latimer several times a day, in either her own chambers or those of the Lady Mary."

Jamie shuddered. "Five wives is enough," he

said, though it was dangerous to speak it. I admired his boldness. He turned with a grin. "The Turks take four wives. Sometimes all at once."

"I know that well," I said. "My late father shared many tales with me of the lands in which he traded." I flashed a wicked grin. "Do you aspire to become a Turk, then, Jamie?"

He laughed aloud. "Nay, mistress, they are braver than I. One wife is enough for me. If she were the right one," he parried. "What other tales did your father tell you?"

"Oh, some from the East. And some of the natural world. But he was a proud Englishman and loved best to tell the story of Saint George. But that, too, is talk for another night, and another audience."

The song soon ended and Sir John Temple touched Jamie on the shoulder and, bearing his greater status, indicated that he would like the next dance with me. Jamie graciously kissed my hand, and I felt the kiss run through me afore he took his leave. In less than a minute he'd partnered a woman who glittered more than I. John Temple held me close, and I suspected that my cool reserve earlier had somehow driven him back to me in a challenge.

Later, I sat at a table and took some refreshment. Dorothy joined me, so I asked her, "Are you fond of Sir Tristram Tyrwhitt?"

"Not particularly. I scarce know him. Why do you ask?"

"I noticed you enjoyed his company," I said.

"I noticed he enjoyed yours," she said a little sharply. "And yet, mayhap you prefer the Irishman?"

I grinned and she saw it and grinned back. Then I replayed in my mind every word Jamie had said, the sound of his laugh, and the most welcome feel of his hand on my back.

Later that night I took in hand the jeweled pins Kate eased from her hair and then returned them to their casket. "Did you enjoy yourself this evening, Juliana?" she asked.

"Oh yes, my lady," I said. "It truly was a marvelous time. There are no words adequate to express my gratitude at being included in your household." She stood to be unbuttoned and I fetched her bed gown whilst her lady maid left the room with Kate's gown. This left Kate and me alone for a moment.

"Court is a wondrous place," she agreed. "I enjoyed the evening too."

"Especially with Sir Thomas?" I teased.

She turned to correct me but saw the grin upon my face, and, I supposed, remembered my own connection to Sir Thomas and softened some. "Yes, yes, especially with Sir Thomas."

"How did you become acquainted with him?"

"My brother, William, was in the household of the Duke of Richmond at the same time that Thomas's older brother, Edward, was. I had occasion then to begin our . . . friendship. And it grew with stops and starts through the years."

"He is not yet married," I ventured with care. "Nor are you, since the passing of Lord Latimer, God rest his soul."

Kate closed her eyes for a moment and finally said, "My mind is fully bent to marry Sir Thomas before any man I know." The maid came back into the room and Kate, startled by the noise, wakened from her reverie and perhaps recognized that she had disclosed more than she had intended to.

"Yes?" she asked in a faintly sharp tone.

"The king, His Majesty, has sent this for you," she said as she held out a box. Nestled within was a pair of pearl drop earrings.

FOUR

Spring and Early Summer:
Year of Our Lord 1543
The Palace at Whitehall
Hampton Court Palace

Nearly every day after the masque an invitation came to Kate from the king. He might invite her to a hunt or to join him at cards or request her presence in his dining chamber. She oft reciprocated, as she knew she must, with an invitation to join her in like manner. One night she invited His Majesty and his men to dine with her maidens and ladies, which still numbered few, in her chambers.

The king arrived last, as was fitting, and none could depart thereafter till he gave them leave. We knew that our gowns and persons must please the king's eye, which was ever drawn toward all that was beguiling. Kate had asked me to lightly sugar the claret whilst she talked with the king. Discussion turned toward the laws Parliament was about to pass, on the king's behalf, banning certain books and Bible translations that we all knew to be dear to Kate. As her voice grew more strident the room grew more still.

"Your Majesty has done much good in this realm, the most good done of any king ever, truth be told," Kate said with sincerity.

The king's face warmed quickly. "We are well pleased with your opinion of us, Kate."

I glanced at Dorothy. She'd caught it too. "Lady Latimer" had been replaced with "Kate."

"We've insisted that anything hinting at heresy shall be made illegal. Tyndale and Coverdale's translations of holy writ will soon no longer be allowed, only the Great Bible, and we have made changes in our own hand on the *Necessary Doctrine and Erudition for Christian Men*. Luther's repugnant thoughts have been refused."

He then clapped his hands together for more wine and Kate nodded to me to serve him, as his cupbearer, Edward Askew, was not present. I approached him carefully. I stood close and could hear him breathing heavily, ignoring the faint but pungent scent of a rotted tooth. I smiled down at him and he smiled back at me but just as quickly turned back to Kate, who was speaking.

"And yet, Your Grace has himself instituted great reform," Kate said rather bluntly. "Turning the realm away from all things of a superstitious manner and allowing prayers to be said in the mother tongue of your subjects, by your subjects, great and mean." I stepped back and Lady Herbert grimaced. But the king seemed delighted that Kate could hold her own in conversation with him.

"And we shall continue to determine the boundaries as is our place as Defender of the Faith. We expect our subjects of every rank and station to bring themselves unto strict obedience to the new law, as is meet." The king had brought the conversation to a close.

Kate opened her mouth to speak again but I saw her sister shake her head slightly. Kate instead turned the conversation to the merrier topics and insisted on playing dice. She beat him handily and he seemed glad of it. "This is one debt we shall be glad to pay," he said, taking her hand in his and raising it to his lips. Before he took his leave that evening he drew her into his arms and kissed her on both cheeks. "You are sweet and pure, Kate," he said. "Your very goodness exudes from within." He still maintained his courtly manners and indeed showed interest in all present in some small capacity or another, a warm touch, even to those of lower status. This was more than could be said for many men of lesser rank.

One afternoon a week hence, Kate returned from dining in his apartments and drew her ladies together.

"The king has extended his hand to me in marriage. He has given me some time to think upon the matter, though he made no secret of what his earnest desire would be."

I looked at Dorothy and she looked back at me—we were both horrified. His earnest desire! Enforced with the point of a sword? Mayhap not, but the king was hard to resist; none had ever done so that I could tell. Many former queens had sought his favor but, once they'd captured it, rather found that it was like taming a tiger. Kate had neither sought nor wanted his attentions, I knew.

I gave Dorothy a meaningful look, and though we both held our tongues and kept our peace, I knew we'd discuss this in detail later in our chamber. I determined, if I could, to speak of my fears to my lady, to reassure myself, if not to inform her of anything new.

Some of Kate's greater ladies gathered round

her to offer solemn congratulations, but shortly thereafter Sir Thomas Seymour and many of his household, though not Jamie, arrived to play cards. Kate dismissed most of her household, but Lady Margaret Neville and I remained to assist in putting away the cards and dice that would no longer be needed. She then drew Sir Thomas aside.

Dorothy looked at Sir Thomas and Kate, and then me, with a knowing glance before she took her leave. While I was glad to have been chosen to help Lady Margaret Neville, I grew irritated at Dorothy. *She is jealous,* I told myself. I had to wonder why the questioning of Sir Thomas made me behave with uncharacteristic rashness. And why did Dorothy insist on so easily questioning Sir Thomas when she knew him to be my patron and my father's friend?

Kate and Sir Thomas spoke softly by the fire and we took care not to draw too close, but I was young and my hearing was sharp. I knew Margaret Neville's was too.

"I will have none but you, Kate," he said.

"I wish none but you, Tom," she said. "It is my fondest wish and desire to marry you. But it cannot be."

"It need not remain so, but can indeed become a fact." Seymour took her hand in his and slowly kissed each fingertip and then the inside of her palm. I turned away from the intimacy of it and withdrew to her dressing chamber with Margaret Neville. I wondered what Lady Margaret Neville thought of this, only months after her own father's death. But she had always remained resolutely loyal to Kate.

When we returned to the room, Seymour was about to take his leave. As he did, the king appeared with his men at the door to Kate's chambers.

"Tom," the king said, a look of surprise upon his face. Lady Margaret, Kate's ladies, and I attempted to make it clear that Kate had not been in the room alone.

"Your Majesty," Sir Thomas said with a deep bow from the waist. He withdrew and the king took Kate's hand in his own, although he still looked faintly bewildered.

"We bring glad tidings," he said. "In addition to those I have already imparted earlier." His eyes gleamed at the apparent memory of his proposal of marriage.

Kate welcomed the king into her receiving chamber. We withdrew to a suitable distance.

"We have decided to raise your beloved brother William to Knight of the Garter," he said. "And thereupon make him lord warden and keeper of the Western March. With all its attendant responsibilities and privileges, incomes, and rooms at court."

Margaret and I looked at one another wide eyed.

"Thank you, Majesty," Kate said in her sweet, moderated voice.

"But that is not all," the king continued. "We have also decided to dispense various favors and privileges upon your sister's husband, Lord Herbert. In Wales."

"You are too kind, sire," Kate said. "Thank you, Your Majesty."

"We shall take our leave," he said. "We know you have much to think upon and shall need quiet. But we shall not stop thinking upon you in your absence," he said, his voice filled with affection. "And shall pray for Godspeed in your decision."

Kate spent some time conferring with her brother and sister over the matter of the king's proposal, and I was sure that they knew of her affections for Sir Thomas. In spite of her misgivings, Kate's siblings were strongly in favor of the king's suit and spent the week encouraging her in that direction. In case she wanted of a push, the king sent that promised girdle of gold and rubies, which she immediately fastened about her waist. He knew she loved rubies above all other gems.

One morning in early May we gathered in Kate's chambers, and after some stitching and gossip Kate indicated that she wanted us to read for a while. Her friends were women with preferences similar to her own: reading, debate, reformed religious discussion. It was not that we didn't enjoy dancing and music, gowns and jewelry, and discussing men; we did that too. Excepting perhaps the Countess of Sussex, who rarely made small talk. I could think of no one who liked her husband the earl. He had a back as firm as a thin leather lash and a tongue to match it; though she were sharply spoken sometimes as well, her back was of oak. 'Twas hard to believe she was but a few years older than Kate.

"Shall you read to us this morning, Juliana?" Kate asked. Dorothy had read, beautifully, the morning before, so it was not unexpected that it might be my turn. I chose Tyndale's translation of holy writ, as I had been spending time reading it in my own chamber and felt most confident with and affectionate toward the material. I opened to a passage in the Epistle of Saint Paul unto the Galatians, and began reading in the sixth chapter. I had just finished the section which ended with, "Let us not be weary of well-doing. For when the time is come, we shall reap without weariness. While we have therefore time, let us do good unto all men, and specially unto them which are of the household of faith."

At that moment, the Countess of Sussex entered the room with Lady Tyrwhitt, Tristram's aunt and Kate's dear friend. Kate indicated for me to stop reading.

Lady Tyrwhitt began. "Parliament has just

passed a law barring Tyndale's translation as a 'crafty, false, and untrue translation.' It also forbids nearly all religious commentary, and indeed, practically every book published with the exception of a very few approved by His Majesty."

The countess snorted. "His Majesty's Great Bible is so alike Tyndale's 'crafty, false, and untrue' one as to be cut of the same cloth."

Lady Tyrwhitt continued. "All lower classes and servants are forbidden from reading holy writ either publicly or privately. And whilst highborn women are allowed to read the king's Great Bible privately to themselves, they are not allowed to read it to their ladies or servants. Only licensed men may read it aloud or publicly."

All expected me, I knew, to close Tyndale's "crafty" and now forbidden translation and for a moment I felt the weight of the king's new law. Then Matthias's father's smug face leered at me from a memory, and my father risking himself to transport it responded in my mind, so I pressed on, courageously and not foolishly, I hoped, nervously turning back a few pages before reading out in a strong voice.

" 'Now is there no Jew neither gentile: there is neither bond nor free: there is neither man nor woman: but ye are all one thing in Christ Jesus."

I closed the book with a flourish. Holy writ itself contradicted the king's new decree. The room remained still. For a moment, I repented of the choice. Had I gone too far? Misjudged the tone of the room? I held my face steady and prayed that I had not overstepped.

And then Kate laughed, and Dorothy next, then the others; I was glad of it and joined in, feeling truly welcome and among my own for the first time in my life.

Later that afternoon Kate sat writing letters, and when she was done, she handed one to Lady Margaret Neville, whom I knew she considered her daughter though she were born of Lord Latimer and his first wife. "Please deliver this to Sir Thomas," she said. Margaret dipped a short curtsey and took her leave.

Dorothy put the books away and I cleared Kate's desk. As I did, next to the draft of the book she was writing, I saw a piece of letter parchment that she had discarded after blotting it with ink. Upon it she'd written,

God withstood my will therein most vehemently for a time. Through His grace and goodness, He made that possible which seemed to me impossible: that was, made me renounce utterly mine own will and to follow His most willingly. It were too long to write all the process of this matter. If I live, I shall declare it to you myself. But I will marry the king.

I looked up to find her standing over my shoulder and grew red with shame. "I am heartily sorry."

"For reading my private correspondence or for the decision I've made?"

"Both, lady, as I have great love for you and wish only joy for you and not the great calamity I fear, and feel, lies ahead," I pled. I had not had a prophetic vision that warned of this, and yet that spiritual sense inside me reverberated.

She took the paper from me and then took my cold hands in her own warm ones and led me to some nearby chairs. "Come, dear heart."

Unexpectedly, tears filled my eyes. My own mother had never referred to me with such a term of endearment, and I had never heard Kate use one with any save Margaret Neville. Until that moment I had not realized that I so long craved that kind of affection and love, as a deer pants for water.

"It was not my desire, as you are well aware, to set Sir Thomas aside and marry the king. And yet as I have written to Sir Thomas, our Lord has overcome my will with His own. It became clear to me after the new laws that the realm is going in the wrong direction, perfectly backward to the gains that have been made. And, of course, the prince's tutors are likely to influence his thoughts upon the reform, and the direction the realm will take whilst in his care, so their continuing sympathetic selection is imperative. As is a mother's love. I feel a call to persuade in the way only a wife can, the most intimate of influences. Queen Anne Boleyn herself strongly influenced the beginning of reform thusly."

"I beg your pardon, my lady." I knelt before her, having felt that same mother's love from her and not wanting to lose it, for her sake, and for mine. Fear rose at the mention of the name of beheaded Queen Anne. "But that queen did not meet with a seemly end in spite of the king's deep affections for her."

If I live, Kate had written to Sir Thomas. She well knew the risks. I was not entirely sure I wished for her to marry Sir Thomas either, as his presence in my vision still unsettled me. But the risks of Sir Thomas were nothing when compared with the risks of marrying His Majesty.

And yet, did she truly have the choice to reject the king?

"You've heard how soft a tone the king uses with me," Kate continued. "And the king has his son, Prince Edward, now; 'twas lack of a son more than forthright speech that undid Queen Anne."

"Perhaps you shall give the king another son." That alone would have saved Queen Anne; perhaps that would save Kate. Since she was set upon this course, I reached to whatever comfort I could offer her and myself, though it was a weak tonic.

Kate's eyes misted over. "There is nothing so desirous within me as to bear a child of my own. I pray that God will bring it to pass, but I doubt that it will, because I have twice married with no quickening of child." She took my hand and lifted me off of the floor. "You, Mistress St. John, shall stay on in my household as a maid of honor, if your mother wills it."

"Oh, she shall!" I exclaimed. "I mean, I hope she will agree."

Kate laughed with me.

"What does a maid of honor do, lady?"

"She helps, like all the queen's other ladies, as you have been doing, except my household will become much bigger and have many more responsibilities. Gowning and ungowning when the ladies require assistance, assisting with the care of all the wardrobe and jewels, fetching physics and other things as I require in my pursuit to be useful. Maids of honor provide companionship as well as partnering at cards and dance, delivering or fetching messages for me, and reading—for which you are specially well suited. My ladies in waiting will pack and unpack as we travel and you can assist. And," she finished, "the queen's ladies of all rank are to be her friends and her protectors, because court is a treacherous and cunning place."

I nodded. "Thank you, my lady. I shall endeavor to be useful in all I do." As I said it, a certain peace and heaviness quickened within me, a certainty that this promise to her, so readily spoken, would be bigger, fuller, harder and would require more than I could yet imagine. My prophecies, those seen and yet unseen, and perhaps my very life would be demanded. The arc of her life was somehow, now, fused with mine.

As I gazed upon her face and basked in her unwavering affection, I knew that whatever was required of me I would do.

Kate smiled. "That is an excellent motto, Juliana, to be useful in all I do. I shall adopt it for one of my own. It rings of your earlier reading today, does it not, to not grow weary of well-doing?"

I delightedly made my way back to my chamber, restraining myself from childishly skipping down the elegant hallway. I rather fancied being a maid of honor!

Within the week the king sent Sir Thomas Seymour to the Netherlands for an extended diplomatic discussion. I was not privy to their good-byes, but I know Kate mourned deeply from the sleeplessness her face revealed, which we powdered over, and the sighs she could not withhold.

Soon thereafter, just four months after my Lord Latimer's passing, the king gathered together a few dozen of those most important in the realm to Hampton Court Palace for the wedding. Straddling one bank of the river Thames, the palace was hugged with lush green lawns of July and trees that were heavy with leaves. The king's gardeners ensured that flowers thrived, and the best and brightest of them bloomed as if at royal command under the welcomed English sun.

Two dozen men were there to support the king, as well as some of Kate's family and friends. Thomas Seymour's brother Edward was there, though of course Thomas was not. Henry was fond of them both, as uncles to his son and brothers to his beloved wife Jane, who'd died afore Henry had a chance to grow tired of her. But Henry had sniffed out Thomas's interest in Kate and sent him away.

I accompanied all of Kate's ladies to the Queen's Closet, which was next to the royal chapel, but did not remain in the exalted company of attendants. The closet was small. Kate, I knew, was hesitant. Although Cranmer had issued the license, Bishop Gardiner, who all knew yearned for the church in England to return to Rome, would preside over the marriage ceremonies.

"Does Bishop Gardiner know of your sympathies?" Lady Seymour had asked her once when there had been but few of us in her chamber.

"Nay," she'd said. "My Lord Latimer was a faithful Catholic till the day he died. Gardiner likely assumes the same of me. When he finds out I am not, he shall become my enemy."

"It seems to me that the king oft plays divide and conquer with his churchmen," I'd said. "Mayhap to keep them off balance."

Kate dropped her brush and looked around the room before speaking sharply to me. "You must become temperate in your speech, mistress, and learn when to hold your tongue. The time for naive girlhood is over. Now."

"Forgive me, my lady." I was deeply remorseful.

Kate nodded. "An astute person does not let her talk become a menace to those around her."

"Yes, madam." It was a maternal reproof but offered with love. I knew, too, by the eddies swirling around the court, that while all were happy to see a woman of her kindness and learning become queen, none knew what to expect from His Majesty. His cycle of affection seemed to shorten with each bride.

I am to be a friend and protector. Useful in all I do. I shall learn to hold my tongue.

We maidens left her there in the Queen's Closet shortly afore the ceremony with the unreasonably merry guests, among whom were relatives of Anne Boleyn, Jane Seymour, and Catherine Howard. On the return to my chamber I walked the long gallery and as I did, I recalled to mind that only a year and a half had passed since Queen Catherine Howard had run shrieking down this very hallway, begging for her life from the king, who'd refused, as was his habit, to see her afore sending her to her death. It made me very cold indeed with concern for my lady.

That evening there was a small but sumptuous dinner. 'Twas held in the great hall, of which Henry was proud, and rightly so. The king's minstrels played marvelously well, the strings groaning and the flute whispering breathily as I imagined lovers might, which was only fit for this eve.

"Kate eats lightly," I pointed out to Dorothy, who sat beside me.

" 'Tis her wedding night," she giggled, and raised her eyebrows. "Of course."

"I noticed that the king is not as disinclined toward the table." I spoke softly.

Dorothy laughed and drew near me. "Imagine waiting in your marriage bed and seeing His Majesty coming toward you." She wrinkled her nose.

"Much like a barge making its way down the Thames. I fancy a rather different kind of wedding night," I replied with a grin. I wanted to tease with her but did have a caution toward idle chatter, due to Kate's earlier rebuke.

"I too," Dorothy said before taking her leave to talk with another friend. I wondered whether Dorothy had a young man waiting for her in her home shire, someone her father had picked out for her, a spoken or even an unwelcome but seemingly unavoidable understanding, as I had with Matthias. In all our time together it had been a topic she'd never raised and assiduously avoided when I had.

Lady Margaret Neville slid alongside me. She looked rather wan, and I urged her to retire to her chamber early as Lady Herbert would serve the queen this night.

"I may," she said, looking off toward the corner and then nodding. "As I can see I'll leave you in welcome company."

She smiled in the way of a true friend, and when I saw upon whom she trained her gaze, James Hart, I blushed. My affections had been made plain enough that Lady Margaret Neville had guessed my feelings, and then I grew white with the shock that he was there at all.

"You seem surprised to see me, mistress," he said as he took my arm and did not release it but used it to draw me near. A most welcome gesture. "You mistook me for a ghost?"

"'Tis unlikely any would mistake you for a ghost," I said. Then I repented of it because I did not want him to think I was looking upon his figure.

"Why is that?" he teased, clearly knowing my thoughts.

"I thought you had left with Sir Thomas." I

neatly turned the subject, which he gallantly allowed.

"I leave to join him soon, after returning to Ireland with my brother Oliver to meet with some who will contract with us for shipping. Have you partaken of enough strawberries?" He waved over one of the king's servers and requested more. When they arrived, he handed the platter to me and I plucked the finest one and held it out to him.

"I am already overfond of strawberries," he said, his voice quiet but rough as he cupped my hand with one of his own before plucking out the berry with the other. "I must have a care 'ere I become overfond of their bearer as well."

I ducked my head to hide the coming pink flush. James laughed.

"I do have a small trunk for Her Grace," he said, looking at Kate.

Ah yes, I must recall to style her that from now on.

"May I give it to you in her stead? It's from Sir Thomas."

"What is it?" I asked. I was not about to take delivery of something that would put her at risk, and while I knew Kate loved Sir Thomas, I was not altogether certain that he might not bedevil her in some unwitting way.

"Books," he said softly. "From the ship that put into harbor late. She expects them."

"Yes," I agreed. "I shall keep them in my chamber

until I can place them in her locked cupboard."

I told him where to find my chamber and he said he would arrive there presently with the books. I quickly made my way down the long galleries, past the courtyard, and to my room.

It wasn't but a few minutes later when James's knock came to my door.

I pinched my cheeks for color, smoothed back my hair, and opened the chamber door. "Come in," I said.

"Here they are." He handed a small case of books to me. I'd look over the titles later; Kate would surely not mind. He took one off of the top, though. "May I take a seat?"

"Oh, of course," I said, sorry that I had forgotten my manners. We pulled the two small chairs next to the fire. He handed the book to me.

"This one is for you."

I opened my eyes wide, and then my mouth, and then shut them both. I tried to speak but nothing came out.

"You make a fine imitation of a puppet," James teased.

I looked down upon the book. It was leather bound, and on the top, in gilt, was written *Saint George and the Dragon.* Brilliant colors and finely wrought drawings completed the magnificent cover. I drew it close to me. "Oh, thank you, James. But you needn't have."

"Of course I needn't have," he said. "But I was

96

carrying books for a client who oft asks me what I'd like for myself. Normally I take nothing. This time I said I'd like this book, as I knew someone who would appreciate it."

"Oh, yes, yes, I will. I mean I do. I mean, thank you!"

He grinned. " 'Tis not every day I get to please a pretty mistress."

"Don't ruin the gift with a mistruth," I advised. At that, he laughed before standing up and growing sober.

"I'd best take my leave," he said. "We sail with the tide."

I stood and walked him to the door of my chamber. "How can I thank you? I do not like to receive a gift without giving one in return."

He pretended to think afore answering. "A kiss . . . ?"

I nodded. He bent near and did not press his advantage in an ungentlemanly way, but kissed me softly on the lips; for a moment, though, I heard and felt his breath quicken and sensed he would have liked to have made the kiss longer.

I wished it too. My thoughts were dismissed and emotions summoned forth and I felt faint and alive both at once.

It didn't seem enough, one kiss for a book, a wonderful book, the book that reminded me of my sweet father. I decided I could offer him some-thing further. Hope. And belief in him.

" 'Till we meet again, *Sir* James Hart."

"I shall do my best to earn that knighthood, Juliana," he said softly. He turned to walk away and then turned back toward me. "Thank you," he said with emotion I'd not heard in his voice before.

FIVE

Summer, Autumn, and Winter:
Year of Our Lord 1543
Hampton Court Palace
Ashridge House
Greenwich Palace

E ven before her wedding Her Grace had begun to assemble her household and its goods, and the ladies and the men who would serve her now that she was queen. She surrounded herself with those she could trust and some she could not. Her uncle served as her lord chamberlain, her cousin as her cupbearer. Among her new ladies was the stunningly lovely Elisabeth Brooke, niece of the poet Thomas Wyatt, who had died the year before. The queen's brother, William, was married to the highborn heir to the Earl of Essex, but she'd abandoned William Parr two years earlier to elope with another man, though her current marriage had not yet ended by divorce or annulment. She thus lived in bigamy, and had brazenly borne a child by her new husband, a prior, no less. William, thus abandoned, was especially taken with Elisabeth Brooke.

Kate took me aside. "Should you mind if I place you into a room with Elisabeth Brooke? She is lively and kind and I believe the two of you would find the arrangement congenial. Because of her . . . *affection* for my brother, I should prefer someone I know to be discreet to share her chamber. And"—Kate's eyes twinkled—"because her father is Baron Cobham, her chamber will be distant from kitchen and stable smells."

"Thank you, madam, that would be delightful," I said. I was pleased that, in spite of my earlier intemperate remark, she viewed me as discreet enough to be trusted with a difficult situation within her family and household, one she had no control over but that could harm all involved if it was not handled with care. I determined I would uphold that confidence at all cost.

Lady Fitzgerald Browne came welcome to Kate's household too. Irish, beautiful, and remaining staunchly Roman Catholic, she was three years younger than I but already married to Sir Anthony Browne and stepmother to his eight children. The Duchess of Suffolk was more inclined to share my lady's persuasions and she was young and witty, but oversharp of the tongue.

One morning shortly after Kate's marriage, we were in the midst of ordering several dozen new pairs of shoes for Kate when one of the king's men appeared on the ground floor of the queen's apartments at Hampton Court.

"Pardon, Your Grace, but the king would like to know if you have need of some babies."

A titter went across the room and the king's man went red. A saucy response was on my tongue but I endeavored to hold it back, promising myself that I would share it with Dorothy later. She had avoided any such pleasant discourse with me since Kate had changed our rooming situation.

"Thank His Majesty for me," the queen answered. "My seamstress has provided everything required." After the door was closed behind him we burst out laughing as Kate explained that some of the king's men called his dressing manikins "babies." I marveled, for a moment, of a man who cared so about clothing that he had dolls. Then I remembered 'twas His Majesty we spoke of and marveled not at all.

Later we returned to the queen's presence chamber, up a long spiral staircase, which lay next to the Queen's Closet and her bedchamber. The rooms faced the park and welcomed the glorious sunlight. Over the next week she ordered gowns and kirtles, sleeves, and then fine linens. Next Kate required pouches of sweet herbs for her bath—and for her bed. I found myself contemplating if His Majesty's wound required an excessive amount of herbs to camouflage the odor and then promised myself that I should better marry soft Matthias than an old man with evil smells about him.

But 'twas not Matthias I dreamt of marrying; others might have directed my actions but they couldn't command my dreams. At night I lay abed, in my empty chamber, and when I closed my eyes I could see Jamie's smile, his blue eyes, his laugh. I could feel his lips upon mine and when I did I held the thought still in time, till mayhap they could revisit me again. I had thought poetry of love, which I had been required to study, perhaps a fancy of the imagination. Now I knew that it was a reflection of truth.

Seeing Kate busy writing her books and devotions had prompted me to write more often, too—to my mother. I had written to ask permission to remain in the queen's service and shared with her news of the court, of my friends, and of my book. I had hoped for a somewhat merry response with news of all that was happening in Marlborough. She replied that I might, of course, wait upon the queen as long as the queen would have me, till I was betrothed. She did not specify when that might be, nor did she add anything of a personal nature, though we'd been parted for a year.

Hugh wrote back to me and conveyed her letter with his. "My studies go well, but I miss you, and would you please find a place for me at court?" I think he misunderstood how little influence I had, but I promised myself that I would endeavor to mention it to the queen till she found a place for him. I kept his letter tucked in my trunk and read it often just to hear his voice.

One day the queen's sister came to her with news that one of Kate's ladies, Lady Wriothesley, staunchly for the old religion, had lost her young son shortly after his birth. "You'll recall Secretary Wriothesley wrote a kind note about you to the Duke of Suffolk after your wedding," Lady Herbert said. "He also wrote kindly of you to William, our brother. Should you send a note of regret to his wife?"

Kate nodded, and whilst I folded her silks she dictated a letter to her secretary indicating that she grieved for Lady Wriothesley's loss. Perfectly proper. Then she added, "It hath pleased God of late to disinherit your son of this world."

Kate stopped and spoke to Lady Herbert. "I have heard that she sorrows overmuch, which is not becoming."

"But, Kate, 'tis the loss of a child." All knew Lady Herbert treaded lightly because the queen had been deprived of bearing a child of her own.

"I well know it's the loss of a child," Kate responded sharply. "Because I have not borne a child of my own does not mean that I cannot sympathize nor understand the grief of those who have."

The room grew quiet. 'Twas rare that Kate lost her temper or dressed anyone down. But when she did none dared meddle, not even her sister, who knew better, having served in the household of each of Henry's six wives. The queen gathered herself and turned back toward her secretary, indicating that he should continue.

"For what is excessive sorrow but plain evidence against you that your inward mind doth repine against God's sayings, and a declaration that you are not contented that God hath put your son by nature, by his adoption, in possession of the heavenly kingdom?"

She nodded for him to finish off, she signed it *Kateryn, the Queene, KP*, and sealed it. No one spoke out again about the unseemly attitude she'd taken toward a young mother in grief. But I knew enough about the court, and women, and grudges long nursed, to fear that this would come back and harm her someday.

The eve afore we left on progress there was a dinner at court and then a reciting of sonnets, which the king both composed and enjoyed. Lady Fitzgerald Browne and I amused ourselves by composing witty sonnets to one another in a corner whilst waiting for the more exalted ones to be read. After some of the poems had been recited, the guests walked about talking with one another, especially as those who would not accompany the king would likely return to their own properties and not return to court till Christmas. I was nibbling on a sugared plum when John Temple approached me.

"Mistress Juliana." He tipped his head, which, strictly speaking, he did not need to do. But 'twas polite, and I bowed mine in return. "How go the affairs of little Marlborough?" His smile was sarcastic, though he kept his tone even.

"I am shocked that you would care to know anything about our town."

"I am most interested in what is new . . . and fresh . . . at court, mistress." His voice had the snap of a just-bitten apple. He continued. "I've found that things are different in the country. More backward in some ways. More forward in others. I find you lovely." He placed his hand on my back; he then slid his hand around the front of my gown toward my waist, but I quickly stepped away afore his fingers could further splay upward.

"Good eve, Sir John." I retreated to the side of the room, next to Dorothy, who looked at me questioningly but said nothing so as not to be impolite. I took a glass of watered wine in my shaking hand. Had he meant me no harm and I misjudged his intent? Just then, Sir Tristram arrived. Dorothy smiled with real pleasure, the affection softening her already pretty face. But 'twas me Sir Tristram wanted to speak with, and as he pulled me to the side I saw her smile slide.

"Mistress Juliana," he said, "I feel I must warn you. Do not do anything to encourage Sir John."

I stepped back in shock. Had he witnessed John Temple's attempt and interpreted it as welcome? "I never would, Sir Tristram!"

He softened and called me by my given name. "Juliana. You are pure, but in want of understanding of the ways of court. Have a care. And please call me Tristram. I shall look upon your return to court with great anticipation."

"I do believe my friend Mistress Dorothy will be in attendance upon the queen whilst I am away," I said. "She's got a strong mind for holy writ and is a wonderful dance partner. I think you would find time in her company to be most enjoyable." He nodded briefly, and then spoke of inconsequential matters for another moment or two. As he took his leave, he neglected to stop and greet Dorothy. She continued to look upon him with pleasure, but when she turned to me, she scowled and then looked away. I blinked away my hurt. I had tried to turn him her way.

Why was she upset with *me?*

Because the greater ladies in Kate's household were themselves preparing to leave on the morrow, and because I had so little to pack and prepare, I was allowed to help Kate ready herself for a visit from His Majesty that evening.

I rubbed a bit of almond oil on my hands and

then through her hair afore I brushed it out. Whilst I did, she leaned forward and, looking into a small glass, plucked her eyebrows into a neat, up-tipped V, using a silver pincers.

"I should like to try that sometime," I said. "I feel that my brows are unruly, and, well, simple."

She laughed. "Set the brush down." She bid me draw near and then one by one plucked the hair from one of my brows till she showed me its perfect shape in the mirror.

"It feels like bee stings!" I rubbed my left brow with a bit of her oil of clove afore she began on the right.

" 'Tis not easy to be a woman," she said. "Surely your mother has told you that."

I cast my eyes down. "My mother does not discuss such things with me, Your Grace."

"Ah, I see," she said. "Well. Now your brows shall appear perfectly obedient when the young men seek to partner you at dance."

"My lady?" I inquired.

"I've watched many seek you out this eve," she said. "And I suspect there will be many more."

I smiled. Courtiers, knights, were interested in me. What would Matthias think?

She looked at the gold and diamond watch hanging from her girdle, one of her many watches, of which she was fond. "His Majesty will arrive presently." I nodded and stood up.

"Thank you for taking the time to assist me,

tonight, Your Grace, when it should have been me assisting you."

She drew me near to her in an embrace. " 'Twas a pleasure, Juliana. *You* are a pleasure, one perhaps your mother does not recognize." Then she let go. "I shall see you upon the morrow."

Late that night Elisabeth and I stayed up packing and sharing excitement over the forthcoming progress. Because she was oft with the queen's brother, and he so highly placed, she flew well above the official station as a maid of honor and was rarely in our chamber. We did not, therefore, discourse much. But when we did, I found her a marvelous friend.

We left the next day, riding ahead of the plague. The king had a particular fear of that illness, though none could blame him as it was a fearsome contagion. He left behind death of his own making, however. Four good men were convicted of acting in conscience against the King's Act of Six Articles, which spelt out acceptable faith and practice thereof, and were sentenced to death. They were burned, reported to have walked to their deaths filled with glee, almost as those far gone in drink. One arranged a coronet of straw on his head so he would present himself to our Lord with a martyr's crown of fire. Kate had told us that she meant to change this, somehow, and set her mind upon it.

Among the silks and perfumes and dozens of shoes that were her delightful perquisites, Kate had begun her dangerous work.

I knew that the king's daughters, the Lady Mary and the Lady Elizabeth, were to join us on progress. I had become well accustomed to the Lady Mary, as the queen often kept her in her company and they were great friends. The Lady Elizabeth had been at the wedding itself but had not attended the festivities afterward, being only ten years old. So I was eager to make her acquaintance. Because she had not long been restored to the king's affections there was not even yet one portrait of her by which her features may have been made known.

It was a shock to me of the gravest nature, then, when I did meet her. Kate called me over, along with Dorothy and Lady Margaret Neville.

"I would like to present the king's daughter, the Lady Elizabeth," she said.

Dorothy and Margaret dropped into an immediate curtsey. I stared, near about to faint. Her fiery red hair, her fair face, her dark black eyes.

Here, now, in front of me, stood the girl in my vision, the very one who would have her gown chopped from her person. There was no doubt at all. The king's daughter!

Dorothy tugged my elbow and I remembered, quickly enough, to drop to a curtsey.

"Lady Margaret Neville, Mistress Dorothy Skipwith, and Mistress Juliana St. John," Kate said.

"It is a pleasure," the Lady Elizabeth responded politely. She was yet a girl, but already unbelievably dignified in presence. I had never known her mother nor seen her mother's portrait—His Majesty had them removed upon the execution of Queen Anne Boleyn—but I certainly knew King Henry. And the Lady Elizabeth was his not only in countenance but in bearing.

Within a minute, the dignified young royal dissolved and a girl of ten replaced her when Robert Dudley, the son of one of Kate's highest-placed ladies, Lady Dudley, tugged on some of that magnificent mane and Elizabeth spun around to repay him. Kate grinned and let them go. " 'Tis good to allow her some time to play as a child might. She's led a difficult life."

Dorothy and Margaret agreed but I was still too shocked about the prophecy to speak much. I stumbled about my duties and muttered something about feeling unwell. Although she appeared to be some years older in my dream, it was clearly the same person. Sir Thomas's hands would touch her with unseemly overtures, and the Lady Elizabeth would without a doubt be under duress and fear, far removed from the sunny, majestic child in my presence.

Presently, we reached Surrey, the first stop of our journey. I tried in vain to push the thoughts aside then. I had not had a vision for over a year. Perhaps something had waylaid their intent and the time of danger had passed. I fervently hoped so, and, in any case, no longer had to feign feeling unwell, as I truly did. My sense of shock and certainty reminded me that my gift may have been at rest these months past but it had not been removed. *What do I do with this now, Lord Jesus? Please tell me, somehow, if this is to come or if this horror has blessedly been set aside.*

In any case, I saw little of the Lady Elizabeth during the next few weeks, and due to her age, she shortly thereafter departed for her home at Ashridge.

After Surrey we visited Oatlands, Woking, Guildford, Sunninghill. August found us at Hanworth near Twickenham, Hertfordshire, Bedfordshire. We stayed but a few days, or mayhap a week, at each place, long enough to indulge in the delicacies of each household, bankrupt our host, and force the replacement of the sweet grass rushes covering the floors. In September, the Lady Mary became ill and returned to London. Kate gave her gold bracelets set with diamonds, emeralds, and rubies as a consolation and promised that Christmas at court would be a family affair and merry indeed.

One morning toward October Kate drew Margaret and me aside. "After the king and I visit, I should like you to remain with the Lady Elizabeth at Ashridge for a short while. It is good for the Lady Elizabeth to become more comfortable with the members of my household, as I intend to invite her to court often. Mainly, I'd like you to make polite conversation about what she's studying with her tutors, as I would like to know if her studies have taken a . . . reformed religious direction. Lady Fitzgerald Browne will remain with you, as her brothers and cousin are in residence with Prince Edward's household at Ashridge right now, and she's been in the Lady Elizabeth's household for some time as well."

I was to be a companion and a spy! I couldn't wait, as it promised both novelty and adventure.

We approached through a thick forest of slim trees standing straight and tall, a company of soldiers with heads like old men's, losing their color and thinning as winter approached. Once we'd traveled through the forest, Ashridge House itself came into view, magnificent and lovely, the shade of weak sunlight. Turrets and arches and carefully carved stone graced each view and approach.

Lady Troy, who was in charge of the household, met us and had someone show us to our chambers. All dined later, in the gallery. The king and queen sat near His Majesty's children Edward and Elizabeth.

I could not hear their conversation in whole, but I did see the queen place her hand on the prince's hair and pet it soothingly; he closed his eyes and near swooned with pleasure. She bent down, before the evening was gone, and softly kissed the Lady Elizabeth on both cheeks before squeezing her shoulder lightly.

"You must both look upon me as your mother," she said as she and the king took their leave to mingle with the other adults. The look of delight on the children's faces was marvelous to behold. Neither child had truly ever had a mother's love, and I understood that; I felt thusly when showered by Kate's affections, too, and yearned for it when 'twas not present, though I was now nineteen years of age, old enough to be a mother myself. Henry beamed with pride and drew Kate near to him in a way that showed all how he desired her company day and night.

After the king and queen left Ashridge, we often dined with the Lady Elizabeth's household and sometimes with the young Prince Edward. As discreetly as I could, I watched the two of them play and talk side by side with no rancor nor ill will. And yet Elizabeth's mother had been beheaded to make way for Edward's mother. Of course, the mother of the Lady Mary had been set aside to make way for the mother of Elizabeth. I'd

112

noticed on progress that while Mary was congenial toward her half sister, she had not been truly warm to any save Kate, the king, and her own ladies. I also recalled that she had called the Lady Elizabeth's mother a concubine upon first meeting me.

"Should you like to play a game of rook?" Elizabeth asked one afternoon after her studies were complete.

"I should, my lady. But I must warn you my skills are sadly unpracticed, not having cause to play of late."

"Then I must warn *you,*" she said with a grin, "that I do not ever forfeit a game nor countenance those who do. A win must be a win. But we shall enjoy the parry."

We sat down at an ivory carved chessboard near a fireplace in the great hall and played whilst Edward did his lessons upstairs. They shared tutors, that much I had learned, and the tutors were bent toward reformist learning but cautiously so.

I held my own for the first half of the game, and then the Lady Elizabeth, spurred by the challenge and desire to win, began to plan her moves most carefully. Of a sudden, she went for the kill.

"Check," she said confidently.

"I am trapped. The game is yours."

" 'Tis mine," she agreed, and met my gaze with a calm smile.

I liked her without reserve. I knew then that my prophecy had been given to protect her—not Thomas, not the highborn woman who held her fast, and not myself, but the Lady Elizabeth, for what greater good, I knew not, and, truth be told, may never know.

SIX

Year of Our Lord 1544
Whitehall
Saint James Palace
Hampton Court Palace

The king had told Kate, upon her marriage, to choose whichever women she liked to pass the time with her in amusing manners or otherwise accompany her for her leisure. The queen certainly did so; we played cards and dice and she loved to hunt with her greyhounds. But His Majesty did not realize, I was sure, the extent to which Kate was about more serious business. Her chambers were oft filled with women who held spirited debates upon philosophy and religion.

Early in January, six months after Archbishop Cranmer had requested His Majesty's marriage license for him, Cranmer was informed that he was to be sent to the Tower upon the morrow for beliefs and activities that were considered heresy.

Tristram Tyrwhitt was near the king's presence chamber when it happened, and he came to tell us that eve in the queen's rooms. One of her footmen, dressed in a claret-colored doublet and hose, opened the doors and showed him in. After bowing, Tyrwhitt began.

"Cranmer appeared, white as mold on cheese and sweating like those who are ill. He abased himself before the king," Tristram said, "and pled, 'Sire, I am always and ever ready to subject myself to your law, justice, and rule.'"

"What next?" Kate asked, deeply distressed. She and Cranmer had become friends since her arrival at court.

"His Majesty looked down upon the heap of bishop and asked, 'Think you to have better luck that way than your master, Christ?'"

At this, the room gasped.

"And then His Majesty did a complete turn," Tristram recounted. "He held out his ring to Archbishop Cranmer and told him that when the council came to arrest him, he should show them the ring and all would be well. It's been said that the investigation of Cranmer and his circle had been going on for months, and at the behest of Bishop Gardiner and his nephew."

At this, Lady Temple glanced at Lady Matthews and scowled. I well remembered that Temple's son was in the service of Bishop Gardiner, Cranmer's enemy. Henry counted both bishops, of opposite leanings, as friends and confidants. I recalled the game of chess in which the Lady Elizabeth had bested me. Her father well knew how to play his pieces against one another.

Kate leaned over and whispered something to the Duchess of Suffolk.

By March, Gardiner's nephew died the ignoble death of a traitor, hanged from his neck like a rooster at market.

The queen's earnest business did not only involve religion. Parliament was meeting at Whitehall. She frequently dined with the king in her quarters, and I or Dorothy was sometimes there to assist her greater ladies, as Margaret Neville was often unwell.

His Majesty sat at the head of the table. "I am pleased to see that Your Grace passed the Christmas and New Year's holidays with your illustrious children," Kate said. Her carver was Thomas Seymour's brother, specially chosen, and he hovered nearby to slice more of His Majesty's venison if required.

" 'Tis you we have to thank, sweetheart," he said. "Never was a wife more bonny and buxom in bed and at board." He indicated the fine spread before him and I glanced down at the intimate reference to their private life. That was the oath that Kate had taken upon her wedding, and although the nuptials were not what she had wanted, she had remained true to her vows. The king glanced up at the carver and indicated that he desired more meat. "How does your brother?" His Majesty asked him.

"My Lord Hertford does well, thank you, sire," Henry Seymour responded.

"Your other brother," Henry said pointedly. "Thomas."

Kate indicated that her wine should be refilled. Her hand trembled as she picked up the golden goblet.

"He does well, sire," the carver answered. "Always ready to serve Your Majesty." Kate did not meet his eye nor acknowledge the subtle menace at the edge of the king's voice.

"Good, good," Henry said. "Kate, I have given some thought to your comments about our family, our children, and the succession, as you ever act upon our best interests. I will instruct Parliament to reinstate our daughters into the succession after the prince, this realm's most precious jewel." He gulped some wine and indicated for more. "Thus they will be placed ahead of the offspring of our sisters." He winked at her, his cheeks pushing up into his eyes, his beard tufted and noticeably thinning. "Unless, of course, there are any children from you."

That was the cue to set the remaining wine on the table and withdraw. Henry Seymour did as well, as did the other servants. Lady Tyrwhitt closed the door to Kate's chambers behind her to the sound of her muffled laugh at some coarse jest His Majesty had just offered, seemed to often offer, far from the noble stories of the golden prince I had heard him to be in his youth.

Within the month, the king had approved the Act of Succession, in which Mary and Elizabeth were restored, in that order, after their brother. 'Twas the first time that the right for women to be sovereign was invested in English written law. How many knew that Kate had urged it, though it was always His Majesty's will that was done? Within the month the Lady Mary sent an expensive gold bracelet to Kate. The Lady Elizabeth sent a letter overflowing with love and affection, which touched the queen even more than Mary's bracelet had.

Edward, a child, did not indicate his pleasure or displeasure at having them included, but by the unmediated affection he showed to Kate at the Lady Margaret Douglas's wedding festivities, he had taken Kate deep into his young heart. He referred to her as his dearest mother. And yet it was his birth mother, Thomas Seymour's sister, the long-dead Queen Jane, who appeared next to the king when he commissioned the first portrait ever of himself with all of his family not long after the Douglas wedding affairs wound down. I suppose that was to be expected, as Queen Jane had been mother to the prince.

Queen Kateryn was painted utterly alone. I wondered if none but I saw danger in this telling isolation. If they did, they kept those thoughts to themselves, but I drew closer to Kate because of it. My affections, unlike many of those in her household, were not based upon His Majesty's pleasure in her but in love for the queen herself.

Each year, on Maundy Thursday, the queen distributed coins to the poor and aged. Kate chose to do so in her chambers, with her ladies there to assist.

"I cannot image Queen Catherine Howard distributing monies to the poor," Dorothy said on our way down the long hallway, "nor sinking to her knees with her ladies to wash their feet."

"But she did," I said. It seemed uncharitable to speculate upon the beheaded queen. Dorothy took my comment as a rebuke. And I suppose it was intended as such. We walked the rest of the way in silence.

We arrived in the queen's chambers and they were already set up; we were to hand linens to her and take the used ones away when she had finished. Kate had chosen some of her finest herbs for the washing water and her softest linens to dry the cracked, dung-crusted feet of some of those brought to her. There would be thirty-two petitioners, who would each receive thirty-two pence, one each for every year of my lady's life.

119

"Thank ye, Your Grace," one elderly woman said, her scarf pulled loosely around her hair, which wisped upward like goose down. When we were near to the end, and wearying, a woman approached Kate and with an unruly, high voice began to jabber.

"Beggin' your pardon, Your Grace," she said, her shrill voice parting the calm in the room in an unseemly manner. Every eye was drawn to her. "I'm here to speak on behalf a Anne Askew," she said. "Mayha' you do na know of her. She is of God."

Kate looked up at the woman and indicated that Dorothy should wash the woman's feet whilst she listened to her. "Go on, my good woman." Dorothy bent down and carefully wiped away the dried mud.

"Mistress Askew speaks often of holy writ," the woman continued. "She speaks not of her own words, but the words of our Lord."

Kate nodded, and whilst I had not heard of Askew I gathered by the look on Kate's face that she had.

"She's about her in preaching and teaching the Word of God. Her husband, Thomas Kyme, has turned her out because she uses her own name, and na his, and because he says she has abandoned her children and her bed by her gospelling. The bishop of Lincoln, he rebuked her, he did, for reading an English Bible."

The Duchess of Suffolk Katherine Willoughby spoke softly. "Her sister is married to my husband's steward."

The old woman continued. "Askew's husband has turned her out, he has, with nothing a'tall. If it pleases Your Grace, I will pass along these alms to her."

Kate nodded and I was at her elbow, assisting, so I could see her give the woman a double portion, closing her hand firmly around it so as not to be seen by the others.

The older woman bowed and scraped herself out of the room whilst muttering thanks. The Duchess of Suffolk, a newly dear friend, said to Kate, "I shall look into it." I recalled that the duchess had once dressed her dog up as a bishop and called him Gardiner, to the great amusement of all when she called him to heel, but to the everlasting enmity of the cardinal himself. There was no doubt which riverbank her loyalties washed up on.

Kate dismissed most of her women after that. Margaret Neville and I were left folding the linens. The Countess of Sussex remained behind. She looked at me and Margaret, and Kate nodded. "Speak freely."

"I have had prophecies of Anne Askew," she said, her voice strong and fueled with anxiety. Kate glanced at me and I rather wondered if she regretted giving the Countess of Sussex leave to speak freely. But the countess pressed on.

"Although she does good, her future does not bode well. I've seen the rack."

At that I sucked in my breath. A highborn woman, racked? Surely not. It had never been done.

I wondered at the countess being bold enough to speak of her prophecies. As her husband was cousin to the king, she might be safe. And then I recalled Father Gregory's warning that none, not even the highest born, would be safe from charges of witchcraft if 'twere truly suspected.

"I shall see what I can do," was all the queen committed. The countess nodded, knowing that her audience was over.

After she left I asked Kate, "Why do you keep some women, like Lady Temple and Lady Matthews, in your household who will seek to do you ill when they can and even spy?"

Kate smiled. "Being one of the queen's ladies is the privilege of many noble families, Juliana. Whether or not they agree with or like me, they must be admitted. And I seek to do good for all, even mine enemies. Mayhap I can turn them from evil to good."

Gospelling.

"They can only turn from doing ill to doing good if they want to," I responded. "And like as not some pleasure in evil and have no desire to turn." I had no doubt that while there were good people on both sides of the religious matter, those who acted according to conscience and firm faith, there were also those on both sides who would do ill if it best favored them. Wheat and chaff grew tightly together in both camps.

I could see by the dreamy look upon Kate's face that she supposed it differently. 'Twas not the first, nor the last, time she would dismiss the plain truth for Sir Thomas More's utopian view, and I worried for her lack of clear sight.

In spite of Lady Sussex's dismal vision of execution at Smithfield, the business of the court was preparing for war with the French. As such I was able to dismiss the whole matter from my mind for a time. I noted, though, that when the queen signed her documents she did it as *Kateryn the Queen, KP,* retaining her given name's initials.

Anne Askew had been maligned for that very same thing. And for gospelling.

In July the king left for war with France. As age and gout anchored themselves in His Majesty's person, all suspected that this would be his last chance for martial glory. Thomas Seymour was commissioned to war, too, as were nearly all able-bodied men. Each time I read of St. George I allowed my heart to stay upon Jamie and prayed that he met with success and his knighthood. When I let my mind settle upon thoughts of men, 'twas not a fancy of Matthias, nor any man at court, such as Tristram, but of Jamie.

The king, showing great honor and trust in the queen, left her as regent, in charge of the realm in his absence. He also left her as both regent and governor over Prince Edward should the king meet with an untimely demise. Although she had a council to advise her, Kate was in command.

"Please instruct the households of the king's children that we will be conveying them, ahead of the plague, to meet us at Hampton Court Palace," she said. Before Kate left Greenwich Palace she dictated a loving letter to the king that she finally brought to a conclusion.

God, the knower of secrets, can judge these words not to be only written with ink, but most truly impressed in the heart.

                                    Kateryn the Queen, KP

In late July we arrived at Hampton Court by royal barge with Edward and Mary. Although Edward remained the quiet, reserved boy with the brilliant mind he was already becoming known for, he warmed noticeably, as did we all, because of Kate's love and laughter, nearly to the point of joy. In August, the king's youngest daughter, Elizabeth, joined us.

The castle was one of Kate's favorites; it had lovely gardens and fountains, and its sturdy red brick was softened by white casements and easements all sculpted most carefully, like dried-sugar syllabubs. Her quarters were sumptuous. I noted with delight the deference all paid her, not only as queen but as queen regnant. She, not the king, sat enthroned in the presence chamber.

I curtseyed as the king's daughter approached that chamber one day. "Lady Elizabeth."

She turned to me and smiled. "Mistress St. John." She'd remembered our chess game, and waved me into the room with a true, rather than courtly, smile and I, thus honored, delightedly sat with her whilst Kate talked to her of court business.

Even as the queen and Elizabeth grew closer, the queen and Mary grew further apart. She did not like the reformed approach of Kate's conferences in her chambers or the preaching of her chaplains. But Elizabeth gladly filled the space Mary's absence created. Kate, for her part, allowed Elizabeth to remain nearby during several meetings with her council. They sat together whilst Kate dictated a letter to the king sharing the celebratory news that they had captured a ship off the Scottish coast bound to aid the king's enemies, the French.

Elizabeth watched as Kate dispatched funds for the war and made arrangements for provisions to be sent. The queen was served her meals by attendants on bent knees. She disbursed funds and executed proclamations in her own name. The Earl of Hertford, Thomas's brother, Edward, was on the queen's council to advise in military matters, and as he was an accomplished soldier, she listened to him well. However, when Thomas Wriothesley, the lord chancellor for the finance of the war, spoke up too often and interrupted Kate, she hesitated not to rebuke him.

"Lord Thomas, I appreciate your concern and advice. I oft lean upon it. But His Majesty has left me, at the final, to make the determinations on his behalf. And I shall carry out that duty as I best see fit."

"Your Grace," Wriothesley replied, and bowed his head with a neat, tight nod. All who knew him understood that was not so much an indication of acquiescence as a hawk biding his time before the kill. I recalled that he held very conservative religious views, contrary to the queen's, and that it was to his wife that Kate had sent her screed about not grieving overmuch a dead child, and I grew chilled.

The Lady Elizabeth, however, did not seem chilled. She seemed, if anything, warmed by this display, writing with admiration to the queen even though they saw one another daily, practicing Italian with her, seeking her affirmation on reading choices as well as on what to wear, and observing as Her Grace both confidently raised four thousand more men to aid the king and shared her thoughts and rationale with the young girl. They clearly held one another in deep love and affection.

I had the distinct impression, whilst watching and admiring them both, that Kate was preceptor in a most unusual Queens' College.

"Victory is to the king!"

Sir William Herbert, married to the queen's sister, strode into the queen's presence a little more than two months after the king's departure for war to announce the welcome news without waiting for the queen to invite him to speak. A great cheer rose among the small crowd and it traveled, like a wave, down the grandest halls, finally washing out in the furthest reaches of the scullery. Boulogne had fallen to His Majesty, a long-desired dream. Kate immediately sent word through the Earl of Shrewsbury to those fighting in Scotland so they might know that England was victorious and gain courage and force the Scots to wilt. Shortly thereafter, Wriothesley sent a letter to the queen asking that three ships, the *Primrose*, the *Jennet*, and the *Sweepstakes*, be sent immediately with provisions.

Kate dispatched the order with happiness. I caught her eye but held back a smile and a tease as others were in the room. Sir Thomas Seymour formerly commanded the *Sweepstakes*. I found it apt. Sir Thomas was in no way a primrose, demure and low to the ground. Nor was he a jennet, though he could be as obstinate as a donkey when he wished to be. Commanding the *Sweepstakes*, however, that was appropriate. I'd seen him at the card table. He was ever ready to gamble, always expected to best others, and did not mind if the stakes were high.

As winter seemed to have settled in early, Kate sent to one of her estates, Baynard's Castle, for furs for all of us and then we set out on a small progress and hunt toward the coast. The king's children were, of course, delighted for his victory. But now that it was over, he, and not they, must take precedence in Kate's affections. She bid them a loving good-bye and went to meet her husband in Kent, and they made merry on their way back to London. The king seemed younger and happier than in all the time I'd been at court and spent a lot of time in Her Grace's chamber, which he hadn't done as often afore France.

I prayed for a prince.

Toward the end of progress the Countess of Sussex, the prophetess, received word that her young daughter, two-year-old Maud, had died of the plague far away at their home estate. The babe would have been quickly buried by few so as not to spread the disease whilst her parents were in London; there was no reason for the expense of leaving and returning to court, and the earl was expected to attend upon the king. The countess mourned, though, excusing herself from many of the festivities that would be held to instead remain quietly in her rooms. This time, Kate sent a letter full of compassion and hope. She'd learnt well since her letter to Lady Wriothesley upon the passing of her son, though she still had no child of her own.

The king had planned a week's worth of celebrations for his war victory. First was to be a wrestling match; His Majesty could no longer wrestle on account of his ulcerated leg, but he was a great enthusiast of his men wrestling and jousting and sporting in every way he once had.

Next there was to be a play, based upon the sacking of Troy, to illustrate England's great victory, and finally a banquet. Kate, having anticipated her husband's victory like every goodwife of any status, had arranged for us all to have new gowns made. We were thus ready to celebrate.

"I've not been to a wrestling match," I confided to Dorothy as we sat in the stands. We were not attending upon the queen that day, as many of her higher-ranked ladies were there for this very public celebration. Sir Tristram Tyrwhitt came and stood by me.

"May I keep company with you?" He looked first at me and then at Dorothy. It seemed to me that his smiles were equal for both of us, and it must have seemed that way to Dorothy too because she lit with joy.

"Oh, yes," she said. She moved over so he

could sit between us and I thought that clever of her; he would not have to choose one of us over the other, thus appearing less gallant. "I've heard you performed wonderfully well in France," she said.

He looked at her with surprise but also pleasure. "From whom did you hear this?"

"Your aunt Lady Tyrwhitt," she said.

"I had not heard," I added. "But I am not surprised. I'm sure the French cowed like maidens when they saw you coming." I grinned.

"A jest, mistress?" Tristram asked.

"I admit to it. But a friendly one, well intentioned," I said. "I congratulate you."

He nodded. "And now, I thought I heard you say you had not been to a wrestling match before. I know Mistress Dorothy has, so I shall concentrate my explanations upon you." With that he turned his back, slightly, to Dorothy and began to explain the rules to me. I tried to lean forward to include Dorothy, but it was to no avail. She leaned back in ill humor and would not be engaged.

Among the wrestlers that day were the Seymour brothers, Thomas and Edward. Edward bested his brother in the first match, but Thomas won the second. Watching them put me in mind of Jacob and Esau.

"A third match!" Thomas cried out, throwing his fist in the air. "To proclaim the victor!"

Edward politely declined, cuffing his brother on

the shoulder, and Thomas eventually, gracefully, accepted a truce. I saw the ring on his small finger; he still wore it. My stomach turned as though I'd eaten bad fish with the reminder of the prophecy. I'd asked after that ring one night, casually, whilst attending to my lady. Kate had told me once that it had been a gift from his brother Edward and that inscribed within were the words, "What I have, I hold."

I wondered if that inscription was a warning from the giver to the bearer. The story of Jacob and Esau did not end happily for either brother.

The next night was the banquet and I wore a gown of peach-colored velvet cut slightly lower than usual, a beguiling plunge. Because my mother sent money I was able to supplement the budget Kate had set with matching shoes and fine pearl strings to weave into my hair. I softened some kohl in the corners of my eyes and plucked my brows as Kate had taught me.

Dorothy looked becoming in a violet gown that made her complexion seem even fairer. "Would you like to borrow some of my essence of rose to lightly tint your lips?" I offered as she stopped by my chamber. Elisabeth had already left and the maid with whom Dorothy shared a chamber was often late. Dorothy nodded and I took a small piece of linen cloth and helped her apply it. "It took me months to get it right myself," I said, so she wouldn't feel bad that I was assisting her.

"For quite some time I looked unwholesomely bruised!"

At that, she relented and willingly let me assist her.

"Sir Tristram will find you irresistible!" I said, and that, finally, coaxed a smile. When we left our chamber and stopped by to inquire if Lady Margaret Neville was ready to attend Her Grace, as we were wont to do, we found Margaret still in a linen dressing gown; her face matched the paleness of the cloth.

"Please give my regrets to Her Grace," she begged. "I have been most unwell and fear that I may faint should I attend this evening's activities."

"Do rest and don't concern yourself unduly. Dorothy and I will tell the queen," I said as she slipped back into her chamber. Later we decided to tell Lady Herbert, the queen's sister, who would pose the news in a way that would not unduly discomfit Kate on this evening. 'Twas the zenith of the king's celebration and Kate must revel with him.

The king's cooks had limited themselves to fifty courses, including the king's favorite dish: roast swan on a large platter, well larded afore being regowned in its feathers and ruffs, presented to the king with a sauce of vinegar and herbs. That was followed by jellied eels, gray and curled like sleeping snails, and black broiled carp with roast porpoise.

I picked at some marchpane and sugared fruit; politely refused a dance with Tristram, suggesting Dorothy instead; and looked for Jamie. Distressingly, he was nowhere to be found. I was surprised when, some minutes later, Sir Thomas sought me out for a dance.

"Certainly," I replied, though I was a bit bewildered at why he had chosen me. I didn't have to wait long to find out.

"How is Her Grace?" he asked me. "Truly."

"Truly, sir, she does well. I know that circumstances have not always been . . . arranged to her preferences. But she has made do admirably. You would be proud of her." As he was my benefactor, and always and ever a champion of Kate, I felt as though I could speak freely. Perhaps I was, as my mother had once claimed, too trusting.

"I am glad of it," Sir Thomas said. "You shall tell me if she has some need, of a private sort, that she cannot share with another?"

"I shall," I said, but thought it like as not that I would take care when trading confidences with Sir Thomas unless there were no other manner to inform myself. I knew he well loved my lady but also was apt to act and speak rashly. And then I went ahead and spoke rashly myself, because I knew of no one else I might ask. "One of your men, James Hart. Has he accompanied you back to court? Did he . . . fare well in France?"

Sir Thomas held me at arm's length. "Unless I am

mistaken, mistress, and I rarely am, you asked about that very same gentleman when we last danced."

"I am surprised that you would remember anything I said," I rushed on, trying to cover my shame, but I only worsened matters with my lack of composure.

He laughed. "I am very interested in what you have to say, Juliana," he said. "James Hart has won his knighthood and, I suspect, returned to Ireland to tell his mother and crow to the local ladies about his conquests. He'll be back at court presently."

"Thank you, Sir Thomas," I said, broken. I'd convinced myself that Jamie had thought of and wished for me on the long nights alone as often as I had yearned for him. Perhaps he'd not given much thought to me at all. Perhaps his nights had not been spent alone. I forfeited honesty for a bright smile as I turned back to dip my head at Sir Thomas.

He bowed and I curtseyed, and as he took his leave Tristram took my elbow. "May I?"

I smiled, glad of his friendly company to distract my mind from Jamie's absence. "You may." We danced and he tried to entertain me with stories of battle and bravery but they were a bit stilted in the retelling, perhaps due nothing to his own storytelling abilities but rather to my lukewarm interest in the one recounting them. Over his shoulder I noted that the queen danced two dances in a row with Sir Thomas. They kept a discreet distance from one another, their hands barely touching, their smiles and voices at a respectable level. But when Kate reached up and smoothed a wrinkle from the top of Sir Thomas's doublet, a loving gesture, I held my breath. I looked to the king, who seemed deep in conversation. I knew, though, in spite of his recently waning eyesight and gray-spiced beard, that His Majesty missed nothing.

What he has, he holds.

Later that month, in recognition for his service to the king on the high seas, Sir Thomas Seymour was made lord high admiral of His Majesty's navy. 'Twas a great honor, but a post that would keep Thomas away from the court, at the king's bidding, for great periods of time, nautical miles away from the queen.

In the three months between the banquet and the New Year's celebration, Sir Tristram often sought me out to walk in the galleries, to play cards, and to make merry in general. I sometimes agreed to accompany him when in a group, but sought to include Dorothy at all times and made it clear by a certain remove that I was not interested in more than friendship. I do not think he paid mind to my assertions, as by the end of the year he was asking after my father and my brother and plans in Marlborough.

In spite of Sir Thomas's reassurances, Jamie did not soon return to court.

SEVEN

Year of Our Lord 1545
Westminster
Greenwich Palace
Southsea Castle, Dover
Windsor

The king, still drunk with French victory, was most generous with his New Year's gifts. He gave the queen a heavy purse of gold, some fine gowns, and a diamond-encrusted clock, as she was overfond of timepieces. He added to her personal jewelry collection, not just that belonging to the crown, and on the second of January I assisted her sister, Lady Herbert, as she sorted through Kate's stones, collars, and chains, storing them in appropriate silk-lined cabinets.

"Place the emeralds here." Lady Herbert pointed to a small, lacquered casket and smiled. She had been in charge of Queen Catherine Howard's jewels, too, before that queen stumbled toward the scaffold. I was inordinately proud because I was the maiden most often chosen to help with my lady's jewels. Lady Margaret Neville had oft helped her in the past but she was unwell of late and took to her chambers more often than not. I knew Her Grace worried on Margaret's behalf and yet she had duties from dawn till dusk most days, and His Majesty did not abide sickness well, not even his own, which had seemed to wax lately. Perhaps his winning efforts at war had been purchased at the cost of quickening his ill health.

Kate sat on a comfortable chair and read to us from the Lady Elizabeth's gift to her for the New Year.

"Exquisitely and thoughtfully done. Brilliant. 'Tis a translation of *Miroir de l'âme pécheresse*, '*The Glass of the Sinful Soul*,'" Kate mused aloud.

At that, her sister looked up, discomfited.

"What, Anne?" Kate responded a bit sharply.

"'Twas written by a princess. I write and transcribe, and the Lady Elizabeth enjoys writing and transcribing and is much skilled already. Surely nothing is amiss with that." Kate seemed to weary at the unspoken rebuke.

"*Miroir* is beloved by reformers and written by a manifest reformer. I do not think the king, her father, would look upon this with favor."

"Ah," Her Grace said quietly. "But *I* look upon it with favor, and her mother, Queen Anne Boleyn, would as well. Who knows but that it may be her copy that Elizabeth translated from? Marguerite was an especial favorite of that queen. I rather admire Queen Anne and I know you do, too, as it was in her household that you first came to be a reformer and shared the like with me. I wish the Lady Elizabeth to know of her, especially as the Lady Elizabeth is growing both

137

astute in and warming to matters of faith and practice."

Lady Herbert busied herself with the jewels, and I did, too, hoping to dissuade my lady from any more talk about Anne Boleyn lest she follow Queen Anne's narrow path.

Inside, though, I applauded Her Grace for ensuring that Elizabeth knew something of what her mother cared for too.

As spring wore on it became clear that Kate's stepdaughter, the daughter of her heart, was ill unto death. The king gave the queen leave to attend more frequently to Margaret, whom she had moved next to her own quarters.

"Come now, dearest. I've had some custard prepared for you," the queen said, sitting near Margaret in her receiving chamber. She looked up at one of her lady maids and had the tray with custards, potage, and other soft foods temptingly arrayed delivered to Lady Margaret Neville's side.

"I shall eat a little," Margaret declared, though out of will to please Kate and not hunger, I knew. I busied myself in the room, as did Dorothy. One lady placed some of Kate's books in her cupboards and another ordered some tables arranged for the afternoon's card game. All affected a semblance of normalcy, but we knew how ill Margaret truly was. She confirmed it for us with her words to Kate.

"I have completed my will," she said. "I've had my father's steward assist me, and of course, dear lady, I have left everything to you. I shan't require the money my father had set aside for my dowry or keep."

"Hush, now, there is many a year to concern ourselves with that," Her Grace said, trying to reassure her. I saw her face pink and she blinked. I looked away.

"Nay, my lady, 'tis not the truth."

Lady Seymour disappeared into the Queen's Closet and aimed a significant look at Dorothy and me. We dared not disobey and followed her in, where she gave us some meaningless duties to leave Kate and Margaret alone.

Within the month, young Lady Margaret Neville had passed away. One night soon after, I took the ivory-handled brush and performed the task that Margaret often had as Kate allowed herself to grieve, wiping her eyes with a nearby linen, tears coursing in disorderly fashion over her cheekbones and down under her golden collar, which had yet to be unclasped.

"I am sorry, Juliana, that you should see me thus."

"Don't be sorry, Your Grace. You were her mother." I smoothed my hand over her head, wishing to soothe her as she so often did for others.

The queen wiped her face again and nodded. "I

was. I was her mother, not just her stepmother. She was my only child."

I set down the brush and pulled her head close to my shoulder, sharing her burden in hope of thereby halving it. "You were a fine mother to her," I said, imitating the calm tone I'd often heard her use. "All knew it, not the least of all Margaret." After a moment of silence I continued. "Someday, when I have children of my own, I will know how to mother them because I've watched you. You mother the Lady Elizabeth, Prince Edward. And though I am older, me," I added softly.

Her Grace said nothing, but did allow herself to quietly weep for five minutes afore collecting her senses. I grieved with her. Lady Margaret Neville had been a friend, a kind and true friend. I had helped her maid to pack her things so that Kate would not have to, and sent them along to the poor.

At court one is not allowed to grieve overlong. Soon Lady Seymour brought news of Anne Askew's arrest, along with a dangerous challenge for the queen.

One of Kate's ladies was reading in the queen's chambers whilst the March wind blew rain across the Thames so hard it tried to breach the windowpanes. I don't recall what she was reading because shortly after she began, Anne Stanhope,

Lady Seymour, entered the room and stood at the back. I could tell by the way she held herself that she had something to tell those of us assembled, but the queen intentionally did not give her leave to speak immediately.

Although they shared the same reformed beliefs and were beautiful in their own ways—my lady with her dark russet hair and Lady Seymour with her icy blond—they did not hold inordinate affection for one another. One was the wife of Edward Seymour. One still carried his brother, Sir Thomas, in her heart.

Dorothy leaned over and whispered, "You do know that the earl was married to someone else before he was married to the Lady Seymour."

I shook my head ever so slightly, so she continued.

"Lord Edward was married to another woman first, but she is supposed to have continued having relations with Lord Edward's father, so her husband put her aside. Many believe Edward Seymour's first two children to be his brothers and not his sons."

I opened my eyes widely and Dorothy nodded wisely. It brought her great pleasure when she shared a fact with me that I didn't know, so I squeezed her hand and whispered that she should tell me the rest later that evening. I was hoping to rekindle our friendship, which had burnt down to a lukewarm ember since I began to room with

Elisabeth Brooke. I felt, at that moment, pity for Edward and how he'd been wronged. His wife had certainly made up for his baseborn children, however, having already given him a handful plus one more, the fact of which caused great pain to my barren lady. I now understood a bit better Anne Stanhope's fierce loyalty toward her husband and her willingness to tangle with any who stood in his way. When I married—and my mind drifted fondly to Jamie—I should be fiercely protective of my husband too.

Her Grace indicated that Lady Seymour should step forward. She did, and seeing that the women were few and like-minded, spoke freely.

"Askew has been arrested again. I've heard that she's being held at Sadler's Hall, and interrogated. She's borne up well thus far but has little in the way of warm clothing, money for foodstuffs, or a word to hearten her."

Sadler's Hall was the guild for saddlemakers; we had one near my home in Marlborough as well. It was not a bad place but also not the kind of place to restrain a highborn young lady nigh on twenty-five.

"We should assist her," Stanhope declared.

I knew my lady well enough to know she was holding back a tart reply about "we" assisting Askew. "What do you suggest?" the queen asked.

"Her brother is the king's cupbearer. Could he be of assistance?"

The queen nodded and dismissed all but a few of us; I was among those who remained, as was the Countess of Sussex. I looked at her closely, remembering her prophecy about Mistress Askew. 'Twas comforting, of a sort, to know there was another woman nearby with that gift. It made me seem less peculiar, and I thanked God for the knowledge of her. There might have been many others, but none of us spoke of it and I was relieved that, these three years past, no further prophecy had been given to me. I oft forgot I had it at all. But it waited.

"Juliana." The queen drew me near. "I have had Margaret run certain discriminating errands for me, in the past. Now that she is gone, I wonder . . ."

"Yes, madam." I spoke up, thrill and fear racing one another through my limbs. "I will serve you however I may."

She conferred with her closest circle of women and then said, "I shall give you a letter and a purse to bring to the king's cupbearer, Askew's brother. If he seems inclined to assist, after some delicate conversation on your part, pass these along to him. If not, you may return to me. I will decide what to do then. You must wear something that indicates you are well-bred, but not something likely to draw undue attention."

I hurried back to my chambers and changed. I prayed quickly that I might be useful for Her Majesty.

• • •

I hid the letter and the small purse that the queen gave me and made my way to the king's chambers, and beyond, to where his men stayed. Further down the hall were the lesser chambers of his lower servants—still all nobly born or gentry.

"I seek Edward Askew," I said to a page. "The king's cupbearer. I am here on an errand for the queen."

"Certainly."

I waited in the hallway whilst he found Askew. I was not going to be seen entering a man's chamber, for certes, ruining my reputation for all time. After a few moments a tallish man with teeth bent upon one another like awkward saplings came to the hall.

"Her Grace would like to ensure that the king's wine is not oversugared," I said. "She has a concern that his health may be better served with less. Until she can speak with his physician, as his wife, she's attending to this matter."

Edward Askew looked at me a bit strangely, but agreed. "I endeavor in all ways to attend to the king's well-being, as long as His Majesty agrees to the taste."

I looked at him. "You seem familiar to me. Are you the brother of Anne Askew?"

He spat on the floor. "Better she should be called Kyme, the name of her husband, rather than

144

spew her unwomanly nonsense and bring further disgrace upon the name Askew."

I nodded and kept the letter and purse well within my sleeve. "I see. Mayhap we have not met before. I shall tell the queen of your sentiments regarding the king's wine. Good day."

"Good day, mistress," he said, bowing his head curtly afore taking his leave.

I returned to the queen's chambers and shared with her and her attendants the exchange between myself and Edward Askew.

"What now?" Kate said. "She's like to be unwell with no one to care for her, nor funds for physic or food."

"We shall find another way to get the monies to her," Lady Seymour said. "I shall send one of my most trusted pages."

"And if they do not allow a man not from the council to see her?"

"Send me," I interrupted. "I shall cloak myself, and truth be told, I am of so little account that few outside of your circle know of me, Your Grace."

They agreed, and shortly thereafter I was met by a young man wearing the blue livery of Edward Seymour's household. I had not been on the streets of London before, only at my lady's properties or with the court, and thus was uncommonly excited. I fixed my hat down low and drew my cloak about me.

We took two horses and made our way down the

freshly paved streets till they churned into mud alleys. I was thrilled to be outside of the palace. The streets were lined with markets and peddlers and all manner of mean people, not unlike Marlborough but many times over. They shouted as they hawked their wares, lark pies, roasted nuts, and spices. Women of a vulgar sort boldly hawked their wares, too, as they loitered outside the taverns, their gowns barely covering their slack skin. I pulled my cloak about me, glad that their life was not mine.

"We've arrived," the young man riding with me said as we pulled up to the guildhall. He brought our horses close to the door and bid me stay with them. I had never been out alone, without a servant, and I admit to a certain unease. Others looked closely at me; it was clear our horses were expensive.

The servant came back. "They've taken her to the Counter prison. Or the Compter, on Bread Street." We rode down that street, slowly. "Next time," he muttered, "if there is one, I shall not ride so fine a horse. Draws too much attention and I've already got difficulties fending off questions from Lord Wriothesley's pages."

We arrived at the prison and the servant spoke to the warden and then returned to me. "A woman can visit," he said. "To offer feminine comfort. But not a man. Be quick." I pulled my cloak about me again and went inside.

It stank of decomposing defecation and the sharp smell of blood. Vermin not only lurked in the corners but raced down the corridors. They seemed overbold to me, their beady eyes not bothering to turn aside as I stared at them, rather taking it as a challenge to come yet nearer.

I saw her; there was no doubt who she was, the only young, pretty, highborn woman there. I came close to her cell and whispered, "I have comfort to offer, my lady. And a coat, and a purse."

She looked upon me, her eyes sharp and focused. I could feel her courage like a weapon at her side and I admired her for it. "Who are you?"

"A friend. Sent by highborn friends."

She nodded. "I know of whom you speak. Yes, thank them."

"How do you fare?"

"Well," she said, not allowing herself the luxury of letting down her guard. "Pray for me."

I handed the bag to her; there was to be no letter or other indication of who her benefactors were. "We will, my lady. Heartily." I recalled to mind the words Father Gregory had given to me. "That you will be able to resist in the evil days that come. And to stand."

At that she smiled, a warm smile that smoothed the zealous edges from her face. I realized that we were but a year or two apart in age and could well have been friends under other circumstances. I said nothing more, not wanting to give her any cause for softening. She would need her calluses.

Later, I reported all to Her Grace in the privacy of her bedchamber, thrilled to have been included in this most important, sacred almost, task. The kind of sensitive task a mother might entrust to a daughter.

"Well done," she said, reassuring me.

"My lady . . . upon what charges do they detain Mistress Askew?" I asked.

"She is not in agreement with the king's Six Articles," Kate replied. "Which is the law in determining acceptable—and heretical—applications of faith."

"Which of the Six Articles?" I pressed. I could not help it; having been drawn into the intrigue I wanted to understand the particulars.

"Chiefly," the queen spoke softly, "Mistress Askew does not believe that the bread and wine, the Lord's Supper, become the actual body and blood of our Lord Jesus Christ during the celebration. She believes them to be representative, symbolic. The king marks *that,* especially, as heresy, punishable by death."

I dared to ask a question; I needed to know the answer if I were to help her. "Do you mark that as heresy, my lady?"

After a moment, Kate responded. "No, Juliana, I do not. I find I now sympathize with Anne Askew on these matters."

After my own readings I too was beginning to

agree. After all, our Lord was neither literal vine nor door, either, though Scripture called Him both.

"And the king?" I asked with dread. "Does he know you believe thusly?"

She shook her head. "He does not. Prince Edward's tutors and, er, uncles, share my sympathies. The Lady Mary is strongly in agreement with her father and devoted to her mother's faith. I believe the Lady Elizabeth lightly inclines toward me, though she is young, and not zealous."

"Excuse me, my lady. But a house divided against itself cannot stand."

"Which is why I seek in all ways to persuade the king in this matter. As does Archbishop Cranmer."

But not Bishop Gardiner, I thought, *nor Lord Wriothesley nor many powerful others. They both seek to do you harm wherever they may.* I had little confidence in my lady's ability to offer guidance and instruction to the king on religion; I thought it rather more likely he would declare her a heretic upon discovering the magnitude of her beliefs.

A few months later, Thomas Berthelet, the royal printer, delivered to my lady a shipment of her book *Prayers Stirring the Mind unto Heavenly Meditations*, which I had seen her quietly working on for months. He had already delivered a copy to His Majesty, who soon made his way to Kate's chambers to proclaim his pride in his wife's learning and piety, under his own strong guidance and tutelage, of course.

Later that week His Majesty held a small feast as a celebration of the event. My Lady Suffolk, whose husband had taken ill, made a special effort to attend and celebrate without him to show support for the queen. All were delighted with her success, and I was particularly proud as I had seen her at work on it late at night. Lady Seymour was there with her husband, Edward, Earl of Hertford. As she viewed her family as nobler, and herself as superior in person, she did not seem to enjoy the well-deserved accolades given Kate as one among the few women to publish in the English language. Lady Seymour, Anne Stanhope, styled herself a writer, too, so 'twas more like sun in her eyes. I wondered, perhaps uncharitably, if Stanhope would do Kate ill if given the chance.

In August, the Duke of Suffolk, who had been the king's lifelong friend and closest confidant, a brother, really, passed away. A certain lightness went out of the king and I do not think that, as he turned that corner, he ever returned. From that time forward his illnesses accelerated. The duke had requested a simple burial; the king insisted that his friend be buried with highest honors at Saint George's Chapel, Windsor. His Majesty informed those gathered that the duke had never brought harm to a competitor nor to an adversary, nor had he spoken a word with the intent of injuring another. "Is there any of you, my lords," the king added, "who can say as much?" I thought it was unlikely there were two such men at his court, ever.

In spite of his dour mood, His Majesty needed to keep up royal pretenses and thus bought fine new clothes for both of his daughters in advance of the Christmas celebrations. The Lady Elizabeth, being young, would not be in attendance all month so he held a series of celebrations in mid-November too. The one I looked forward to the most was a musical evening. The king was a fine composer and several of his songs would be performed by lute and harp; the virginals, of which I was particularly fond because my mother had ensured that I was well trained on them, would be played too.

The great hall overflowed with people who mingled and talked and ate of small fancies whilst the musicians played. I had loaned Dorothy one of my fine rings after she'd come to keep me company in my oft-lonely chamber. Elisabeth had left early to assist Lord William, as he'd held a small reception in advance of the evening in his chambers; she was there more often than not, night and day. She'd invited me to the reception but I did not feel particularly comfortable with that set. Dorothy took special care to find Tristram as soon as we arrived and I prayed that he would be delighted with her company.

To my own utter delight, Jamie was in attendance. I caught his eye across the room and he smiled broadly, then nodded warmly in my direction as if to say he would speak with me soon. I was glad that I had, again, chosen my peach gown with its womanly tucks sewn in becoming places.

"You look in want of company." John Temple came up beside me.

I smiled graciously, as was required at court. "'Tis very kind of you to think so," I said. "But I was just on my way to speak with someone else." He followed my gaze to Jamie, who was deep in conversation with another woman.

"Sir Thomas does welcome the rakehells into his household, does he not?" Sir John said smoothly. "I'm not surprised." With that he took his leave.

In spite of his nod, Jamie did not come and find me immediately thereafter. I saw him speak with another woman, and I joined Dorothy and Tristram and a group of others from Her Grace's household in conversation. When I looked to Jamie again, he was speaking with another group. I tried to catch his eye but could not and he did not seem to be looking for me, either. Dorothy led Tristram away and kept him occupied, although he cast a longing glance in my direction once or twice, which I returned in a friendly but not necessarily inviting manner.

Rather than stand by myself and look a fool if Jamie should glance my way again, I reluctantly sought out Sir John to make happy, if forced, conversation and cheerful, even ebullient, company at dance.

'Twas a singular mistake that I'd wish undone.

"Ah, Mistress Juliana, your Irishman seems preoccupied," Sir John said.

"He's not my Irishman, Sir John."

He nodded approvingly. "At least Marlborough, burg that it is, is on English soil."

"I plan to return to Marlborough after the New Year's celebration," I said, glad for once to speak of home, which felt familiar and warming. "I haven't visited my mother for some time."

He smiled and made pleasant, educated chatter about the music. I drew a bit closer to him when I noticed Jamie looking in my direction. This seemed to please Sir John. "May I bring you a goblet of wine?" he asked.

I nodded, and wished that Jamie would come and sit nearby me in Sir John's absence, but he did not. Sir John handed me a cup overfull, and drew near and talked with me for some time, about nothing at all of importance; the more I talked with him the more I disliked him, but he seemed to take no notice of that and I could not keep up the happy pretense. Finally I said, "I must return to my chamber."

"So soon?"

"As I am alone I do not like to return too late. Thank you, Sir John."

"May I persuade you to let me accompany you to your room, as the hour does, indeed, grow late?"

I nodded. It was a gentlemanly thing to do. We walked down the long galleries, tapers fluttering on the wall sconces, I weary and disappointed. Most doors were shut. I heard a small noise from within Dorothy's chamber; 'twas she or the maiden she shared with, already returned for the eve.

"Thank you," I said when we arrived. Sir John looked at me inquiringly but did not respond. I realized that he had had too many cups of wine, which was why he was presently unresponsive. As I opened my door he forced himself into my room.

"Sir, please, take your leave!"

"I shan't, not until I get what you invited me to come here for," he said, firmly closing the door behind him and blocking me from its path.

"I invited nothing, nor do I want anything from you, but for you to remove yourself." I tried to dart around him in order to open the door of my chamber to show him out, or shout for assistance, whichever should be required to stop his menace. He blocked me.

"I shall, mistress, but not just yet." He took both of my arms firmly in one of his own and then tore my gown down the back.

"Sir John! Have you gone mad?" I struggled to free myself and tore loose. I grabbed the small torch from the wall and swung it at him to set him afire but he knocked it from my hand and stamped it out while twisting my arm behind my back. I was firmly held and unable to move. So I shouted.

"Dorothy!" I shouted for the only person whose chamber was close enough to, perhaps, hear. But the chamber doors were heavy and I did not know if the sound of my voice could penetrate through them.

He clamped his one free hand under my jaw, over my closed mouth, so I could not even bite his hand, though I tried.

"If you free yourself or call out, I shall tell everyone that you invited me in and the noise they heard was rough play."

My eyes were then opened and I knew what he was about to do. He pushed me onto the bed and undid his hose and codpiece. I squeezed my eyes shut and prayed that what was about to happen would not happen, would stop.

It did not stop.

I felt myself somehow drifting away from the situation, like a ghost, even as I was assaulted by stabbing pain and harsh treatment; the blood oozed from between my legs, then coursed along my thighs. His body was heavy on mine and though I had closed my eyes against his face I could not stopper my ears to his noises nor spare my skin from his rough beard and foul breath. The music from the evening made its way from my memory into my head along with the beating sound of my heart and I tried desperately to focus upon it whilst calling out in my heart, *Lord Jesus! Save me!*

To my great sorrow no supernatural rescue arrived and the constant searing pain reminded me that I was there in the flesh. Within a few minutes, Sir John fell back.

"You are a maiden!" he said with surprise. "I, I thought that others had had you."

"Get out." I pulled the linens around me but could scarce move my legs because I suffered. "You have badly misjudged me. It would not have mattered, should not have mattered, in any case whether I be a maid or not."

He looked like a little boy whose governess had never told him no, both pleased that he'd had the temerity to act brashly but afraid of the potential consequences once caught. "None need know this but us. Your own behavior led to this. All saw you willingly seek my company tonight. You cunningly informed me that you would have the chamber to yourself and, therefore, the privacy we required. I should make sure others believe that you decided to cry rape once I declined to proceed further toward any binding relationship."

"That is wholly untrue!" I protested. "And I shall not allow others to view it that way."

"It's all in the mind of the beholder, mistress, and in how it's presented and by whom. I daresay it will surely bring sly and nasty comments upon the queen's morals, after all, to have both you and Lady Brooke acting in such a vulgar manner— perhaps that's why Her Grace chambered you together, hmm? And mark me, no good man will want you once you've been . . . sampled. I know I wouldn't. And I know how men talk behind closed doors."

That Kate's morals and the running of her household would be slandered I knew to be true. She had many enemies sniffing about for a reason to give the king to question her. I did not know the way of men. Could Temple's conclusion about no good man desiring me now perhaps be true?

He pulled on his doublet. "I told you once, mistress, that reputations are lost quickly at court. They can be best lost through whispers. They can be best retained by silence."

I recalled Dorothy's tale of the woman Sir Thomas was accused of debauching, and the shunned and sorry life she'd lived thereafter. 'Twas the unfair and startling truth that whether or not the story was true the consequences certainly were.

He finished dressing. "Justice at court is the domain of men, not women."

He slammed the door behind him but within a minute, I heard a knock. It became persistent and I knew I must answer but I was so stunned I scarce knew what to do. "Yes."

Dorothy pushed the door open; I had not gotten up to lock it. "Juliana. I heard the door slam and . . . oh. Oh," she moaned. "What happened? Has someone harmed you?" she looked upon the bloody linens and my ripped gown thrown on the floor.

I nodded and answered dully, "John Temple." She looked once more at the disarray on my chamber floor and then quickly left, pulling the door behind her. Shortly thereafter the midwife came to attend me. I allowed her to, as if in a dream, examine me, though each touch she made bruised me again within and without. I sobbed silent sobs, my body shaking with fear and pain and chill and shame as she finished her work.

The midwife kindly drew me into her ample bosom when she was done. "You will heal."

"Shall I, shall I get with child?" I asked with dread.

"I'm sorry ta say it may be difficult to ever bear a child due to the damage done ta yer innards. I canna tell just yet. Later, yes."

"I may never bear a child?" A new and terrible horror followed the one I'd just endured.

She took her hand in mine. "Perhaps. I do not know. Though you shall, after some time, be able to lie with a man again, 'twill perhaps not bear ripe fruit. I can help ye affect a maidenhead later if ye need. You just call upon me." She gathered up the bedclothes. "I shall dispose a these—no one comments on bloody linens from a midwife—and have new ones sent to you. I shan't tell anyone of this and I advise ye to keep your peace as well. Men run our world, mistress. It favors a man's word, and even if some believe that this was not of yer choosing—and I can certainly see that 'twere not—not all will believe it, they won't."

I well understood what she said. "I shall keep my own counsel upon this."

She nodded. "That be wise. Your friend who came quickly ta fetch me, I've warned her to speak naught of this again for your reputation's sake. We three—and the cur who did this—are the only ones who need know of it."

I nodded quietly and she took her leave.

There was no way to lie down that did not bring pain. I did not sleep for hours, speaking harsh and hot words in tear-stained prayer as to why a prophetic dream could not have been given me or anyone else to forestall this attack when dreams had been sent to help others. I lay chilled, wishing for the comfort of my own home, the laughter of my brother, the security of my childhood, the arms of someone I could trust, all of which had now been thieved from me forever by John Temple.

God rot him.

Is this why I have been brought to court? I next accused our Lord, though I knew one must not. *Is it?*

My sobs slowed to choking, then to panting, then to breaths before I fell into a restless sleep.

Dorothy did not appear at my chamber the next morning, leaving me to privacy and peace, which I felt certain she viewed as a kindness. We'd all been well trained to turn a blind eye to misdeeds at court and if one wanted to survive one continued to do so. Her silence only reinforced my conclusion that the situation would be viewed as my shame and that pretending it had never happened was the only sure path to retain my dignity. I did not want to be on the receiving end of pointed fingers, the recipient of pitying stares by others gladdened not to be me, nor the topic of conversation transpiring behind mouths shielded by hands. John Temple may have robbed much from me, but he would not steal my dignity nor my pride.

I got myself dressed and painfully made my way to Kate's chambers. She was still being gowned.

"Your Grace," I spoke carefully. "I have received news of illness. And injury. May I return to Marlborough and my mother rather sooner than I had planned?"

She turned toward me and I longed to fling myself into her arms and cry out with pain and sorrow, to have her reassure me that all would be well. But I was there to serve, not to bring misfortune or gossip upon her. If I were to seek unlikely justice, I should have to publicly reveal that Elisabeth had left me alone in my chamber most nights; this would bring shame to the queen, because Brooke's married paramour was the queen's brother. Sir John would certainly speak his lies. They would then spread like contagion to harm Kate, stirring up her enemies even more against her through her family, her ladies, and her religious belief.

There was also my unspoken shame, which had been whispered to me continuously in the night, endeavoring to take root. Had I, by seeking out Sir John, by sharing his wine, by keeping his company when Jamie had eschewed mine, by wearing a becomingly cut dress, and by my intemperate speech, brought this upon myself in some manner? I had no one to ask. Kate might perhaps no longer see me as the daughter I'd become to her, but as unchaste, and if not that, then perhaps pitiable. I could not abide her thinking of me thusly.

"You may take your leave." She drew me in for a quick embrace and I took the sip of affection offered, though I greatly desired to beg for a goblet full. "Just return to me shortly after the New Year. I shall miss you terribly."

I nodded, but it was a lie. I did not intend to return at all.

EIGHT

Yuletide: Year of Our Lord 1545
Winter: Year of Our Lord 1546
Brighton House, Marlborough
Hungerford Manor, Marlborough

I'd quickly written a letter to my mother and sent it with a swift messenger, to alert her to my early arrival. The queen sent me home in a fine litter at her own expense. When I had last made this journey, in reverse, my heart had been filled with girlish joy and the delightful expectations of a life of glitter and promise and escape. Now it was shot full of the lead of the court and the heavy weight of adulthood. The hours passed, snow-topped tree by snow-topped tree, as the landscape relaxed from city to clearing and then home. I breathed London out as a mist that dissipated in the cold air. I looked upon my return home with fondness and urged the driver not to tarry.

I alighted from the litter and Hugh ran from the house, a man now, though he still leapt into the air at the sight of me, as a child is wont to do. I fell into his embrace; he was large enough now to encompass me. "Dear Juliana," he said, "how I've missed you. Even our mother has missed you. We are glad you have returned for a stay."

He drew near to me and lowered his voice. "And

please do share the welcome news that you'll be taking me back with you to court upon your return."

I choked back the sobs that wanted to be loosed, not wanting to scare him. Instead I buried myself in his embrace for a moment and let myself revel in the thought that I was safe, boringly, welcomingly safe. I hadn't the heart to tell Hugh that I had no plans to return with or without him, and then our dog Brise came running from the stables to greet me. I pulled away, bent down, my garments already well dusted from travel, and allowed her to put her paws on my shoulders whilst she licked my face and my ears. Before long a litter of puppies came yelping, streaming out behind her. She nuzzled on them and looked upon me for my approval, which I readily gave.

I reached down and patted each in turn, so she'd know how proud I was of her brood, especially one overbold male who made it his cause to draw as close to me as Brise. By the time I left her to romp with her litter I had regained my composure.

"They'll be good for the hunt," Hugh said as he took my hand and lifted me up. My lower body was still sore and achy from John Temple's attack, but Hugh mistook it for weariness from my journey. A welcome mistake.

My mother waited at the door for me. When I looked upon her countenance I was shocked, though I did my best to hide it. She looked old and weary, though still fashionable. In my mind's eye she had only ever appeared powerful and disapproving, but I pitied her somehow and promised myself I would endeavor to be kind.

"Welcome." She took me into her arms, though rather stiffly, and kissed both of my cheeks. "You'll want to change afore we sup. Lucy is upstairs waiting for you."

Hugh had one of the men of my mother's household deliver my trunks to my chambers and, indeed, Lucy was waiting for me.

"Mistress, what be wrong?" After greeting me with delight and affection, she took my cloak from me and looked into my eyes. Of course Lucy would know right away that all was not well with me. Though it had been nearly three years since we'd parted company, she still knew me better than anyone else did.

" 'Tis only the journey and the demands of the court," I said, and softly warned her with a look not to ask more. She was glowing and happy to have me back and I did not intend to demean the festivities.

She eyed me warily but accepted my explanation. "Let me help ye wash," she said. "And I shall bring out one a yer fine gowns for the meal."

After the meal that night, my mother sat with me whilst Hugh directed the man who'd brought me to a warm corner in the stable whence he could return to London on the morn.

"You're different, Juliana," she said plainly, but not unkindly.

" 'Tis the sheen of the court, Sir Thomas says," I answered.

"I would rather say it's womanhood. And perhaps the need to rest. How does Sir Thomas?" She nodded for one of the men-servants to stir up the sea coal heating our home. My father never allowed wood to be used; he'd preferred the costly coal. "I have sent him letters inquiring of placement for Hugh, but he has not deemed it necessary to respond to my correspondence."

"I do not see Sir Thomas often, Mother, but when I do, he seems well."

"Word has it that he is in love with the queen." My mother sipped from her goblet.

I was surprised that news had traveled this far, but then not surprised when I considered how close we lived to the Seymours' estate, Wulf Hall. "I do think he cares deeply for my lady, but she is in all manner discreet and honoring to His Majesty." I found, and noted, my ire rising in defense of Kate toward my own mother, an unexpected reversal of loyalties.

"I'm certain that she is," my mother said, but her tone of voice did not seem bent toward charity. "Sir Matthias and Lady Hurworth have invited us to celebrate the New Year with them. I am sure young Matthias welcomes your return visit. And you must welcome the opportunity to see him?"

Yes. Now that I was home, I had to face the question of Matthias; I could no longer avoid the topic by remaining at court. I could not tell if my mother had spoken a question or a command. "I shall look forward to the event." I did not lie and say, "With pleasure."

She bid me good evening. My mother was right. I had indeed matured into a woman, completely, with my eyes wide open, though certainly not by the means I would have chosen.

Within a few minutes, Hugh returned and took our mother's place by the fire in the large, paneled hall. "I must know. Are there jousts every day? Cockfights? All manner of food and wine and beautiful women much in need of a knight's son from Marlborough? Intrigues?"

I smiled at his enthusiasm and naivety, pleasures I had been allowed till they had been sanded away by the court slowly, day by day, year by year, till ultimately nearly all was stolen from me. My mother had noticed, but had not taken me in her arms, crooned over me, or promised to set things aright. She could not, of course. But I yearned for her to have tried.

"Yes, there are often jousts, and wrestling matches, and many beautiful women, though none have spoken to me directly of a pressing need for a knight's son from Marlborough. And there are intrigues, of course. But most of them are of a religious nature."

"That sounds dull." He looked crushed, of course.

"As dull as an axe blade." I leaned over and took his hand. " 'Tis good to be home, Hugh. In many ways, the court is like the story of Saint George, with the dragon always looking for a new and beautiful maiden who will be sacrificed to him. All seek to placate him but he is never satisfied."

Hugh leaned closer. "Do you mean the king?"

I shrugged, aware of Kate's warning to be discreet, and knowing of Hugh's youthful lack of discretion. " 'Tis hard to tell who the dragons be, and who be the knights."

"I should know immediately," he said with bravado.

"I am certain that you would," I jested. "And now, dear brother, I am tired from my long journey and must retire for the eve."

I had worried that, once home, my visions would return to torment my sleep but blessedly, they did not, though I woke often every night with terror come upon me after seeing John Temple's face or feeling his spent breath upon my face in my mind's eye, or just the rustle of a noise that I feared was someone breaching my door. After some weeks resting, riding, and reading from my father's library near a warm fire, the terrors waned. I was therefore recovered in body, but not in spirit, by the New Year.

. . .

Lady Hurworth had invited us to a large New Year's celebration she held at Hungerford House, replete with fools, jesters, and a play. Her tables, as always, were laden with delicacies. I indulged myself lightly, though stayed myself from the strawberries, which I had not seen in our town before.

"This is a lovely evening and celebration," I commented to her as we waited whilst the players assembled themselves afore the second act. "I am glad to be home again."

She smiled at me, though not warmly. " 'Tis not at the level you are used to at court, I am sure, but we do our best." I dipped my head and took my leave, and as I did Matthias came alongside me and took my arm.

"Let us sit for a while," he pleaded. "I've had naught but a few hours of your time since you've returned from court."

I reluctantly agreed and he drew me to a softly covered bench at the edge of the large room. The fireplaces, taller than a man and twice as wide, kept the winter out of the room and the marble held their heat.

"Are you well pleased to be home?" he asked. He looked little different from when I'd left. I noticed that his dance was more waddle than rhythm and yet his constancy in his affection to me was endearing, as a brother's might be, but I certainly felt no passion toward him, nor a desire to remain with him for life.

"I am. Court is a hive and 'tis sweet to have quiet and to repose."

"I should rather hope that you'd be ready to remain home in repose," he replied. "I know that my father desires to speak to your mother about . . . my future, your future. We have not spoken of this together afore, but I would do so now. Do you wish to remain here, which I think best, with your family? And with me? Or will you be returning to court?"

I had not expected him to speak to me so directly, and yet I'd been at court for more than two years so 'twas not surprising that he'd like to settle his plans.

"I had not given it much thought," I answered. I would not hurt him. And yet I had little choice in the matter. Whom I would marry was up to my mother, and, to some lesser extent, my younger brother. "I have only just returned."

"You've been back for more than a month," he said, his tone nasal and high. "My younger brother will like as not be married within six months' time and will shortly thereafter get him a son. I shan't like to follow where I would better lead."

"Whom shall he marry?" I turned the subject to give myself time to think my way. Although I was mildly repelled by the thought of a plodding, dull life with Matthias, I had no desire to deceive him; in fact, I would not do so. And, yet, if I agreed to marry him understanding I likely would not bear children, that's certainly what I'd be doing. But 'twas not in my power to tell him I would or would not marry him; that rested with my mother.

"She's the young daughter of a knight; they come from York. She's lovely, and brings a fine dowry. Though not as fine as yours." He belched and though he covered his mouth with his hand a hammy vapor escaped. "Some women with large dowries desire a title in exchange," he continued. It clearly troubled him.

"I am not one of those women, but I cannot speak for what my mother desires," I said. "Though she contented herself well with a gentry man of means."

"And that I am," Matthias said. "Till your brother comes of age, my father and I will take care of all the details. Sir Thomas Seymour is having one of his associates deliver another shipment from the East next week and I, not my father, shall meet him, take ownership of the goods, and disburse the funds accordingly."

The languor that the fire and good food had blanketed me with was suddenly stripped away and the immediate problem at hand, how to be honest with Matthias whilst protecting myself and my reputation, dissipated.

"What is the name of this associate?" I asked.

Matthias looked startled. "Sir James Hart. Do you know of him?"

I steadied my breath. "Indeed I do." I caught his querying look and sought to soothe it. "From court, of course, as I first came at the request of Sir Thomas. And now your mother's players are back. We should honor them with our attention."

I turned toward the play, but I did not stay my mind upon their lines, resting instead upon the fact that Jamie would be in Marlborough within the week.

He arrived eight days later. Lucy was in my chamber, sorting through my jewelry, both paste and proud, and then rubbing them with silk, when she glanced out the window.

"Mistress! He's here. Tha one who brought you tha strawberries."

"Thank you, Lucy."

"You do na seem enthused." She knew how happy I'd been when Jamie had come to see me in London and had most likely overheard our kiss.

"I'm not, really," I lied as I froze in place. I had wished to be indifferent toward him but I'd still chosen to wear my best gowns day after day in case he should arrive unexpectedly. My mother had commented that we were, in fact, in Marlborough and not London and there was no need for me to array myself in finery at all times.

She did not know that I dressed in feminine anticipation.

I glanced out the window and saw him greet and win over Brise and her pups. That brought an unplanned smile and an unwelcome softening. Matthias did not like dogs, not even at hunt, though he had to use them when he did. I heard Jamie speak with my mother's steward, who soon climbed the winding stairs and knocked upon my chamber door.

"Mistress Juliana, there's a man here from court that says he has correspondence for you from Her Grace the queen."

I looked in my glass to ascertain that my hair was not unruly; indeed, 'twas not, as Lucy had recently finished fixing it. Then I opened the door. "I shall see him presently. Please inform my mother that we have a guest."

The steward nodded and left and within a minute I descended the circular staircase and went into my mother's receiving chamber.

Jamie stood when he saw me, and I inhaled deeply as I looked into his eyes and held his gaze and offered him my hand. He kissed it, and for a moment I felt the warmth spread and then my body, against my will, clenched tight like a fist. I withdrew my hand.

"I hope the New Year finds you well," I said, keeping my voice as even as possible. "I am well pleased to hear that you have earned your knighthood, not that 'twas ever in doubt. Congratulations."

"Thank you, Juliana. The New Year does find me well, but I admit to being better of it now," he said, his voice lightly jesting but tender all the same. I indicated that we should be seated and I chose a seat not next to him but not too far away, either. I did not want us to have to rely upon raised voices but did not want to be so close as to lose my sensibilities.

"I've missed you at court," he said. "When Seymour mentioned that he was coming to Marlborough to meet with an associate and make a delivery, as well as bring a letter to you from the queen, I asked if I could come in his stead."

He had sought me out.

My heart reached toward him, wishing, wanting him to say more, and yet my mind wished his lips to still because I did not want to be forced to give the answer I knew honor demanded I must.

"What did Sir Thomas say?" I asked.

"He agreed. He was not surprised. I—I think he knows that I am soft toward you. He indicated that you care for me too."

"I do." Endeavoring to keep my voice steady so I did not sound like a petulant child, I spoke. "The last time I saw you, Sir James, you did not seem to prefer me to the company you kept, nor even make time to speak with me."

"I am heartily sorry," he said. "I grew

173

distracted talking with many I hadn't seen in overlong. When I saw that you had retired for the evening without my having had a chance to seek you out, I repented of my wasted hours. I sought you several days hence, when I had leave to do so, but was told you had returned home to Marlborough."

"It rather seems to me that you are like the pit of a peach, Jamie. Always completely surrounded by soft flesh." I could not keep back the smile that twitched upon my lips.

At that he laughed. "I should take offense, lady, but you put the barb so prettily that I cannot. 'Twas true of me, at one time, I admit. And most recent, though I shall not own up to even a tithe of what I am certain to be accused of. Yet, of late I find myself changed in that. When I returned home I found my friends married and with sons of their own, enjoying the comfort of the hearth. I find that I no longer take pleasure in the superficial company of insubstantial ladies. I much prefer the beautiful, congenial, and forthright charms of only one unspoilt maiden. Her name is Juliana St. John. And I hope she'll let me pay heed to her when I am not at sea."

He took my hand in his and I allowed him to hold it, though I still felt tense. *I am no longer an unspoilt maiden.*

"I have a letter from the queen." He withdrew it from a leather pouch. "She's told me that she desires to have you back at court and hopes that she can convince you to return."

I took the letter from him, but did not open it.

"Do you plan to return?" he asked.

"I do not yet know."

He moved to the seat next to me. "When I was completing the delivery of goods to your father's business partner, Matthias made it clear that he hoped that you would remain here. Do you have an agreement with him?"

"There is no agreement presently, though 'tis possible that my mother should prefer to make that arrangement shortly, which would forestall my leaving for court."

He said nothing. I could hear the deep stillness of someone listening out of sight, behind the doors.

"My father wished otherwise for me," I finally admitted.

"I wish otherwise too," Jamie answered. "Greatly. Do you?"

"What I thought I knew, I know not. My heart is unclear. I have been praying for direction, but the answer has tarried."

It was not the answer he wanted and it was not the one I truly wanted to give, and yet it was the one I felt was right then, and so I offered it. I could sense that his heart fell, along with his countenance, in tandem with both of my own.

A moment later, my mother joined us and

insisted that Jamie dine with us afore his long ride back to London. She was a perfect hostess and did not seek, this once, to overshine me. He made good conversation and shared tidbits of court news, including that the king was growing ever more ill and cantankerous and had to be pushed about in a chair upon wheels and hoisted up the stairways. I knew the king's mood would be trying for Kate.

My mother withdrew and left us to talk for a while. He told me more of his family, especially his nephews, whom he clearly adored, though he referred to them as Rascal and Scamp. I told him more of my father and my childhood and for a few hours I forgot my demons long enough to allow myself to laugh and be young again.

Jamie finally brought the early afternoon to a close. "I must take my leave as 'tis a long, hard ride back to London and I leave to sea shortly. When I return to court, I shall seek you, and hope to find you." He took both my hands in his own but I felt little. I longed for, I yearned for, the pleasure and joy and yea, the flush of heat and passion and restrained desire I had felt some months back when he had touched me. No matter how I tried to summon them, they would not come. John Temple had robbed me of more than my maidenhood.

I stood at the door and watched as Jamie rode away, trailing dust behind him.

"I thot ye were not enthused for him," Lucy said, coming up behind me.

"The day may come when I am unable to appreciate a fine man upon a fine horse as he takes his leave," I snapped. "But that day has not yet arrived."

She grinned and as I looked at her I knew she was happy to see my vinegar stirred.

Jamie had not kissed me afore he left.

I knew not whether that was because he thought I might be spoken for by Matthias, or whether he sensed my tensing to his touch. I was not certain if I was pleased or sorrowed by the lack of his kiss, as nothing good could come of knocking upon a door that would never be opened. Would I ever feel desire again? And even if I did, what man would want to live without the hope of sons to inherit his hard-won purse, his lands, his titles, and provide said pleasure at hearth? None I knew of, nor had ever met.

I was also uncertain if a man could change, as Jamie had said he had. I recalled a motto one of our tutors had Hugh and me memorize from Euripides. *Time will discover everything . . . it is a babbler and speaks even when no question is put.*

That night, I took Kate's letter to my chamber but before I read it I closed my eyes and held in my mind the wondrous picture of Jamie's face and the resonance of his laughter and words.

And yet, I was no longer who he thought me to

be; I wanted both the man and his good opinion. As it seemed unlikely that I could have the former, I would do nothing to disabuse him of the latter, which I then might hold dear forever.

"Lord Jesus," I whispered, after reading the day's passage in my neglected book of hours, the scourged holy intimacy between Him and me having begun to scab and heal. "Show me. Guide me. I trust in You."

I will never leave thee, nor forsake thee.

The Lord is my helper, and I will not fear what man shall do unto me.

Presently, I slit the wax on Kate's seal and read her letter twice afore falling into vexed sleep.

There was no face to the man who carried the leather pouch, which was wrought with gold and stuffed with scrolls, but the hand, gnarled and beringed, was visible. His sleeves were of the finest fabric, the dark ruby color of congealing blood, slashed to show the ivory underneath. He hurried down the hallway, sun streaming into the long windows aside the Thames.

The Palace at Whitehall.

One of the scrolls dropped out of the pouch and began a long, slow descent to the floor. A hand reached out to catch it afore it reached the filthy rushes, and as it was caught, it unrolled. The signature, *Kateryn the*

Queen, KP, was running, the ink dripping and coursing down the document to the floor. The ink was the same bloody color as the man's sleeve. I ran to my lady's chambers and when she read it she began to shriek. One of her men quickly closed the doors to her chamber.

The hand that had caught the errant scroll was instantly recognizable.

'Twas my own.

"Are you all right?" Lucy shook me awake. She'd already lit a candle after coming from her room.

"Yes," I said. "Yes, I believe I am."

"A dream?" she asked.

I nodded.

"I fear for ye, lady. I do. I know something happened a court, though you won't say wha'. And now this, then, again."

I sat up in my bed. It was true, I had not had a prophetic dream in some time; therefore His sending one now had clear purpose. I felt a strange peace and calm. I picked up my copy of holy writ and opened to one of the passages marked by a thread from Father Gregory's vestments. Lucy was already privy to the goings-on and had become, in a way, a protector. It seemed only fair to be straightforward.

I softly read, "'And he said, Hear now my words. If there be a prophet among you, I the Lord will make myself known unto him in a vision and will speak unto him in a dream.' "

Lucy's eyes opened wide and I put my finger to my lips to indicate that she must hold her peace about this, now and forever. She nodded.

"I must return to court."

"Must ye go? I fear for ye," she admitted softly.

"I must, though I admit to a little fear as well. Listen well to what Her Grace had to say." I reached for her letter and, after opening it, read a selected portion. " 'The king has given me a fine New Year's purse, as is his generous nature. My lively faith maketh me bold, though I know how vain, foolish, false, ingrate, cruel, hard, wicked, and evil the world is. And 'tis closer to me than ever.' "

"She sounds afraid," Lucy said.

I nodded. I had not shared the portion of the letter wherein Kate told me she missed my companionship and the steady presence of the few whose fidelity she never questioned in her small circlet of safety. I had promised to serve and protect her. And my new vision showed me I was being called back.

The following morning I asked my lady mother if we might sup alone after church, and she agreed. I liked the new clergyman at St. Peter's well enough, he seemed a kindly sort, but he could not fill the heart space left by Father Gregory.

After the servants had set the platters on the

table, refilled the goblets, and left the room I spoke up. "As you know, Sir James delivered a letter to me from the queen."

My mother nodded but did not set down her knife, though her portion was tiny.

"She requests that I return to court. If you do not object. And she says she has a place for Hugh in the household of Sir William Cecil, who is placed with Edward Seymour."

At this my mother showed some pleasure and surprise. "Ah. Edward Seymour." She set her cup down. "What do you wish, Juliana? You are a woman now."

"I . . . I wish to return," I said. "Though I am grateful for a good home and the peaceful repose I've had whilst here, I believe 'twill be good for Hugh. And the queen needs me."

"And you must fly like the homeward pigeon when Kateryn Parr recalls you," she said, quickly shifting to bitterness. And though she did not show me kindness but a handful of times during my childhood, and I could therefore not see how she would be jealous of my affections for Kate, I did not wish to inflict additional pain upon her.

"Do you wish me to stay, then, Mother?"

She shook her head. "No. Of course not."

I bit down on the inside of my lip and tasted blood. 'Twas as it ever had been.

"I had already had both you and Hugh and lost a babe in between by the time I was your age. And what of Matthias?" she asked. "Do you wish me to speak with his father? He grows impatient, I know. And I believe him to be an excellent match for you. But I also know your father had not wished him for you, and that gives me a small pause."

I risked a question. "Did my father ever explain to you why he did not wish that?"

"He did," she said sharply. "But no one should be privy to the conversations betwixt a man and his wife."

"I'm sorry, Mother, I did not mean to offend."

"We shall tell Matthias that the queen has summoned you to return," she continued. "He will be glad, I know, of your connections at court and how they may advance his causes in commerce later. But he will not wait long. There are many who would be pleased to be bonny at bed and at board with him."

I nodded my agreement. *Thank you, Mother, for securing this honest solution, however temporary it may be.*

She sipped from her goblet. "Sir James Hart seemed beguiled by you. He never took his eyes from you except to politely acknowledge my comments at dinner."

"He's . . . a fine man."

"Do you know anything of his family?"

"I do. They are a good family of means who ship and do other business with the Seymours and other of the king's men. But I have no intention of pursuing my . . . friendship with him any further."

"You may not, Juliana, but he might. Sir James seems to be a man of the world. Have a care. He does not look like one who gives up pursuit easily. I well recognize those who do, as well as those who don't."

After the meal, I retired to my chambers to pack. Within an hour, my mother appeared and Lucy discreetly left the room.

"I have some jewelry for you." My mother handed a small casket to me and when I opened it I found several necklaces, including one of emerald and gold and a string of pearls. There were rings and some diamond hairpins. There was also a long string of polished jet, set in silver, which I knew had come from Constantinople.

"Your father saved these for when you were married. But I believe he would want you to have them at court, so that you do not feel out of place with the others. I've also prepared a purse for you, so you needn't depend upon the queen for your clothing and expenses."

I curtseyed to her and she took her thin hand and put it aside my face for a moment, and then took her leave. It occurred to me, as I looked through the treasures, that her way of telling me she had a care for me was to phrase it in terms of what my father wanted for me, though it was what she wanted for me too. I did not know why she could or would not speak plainly of her affection. It would not be the prickly method I would use with my daughter, but it was what she chose, nonetheless, and I would accept that.

Late that night, as I packed the jeweled crate, I stopped of a sudden and bit on my fist to stop myself from crying out. It had abruptly occurred to me that I might never have a chance to gift these jewels in a kind and loving manner.

I would likely never have a daughter. Nor a son.

NINE

Spring: Year of Our Lord 1546
The Palace at Whitehall

Within some weeks I saw Hugh settled with William Cecil, in Edward Seymour's household. A few days later the king held a tennis match to be followed by a private dinner in his chamber for the queen and a few of his favorites. The queen had asked me to be among those who served them, as she'd missed my company and wanted me near her often. I had not attended a tennis match, and looked forward to it. I knocked upon Dorothy's door to see if she wanted to make her way to the recreation hall with me, but when I arrived she had already left without me.

There was a longish viewing chamber that ran alongside the court, and most of the courtiers were already seated. Kate was at His Majesty's side in the center. He looked in a foul mood and his face looked as if 'twere blackening. Once he had been young and agile and on the court himself. Now he was corpulent and ill tempered. I could see that Kate kept her hand on his good leg and patted it from time to time.

I smiled broadly at Dorothy, who offered a wave back but then turned away; Tristram sat next to her but he did not meet my gaze. I scanned the crowd quickly to see if John Temple was there, and when I didn't see him, I relaxed and settled down next to Lady Fitzgerald Browne, who welcomed me with an eager smile. Her husband, Sir Anthony, was not yet present so till the match began, we made small talk about her stepchildren and her reading and my visit at home. She was still a wit.

"There are so many tennis balls in that bucket." I pointed to a large holding vessel near the court.

" 'Tis because there are so many old men here losing their hair," she quipped, and I laughed with her, knowing that the tennis balls were stuffed with hair, lost or cut. Just then her kindly husband joined us and she made a brief, glancing look upon his thinning hair. I hid a smile and she barely did too. To his favor, he did not leave me out of their conversational twosome but made me welcome. I was grateful, and yet missed my normal circle of friends. It was most enjoyable, though, and I made a note to seek out her company more often.

The game began, and it was pleasant to watch the young men bat a ball back and forth with the paddles made of wood and strung with dried sheep gut. Much better than bearbaiting, which I did not prefer. Sir Thomas was not in attendance, nor many of his men. I did see Lady Seymour and her ladies and sought her out afterward.

"My lady?"

"Yes?" she said. She was not welcoming, she never was, but she looked at me overcuriously. Perhaps she was unused to being approached by those she did not know well.

"I wanted to thank you, on my mother's behalf, for taking my brother, Hugh, into your household through William Cecil when Her Grace inquired."

"Certainly," Lady Seymour responded. "When the queen asks, we of course comply." She made it sound perfunctory and her voice was neither warm nor cold. "And your brother's name and mother's name are . . . ?"

"Lady Frances St. John, of Marlborough," I said. "And my brother, Hugh St. John."

Lady Seymour's smooth expression didn't break as she responded, "Oh, yes, that is right. Tell her she is most welcome. I know Her Grace is delighted to have you return."

It was a dismissal, I heard it in her voice, but that was fine. I'd done my duty and expressed our gratitude, and I did not expect her to be over-friendly to me when she and my lady were often at odds.

After the match I made my way down the halls and through the palace to my chamber as quickly as possible, so I could change afore going to serve Kate and the king.

I left shortly thereafter to assist Kate, but when I got to the queen's chambers Lady Dudley met me.

"Her Grace will not need your assistance this evening. The king is unwell and the queen is tending to him privately." Her face had a warranted shadow of worry. "I only hope she keeps the conversation light and does not stray, again, to theology."

I nodded my head in fervent agreement. His Majesty was not a patient man even when he was not in decline.

I returned to my chamber, which showed little sign of Elisabeth, who was likely with William Parr. I had slept well at home, with Lucy nearby but far from court. Now that I was back I startled easily, like my lady's pet birds with their night frights, and awoke not refreshed at all.

One evening shortly thereafter I helped Lady Herbert, the queen's sister, sort through Her Grace's jewels in the tall, wooden coffers in which they were kept in drawers nestled one upon the other. The queen was in the next room getting ready for an evening in the king's chambers.

"Excuse me, lady," I said in a soft voice to the queen's sister. "I have a gift for the queen. May I take my leave for a moment and present it to her?"

Lady Herbert smiled. "Of course, Mistress Juliana. Please do."

I made my way to the queen, who was reposing in one of her chairs whilst another lady helped with her shoes. "Your Grace," I began, "I can never begin to repay you for the kindness and affection you have shown me by keeping me in your household, and for helping to place my brother, Hugh. But I would endeavor to give you a token, if that meets with your approval."

She beckoned me forward. "Of course, Juliana, though none is required."

I handed a finely wrought case to her, one from the cache in the coffer my mother had given me afore I'd left Marlborough. She took it and bid me sit next to her before she opened it.

Ensconced snugly within was the string of jet beads strung with silver. "Oh, Juliana, these are lovely!"

"I know they are not as dear as precious stones, but mayhap because they are from the East, and unusual, you will find some mean occasion in which to wear them."

"They are delightful, and I will carefully plan when to wear them so they may be shown at their best," she said. She drew me near to her and embraced me; her sweet perfume enveloped me and her soft hair brushed against my cheek. "I am ever so pleased that you have returned to court. Elisabeth Brooke has told me that she is gladdened that you have returned, too, and indeed, my readings will now be much livelier. Should you read to us tomorrow?"

"I would be honored, lady," I said, delighted and humbled by her warm response.

" 'Twill be a bit later than usual," she said. "As I shall spend the night with the king."

She did not do that often, but there had been rumors of the king muttering about the decided lack of a Duke of York, a title he cherished as it had once been his own, as a second son, whilst his elder brother, Arthur, had still lived as Prince of Wales. As His Majesty grew more ill, his desire to anchor his legacy grew more insistent.

"I shall pray for a prince," I said softly.

"I too," the queen said. She looked more wan than she had before I'd left court. "I have also received some most loving correspondence from another prince, my beloved Edward." She showed me the letter, which lay on her table next to the New Year's gift she'd received from the Lady Elizabeth, a translation into French, Latin, and Italian of the queen's own *Prayers and Meditations.*

"I should desire to guide Prince Edward well

into adulthood," she said, and her sister came up behind her and put a hand on her shoulder, a warning hand, no doubt. "Come what may."

I kept my face steady and expressionless—I had learnt my court lessons well—but I knew what she intended; indeed, her ladies had whispered it among themselves. Her Grace meant for the king to name her as regent should the king die afore Prince Edward reached adulthood, which was likely. Should she bear the king a second son, that would be a near certainty.

Two of Kate's little spaniels were quarrelling about her feet and she lightly kicked in their direction to temper their misbehavior.

"Should you like me to walk them for you tonight?" I asked. "I have no other duties, if Lady Herbert gives me leave."

"That would be delightful," Kate said. "You are thoughtful, dear heart."

I am here to be useful in all I do. Kate brightened her countenance and took her leave to charm an ill, restless, and often intemperate king.

We gathered in her chambers a bit later than typical the next day, but many of her ladies were present; oft times we were a small gathering, as many tended to their own households and children. Lady Seymour was there and, after ascertaining that the ladies present were friendly, made a soft announcement. "My husband has heard that there are letters being circulated about you, Your Grace, and that they pertain to your nourishing heresy."

"Who dares write such a thing?" Kate whispered angrily.

"Wriothesley," Lady Seymour said. "But there are others."

Kate waved her away with her hand. "I have just spent a most satisfactory night with His Majesty and find it difficult to believe he would lend an ear to slander against his wife."

Wriothesley had tended the fire of his hatred toward the queen since she had penned that unfeeling note to his wife after the death of their son.

Lady Seymour shook her head and though she were no particular friend to me, I sympathized with her as she had undertaken to share a confidence with the queen at risk to herself—a confidence that had been lightly dismissed.

"Mistress Juliana?" The Countess of Sussex put her hand on my shoulder and shook me slightly. "The queen has just asked you to read."

"I'm sorry, my lady. What shall I read?" The queen, confident of her sway over His Majesty, handed a copy of Tyndale's forbidden book to me. I locked eyes for a moment with the countess afore choosing a selection that Father Gregory had marked for me some years before with his vestment threads, in the Acts of the Apostles.

" 'And we entered into the house of Philip the Evangelist, which was one of the seven deacons, and abode with him. The same man had four daughters, virgins, which did prophesy.' "

I glanced again at the countess before continuing on through the passage that prophesied about the terrible death of Saint Paul, who was to be delivered up to his enemies.

" 'Then Paul answered and said: "what do ye weeping and breaking mine heart? I am ready to be bound, but also to die" . . . after that, we made ourselves ready.' "

"Thank you, Mistress Juliana, that is satisfactory." Lady Herbert came and took Tyndale away from me. I held my suddenly empty hands out in front of me but for a moment and then curtseyed and stepped back. As I did, I noticed Lady Rich, a friend of Gardiner, had stepped into the room.

I did not know if I had been immediately relieved of the reading because of the sudden presence of one of the enemy, Lady Rich, or because of my melancholy choice of passages, which, I realized too late and to my horror, might have presaged the mortal level of danger that the queen was in. The other ladies soon went about their business, fading into and out of the queen's chambers.

The Countess of Sussex, who I knew had prophesied, drew near to me so only we two could hear one another. "Did you choose that passage because of my presence?"

"In part." I cast my eyes down.

"Those so called have the duty to act or speak when so compelled, depending upon if they have a word of knowledge kept private or that of utterance shared with others," the countess said softly.

"Yes, my lady. I understand."

Her Grace called her sister to her later that night when the chambers were nearly devoid of other ladies, then one of them called over a page, who gave her a letter opener. Lady Herbert took the opener and, out of his sight, used it to twist and befuddle some of the locks in Kate's jewel cases till they no longer moved smoothly. Then she gave it back to him.

"No matter how I pry, I am not able to fix some of these worn locks. Please call for His Majesty's locksmiths that we may have new ones installed."

Within a week the locks on her cases had all been changed; only the queen and Lady Herbert had the keys. This was provoked, I was sure, by the alarming news of the circulating letter. All copies of forbidden books, religious and otherwise, were placed in the lower drawers of the jewelry boxes and from that moment on we kept all of our reading to that which His Majesty approved.

I was relieved that Kate was out of apparent danger.

I stopped by Dorothy's chambers on my way to my room one day after dining and knocked. I'd missed our friendship and suspected that she felt awkward for having found me after John Temple's assault. I wanted to put her at ease, and enjoy our friendship once more.

"Oh, Juliana." She stood by the door, not moving to make way for me to enter.

"May I come in?"

"I'm so sorry, but I am about to leave on an errand for Lady Tyrwhitt."

"Dorothy," I began, in a quiet voice, "I am right sorry you had to stumble upon me after Sir John's terrible assault. I know it's made things uncomfortable between us, and I wish them to be as they ever were."

She grew even paler, if it were possible. "Oh, yes. Well. We shan't talk of it again."

"I know you shan't tell a soul, don't worry. And I haven't either," I reassured her.

"We shall have to find some time to read together, or sew, soon," she said. "But I fear I shall be late for Lady Tyrwhitt, so I must take my leave."

"Certainly," I said afore continuing to my room. I feared that, rather than make things better, I had instead made them worse.

I made my way to my chamber, expecting another dull afternoon and evening as the king had no entertainment planned, but to my surprise,

Elisabeth was there waiting for me. "Sir William has taken his leave for Baas Manor and I find myself free for some time. Should you like to ride?"

"I would indeed," I said, and we dressed in our riding outfits and made our way to the stables. Because her father was noble and rich and her paramour was the queen's titled brother, she had ready access to the horses and she took me through St. James's Park. We returned to sup in our rooms and gossip, and we made plans to have the seamstress visit us the very next week to order a new gown each. I gave silent thanks to my mother for her gift of a purse. I was gladdened, too, for the gift of Elisabeth's friendship and the promise of her more constant company. That night I slept deeply for the first time since I'd returned to court.

In May, my Lord Norfolk's son, Henry Howard, Earl of Surrey, one of the highest-born men at court, spoke up loudly against the conservative preaching during Lent. The king, tired and ill and in no mood to brook impertinence from the Howards, had Surrey examined before the council at Greenwich.

"The council asked, specifically, about the queen," one of the ladies relayed to a small circle of the queen's household in a private dinner one evening not long after. Gossip of the matter had already popped up like smallpox throughout the court so we were not surprised.

"Did his own father lay the trap?" Elisabeth asked her.

"Possibly. They will be battling bitterly till the axe whispers one of their names, or like as not, both, for their right wages. Surrey was told that he would be offered clemency if he would confess other talk in the queen's chambers."

This boded ill for my lady. And yet it gave us a red-sky warning afore the storm. After almost everyone had left the rooms, the queen had her uncle take all of the contraband books from her newly locked jewel case and remove them from the court entirely. If it could be proved by any of the queen's enemies that she was harboring and distributing forbidden literature, much less leading those under her care, including and especially the royal children, astray with them, there would be evidence enough for her to be prosecuted and then perhaps not even the king himself would save her. With all the material removed, Kate announced that she now felt safe, and happiness crept back into her countenance, and mine.

TEN

Summer: Year of Our Lord 1546
Greenwich Palace
Smithfield

In June, the matter of Thomas Seymour marrying the Duchess of Richmond was broached again by her father, the conservative Duke of Norfolk.

"Norfolk knows he is losing power, and when the king dies, it might well rest with the Seymours, who will always have the prince's best interests, as his family," Elisabeth said as we whitened our teeth with chalk in our chamber. "Norfolk, on the other hand, covets the throne for himself or his kin. 'Tis unlikely his family shall give that cause up."

"Shall he meet with success?"

Elisabeth shook her head. "I do not believe so. The king is not inclined to give him any more power by marrying Norfolk's daughter to the prince's uncle. And curiously, Henry Howard, Norfolk's son, dislikes the idea."

"Father and son butting heads once again," I said.

"Indeed." She motioned for me to help her with her laces, as we had no maid to assist us that day. "Whilst they still have them."

197

I was glad for the queen. All knew that the king approached midnight and that she likely had many more years to live, as did Sir Thomas, who had remained strangely unmarried for a man of means and title. I put it to his love for Kate and it softened him in my eyes in spite of what I feared about him. I expected they were biding their time.

Within a few days of the quiet announcement that no marriage arrangement would take place, Kate hosted a feast for the king and his courtiers on the grounds of Greenwich. It was a risky thing to do in June, when it rained more oft than the sun shone, but this day the clouds obeyed and being outdoors in the gardens among the flowers put everyone in a merry mood.

The men played bowles on the lawns and Kate had tables laden with sweetmeats and comfits and delicacies of all manner. Minstrels wandered about and the blossoming trees sent delicately perfumed missives to land on gown and doublet alike. "I have not seen you keep company much with Tristram Tyrwhitt," Kate said to me, quietly, as she made her way among her ladies and the other guests.

"He has not sought me out since I returned to court," I said. "But we were naught more than friends, after all."

"He has been occupied," she said. "Go seek him. You are not unable to speak up, methinks." A twinkle brightened her expression. She was glad that Sir Thomas would not be marrying Mary Howard, though she could not, of course, share the reason behind her merriment and hoped for romance for me too.

Though I was uninterested in Tristram, to honor my lady, I came up beside him as he was speaking with a group of other young courtiers. Many of them smiled and parted, and all conversation stopped. I nodded my head slightly. "Sir Tristram?"

He looked discomfited. "Mistress Juliana."

"I have missed your friendship," I said.

He smiled weakly, took my arm, and walked me toward a far table, alone but for the festive ribbons tied on it, streaming in the air.

"I have been remiss in not speaking to you, I admit. And I hope you'll forgive me," he said. We took a seat near one another and he kept his voice low though the minstrels would have covered our conversation in any case.

"After you left court, afore Christmas, I sought out your company. Mistress Dorothy told me that you'd gone back to Marlborough. She and I passed the season together and we grew . . . close. When I asked of you again and again, and she knew of my great affection toward you, she, as a friend to us both, sought to put me out of my misery, though more misery followed upon the disclosure."

I looked in his eyes and I knew what he was going to say afore he said it. The flute in the background mourned, and I forced myself to take deeper breaths and wished I'd have worn looser stays.

"I am sorry that you were so cruelly attacked," he said. "But I did warn you not to give John Temple any reason to believe you favored him."

I drew away. "And what makes you believe that I showed him any favor at all?"

"I saw you dance together many times that evening. I saw you leave with him, arm in arm."

He'd been watching me! "As you and I have danced and walked many times. And as you and Dorothy no doubt do even now."

"Ah yes, but I am not John Temple."

"And I am not the fair Dorothy—is that your next thought, Sir Tristram?"

He drew near. "I have my own reputation to think of as a man of integrity and a reformer, should this ever circulate," he said coldly. "I do not desire to plant where another man has plowed."

I recoiled from him in disgust. "You are detestable."

"Come now," Tristram said. "Mayhap this is all a result of you rooming with the harlot Elisabeth Brooke."

"Harlot?" I could scarce keep my voice at a level that would not draw an unwelcome gaze.

"She cavorts with a married man most nights. It's a wonder her father allows it to continue, but mayhap not, as his sister was notorious as well. She will be ruined if Parr turns from her."

"I do not know what Lady Brooke does or does not do when she is not in the chamber with me," I said. "But I do know that Sir William's wife abandoned him for another man, committing the sin of adultery, and lives with him even now as man and wife. According to the Lord himself in the book of Saint Matthew, she has broken her wedlock. Sir William may not be free to remarry according to the king's law, but he is according to the Lord's. It is the latter you seem so concerned everyone live by, Sir Tristram, and not the former."

He was caught and knew he could not both argue the point and keep his lofty ideal of himself. He stood up. "Good day, mistress." He bowed properly, slightly, and took his leave.

I made my way back to my chamber and stayed there until I knew Dorothy would be back at hers. When that time came, I made my way to her room and knocked sharply.

"Juliana." She opened the door and looked at me as a cornered mouse might.

I made my way into her chamber and saw that she was alone.

"You told Tristram."

She said nothing.

I gazed upon her, our once promising friendship now broken into shards, as a dropped vase might be, never able to be reassembled. " 'Tis nothing on earth I have ever done to you to earn such disloyalty, such disfavor, such a lack of charity. If there was, tell me now so I can repent of it," I said, holding back my sobs.

"You were haughty from time to time," she said in a pleading tone. "You have money and Kate's favor and you shall find another man and I shall not. Tristram is my only hope and he favored you over me. But I knew he, like any of my brothers, would not want a woman who had been . . . tried."

"Tried? Tried? Raped! You had been trusted with a most urgent secret, and you have not held to that faith." I ran both of my hands through my loosened hair and then placed one at the back of my neck to steady myself.

"He will tell no one," she said, her voice softer now. "He will shortly speak to his father and mine about being married; we will retire to his family's estates, and the secret will go with us." She drew close to me. "You did not want him, Juliana, so there is no harm done."

I closed my mouth and did not respond till I'd mastered the sharp retort I wanted to unleash. After a minute I said, "Please return the blue gown I *loaned* to you."

She walked to her cupboard and took it out and

handed it to me gingerly. "I am sorry," she said. "I hope one day you will forgive me."

I took the gown from her and let the tears rush down my face. "I loved you not a little, Dorothy, but very much. I wish you well."

I returned to my own chamber, glad for the fact that Elisabeth would likely not return to it that night, and cried myself sick into the returned blue gown.

Tristram's response proved that, like one of the king's coins, I'd been clipped, debased, lost some of my worth through no fault of my own, never again to regain my full value. No matter how I pressed on, I was kicked back. I was tired of trying and didn't know how much longer I could persevere. After a time, I read in my book of hours, prayed for comfort, and fell asleep without first undressing.

It was a cliff, and next to the cliff, a tiny patch of green upon which grew some flowers. They were bright and bold, *flos solis*, sunflowers, with beautiful faces that turned toward the sun as it arced across the lustrous blue sky, and I felt a sense of peace and contentment.

Toward the end of its arc, a seed dropped from one flower's bosom and implanted itself deep within the soil. Within a moment, a tiny shoot sprang forward, steady and green.

• • •

We were in the queen's chamber sewing, a week or so after the feast, when her brother, Sir William, arrived. He drew near to his sister.

"Kate." He looked around the chamber. I was there, and Dorothy, though we sat far apart and spoke perfunctorily and coolly. None from the faction opposed to Kate were present. They had been keeping their distance from her.

"Speak freely," she said to William.

"A letter has been intercepted, from Mistress Askew, which has led to her rearrest in London and another imprisonment. There is a rumor that the letter's content may implicate you." He looked around the room. "And others. Though that may be but an excuse to question her about you and your ladies."

A hush traveled from one lady to the next.

"Gardiner is already attempting to poison the king's mind against you, and he is sniffing every hedgerow to find further evidence to add to his case."

"Should I speak with His Majesty about this?" she asked.

Sir William shook his head. "I think that would be unwise. He is in a foul mood."

"You should speak with him," Kate said. "He trusts you, always has. Hasn't he nicknamed you his Integrity, for you shall always tell him the truth no matter the cost?"

William sat down next to his sister and took her hand in his own. "He has already spoken to me, Kate, and expects me to tell him the truth—no matter if the cost be my own sister! He has appointed me to the council that is to interrogate Mistress Askew. And not only I, but John Dudley."

"He appoints you, my brother, though I be implicated in her letter?" Kate's voice, and my pulse, rose.

"Yes," William said. "I am sore vexed about it. It be a test, I know it. Have a care." He turned toward Lady Tyrwhitt. "Because your husband served with Mistress Askew's father, and they are known to be friends, I should have an especial care for your family, too, lady."

At this Dorothy's face lost color and I was left rather wondering if she still thought Tristram was such a marvelous match. I did not wish for the king's wrath to spill upon either of them, though, nor anybody. Save John Temple.

The queen's brother would not return to the queen's chambers for many days so as not to draw attention to her whilst the investigation was under way. But Elisabeth heard the details from him, and she shared them with Kate privately, and with me in our chambers, as she knew where my sympathies lay.

"Today they asked Askew what her views are on the Eucharist," she told me.

"What did she answer?" I asked, knowing that was the one question which, if answered wrongly, would lead to her death.

"She replied, 'I believe that as often as I in a Christian congregation do receive the bread in remembrance of Christ's death, and with thanksgiving, according to his holy institutions, I received therewith the fruits of his glorious passion.' "

"She did not answer," I said.

"Exactly," Elisabeth agreed. "Gardiner then told her that she should answer directly and stop speaking in parables. She told him that even if she did he would not accept it. He became vexed and shouted to her, 'You are a parrot!' "

I said nothing, but admired her tenacity to her faith whilst under duress.

"She did not give up any names," Elisabeth said. "Even when the counsel had her put on the rack, and Richard Rich himself turned it so that her bones and members were disjointed like as to never return to their abilities again. Then they dumped her on the cold floor, half blinded, for hours." I recalled the countess's prophecy.

I grew ill while envisioning the racking and determined to continue praying for Mistress Askew daily. "They did not mention the queen, did they?"

"Not by name—they dared not. But all knew they were trying to strangle Her Grace by implicating a necklace of women in her household. Gardiner has well planted a thought in the king's mind that Kate is undermining him, and His Majesty has given Gardiner permission to explore this."

"Did His Majesty know of this whilst it was happening?" I asked, although I knew he must have. Little of consequence happened in his realm without his knowledge or approval, and he did not shy from torture. But racking a woman? It seemed beyond him even.

"He did," Elisabeth answered bluntly. "The lord lieutenant of the Tower sped to him by the river and told him. But he did not stay their hands. This is not about religion, no matter how it's cast, on either side," she continued, whilst clasping a diamond bracelet about her wrist. "'Tis about power."

Then I understood. All of the wives implicated were married to men in the rising faction in the king's household: those who had his ear, his purse, his stamp. And then there was the queen, who was named in the king's will as regent over the prince should something befall His Majesty. Religion might be the arena the game was played in, but the prize, no doubt, was earthly power.

As for Anne Askew, as a woman in opposition to the men at court in power, she had no recourse whatsoever. Her execution by burning was set for July 18. We were numb with apprehension on her behalf and despaired of our inability to help her.

• • •

Shortly thereafter the Countess of Sussex sent one of her lady maids to my chamber. "Mistress, the countess would like to see you, if you do not object."

It was not every day I was summoned by a countess. I was afraid for what she might beseech of me and made my way on weak limbs with racing thoughts toward her chamber.

We made our way down the halls, still dimly lit with the declining summer sun, and near the center of court where the grander courtiers lodged. The lady maid knocked on the door first and then pushed it open. The Countess of Sussex was waiting in her receiving chamber just within. "Thank you, that will be all," she said, dismissing her servant. She indicated that I should take a seat near her and offered me a glass of wine. I took it but I was not thirsty.

"Anne Askew is going to be martyred," she said without polite prelude. "We cannot forestall that, but we would like to ease her journey as we might. It is known that they often cause the fire to burn slowly, building with little wood and not high up, for those that displease the council."

I shuddered. I had never known a person who had gone on to be executed, and now came a woman nigh on my own age, with two small sons, about to be roasted slowly, like an ox on a spit. It seemed unbelievable.

"Will you help?"

I considered it for a moment before nodding cautiously. "How can I not? If Her Grace gives me leave, that is."

"She does."

I knew I should not speak of this with the queen herself due to the danger of the situation.

The countess went on to say, "Lady Hertford's page brings Askew some monies to buy food whilst she is in prison, to strengthen her. But he cannot be seen going there again. We plan to deliver gunpowder to the executioner."

"What for?"

"To place upon her body so she will die quickly. Would you be willing to assist by riding the funds to Smithfield and delivering them to the man providing the powder? You are little known and not like to draw attention. You understand the route to Smithfield better than most because it lies adjacent to Charterhouse, where you lived with your lady whilst she was married to Lord Latimer. You must go alone, but I would provide servant's clothing. If any question you, as a last recourse, show them my husband's chain of office and that should forestall further questioning for the moment, though it may lead to more later. Use it if all else fails."

I nodded, as my tongue had become too dry to speak. This was a mission fraught with danger. If I should fail, she would die badly. If I were found out, I might well end up in the prison, or worse, like Anne Askew.

And yet I recalled her courage, her fearlessness, her willingness to press on for her faith. I assumed she knew that help would be provided, though all peril not forestalled, because the One whom she served would not leave her unaided though it might appear that way to others.

"I will never leave thee, nor forsake thee."

The Lord is my helper, and I will not fear what man shall do unto me.

"Will you assist?" the countess asked me.

Are you afraid of battle? I'd asked Jamie.

Nay, he'd replied. *I am eager to prove myself.*

"I shall assist," I agreed, gaining courage by doing something I knew would make him proud. In my head and in my heart, he smiled at me and urged me forward.

The countess nodded. "I knew you would."

I presented myself to the stable boy, who looked at me oddly, in the mean dress and linen scarf that the countess had provided for me. The garments smelled of fire and I wondered who their owner was, mayhap someone who worked in the kitchens. The boy recognized me from my many rides with Elisabeth Brooke and brought round a fine mare.

"This'll do ye," he said, and I shook my head.

"I should prefer to ride with less attention," I said. "Not a nag but—"

"There be no nags in the king's stables, miss."

"Something sturdy but with a plain saddle and no silver markings," I said.

He nodded and brought out a gray mare, which would blend in with my gray cape, allowing me great anonymity. He seemed to understand and kindly asked no further questions.

After he helped me up, I pulled the light cape tight round me and took off out of the palace's grounds and along the south bank. I knew I could follow the south bank all the way to the bridge where I must cross over. Although my lady did not have us ride in the sickly, crowded streets around Charterhouse, I could often see them from the edge of her property.

Greenwich was southeast of the city, and Smithfield, where the burning was to take place, was in the northwest portion. The south bank was a stench; fishwives cleaned their wares, knifing slippery guts into the river Thames afore tossing the gaping fish into wicker baskets under the hot sun. I heard the competing shouts of the boys selling water and wine and wished I could stop and avail myself of either; though the day was young the July heat was already stifling. Women, tired and poor, offered their bodies, young and firm or old and slack, and I prayed on their behalf.

I soon passed the Tower; even from a distance I could see Traitor's Gate, where Queen Anne Boleyn had been rowed in but had never left. High atop the tower, with its gap-toothed turrets, perched several ravens and I recalled to me the vision of the Lady Elizabeth's chopped gown. A cold sensation ran through my chest, and I felt like one taken with illness.

As I grew closer the noise grew louder. None stopped to take account of me; like beasts of burden they kept their heads down with their own day's load, I supposed. I could soon see the wooden spire of St. Paul's rising above the city.

I slowed my mare; she clopped across the bridge with the others, some on horseback, some in litters, most on foot. As I reached the outermost corners of Smithfield, where the livestock was sold and butchered, I could smell the tine of boiling bones. The fat melting down into tallow for poor households left a greasy residue on the wind and the loud voices bartered whilst the animals bleated afore being led to a shambles for slaughter.

Once I reached Smithfield's west gate I handed my horse to one of the boys loitering nearby hoping to earn a coin. "Keep my mare here," I said, handing a small coin to him, "and let none harass her. When I return, you shall have two more of these."

"Yes, mistress, I will. Shud be a good show. A lady's burnin' with 'em and the highborn are here for sport as well as us folk."

I handed the reins over to him, suddenly

212

thankful that he had not noted my speech to be highborn. There was already a thick hedge of people surrounding the stakes, which were in the center of a long row. I was to find a certain copper merchant and hand the purse to him, and he was to hand the funds collected by the ladies, especially Lady Seymour and Her Grace, to the executioner—who would then hang bags of various lengths under the stained ivory gown of Mistress Askew. I soon found the copper merchant, his mean shop guarded by a handful of belligerent hens.

"Do you fashion pots on request?" I asked him. His long red beard matched what the countess told me I should find.

"I do, mistress, with half the funds up front and half upon delivery."

Having stated and received the proper words, I handed the purse over to him.

"God be with you," he whispered to me. I nodded, but dared not speak more than required lest others about us hear my inflections and know I was not common townsfolk.

At that, my requirement had been met. I was tempted, of a moment, to return to my mare and quickly make my way back to the safety of Greenwich, away from the bloodlust of Smithfield. As I passed near the stakes again, I overheard some who were sitting on a bench nearby. I pulled my stained scarf close to my head to allow me the chance to view who 'twas speaking.

Wriothesley, for one. Norfolk, who'd gladly sent his own niece Queen Anne Boleyn to the block almost exactly ten years earlier. And Bishop Gardiner.

I quickly moved away from them but it was unlikely they would ever glance at so mean a person as I. Although I was weak with fear and revulsion and desired nothing more than to flee back to court to pray to have this scene removed from my mind, I determined right then to stay, in case Mistress Askew looked up and saw no friendly face in the crowd. I did not want her to die alone but for those being martyred with her.

An hour later they carried her out in a chair; her joints and bones had been so badly racked that she could no longer walk, and her hair was shorn to her scalp like a badly handled sheep. I endeavored to make eye contact with her, for comfort, but she could not lift her head and I doubted that she would recognize anyone at all.

Once at the stake they bound her to the two men who were to die with her, chaining her middle to the post as well, as she had lost all ability to sit upright. I swallowed back some bile, some of which remained to coat my tongue. As they lit the bundle, Nicolas Shaxton, who only weeks before had been arrested with Mistress Askew, then released when he recanted, began to boldly speak.

As a condition of his freedom he was to preach the service whilst his former friends burned. I turned away from his harsh and hypocritical words; he had only received any position at all at court through the kindness of Queen Anne Boleyn.

The men began to moan and cry immediately and I closed my eyes and prayed for them, the words formed upon my silent, moving lips. Askew herself did not scream until the fires hit her face. Instead, till the end, she corrected Shaxton on his Scripture. "Yes, he's got that right," she'd boldly call out of a passage, or, "No, there he misseth and speaks without the book." I was strengthened by her courage and forced open my eyes in order to honor her.

At the end, she too began to scream, and then the gunpowder blew small bits of sticky wood and flesh onto the crowd, which had held itself at a shouting distance. Some pieces struck my cloak and I patted them out in horror, and tried to hold back the rising gorge in my throat but could not contain the tears running down my cheeks. I now understood why the garments of someone who tended fire had been chosen for me.

Take them quickly, Lord Jesus.

Justice at court belongs to men, not women, John Temple had said, leering, and his bitter comments came back to me among the wailing of those around me, which echoed the wailing in my own heart.

If I had been more devout, I would have prayed for mercy upon the souls of the men who sent Mistress Askew to the stake, and for John Temple. But I did not want mercy for them. I coveted justice, instead, for myself, and for Anne Askew and those burning with her, and for all others who are harmed at the hands of ruthless men.

I rode home in shock, my horse, thankfully, mostly guiding herself, and she made her way quickly. I did not eat or drink or sleep that night, fasting from all, grateful that Mistress Askew was now at peace but sickened at how she'd died.

Within the week all of the highborn reformers, including Bishop Cranmer, fled the court for the safety of the countryside and even for France, leaving Her Grace alone and undefended at court.

ELEVEN

Summer: Year of Our Lord 1546
Palace at Westminster

The queen's chambers were quiet that season, and the air held the awkward tension of those picking their way through the forest whilst avoiding trap holes, leafed and twigged over.

"I am glad that the Lady Mary was here to visit with you earlier," I said, making polite conversation whilst Kate and her sister, Lady Herbert, sewed linens for the poor. "She has oft been away."

"Yes," Kate said. "She has drawn closer to me now that the king is oft given to melancholy. He is tired afore the day begins. He does not walk in the gardens as was his habit during the afternoon. He eats but little, compared to his former appetite."

All knew the king was ill unto death. 'Twas only a matter of time, though none knew if that would be weeks or a year. And as he grew sicker, he grew more troublesome and impatient.

"Perhaps you might send him a physic," Kate's sister suggested, "as a show of your continuing concern for his health?"

Kate brightened at that. "Yes, yes, that is an excellent idea." She called her secretary to her and dictated a quick note. "Juliana, will you please deliver this to the king's physician and wait for a response?"

I nodded, glad to be of help. I took the letter and made my way past the king's chambers and down the long hallway where I knew Dr. Wendy might be found. I knocked upon his door, but his associate told me that he was already with His Majesty. I left the letter for him to deliver upon his return and began to make my way toward the hall back to the queen's suite. As I did, I saw another figure, blocky and bold, just ahead of me. He seemed to have just come from the king's chambers.

It was Sir Richard Rich. I wondered if he'd washed Anne Askew's blood from under his nails.

A certain dreaminess overtook me. I saw a scroll drop out of his leather bag and fall toward the rushes. I knew it was the one in my vision, with the queen's name written and dripping blood, and that I was to act and take the scroll in hand.

Rich stopped for a moment, but I dared not move lest he hear me and discover his loss and turn back afore I reached it. I knew I was in danger by taking what clearly belonged to him. He hastened to his destination and seemed unaware of the fallen document. I picked it up, tucked it into the fold in the front of my gown, and held it there with my hand whilst making my way back to Her Grace. As I did, the words spoken in the book of Esther whispered to me.

Who knoweth whether thou art come to the kingdom for such a time as this?

I quickly made my way to the queen's chambers.

"Did you find the doctor?" she asked.

"No, lady. But as I was returning, Sir Richard Rich was leaving the king's chambers. He dropped a scroll. I did not read it," I said, my hand and voice trembling. "But the scroll had not been waxed and has slightly unrolled."

"Hand it to me," Kate said. She opened the scroll. Her face went from rose to ash and then she quickly spoke high and loud. I had never seen her so vexed.

" 'Tis an arrest warrant! For me!" She began to cry.

This could not be true! I did not know whether to give her margin or to come alongside for comfort.

Immediately her sister raced to her side. "Surely not," she said, taking the scroll from Kate's hands. Kate, meanwhile, was close to shrieking.

"It's not stamped!" she said, making no sense. "It's not stamped!"

I brought my arm around her but she nearly flung me off.

"What do you mean," one of her ladies asked, "by 'It's not stamped'?"

"It is signed in his *own hand!*" Kate shouted afore falling to the floor. "Woe to me. I am undone." She continued to bewail and babble and her sister helped her to a comfortable chair, but Her Grace would not, or could not, sit still.

"I am like as dead," she said. And then she wept in a loud voice. It was loud enough that I knew it could be heard in the corridors but none could calm her.

I was shocked and horrified that I had been the woeful messenger of this terrible news. A warrant for her arrest, signed in his own hand. And the king did not shy from executing his wives.

Kate glanced at her little dogs, scrambling about

her feet, but did not reach for them. Instead, she wailed, "The companies of the wicked bark at me. They beset my hands and feet round about." And then she began crying again.

"Fetch His Majesty's physician," Lady Herbert told me.

I stumbled to the king's rooms and, shaking, babbled to one of his men that the queen required the doctor, if the king could spare him, as she had taken ill. I returned to Kate's chamber, where she was still completely disassembled. You could hear her pitiful cries in the hallway, through the closed doors, and I waited but a moment before the doctor arrived.

I echoed those pitiful cries, as did many of her ladies.

"What is it?" he asked Kate once he entered. She, knowing that he shared her religious sympathies, told him about the arrest warrant and how she was undone.

Of a sudden, the king, having heard from his man that the queen had taken ill, appeared in her chamber. I silenced myself, curtseyed deeply, and did not look up at him because I did not want to meet his terrible gaze.

"Kate, what be the matter?" he demanded. "We are concerned for your health and well-being."

She stood up and then fell to her knees in front of him. "Oh, sire, I have had ill tidings delivered to me. I do not know who would besmirch my affections for you, but I have heard that you, my sweet husband and lord, are displeased with me."

The king did not answer right away, and it was interesting that he did not ask by whom these tidings came. "You must be misled, Kate," he said, but his voice was not tender. "Come now, sit with us by the window and regain your senses."

After a few more moments of reassurance, His Majesty took his leave, allowing his physician to remain behind to attend to her.

I was terrified. Having seen what he approved for Mistress Askew, and knowing what he'd allowed, nay, commanded, to happen to his other wives, I had no doubt he would dispatch of Kate if he took a mind to do so.

The doctor, still present, drew near to her. "Gardiner has taken every occasion to speak ill of you to the king. He told the king that you seek to undermine and rule him on every occasion. He has told him that if Henry would agree to protect him, he, along with other counselors, would expose such treason, cloaked in heresy, that His Majesty would perceive how perilous a matter it is to cherish a serpent in his bosom."

Kate said dully, "And His Majesty gave him leave to find out, hence the warrant for arrest."

"Yes. However, madam, the king did come to visit you, though he be cold in manner, something he never did for Queen Anne Boleyn nor Queen Catherine Howard afore their arrests."

Relief swept through the room like a breeze on this hot day. Mayhap there was yet hope!

"What shall I do?" Her Grace fretted.

"My lady, all is not yet lost, though the situation be grim," he said. "Show humble submission unto the king, His Majesty, as is meet and required, and mayhap he once more will find you gracious and favorable."

The doctor took his leave, and Kate sent a note to His Majesty asking if she might dine with him as she had recovered after his tender ministrations.

The king replied that yes, they might dine together.

The queen's sister took especial care in dressing her that night. Although Kate normally preferred ruby-colored gowns, this night she chose one of a pale violet with soft slippers to match. She could not, of course, wear her hair down about her shoulders but especial care was taken to make it look flowing and womanly. Her rubies were replaced with a gold necklace with a diamond drop, which had been given to her by the king. Her sister would serve as lady in waiting but I was allowed to carry the candle down the hall and serve Lady Herbert, whilst she assisted Kate as required.

The king had not many servants in attendance, either, and whilst he was courteous in welcoming Kate to table he did seem indifferent.

The table was set with beef stuffed with forcemeat, soft white manchet bread, and the tarts of jelly and cream-of-almond that the king preferred. He had Edward Askew pour Kate's wine and then asked her a question of a religious nature.

"Tell me, Kate, because you are so learned in this matter. What think you of auricular confession? We hear there are many varied opinions of this at court and we should value your counsel."

Lady Herbert did not move her gaze but I could tell by the tensing of her neck that she found this line of conversation unusual and dangerous.

"Sire," Kate responded, "you know as I do that women were created as inferior to men in these matters, and being little able to make wisdom of these issues, which are weighty, we better turn to our husbands to advise us. I thank you right kindly for tolerating my womanly weakness and imperfections, but I would rather be guided by Your Majesty on this matter than offer my own unworthy opinion."

The king set down his goblet. "Not so, by Saint Mary, you are become a doctor, Kate, to instruct us, not to be instructed or directed by us."

I slid back into the shadows and even Lady Herbert stepped back. The queen was on her own now to claw her way up from this trap.

"Sire, I am sorry if I have misled you otherwise,

but in this, you are mistaken. I seek to follow your counsel and wisdom in all matters. And where I have, with Your Majesty's leave, heretofore been bold to hold talk with Your Majesty, I have not done it to maintain opinion but rather to provide lively conversation which may, for a time, distract you from the pains that beset you. I also, by hearing Your Majesty's learned discourse, might even receive to myself some profit."

She bowed her head becomingly. A minute passed. Then another. Then he grinned afore taking a large drink of wine from his golden goblet.

"Is that even so, sweetheart? And tended your arguments to no worse end? Then perfect friends we are now again, as ever at any time heretofore." He patted his good leg and she made her way round the table to sit upon his lap.

I closed my eyes for a moment and swooned with relief. The rest of the evening was forced merriment, and Kate spent the night in His Majesty's chamber.

There was no certainty that reinstatement in his affections was permanent.

The next day when His Majesty and the queen were walking in the gardens, which he had not done for some time, Norfolk, Wriothesley, and forty guards approached them. "Stay yourself, sweetheart," the king said to her. We, her ladies, remained behind whilst she sat on a bench.

We saw them look as Wriothesley tried to hand him a piece of paper that the king snatched out of his hands and tore up afore motioning for Norfolk to humble himself and bend down to gather the pieces. "Errant knaves! Beasts! Fools!" the king shouted at them, and sent them on their way with a boxing to the ears.

The king then made his way back to the queen, whilst we ladies withdrew to a discreet distance. I could still hear Kate, though, pleasingly telling the king that he should be kind to his men, who only loved him. She acted her role well, not letting on that she knew anything at all of the plot against her.

"You are too kind, sweetheart," he said. "You know not what they had planned. But an unwarranted attack upon a wife is an attack upon the man, and we shall not forget this."

In the days that followed, the king began, once again, to shower his wife with all manner of affection and treasure. And, rewardingly, she did likewise with me. One afternoon after she had dismissed most of her ladies, she called me into her private dressing chamber.

"Yes, Your Grace?" I curtseyed afore standing in front of her.

"Come, Juliana," she said, patting the seat next to her. "First, I must apologize to you for the ill-mannered way in which I pushed you aside after you had delivered the scroll to me. I was quite beside myself and not in my right senses."

"My lady, there is never a reason for you to apologize to me," I quickly said, my ear tips growing warm. " 'Tis perfectly understandable that you would react thusly, especially as someone had besmeared your name with the king—to terrible consequence."

She drew near me. "I do believe our Lord made providential arrangements for you to come upon that warrant, and in so doing, save me."

"I, too, Your Grace, I heartily believe that," I said. "And I thank Him." *Thank You for using me to help Her Grace,* I prayed.

"I have not forgotten the lovely gift you gave me from your father's treasures. I should like to give you a gift in return." Kate handed over a large silver box to me. I took it in my hands and looked at the elaborate carvings on the lid, running my fingers over the top.

"Open it!" she said with delight.

I lifted the box lid; the inside was lined with blue velvet and there were tiny compartments in which rested treasures. "My own pincers!" I said. "I shan't have to borrow Elisabeth's any longer." I moved to the next section, in which was a jewel-studded case; inside was carmine powder for the lips and the cheeks. One long case held sticks of kohl. There was a tiny case of cinnamon-scented drops, the very kind she had the physic prepare for herself to keep her breath sweet. And loveliest of all, a small glass, dear and rare.

"Your Grace! I cannot express my gratitude enough," I said with deep affection. "I shall never forget this favor; I have never received anything so dear. I am so very glad that you are back in His Majesty's good favor."

"I too," she said afore sighing deeply.

I finally have a mother who loves me. I cherished the thought, in the quiet or lonely moments, along with wistful longings for Jamie, his laughter, his jesting, his hand upon my back. His lips upon my own.

Early in August, the lords Hertford and Lisle were back to claim their rightful places in the privy chamber, and a celebration was being planned to honor the French admiral who would be visiting London. The queen's brother, William, would hold a prominent place in the welcoming ceremonies.

Thomas Seymour would attend. Would he put the queen in danger? I had still not forgotten my vision of him and the Lady Elizabeth. Now that the vision with the scroll had come to pass, I felt more certain than ever that the garden prophecy would too.

Prince Edward and the queen had kept up their warm correspondence. The prince was particularly desirous of making a good impression, as his father had arranged for him to play a large role in greeting the French admiral when he arrived at Greenwich. The prince wrote a tender letter to the queen asking for her advice. Prince Edward, who, at the king's behest, would remain under her care after the celebratory events, was reassured that his Latin was excellent, his presence was royal, and he had nothing at all to fear. Rather, the French admiral would note that England's future king was someone to be reckoned with and would therefore very carefully abide by the treaty.

Her Grace signed the letter, had me sand and seal it, and sent it off. Like any mother preparing her son for a challenging future, she built him up at every occasion.

"The king named me his regent in 1544 when he took Boulogne," Kate said, "the very war we are signing an agreement over now. And he has not rewritten it since." She felt confident, especially after her rekindling of affection with the king, that she would guide Edward and his realm into adulthood even though it appeared that her dream of having a child of her own would not be fulfilled.

The young prince, a lad of only eight, performed admirably, and after greeting his guests with a retinue of two thousand on horse, escorted them to Hampton Court Palace, where the king, and Kate, and all the courtiers and households awaited.

There was no one Henry desired to impress so much as the French, excepting the Holy Roman Emperor, and he had spared no expense for this lavish event. There was banqueting and hunting and masks every night.

Though I knew it could never again be as it had been, I rather wished I had Dorothy with me; I missed her companionship. Lady Fitzgerald Browne must have noticed that I looked out of sorts and included me in her circle.

On the third evening of celebrations I had eaten of roasted hare in French mustard sauce and was drinking a delightful wine that the French had brought with them from the Benedictines when someone came and touched my shoulder from behind.

"Juliana."

I turned around, nearly spilling my wine. When I saw who it was, I had to stay myself from throwing it upon him. "I have naught to say to you, John Temple." I denied him the title of *sir,* as he was in no manner chivalrous.

"Do not draw gazes that stay upon us, unwelcome attention, and gossip," he said. "I only wanted to share that I find you as lovely as ever. And as you are alone perhaps you'd like to join me—"

"I would most certainly not like to join you in the gutter from which you slithered," I interrupted. I did not bid him good-bye, I simply walked away.

My hand was shaking and I set my goblet down lest I spill it. I felt an acid rise in my throat reminiscent of the taste of the hare I'd just enjoyed. To the far side of the room I spied the welcome face of Sir Thomas Seymour, who was providentially alone. I had not had occasion to speak with him since the event began but he was at least someone I could approach as I fled Temple, so I made my way to him.

"Juliana!" he said, his face lighting with real joy. "You look lovely. Beautiful. Your mother would be most pleased and proud."

It was clear he did not know my mother well. I could not even get her to respond to my infrequent correspondence.

"And"—he held up his hand—"before you ask me, Sir James Hart is not with me this time."

I smiled warmly but did not allow my face to betray any emotion. "Thank you, Sir Thomas, but I was not going to ask after James Hart. I was about to ask after you, your interests." I lowered my voice and whispered. "Outside of the queen, that is."

He laughed aloud and led me to the dance floor. "She is as lovely as ever, isn't she?" he asked, holding me so close I could hear his voice above the music, dance, laughter, and loud repartee in both French and English. "I have been asked many times why I have not married, not even once, though my brother be married twice with many children. And I shall tell you the reason, Juliana. 'Tis because I desire to marry only Kate, have ever desired only Kate. And soon, I shall have my wish."

I pulled back from him and, before others could notice that I was agog, he drew me back to him. 'Twas treason to talk of or predict the king's death, which is what he had just done. I knew that Sir Henry Norris had gone to the block because someone had mistakenly whispered that Norris hoped to replace the king in Queen Anne Boleyn's affections once the king were dead.

"Now, Juliana, you know how to keep a secret," Sir Thomas said.

"I do," I said, though I was tiring of keeping so many.

"Then I shall tell you another," he said, waiting for the music to strike up afore continuing. "Sir James Hart will be back to London for the coronation."

I unwillingly smiled.

"Aha! I have caught out one of *your* secrets, mistress," Seymour said, jovial and charming. It was hard not to like him.

"Sir James is a friend," I replied. "I shall be glad of his visit . . . whenever that may be." I was certainly not going to be heard talking about a coronation that must, by treasonous definition, happen after the king's death.

"Perhaps you'll be more interested in seeing Sir

Matthias and his family, from Marlborough, who will certainly be in London for the festivities as well." He grinned. " 'Tis fine for an old sea dog like myself to remain long unmarried. 'Tis not becoming for a mistress, especially at court." He glanced up at Elisabeth, firmly attached to Sir William Parr, the queen's brother.

"I shall be glad to welcome them all." I sidestepped the talk of my marriage potential since I felt there was little if any possibility of a wedding happening. "Whenever they may visit. I wish my mother would visit, too, as Hugh is here as well. Alas, she will not."

"She may change her mind," Thomas said. " 'Twill be an event not many shall want to forswear; we Seymours shall see to that. And then, mistress, there will be decades of plenty." He led me from the dance floor and availed me of a fresh goblet of the bubbling wine. "Are you well contented here?" He seemed to genuinely care. "I have spoken with your brother, Hugh, and he does well with Cecil."

"I am contented," I replied carefully. I should not have liked him to think that I was ungrateful, or that there had been some falling out between Kate and myself.

He smiled. "Do not allow the sheen of the court to become a shell, mistress." After a few more pleasant words he kissed my hand and took his leave.

I danced with a few others that night, but I thought carefully upon his words. Had I become sheathed in a shell? Whom had I shared my feelings with completely since Dorothy and I had been estranged? Whom did I trust? Whom could I hold on to and laugh with unreservedly?

No one save one. Jamie was coming to London!

TWELVE

Winter: Year of Our Lord 1547
Greenwich Palace
Whitehall
Baynard's Castle
Seymour House, Syon House
Chelsea

The king and queen passed the autumn at hunt, comfortable in one another's affections, though 'twas clear by the king's panting breath, restless nights, and quick temper that he struggled with unwellness. Though I knew Kate reserved her heart for Thomas, she most clearly enjoyed the king's companionship and he hers. She spoke softly and blushed at his jests while holding his arm tenderly. I thought back upon His Majesty's physician's comment that the king had not offered his other wives the chance of a visit once a warrant of arrest was signed. Her softness was perhaps the reason why.

So it came as a surprise when we were to take our leave from the king's lovely, though incomplete, palace at Nonsuch, so named because there was no such place like it in the world, to return to London.

Kate was clearly upset that we were packing.

"What is wrong, Kate?" her sister asked.

"We are to go to Greenwich, where the Lady Mary will join me. The Lady Elizabeth and Prince Edward will return to their household. But the king goes to Whitehall!"

"Whitehall?" Lady Herbert inquired. "Afore Christmas? His Majesty always celebrates Christmas at Greenwich. Whitehall is for governance."

"Edward Seymour has advised the king that they must spend a considerable amount of time, now that all the nobility are in London, reworking His Majesty's will. To ensure that the prince is well provided for. 'Tis my belief that the prince is already well provided for in the current will, but Seymour has apparently persuaded the king differently."

Ah. So then I knew why Lady Seymour was not in attendance at the moment. Kate suspected that Seymour was turning the king away from Kate's influence in the prince's regency and toward snatching power for himself.

I did not know what to think. Time, though, is a babbler.

Once at Greenwich the queen and the Lady Mary set about planning festivities for the other women and most of the court through the Christmas season and the New Year. The queen gave Edward Seymour a most conspicuous gift, a double portrait of Henry and herself as king and queen.

The king did not allow the Lady Mary nor the queen to visit him, which caused not a little talk. It was the first time that the king had left the queen on a solemn occasion.

As he grew more ill, the king struck harder, clearing the forest of all obstacles so his son might have a straight ride into manhood and kingship. He had Norfolk and his son, the Earl of Surrey, imprisoned for treason. The first thing Norfolk did was cry self-pityingly to the king, telling him that whilst his son was surely a traitor, he, Norfolk, was not.

Norfolk's son, Surrey, was executed in a matter of days whilst his father moldered in the Tower.

The queen kept busy at sewing and reading, though with material not controversial, as she waited for a summons from the king.

"Your Grace." Lady Seymour strode triumphantly into the chambers one day and spoke afore being asked to by the queen. "I thought it would bring you some comfort to know that the king has completed the changes to his will, and has entrusted the entire document into the safe-keeping of my husband."

"Thank you, Lady Seymour," the queen responded coolly. "And now, if you will excuse me, I'm going to sup. I would ask you to stay, but I know you have comfortable quarters of your own and therefore have no need of mine."

'Twas the first volley in a gowned skirmish.

The king was confined to his bed, and still not having been recalled to his side nor having had her pleading letters returned or acknowledged, the queen retired to Baynard's Castle to wait. All of us lived as though on the edge of a cliff. The great king was to die, he who had completely dominated and subjugated our realm for as long as most could remember. Would young Prince Edward likewise dominate? I somehow doubted it and feared, as I knew the others did, what lay ahead. The young boy had not the strength yet to hold the reins.

On January 27 an especially dear friend of the queen came to visit her late at night with a small retinue. "My lord husband has spoken with His Majesty," she said, once inside the warm great hall. "He has brought him ill tidings from the doctors. They have told the king that in their opinion, he is not like to live."

The next morning came a messenger from Whitehall to Kate. The king, at the end, could not speak. He had Cranmer, and not Gardiner, by his side as he died, at the age of fifty-six. He had been omnipotent in the realm for thirty-eight years. Sir

Anthony Browne, Lady Fitzgerald Browne's husband and a religious conservative, and Edward Seymour, Lady Seymour's husband, a reformer, went to deliver the news to Prince Edward and the Lady Elizabeth, who still lived together. Power was beginning to settle like stones cast into the Thames. The heaviest got there first.

Kate slumped and began to weep, for His Majesty, for herself, too, I was sure. The fact that the king had kept her from his side at the end likely meant that he had made changes which she would not find pleasing; the king oft distanced himself from those he was about to do some disservice or harm.

I tried to bring her comfort and cheer but, in truth, had little to offer. Kate had lost her greatest danger. But she'd also lost her only protector. 'Twas not for no reason that a group of courtiers is referred to not as a flock, nor as a pride, but as a threat.

On the last day of January Prince Edward was proclaimed king. There was a great procession to the Tower, and once there all persons of high or noble birth and all knights present greeted him and pledged loyalty, fealty, and deference. Kate could not have been a prouder mother, and she carried on about him when any could listen.

Shortly after the new king's reception, the old king's will was formally opened, though there had been whispers that Edward Seymour had opened it first, afore the old king even died, so that if he did not agree with the final contents he could vex the king further till he did.

As expected, the king had nominated sixteen council members to guide his son and the realm during his son's minority; these sixteen were nearly equally divided among the religious factions. No one man was to be lord protector; each was to be an equal and thus preserve Edward's supremacy.

The queen had ridden to Whitehall and had waited outside of the council room so as to be present when the will was read, but Edward Seymour would not let her in. Instead, he met her in the hall.

"I presented myself to him." She recounted the situation to us later that evening, at her manor in Chelsea. "I wore my finest gown and jewelry, as is befitting a queen. 'Why have you come?' Edward Seymour asked me. 'I come to hear my lord's will be read, to hear my rights, and to know what shall happen to my son, Edward,' I answered."

She becalmed herself afore continuing. " 'He is not your son,' my Lord Hertford responded. And I replied that, indeed, Edward had addressed every letter to me as 'beloved mother' and signed them as 'your son.' 'He may give you the honorary title,' Hertford replied, 'but he is my sister's son.

Not yours. As such, I am in the best position to look after his interests, not you.' And then he proceeded to tell me that the king had left me as queen dowager, with his deeply held affection, as his entirely beloved wife. He has left me no small amount of plate and I am to retain all of my jewelry, anything else I desire to take, my jointure, and further monies each year that shall allow me to live in a manner befitting a queen. My status, before all, is to remain as queen dowager."

She stood up and then sat down again, defeated. "But I shall have no input over Edward, nor the realm. Indeed, unless there is a public function, I have to apply to the council to visit my son at all."

"It was not what you expected," Robert Tyrwhitt, her master of horse, said. "I know."

"Then, when I asked to speak to the council members, I was denied. They put the door closed in my face after quickly bidding me good day."

I felt her pain, and her shame, both of which were undeserved.

Thomas Seymour made his way within a day's time to pay his respects . . . and to complain.

We dined at her long table in Chelsea. There were only twenty or so of us present, those closest to my lady, as her royal household had been dissolved. Whether Sir Thomas had decided that all were safe to unburden himself in front of or

239

whether such consideration had never occurred to him I knew not, but he spoke overfreely.

"The very first thing the council did, in direct disobedience to His Majesty, was appoint my brother, my *brother*," Sir Thomas said, "as lord protector of the realm and governor of the king's person. And who do you suppose suggested this course of action? None other than Edward Seymour himself." He gulped his wine and rapped it hard on the table to call for more.

"It was necessary 'so ambassadors and the like have direction and know with whom to speak,' he said, though he promised he would not act afore getting consensus from the others. If I had been nominated to the council"—his voice rose—"as was meet and right, I could have spoken freely from a lifetime of experience and shown them that my brother did not, does not, and will not gather consensus unless pressed. What he wants, he takes. What he has, he holds."

"He has named you as Baron Sudeley; taken the lord high admiralty of England, Ireland, Wales, Boulogne, and Calais away from Lord Lisle and given it to you; and added greatly to your incomes," the queen commented quietly.

"Yes, but he has made himself Duke of Somerset, a duke—the highest rank of nobility. And he has kept all power for himself. We are both the king's uncles; we should divide that power between us."

The conversation died down then, and to more somber matters as was expected so few days after the king's death. Indeed, he still lay in his leaden coffin, surrounded by long burning tapers, in his privy chamber at court.

Later, as I talked quietly with the queen's guests, I could hear Thomas raving about how the council had power over not only King Edward, but the king's sisters too.

"Should Elizabeth marry without the council's, meaning Edward's, consent," he said, "she will lose her place in the succession."

"But not Mary?" Kate spoke up with surprise.

Thomas stopped, silent, for a moment. "Yes, yes, Mary too, I suppose."

That night I helped ready the queen for bed, as her greater ladies who had served her whilst she was at court had mainly now retired to their own homes. The queen's household still numbered nigh on one hundred, but her personal ladies and womanly attendants had been trimmed to but few.

We sat first together in her chamber whilst her lady servant fetched and warmed the washing water.

"Will your brother and mother repose here at Chelsea for the coronation festivities?" she asked me.

"I sent a swift messenger to Marlborough as soon as you extended the invitation. My mother sends her grateful regrets. My brother, Hugh, would like to stay a night or two here so he and I may spend some time in one another's company." I felt badly that my mother had refused the queen's kind invitation and hoped she would soon turn the topic. Graciously, she did.

"Should you like to return home to Marlborough after the coronation? I have grown fond of you, as you know, and should miss your companionship. But you are a woman ready to be wed and bearing children."

She put her feet upon the stool and passed a tray of sweetmeats to me.

"I do not wish to marry . . . yet," I replied tentatively.

"Ah . . . I did not know that Sir Tristram was of a mind to marry Mistress Dorothy," she said. "Or I would not have sent you to him in the gardens."

"It was a surprise to me, too, Your Grace. But I wish them happiness."

"They will be in London for the coronation," she continued. "They will be staying with his aunt and uncle, of course." She softened her voice. "Lady Dorothy is with child. They have asked me to stand as godmother when the babe is born."

I was overcome with dark misery, like a sudden eclipse of the sun. Kate reached out and took my hand in hers, believing my longing was for Dorothy's husband when it was, in fact, Jamie and our own child I wished for. When I looked in my lady's face, I saw it was writ with sorrow too. She had been godmother to many babes but had borne none of her own.

"You may remain in my household as long as you desire, Juliana, as an especially beloved. But I wish more for you. When the time comes, I shall be glad to stand godmother for you as well."

I squeezed her hand. "Thank you, Your Grace. I shall never be able to repay your kindness." But I would endeavor to, if I could.

We held hands for another minute till her maid came back with the wash water. I left to her dressing chamber to fetch her bed gown. When I came back, the maid had finished her duties and we were alone again. "Kate, forgive me," I said. "But it seems to me that, whilst 'tis a sorrowful thing for you to lose the ability to guide King Edward, you do now have the ability to marry whom you choose, make a family of your own, and live in merriment without the burdens of the court."

She looked up at me abruptly. "That is what I had concluded, too, Juliana. At first. But Thomas has shown me that I have been badly handled and mistreated in this matter. I am a queen, and he convinces me that I must agitate for equitable treatment. He is certain that his brother will further move against me. On the morrow, I will request my jewelry be removed from the Tower, where it has been held for safekeeping, and returned to myself."

She looked at my face, which must have conveyed my doubt, and continued. "Lord Thomas has, and has always had, my highest interests at heart." Ah yes, Sir Thomas had now become Lord Thomas, because of his brother's advancing him.

Lord Thomas had goaded her, then, to move along the direction he wanted to travel. It was not my place to say more, so for once, I did not.

Shortly thereafter, there came news that the queen's brother, William Parr, had sided with Edward Seymour on the matter of the protectorship and had been rewarded by a strengthening of their friendship and "common concerns." The lord protector ensured that Sir William was raised to Marquess of Northampton, a high status indeed.

Then the queen's sister, Lady Herbert, shared news that her husband, Sir Herbert, had renewed his friendship with and support of Edward Seymour as well. In return was the tacit understanding that they would support him against all comers, including her sister, Kate, and his brother, Thomas.

On February 16, His Majesty was solemnly installed next to his most beloved wife, Jane Seymour, in St. George's at Windsor Castle. Sixteen yeomen used sturdy linen sheets to lower the massive coffin containing the bloated sovereign into Jane's grave.

The queen dowager, dressed in dark velvet and wearing the jet beads I had given her as well as a widow's ring with a death's head on it, watched as her third husband was buried. Few mourners likely knew that there was one man determined to see her marry a fourth as quickly as night overtakes eventide.

Whilst at Windsor Castle with Kate, for the funeral, I slipped away to seek the midwife who had tended to my wounds in this very place after the violence of John Temple. The ladies and mistresses all knew where to find her, as someone oft was either with child, was miscarrying a babe, or had a troublesome monthly flux.

I knocked on her door, and, thankfully, as all court was present, she was too.

"Yes?" She peered out of the crack of her door.

"May I please come in?"

She looked me up and down and then opened the door unto me. I suspected she had been sought after by other young women before, as she did not seem too surprised.

"How may I help ye?" she asked.

"You may not recall, but some years back after I was . . . assaulted . . . you tended to me and took away my bloody linens," I said.

She nodded. "I do indeed remember ye, mistress. Do ye need to affect a maidenhead, then? I can help ye with tha'."

I shook my head. "Nay. I was wondering, well
. . . you'd said that I might not be able to bear a
child, and that you'd be better able to tell after
some time had passed. Might you examine me
again and see if that be true or not?"

She nodded and stood there. I finally realized
what she wanted and handed a coin to her—much
more than was necessary, actually, because she'd
charged me naught the last time she'd assisted.

I undressed and lay down on a narrow bed in
her chamber. She examined me carefully and
afterward, I sat up.

"I'm sorry to tell ye, mistress, 'tis still unlikely
you will bear a child. There be too much scarring,
there be. I have been wrong before. But I have
seen many a maid, a lady, a strumpet, and a
mother, and I do na think I am mistaken."

She quickly moved the coin I'd given her out of
reach, fearful, I supposed, that I might demand the
fee back after hearing ill tidings.

"Thank you," I said quietly. I left her chambers
and mixed in with the mourners; my mourning
was multiplied many times over. I found a quiet
corner and squeezed shut my eyes for a moment,
letting my hopes fall through the grate of the
horrible truth. I would never marry. I could never
marry. I could not tell a man what happened to me,
as Sir John and Tristram had indicated good men
did not desire soiled goods, which is what they
both considered, and perhaps others might

246

consider, me to be after learning the truth. I would not marry a man in good faith knowing I would likely never bear him a child. My mourning gown for His Majesty had become a shroud, concealing a person who was once full of life and now had no spirit left.

Later that night, back at Chelsea, I cheered a little when I considered that I might marry a widow who had already had children of his own and therefore would be someone I could honestly marry, he having already acquired the heirs he might want and need. I could be a loving wife, and a mother for his offspring, as Lady Fitzgerald Browne had done. There weren't likely to be many widowers in Marlborough; I would come across more by remaining in my lady's household.

But marrying a widower was not what I wanted, and my false cheer faded. I wanted to wed an Irish knight who loved me, I knew, for who he thought me to be, but who wanted lads of his own. I prayed that night for the strength to follow through with what I knew I must do during the coronation festivities, for his sake much more than for my own.

Hugh had arrived to stay with me at Chelsea with the news that whilst our mother would still not be coming to London for the coronation, Matthias and his family had already arrived and were staying at a nearby inn.

"Matthias rode with his mother and the other ladies in a litter," Hugh told me with a smirk. "Instead of riding a horse."

I grinned with him. Mayhap it was not a terrible fate to let Matthias pass me by.

"How fare you?" I asked.

"Well," Hugh said. "I have made many good friends and met lads more high-flown than peregrines. But I tire of the womanish intrigue, honestly, of court, and yearn for the manlier world of our father. I suspect that I, like St. George and our father, will someday soon set off for the East and leave the financial matters to Matthias and his father."

"Afore finding a lady of your own?"

He blushed. "I may have found one already." He told me of his young lady, of a knight's family, and connected with Cecil's household. "You would find her most congenial."

"Indeed," I said, smiling. Hugh had shared that our mother grew frailer and that Matthias had all but taken over the finances of the business from his father whilst Hugh would now return home and run the portion that had been our father's.

"Shall you marry Matthias?" he asked me.

"Not unless you compel me to, which shall be your right now, as a man full grown and head of our household. And then I shall."

"I should not make you do anything you do not want to do, Juliana," he said softly. It was an odd moment, our role reversal. "I shall tell Matthias that there will be no negotiations . . . if you be certain."

"I am certain," I said. "I do not think I shall marry for some time." I paused. "When Lady Neville's father died he left her either a dowry or a stipend for life in case she should not marry."

We let the fire die out in companionable silence. "You are always welcome at Brighton," Hugh said. "And if you prefer a stipend over a dowry I shall ensure that you receive it."

I tightly embraced him. Nothing more needed to be said.

On February 19, Edward rode from the Tower to Westminster Abbey, where he was crowned king. The week following was full of celebrations, beginning with jousts, at which Lord Thomas excelled. Kate wore her mourning gown but she had cheer about her, and, unwillingly, I did too when I saw Sir James Hart as a challenger.

He found me after his first joust and I decided, on the spot, that armor was most becoming on a man even if he smelt as if he were roasting within.

"I hoped I'd see you here," he said. "I am a man of few prayers, but if they be answered as quickly and as positively as this one has, I shall become devout."

I grinned. "I am glad to be of some use in the deepening of your faith, then, Jamie."

He took his helmet off and walked with me to the side of the tiltyard where tables with small beer and food had been set up.

"Juliana." He took my hand in his own. "How fare you?"

"I am well," I said.

"You look well," he said. "You look beautiful. Come, let's have a seat and I shall tell you all about my dangerous mishaps at sea. You shall be so relieved that I survived them that you will never want me to leave your sight."

I smiled. 'Twas the truth, but also a dream, and one I dreamt on my own and not by the Spirit, which left no reassurance that it would come to pass.

We sat among the others and after an hour's conversation a tall man with a finely dressed woman approached us, two boys accompanying them.

Jamie stood, so I did too. "Mistress Juliana St. John, may I present my brother, Sir Oliver Hart; his wife, Lady Rosemary Hart; and my two nephews, Master Scamp and Master Rascal."

"I be no rascal!" the youngest called out.

"Then you must be Master Scamp," I teased. I then held out my hand to Sir Oliver, who took it in his hand. His eyes were kindly. I dipped a small curtsey to his wife.

"Oh, come now," she said with a lovely, light Irish lilt. She took my hand in her own for a squeeze. "I'm pleased to meet the fair mistress who has anchored young Jamie."

Jamie blushed at that.

"Are you here alone?" his brother asked with concern.

"Oh, assuredly not. I am with the queen dowager's household," I said. "And my brother is nearby."

"I just stole her away," Jamie said. "Now, I have heard that each man may tilt twice if he does it for a lady's favor. May I?"

I unthreaded a ribbon from my gown and handed it to him. *There is no harm in that,* I convinced myself. *'Tis a ride and not a promise.*

He took off and I stayed for a while and made polite conversation with his brother and his wife. Scamp and Rascal, rather Oliver and Stephen, grew restless waiting for their uncle to tilt and so I made a suggestion.

"When my brother, Hugh, was a boy, and even older than you two be, I would oft tell him the story of St. George. Should you care to hear that?"

"Oh, yes, please!" they cried out, and Lady Rosemary looked at me with pleasure and nodded her head in approval.

"Now, the good knight had fought well, and when he was finished, he sought to return to his noble home. But the path home was thorny, and a difficult climb up hill after hill. So he decided to draw his horse aside for water and when he did—"

"He spied the townsfolk in distress!" Stephen called out. His mother shushed him with a look.

"You are correct," I said. "And they bewailed the terrible fate that had befallen the maidens in their town, a fate that no one could halt."

"Except for Saint George," Oliver added wisely. It was not difficult to see which was the older son. I wondered if he and Stephen wrestled, or did Oliver and Jamie, as the Seymour brothers did.

Just as I finished the story, the joust began. They were meant only for display, so there were no true winners. But I held my arms close about me in a tight embrace and fervently thanked God that I had, at least once in my life, had a man ride for my favor.

Late that next night, the Countess of Sussex, who was staying with my lady for the festivities, knocked on my chamber door. My hair was already undone and I was in a dressing gown. I had dismissed the serving girl and therefore was alone.

"Countess," I said with a short curtsey. "I am sorry to greet you whilst I am disheveled."

"It matters not," she said. "May I come in?"

I opened the door wide and indicated that she should take the better of the few chairs by the waning fire.

"I shall make my visit brief, mistress. But in the days ahead I do not know where your lady's household shall be, nor if I shall be oft in her company. But you will be. And I must tell you of a dream I have had given me."

I sat down next to her. "Go on." It was strange that I, an unknown mistress of little account, would press a countess to speak.

"I began first to dream, like Joseph in holy writ, of fat cattle, and then thin. You shall recall that he was given a prophetic dream of seven fat cattle, which meant seven years of prosperity, followed by seven lean, which meant seven years of difficulty."

"Yes," I said. "I do recall."

"The cattle in my dream numbered five. Five fat cattle. And then they were slaughtered, one by one. At the last, Potipher died."

I shook my head, not comprehending. "Forgive me, my lady; I do not understand your meaning."

"There shall be but five years before the king dies," the countess said directly.

I stood up, shocked at her pronouncement, and then sat down again before whispering, "Be you sure? And then the Lady Mary shall be queen?"

"Seems likely, though that were not given to me," she said. "But if it is true, we can expect a return to the burnings like Anne Askew's for all who believe as she did. The Lady Mary was quietly, but clearly, supportive of those measures."

I sat silently afore speaking. "Prophesying or

predicting the king's death is treason punishable by death."

"Yes," she said.

"I do not want to know this," I replied firmly.

"I do not either," she answered bluntly. "But 'tis not our prerogative to choose, is it, mistress? I have been compelled to whisper it into a few ears. Keep the information to yourself and pray about how you are to use it."

She stood up and nodded her head in my direction, though her tone was kindly. "I bid you a good eve." She took her leave and closed the door fast behind her.

It may be forestalled. After all, nothing has yet come of the dreadful vision of Lord Thomas harrying the Lady Elizabeth to her extreme discomfort and compromise.

THIRTEEN

Early and Late Spring:
Year of Our Lord 1547
Somerset House
Chelsea
Baynard's Castle

The Duke of Somerset, Edward, Thomas's newly titled brother, held a grand celebration at his enormous and extravagant household on the river Thames. I had some fear about attending, but then I remembered that the duke was unlikely to invite lesser members from the household of Gardiner, his enemy, and I felt more at ease. John Temple would not be in attendance.

I arrived with others of Kate's household and was seated for the many-course meal. After we ate, the Duke and Duchess of Somerset had music and dancing such as was never seen outside of court. The king, still a child, had long been put abed. Kate, as queen dowager, was the highest-ranking woman in the room and so danced first, with her host. After Kate danced with the duke, she danced with his brother, the lord high admiral, Thomas Seymour.

I hoped that Jamie, as a colleague of Thomas Seymour, would be in attendance. I wished I didn't care, but I did. I had dressed with care in case he attended, in a gown of rose shot with gold and had worn a strand of pearls. On my finger I wore a matching band of gold and stone.

I felt a hand upon my shoulder from behind and heard his voice as he sweetly spoke my name. "Juliana."

I turned to face him.

"You will have, I am certain, noticed that I am alone and not surrounded by peach flesh?" Jamie pressed a tease. "Should you care to dance?"

I let him kiss my hand and lead me out; we danced and talked, and whilst I tried to refrain from flirting with him and offering undue affection, he drew it out of me like a lodestone to iron shavings hour after hour. He most certainly did not smell of armor then, but of musk and spice and faintly of mead. I could not but laugh and talk and pleasure in his company for hours.

"I am well pleased to see our relationship restored to one of joy and ease," he said. "After I last visited your home I was uncertain that you were still pleased with my company. I should like to speak with you privately," he said insistently as the night grew late and the guests retired.

I hesitated. I knew where the conversation would lead and I did not want to hurt him. It might be that he'd press his suit here if need be, though, so perhaps it would be better to speak with him in private. "A suite of rooms has been provided for the queen dowager and her household." I told him where to meet me, and said he might find me there in thirty minutes.

I made my way down the long hallway and, once there, was gladdened that the servants were well trained and that my fire was still lightly stirred on this cold night. I pulled the chairs near to it and poked the embers myself afore throwing in a pack of sticks and one large log. Shortly thereafter, a knock came on my door.

I stood for just a minute, crushed in spirit, and thought how different this might have been if not for John Temple. I walked to the door and opened it and he grinned. "May I come in?"

"Yes, of course you may." Once I closed the door he took my hand in his. I let him hold it for but a moment and then withdrew it. "Please, have a seat." I struggled to keep my voice cool and my manner aloof, berating myself for my inability to do that earlier in the evening, disallowing myself the sheer joy of reveling in his company, which had given him false hope. He, among all people, was the one I cared for most and therefore wanted least to hurt.

Jamie sat down. "My nephews gaily recounted your telling of St. George whilst they waited yesterday," he said. "It was their first joust. My brother thinks it's time they become men," he said with a twinkle in his eye. "Both boys were besotted with you."

"Seems only right, since you gifted the book to me, that I share the story with your kin."

His face looked a little bewildered at my unseemly remove, I guessed, but I could not change that. It would do more harm than good to act otherwise.

"My brother and his wife find you delightful."

"As I did them."

"I told them I intend to marry you," he said. "As quickly as I may, and then, with the woman I love, quickly begin producing Scamps and Rascals of our own."

"Marriage." The truest desire my heart had ever known.

"You are not the only person who can speak forthrightly, Juliana," he said as he drew his chair closer to mine. "Though I be delighted that I can still surprise you."

"You do indeed," I said, wishing that I could find joy in this news.

"I should like to speak with your brother, if he is here for the coronation."

I nodded. "He is in Cecil's household for a while longer; then he returns to Marlborough to attend to our family business."

"I know of it," he said. "I have seen Sir Matthias in passing whilst in London, though I am sure he would not recognize me. Has there been . . . an arrangement made with his son?" he asked softly.

I shook my head. "I told my brother that no arrangement should be made with Matthias, if that were meet with my brother, and he agreed."

"Excellent! Then I am free to speak with your brother, and your mother, if need be."

"I cannot leave Kate's household. She has need of me."

He seemed slightly taken aback. "Well, I suppose you must stay with her for some short time, whilst she transitions to her dower estates."

I took his hand in mine and allowed myself to twine his fingers through my own. "I do not intend to marry for some time, if ever, Jamie," I said softly, and with sorrow.

He withdrew his hand in surprise and then took

258

both of mine in his own. "Why not? Is there another?"

"There is no other," I said gently. "I promise you this."

"You shall take religious vows, then?"

At that I giggled, and broke the tension. "Nay, Jamie."

He laughed himself, nervously. "Well, I thought not, as I believed your religious thoughts veered away from the traditional. But then, is it me, have I misread the situation? I have done as I promised you at your mother's home. I have not lived as a Turk with many wives." He wiggled his eyebrows and we both laughed again. "I desire, as I once said to you, only one wife. And that be you."

I kept my hands in his. "If I were to marry, Jamie, it would be to you. I prefer you above all others. But I cannot, and that is all I can say of the matter. I grieve too."

He stood up. "And you have nothing further to offer? No reason? No explanation?"

"Alas, I fear not."

"If I wait?"

I shook my head no, my chest suffocating in sorrow as one closed in a coffin.

"And yet you are firm upon this course?"

"I am." I left no room for wonder in my tone of voice. It was for his good. I would not force him to make a choice, and should he choose against me, in truth, I did not want to know.

He grew warm in the face. "I do not understand, Juliana, but I will take you at your word and press you no further. I shall sorrow, though. I have a fine manor in the north of Ireland and I desire a family to share it with. As I cannot have the wife I desire, I shall have to soon take one I do not."

He reached into the pocket of his fine leather coat and withdrew a box. "I had come expecting a better outcome," he said, "and had this made for you to keep me in your mind whilst I was at sea after we finalized our marriage." He handed a small black box to me.

I took it in hand and opened it. It was Jamie, a faint scruff on a browned face, blue eyes creased at the corners where his hair met his lashes. I looked at it for a moment and my eyes filled with tears. "I'm sorry." I stood and then held it out to him.

He refused to take it. "No. I had it made for you. You may keep it. You told me once that you do not like to receive a gift without giving one in return." He took my face between his hands and ran them over it, then pulled me close and kissed me. His rough jaw scratched against my smooth one, his cheek bone pressed into mine. In spite of myself I responded and reached my arms around him till we melded together.

A minute later I pushed him away at last, lest we be further tempted to more.

"You respond with love and desire. I sense it," he said. "I am confused."

I opened the doorway afore speaking softly again. "I am so sorry, Jamie. I shall pray for you to have the life of love and happiness that you richly deserve."

He did not ask a further question and I quickly closed and locked the door behind him before I could change my mind. I sat on my bed before I let the tears course silently down my face, then my chin, then trail onto my chest. I unfurled my fingers from his miniature, which I clutched in my right hand, and met him eye to eye for a moment. He smiled. I grieved.

I could not marry him. He deserved his own Scamp and Rascal whom he could teach to joust and tell stories, who could inherit his purse and lands. These were things I could never give him and things I knew he deeply desired. My gift was not the kiss, but his freedom to have the life he deserved.

'Twas more a sorrow than a pleasure, then, to have learnt that our kiss had rekindled the desire I thought had been permanently snuffed out. I allowed myself the reluctant pleasure of thinking what might have been before lying down to bed, caressing his face once more before gently closing the small black box.

In the main, Lord Thomas had been right: his brother had given him lands and titles and honorary fripperies, but he kept him far from the circle of power. Too, the council understood the motherly sway that Kate had upon King Edward, a solemn boy of but nine who needed, I suspected, to be told the story of St. George rather than rule over the castle that held the chapel named in St. George's honor. Thomas's brother kept Kate far from court, too, lest her influence on the king, which he sought to wean him from, should wax instead.

This left Kate and Lord Thomas an inordinate amount of time on their hands in the distant properties of her dower homes and his own home without the watchful eyes of the council.

In March Kate wrote a long letter to Thomas. "I told him within that we should write but once a fortnight," she said to me, handing the letter over to a page to be delivered to Seymour Place. The next day, though, and the next, she handed me similar letters to pass along to her messenger.

"My lady, are you certain?" She dismissed my concerns and bid me obey. Lord Thomas's came quickly, too, in return. I saw them on her table and near her bed.

In April, Thomas began to dine with us regularly at Chelsea. They kept about them only the few whom they knew would be constant in their affection toward one or both, and whilst I was still vexed that he led her to grow ever angrier over her treatment after King Henry's death, I also rejoiced to see her so happy. After having had three husbands chosen for her, it was only right that she would choose the fourth for herself, even if he were not the man I should have chosen for her.

One night, whilst I made my way down the hallway toward my chamber, I heard Thomas plead that he be able to spend the night.

"Not afore marriage," Kate said insistently. "It would not be right. And with the Lady Elizabeth coming within a fortnight to live in my household, I must have an eye to propriety."

"But you have said we may not be married for two years!" he wheedled. "If you be certain we must wait, then let it not be two years but two months." I heard no more after that but giggling and low voices. Aware of the impropriety of my own eavesdropping, I quickly moved on. But one day, not a week later, I was up afore dawn with a painful flux and I happened to glance out my window.

A man approached the manor house and made his way in, quietly. I was still at my window two hours later when he took his leave. He kept his head down but I recognized the jaunty walk. Lord Thomas.

'Twas a most joyous time for all when the Lady Elizabeth and her household arrived at Chelsea. Kate was merrier than I had seen her in some time; she looked upon Elizabeth as a daughter, I knew, and if she could not dote upon the king she would dote upon his sister. The Lady Elizabeth had the finest suite of rooms in the house, after Kate, of course. She had household servants and maidens and gentlemen, and of course her governess, Kat Ashley. Kat was the sister of Kate's good friend Lady Denny, so it was a most congenial mixture. Elizabeth and I oft played rook or cards, though the times were but few when I bested her at any game. Thomas had a kindly word or two for me, asked about my family or my reading, partnered me at dance or cards.

One day he did not even speak to me afore making his way directly to the king's daughter. "My Lady Elizabeth." One of Kate's men took his coat and Thomas sat near the fire, where Elizabeth practiced her letters.

"Lord Thomas," she said, a grin on her face. At shy of fourteen she was not yet a woman but no longer still a girl. I kept in mind that my lady mother had been but two years older than Elizabeth when she had married my father and, shortly thereafter, bore me. It put me on guard. He spoke to her softly for a few moments before I heard him challenge her.

"You shall be sure not to bedevil the queen whilst a member of her household," Thomas said, grinning wickedly in her direction. "Or you shall have to answer to me, my lady, and ye shall find the discipline not to your pleasure at all."

Elizabeth's white skin grew red and her freckles darkened. But her black eyes remained calm and resolute, blinking not at all behind their hawk's hoods. "I shall keep that in mind, sir," she said with a smile. Then she turned back to her quill and parchment.

Lord Thomas grinned and moved away, but I had the feeling that he did not like being dismissed; rather, he preferred to decide when to draw a conversation to a close. Shortly thereafter, he went to find Kate and once he did, put his hands on her hips in full view of the others in the room. I turned away lest I grow red myself.

One day, the Lady Elizabeth's governess, Kat Ashley, found me as I was making an inventory of the queen dowager's gowns as well as her few remaining pieces of jewelry afore she pressed her case to Lady Seymour, to speak with her husband to have Kate's jewelry returned. Although the queen had them placed in the tower, and the lord protector himself had read the king's will that gave them to her, Edward Seymour had not allowed any to be taken: not gifts from Kate's mother, nor her wedding ring from His Majesty, nor any other of her personal possessions.

"Excuse me, Mistress St. John." Kat Ashley spoke up. "Do you by chance know what Lord Thomas's marriage plans are?"

I set the gowns down. What an odd question.

Had word leaked back to court already that Thomas was pressing Kate to make a quick marriage? Or had Kat seen one of Thomas's early morning visits?

"I'm sure I don't know," I said. She nodded and we made small talk and soon after, she took her leave. I thought it unusual, but perhaps she was concerned for the Lady Elizabeth's reputation should the household fall under scrutiny. I dismissed the concern.

The next week we all dined at Baynard's Castle, which Kate had given to her sister, Lady Herbert, and her sister's husband, Lord Herbert. It was to be a celebratory event, a way to honor the Lady Elizabeth, daughter to one king and now sister of another. She was given precedence after the queen dowager and afterward there was a small musical reception with players Lady Herbert had hired.

"I hear you've bought the wardship of Lady Jane Grey," Herbert boomed out toward Lord Thomas from across the room.

"I have indeed, and it was no small purchase," Seymour answered.

"Two thousand pounds is what I heard," Herbert said.

At that, Kate gasped. I suspected Thomas had not discussed this with her.

"A bold man takes risks where the dividends will pay handsomely," Lord Thomas said.

"Do you mean to marry her to the king, then?" Herbert spoke up.

It was exactly what Thomas intended. All knew that whilst he could not control the king directly, he sought to curry favor with all others who had a claim to the throne. He intended to marry Lady Jane Grey to the king; if he succeeded, he, Thomas Seymour, would have great power as her ward. "My brother may have tied the council's hands," he had told Kate, "but I shall hold the children's hearts."

" 'Tis entirely possible the council will tie *your* hands when they find out," Kate had replied, and he dismissed it with a wave of his hand, a merry dance, and a kiss on her lips.

I turned back to look at Herbert, who had handily discerned Thomas's plan. He was waiting for an answer.

"The king's daughters marry only upon the *approval* of the counsel," Thomas said. "But the king himself only needs rely upon their *advice.*"

For some reason, the talk of Lady Jane Grey clearly upset Kate's sister, and I was nearby when she pulled Lord Thomas aside and spoke. "A better question of marriage may be, are *you* about to marry my sister?"

"Nothing could be more satisfactory to me. Alas, she keeps me at a distance," Thomas answered.

"Nay, 'tis not the truth. I hear that there be many

midnight visits to Chelsea and some lasting hours."

At this, Thomas blushed like a maiden and owned up that yes, he did visit her but 'twas nothing improper. Lady Herbert raised her eyebrow, after which I kept my eyes fixed to the ground.

In mid-May, Kate and Thomas were secretly wed at Baynard's Castle, with her sister and brother as witnesses and a priest with reformist beliefs marrying them. They stayed there, as guests, on a honeymoon of sorts whilst the rest of us remained at Chelsea, and Lady Jane Grey and her household at Seymour Place, so it would seem all was normal. They could not tell anyone, of course, till they had the favor of the lord protector and the king on this matter, which they set about to quickly secure.

Kate radiated bliss, and I was delighted for her because this was the first time she'd promised to be bonny at bed and at board where she meant it of her own free will and not as a duty. I could not but be a bit envious of her radiating happiness, wishing I had a wedding day of my own to look forward to. I had some reservations about Sir Thomas, though. Kate looked as though she had just conquered an army, but as I had now seen Thomas's recklessness regularly and in increasing strength, I feared that she would soon be undone.

• • •

There was a night whilst Kate was still at Baynard's that I awoke to find Kat Ashley standing over me, her hair in her sleeping cap and a candle in her hand.

"Mistress St. John, are you all right?"

I sat up in bed and gathered my senses as I took in my surroundings. It had been a long while since I'd had my prophetic dream, and this strongly, and it had taken me by surprise.

"Yes, I'm all right. 'Twas merely a night terror," I said, and she returned to her chamber.

It was the dream of Lord Thomas with the dagger that I already knew. And the Lady Elizabeth under duress. Now, dishearteningly, I saw that it was Kate who held Elizabeth firm.

What shall You require me to do?

FOURTEEN

Summer and Autumn:
Year of Our Lord 1547
Chelsea
Syon House

One evening in June I was in my lady's dressing chamber sorting through some gowns and slippers, determining which would be stored for the summer and which were still appropriate for wear, when I heard a knock at the door. Kate opened it. I could not see who it was, but by her words I knew it to be Thomas. She was still dressed for the day so merely asked him, "Could you come back in thirty minutes, husband? I must finish dressing for bed."

He grunted and then left. Within a minute, there came another knock at the door and I could hear my lady allow her groom of the chamber in to provide coal for the evening's fire. Before allowing me to help her into her bed gown she asked me to finish my sorting task.

"I shall soon be finished," I said. "You have so many gowns!"

She laughed. "Yes, and His Majesty kindly left me money enough to indulge that passion without tapping my purse, so that is likely to continue. Do not rush, I have important correspondence to attend to."

She returned to her desk in the other room, where she'd told me earlier she was penning letters in her own hand to build support for her marriage. Shortly, a knock came again.

Kate opened it and Thomas burst in. I knew it was him just by the sound of it as Kate never thrust shut a door.

"So your husband is told to leave so you may change in private, and yet I tarry but a little down the hallway and what do mine eyes see? A common man, though well built and pleasing for a woman to behold, comes when I was denied!"

"Thomas!" Kate protested. "I had not yet changed when the groom of the chamber came to replace my coal. Are you truly displaced by a servant going about his duties?"

I could hear Thomas exhale and then finally speak. "Sweetheart. 'Tis just that I do not care to see you in any man's company alone, without me. I have had to wait so long, you see, and endure you in the arms and the beds of others that I grow anxious that such may happen again."

"Do you accuse me of keeping private company with another man? And we so newly wed?"

"Nay, nay," he said soothingly. "I repent of my outburst. Forgive my misplaced anger. I have just had a letter from the Lady Mary."

I could hear Kate's tone relax. "In response to your own, asking her to approve of our marriage?"

"Yes," he said. "And here is her response: 'I have received your letter, wherein, methinks, I perceive strange news, the sooner obtaining whereof, you seem to think that my letters might do you some pleasure.' But she begged to differ. Apparently she found it abhorrent and lacking respect that you have so quickly married after the death of her father."

"And yet her father pressed me just as quickly to marry him after the death of Lord Latimer!" Kate responded with a little frustration.

"Exactly," Thomas said. "Last week I bribed

John Fowler to allow me some time with the king."

"Should you be bribing, Thomas?" Kate's voice turned worried.

"How else shall I see my own nephew? 'Tis an injustice that I cannot see him when I like!" Thomas near shouted. Then he lowered his voice. "I bought him some gifts and sang some sea ditties. And then I was able to turn the conversation to help him see, of his own, that 'twould be better for you to not remain a widow, as Saint Paul hath spoken, and that it would be better that you be cared for by someone he trusts. I began by telling him that I needed a wife."

"And his response was . . . ?"

"At first, he suggested Anne of Cleves."

Kate groaned.

"And then he suggested his sister Mary, so I may turn her opinions from Catholicism to reform."

"Not likely she'd have you and not likely she'd change," Kate said.

Not likely he'd know enough of either to convince the Lady Mary, I thought uncharitably. Kate held daily church services and lively debates at her dower houses, too, but I'd not seen Sir Thomas present for any of them.

I could not see them but I could hear Lord Thomas kiss her. It was far too late for me to leave the room now without causing extreme discomfort to all involved. I should have left immediately but

I knew Kate would not want Thomas to know I had overheard his pique of temper. I could only pray that they left things at a kiss.

Thomas continued. "But since His Majesty had suggested Anne of Cleves, the king's sister, I put it to him that an even better turn would be done by having a good queen not long remain a widow, as was meet, and provide a godly wife for me as well."

"And the king . . . ?"

"Delightedly agreed. In fact, he said he would share his good opinion of this with the lord protector upon his earliest opportunity."

Kate said nothing for so long that Thomas pressed her. "Well, Kate?"

"I do not like twisting Edward's mind and actions so, to manage him thusly when he has no indication of our motives. He is, after all, as a son to me, Thomas."

"And a nephew to me," Thomas said, a slight edge to his voice. "If there were another way, I'd avail myself of it."

"But there is not," Kate said quietly.

"There is not," Thomas agreed.

She told him she was going to complete her correspondence and he said he would be back within an hour. As soon as he took his leave I made some loud noises in gathering up her gowns and Kate came to join me in the dressing chamber.

"I had forgotten you were here, Juliana," she said.

"'Tis of no concern. I had so much to busy my hands that I lost track of time." I made my way to the door. "Shall I come early and help you dress afore tomorrow's hunt?"

She nodded and then held my elbow. "Lord Thomas does not mean anything by his spells of choleric. 'Tis just that his brother has set himself up against us at every turn."

I nodded in return. "I understand, my lady."

Mayhap as close as she was to him she could not see that in a few years' time Sir Thomas had gone from sailing in mostly placid water to mostly turgid and let every wind and wave whip him into frenzy now that he sensed victory at hand.

A fair portion of the queen's household and guests, including the Lady Elizabeth, rode out to hunt with us the next day. The Lady Elizabeth was already an excellent huntress, but not quite as fine as Kate, and the queen dowager wanted to ensure that Elizabeth's education progressed in all manner whilst in her household.

"Someday soon," Kate told her, "your brother the king and the council may arrange a fine marriage for you with a prince in another land, and I want you to be well prepared, though I shall miss you when you take your leave and you must promise to write to me weekly."

Elizabeth shone at this display of affection.

Indeed, Kate had arranged for the Lady Elizabeth the finest of tutors, the best dance instructors, and the most competent musicians. Whilst she also arranged education for Lady Jane Grey, she, being farther away at Seymour Place, was not quite as easy to manage. And, I knew, Elizabeth held a particularly dear place in Kate's heart.

Our midmorning repast was held on the hunting grounds, as was Kate's preference. She sat alone whilst Lord Thomas wrapped his arms around the small frame of the Lady Elizabeth some yards hence to better teach her the right manner in which to hold a bow. My lady looked sorrowful, and who could blame her?

I drew near. "Are you well, Your Grace?" I glanced up at the embrace Thomas held Elizabeth in. She saw my gaze.

"Oh, that, 'tis nothing." She motioned for me to sit. "But Thomas has this morning shared with me disturbing news that he received in a letter from the king. He first thanked Thomas for marrying me, but then he shared that both Edward Seymour and his wife were much offended with the marriage. Thomas's brother Edward, as self-appointed lord protector, has that right, I suppose, though if His Majesty seems happy that should be the end of it. There was no requirement for me to get the council's approval before marriage. But it is no business at all of that hell Lady Seymour to be offended."

I was taken aback by my lady's language and my face must have shown it.

"My sister tells me Lady Seymour is wearing the queen's jewels now," Kate said. "The ones that were stolen from me, and of course, there be no queen in this realm save I. She does not yet have the gall to wear my personal jewelry, which I hope shall shortly be back in my possession."

In the distance, Thomas laughed with Elizabeth and kept his arms round her, though the lesson should long since have ended. Even Kate now looked discomfited. She stood up and smoothed her skirts and said, afore making her way to Thomas, "My husband wants me to bring the matter of my jewelry up to his brother myself, at a banquet they are holding next month, at Syon. I believe that I shall."

Later that week she received a letter from the king. He did not refer to her as mother, nor sign it as her son. He did indicate some growing distaste over her hasty and unseemly marriage to Thomas. Whether that thought grew as he recognized that Kate and Thomas had deceived him, or whether Edward Seymour had harried him for his own purposes, I knew not. 'Twas a shame the boy king, without mother, without father, was so ill used by all who were interested only in their own power and the advancement of their own desires.

A month later Edward Seymour and his wife held a fine evening banquet in the gardens of their Thameside residence, Somerset House. I worried no more about seeing John Temple, as Gardiner had been thrown into the Tower after refusing the new directions the king's council took with religious matters. Edward Seymour had been the force behind that action. The Duchess of Suffolk, Kate's dear friend, quipped, "It be merry with the lambs when the wolf was shut up." I hoped, for her sake and Kate's, that he would remain shut up, for he was like to hear of his enemies dancing upon his grave and return the favor with interest should he ever be freed. Certainly his boundless pride had not allowed him to forgive the duchess for naming her spaniel after him.

As to the banquet, no expense had been spared. I had heard my lady speculate about where such wealth was coming from; the seizing of funds from chantries meant to say prayers for the dead, now outlawed, certainly, but there must have been more sources as well. Several of my lady's household rode in fine litters to the event; Thomas and his men arrived via horseback, of course, but they traveled alongside of us.

There were wandering minstrels and jugglers of all sorts; their painted faces were meant to enchant but I found their false, leering smiles a horror and representative of the evening as a whole. I had many friends present, for though we had scattered when Kate's household was broken up we came together infrequently for such events. And yet, as I wandered away from the torches meant to light the night, I felt despondent. My lady would return to Chelsea with Lord Thomas, and the Lady Elizabeth was there with her household; my Lady Tyrwhitt and her husband, Sir Robert, would return to their rooms together, as would various others who resided at Chelsea. Yet I would retire alone, perhaps forever.

I turned to walk back toward the festivities and saw Kate talking with Edward Seymour, who seemed in rather a hurry to remove himself from her company. She followed him for a few steps but he did not turn back toward her. Realizing it was unseemly, I suspected, for a queen to chase after a duke, she stopped her pursuit. Later that night she and I rode back to her estate with the litter curtains pulled back to display the tiara of starlight, as the evening was warm.

Robert Tyrwhitt rode alongside us, as did the other men in her household, but Lord Thomas had ridden on ahead, alone, and in great haste.

"Has Lord Thomas taken ill?" I asked.

Kate shook her head. "He is angry with me. I began to speak with his brother about the return of my jewelry, and Edward put me off, saying this was not the occasion for such a discussion."

"Then when is?" Lady Tyrwhitt asked. "He

refused to return your correspondence and does not provide a time when you may come to meet with him at court or any other place."

"I know it well," Kate said. "He promised that he and his wife should be my guests at a banquet at Chelsea within the month, and we would talk of the matter then, in a more intimate environment."

"And Lord Thomas is angry because . . . ?" Lady Tyrwhitt asked.

"Because I did not insist," Kate said. "But there was little I could do."

I reached over and threaded my arm through her own, sorrowing to see her miserable so quickly into a much-longed-for marriage.

"Lady Seymour wore your ruby and gold garter," Lady Tyrwhitt said. "The one His Majesty gave you as a personal gift, not a jewel belonging to the crown."

"I noticed," Kate said. "She wore it knowing that I, and many others, would understand the message she sent with that gesture. She has taken the pearls my mother left me upon her death, as well."

We arrived home late, but as I made my way down the hallway I noticed that the candles were still lit in the Lady Elizabeth's rooms. I thought I heard the voice of a man, so I stopped outside of her chamber for a moment, but then, hearing only the voice of Kat Ashley, went on my way.

• • •

The next month Kate prepared a festive banquet by which she and Thomas meant to mend fences with his brother Edward and Edward's wife. Kate had invited her sister and her husband, and her brother, William Parr, was to come, too, without the Lady Elisabeth Brooke, though they were as much in love as ever. Kate had gone to great expense to make sure the evening would be perfect, and even the Lady Elizabeth would be allowed to attend.

I suspected that was Kate's way of showing that she, too, had care of a royal child. She rarely saw the king, and the Lady Mary had made a wide space between them since Kate's marriage to Sir Thomas. The queen dowager had also taken her young nephew by her sister, Lady Herbert, into her household to educate him at her own expense.

Four hours afore the event a messenger came hard riding and asked to speak with Lord Thomas. I was in the great hall, next to the receiving hall, ensuring that the final details were being carried out according to Kate's instructions.

"I come with news from your brother," the messenger said. There in the receiving hall he handed over a scroll. Thomas opened it, read it, then ripped it in half. He stared at the messenger, who had taken a few steps back.

"Sir, do you care to send back an answer?"

"You have it, man." Thomas pointed at the torn

280

letter on the floor. "Right there, you have my response." He took his leave and made his way to Kate's chamber.

The banquet went on as planned, but without the guests of honor. Kate explained that the lord protector was unable to attend, as he was raising the troops necessary to invade Scotland and put down the recent French-backed attack planned upon His Majesty's realm. Privately, she told her women what had really happened.

"This is the doing of Edward's wife, Anne Stanhope." Kate rarely referred to her nemesis by her exalted titles. "She has oft promised to invite me to a reading or a gathering of women working for reform. And yet, an invitation never arrives. She promises many comings and performs none."

It was doubly bitter, then, in October, when Kate had some letters from several of the men administering her dower lands. Each reported that her brother-in-law Edward Seymour had directed that the monies from the leases on said land were to be turned over to him, and not to the dowager queen, their rightful owner. The lord protector further informed them that they were to take their instructions from him, and not Kate, on pain of consequence. He did not need to threaten them. They knew who was their true master.

The lord protector was stealing from Kate and no one would stop him.

Kate shut herself up in her chambers upon

hearing the news. She turned me away for a few days, only having the use of her servants.

I spent my time reading, and one day the Lady Elizabeth found me in front of the fire. Master Grindal, her beloved tutor, had given her leave to have time for herself.

"Mistress St. John?" She approached me and I set my book aside.

"Yes, my Lady Elizabeth. How may I be of service to you?"

"Next month the dowager queen's new book will be delivered."

I nodded. We were all anticipating the delivery of *The Lamentations, or Complaint of a Sinner.*

"Lady Ogilvy, whose husband is an associate and financial backer of the book's publisher, is going to deliver the books to the queen, and the queen shall hold a reception for her friends that day."

"Yes, my lady, I am aware of this," I said softly, not knowing where she led.

"Lady Ogilvy was a particular friend of my mother." Elizabeth stared in her lap. I had never heard her mention her mother before. "Kat is a wonderful governess in all manner but she does not have as much experience in gowning and adorning as a lady in waiting might have. I know you have long been at court; you assist the Queen's Highness with her wardrobe even now. I should like to be beautifully presented when Lady

Ogilvy arrives. She has"—she held her hands together, the long white fingers restraining one another from shaking—"indicated that she would like to see me, particularly and privately."

"It would be my distinct privilege," I responded, bowing my head slightly.

The Lady Elizabeth smiled, retaining her composure. "Thank you, Mistress St. John. That brings me much relief."

I made my way to Kate's chamber the next day. Whilst I helped her I asked, "Do you think there might be money for the Lady Elizabeth to have a new gown afore your reception? Like as not many courtiers will be here, and 'twould be good for them to see what a fine lady she has become under your tutelage."

"Yes, yes, that is a splendid idea," the queen said with enthusiasm. "I shall have the seamstress called immediately. Should you like to assist us?"

"It would be an honor." I clasped a collar around her neck. "I have not met Lady Ogilvy, who delivers the books."

Kate shook her head. "She was sometimes at court events, but there was no occasion for you to have met her in particular, as she was not one of my ladies. She was, however, close to Queen Anne Boleyn and even attended her at her execution. Lady Ogilvy especially requested that she make the delivery for her husband, who backs Thomas Berthelet, the publisher. She has written to me that she has some items to give to the Lady Elizabeth, with my permission, items she did not feel were appropriate to convey whilst King Henry lived. I have, of course, given her my leave."

Over the course of the next month the seamstresses completed two gowns for the Lady Elizabeth, one in dark blue with ivory damask underneath, stitched in gold, which set her red hair off to its finest, and one in black. I did not care for the new black dress, which I instantly recognized as the one in my vision. Thinking that perhaps I could forestall the prophecy by removing the possibility of the gown, I spoke up at the time about ordering a different dress instead, but Kate believed it to be becoming and proceeded with having it made.

On the evening of the reception I finished with Kate and then asked, "May I help the Lady Elizabeth with her hair? I know she has attendants of her own, but perhaps it would be an especial privilege to have the lady who assists the queen dowager assist her as well?"

Kate agreed, and I did Elizabeth's hair up in a fine net of gold and pearls and a dark blue French hood very much in the style her mother was famously known for. When we were finished, she looked at herself in a looking glass and broke out in a delighted smile. "I am become a woman, Mistress St. John."

"A beautiful woman, my lady," I agreed. She was now past fourteen years old and marriageable. I grinned and Kat Ashley clapped her hands and we made our way to the hall where the reception would be held.

As it was November, the hall was ablaze with candles and the fires roared at each end of the room from hearths much taller than a man and twice his height, sidewise. There was a small group of musicians in the back, near the virginals, and they played softly. Mead and wine were passed by Kate's household servants.

I knew most of the guests—Kate's sister and her sister's husband, and her brother, William Parr, who had financed the book with the Duchess of Suffolk, who was also there. I had not seen so many highborn nobles since King Henry had died, though my lady often entertained nobility with dancing and the like. All made polite conversation with Thomas but 'twas clear they were there to celebrate the queen dowager and her new book. Cecil had written the preface so he and his wife were there. I had written a letter to my brother and handed it to one of Cecil's pages to deliver to Hugh upon his return. I inquired after our mother, who wrote to Hugh but not to me.

In the center of things, next to the queen, stood a lovely woman who was perhaps ten years Kate's senior, clad in a rich gown of silver crushed velvet that set off her auburn hair, now threaded with

285

silver that matched her dress, and tied back in a becoming knot. Kate called me to her.

"Lady Margaret Ogilvy, may I present Mistress Juliana St. John?"

I dipped a short curtsey and Lady Ogilvy smiled.

Though children were not often allowed to events such as these, Lady Ogilvy had brought her son, William, a lad of about ten, who stood by stiffly until the Lady Elizabeth called him aside and made small talk with him of a common nature. He drew her near and whispered something in her ear and she burst out laughing, the girl again, and he laughed with her, shaking his head of brown curls. I knew not why, but the sight of them together caused Lady Ogilvy to quickly wipe away a tear.

Lady Ogilvy turned to the table where the white, leather-bound books lay and spoke with others about Kate's newest work, which had been delayed until King Henry's death, lest he find its bold reformer pleadings to be heresy. My lady had escaped the first trap laid for her but may not have escaped a second. I had read the book myself and found it deeply moving, a bright beacon of a personal call to faith in the religious fog in which we oft found ourselves. I made my way to Elisabeth Brooke and spent much of the evening in her company. I missed sharing a chamber with her.

"William and I have married," she whispered to me. "He shall tell the king, and the lord protector, at Christmas. I cannot see how they may find it disagreeable now that reform is the triumphant faith."

I embraced her for a moment, sharing her joy. And then I looked toward the hearth.

Thomas seemed to go from jovial to sullen as the attention was focused upon his wife and not himself. I saw him make his way to the Lady Elizabeth, who was, of a sudden, alone.

He coaxed a smile from her and put her hand in the curve of his elbow. Within a minute I saw Lady Ogilvy approach them, personally untangle Lord Thomas's arm from the Lady Elizabeth's as a mother might, and lead her away.

The next morning, the Lady Elizabeth knocked upon my chamber door. I opened it and curtseyed. "Yes, my lady, please come in."

She did, and closed the door behind her. I noticed that she came alone; she rarely moved about without attendants or other maids of her household. "Thank you for your assistance, Mistress St. John," she said. "My mother was well-known for her beauty in person and in dress. As Lady Ogilvy was not only her friend but her mistress of robes it was particularly important to me that I be well arrayed."

"You looked beautiful, my lady."

She nodded slightly. "Lady Ogilvy delivered

unto me some pieces of my mother's jewelry, including her pearls, her personal favorites, which Lady Ogilvy had saved for me. She also relayed some . . . words of comfort and affection."

I knew this unusual disclosure was her way of thanking me and also a display of trust, because Elizabeth was circumspect and shared very few of her personal thoughts or feelings. "A true blessing," I said.

She nodded and a rare soft look passed across her countenance afore she took her leave.

I never heard her speak of her mother again.

FIFTEEN

Yuletide: Year of Our Lord 1547
Winter and Spring: Year of Our Lord 1548
Hanworth
Hampton Court Palace

Shortly before the Christmas season was about to begin, Kate and I were reading in her room whilst the snow swirled outside of the lead cross-panes when she said, "After the New Year's celebrations, I should like to hold a fine banquet and dance to which I shall invite unmarried young men of good birth and knighthood for you to meet." She set her book down and looked at me. "I daresay it is time."

"I should like that, Your Grace." I pushed aside

memories of Jamie. She was right. "And mayhap you can invite some widowers?"

She looked at me strangely. "Of course, but why ever for?"

"I believe that Lady Elizabeth Fitzgerald finds life with her husband, Sir Anthony Browne, to be most congenial. I should consider all."

The queen nodded, agreeing. Soon the conversation turned toward planning the gifts and clothing she would take to court for Christmas.

Although her household numbered at about one hundred, only twenty or so of us accompanied her and Thomas to court for Christmas. She was still the highest-ranking woman at court, which piqued her sister-in-law Lady Seymour. Thomas, of course, shared her exalted chambers. One night as I was unfastening her stays and handing her gown to her lady maid she seemed particularly vexed. "Quickly!" she said. "Lord Thomas will shortly arrive and he is not well disposed."

"Why not, Your Grace?"

She hesitated afore speaking. "He has seen the king, and asked the king to copy, in His Majesty's own hand, a letter that Thomas has written, and then sign it as if written by the king himself. His request was denied. Then Thomas argued to His Majesty that it were no ill thing he be requesting."

I stopped what I was doing and nearly dropped her gown. "What did this document say?"

"It was a request by the king to the council for

Edward Seymour to be replaced by his brother, Thomas, as his governor."

"And the king's response?"

"He refused. He said if it were good, the lords would already have made such a move. And if it were ill, he, the king, would not write such a thing. He warned Thomas that it was treasonous and pointedly dropped the matter."

I knew Lord Thomas would have taken poorly to being rebuked and chided by a ten-year-old boy, king or no. Had he not considered that the council was like to inquire of the king how he came upon this line of thought, and when pressed, His Majesty should speak the truth? "This is dangerous work, madam, when the king himself calls such an action treason. Will Lord Thomas now let this madness lie?" I heard him approach and quickly finished my ministrations.

"I think not," she said softly. "He oft acts rashly and without forethought."

I stuck myself with a hairpin and the sharp shock of it reflected the pain in my heart over Kate's husband.

The New Year began with mishap but followed with merriment. The Lady Elizabeth's tutor, Master Grindal, who was beloved by all in the queen's household and especially by the Lady Elizabeth herself, died of plague. The plague had been better behaved under the last king, but had reared its death head more regularly under the new monarch and began boldly picking off men, women, and children. Though sorrowed, we were also relieved that Master Grindal had taken his leave afore Christmas and therefore had not had time to pass the contagion.

I came upon the queen dowager and the Lady Elizabeth having a disagreement, as mothers and daughters do, about who should replace Master Grindal. Kate desired Master Goldsmith, the Lady Elizabeth, Master Ascham.

"Come now, Kate." Thomas strode into the room mid-discussion. "I believe Elizabeth is now of an age to choose her own tutor. I rather prefer Ascham myself."

Shortly thereafter, Master Ascham was engaged, though I know Kate did not like being rebuked by her husband in front of her ward, especially as he'd sided against her.

More trouble ensued when Elisabeth Brooke and her small household arrived to stay at Hansworth. Though she was married now, the lord protector declared it was not valid, and I again shared my large chamber with her.

"William is forbidden from seeing me on pain of death," Elisabeth said bitterly whilst her lady maid unpacked her clothing. "The lord protector has set aside our marriage."

"What happened?" I asked, sitting in a chair nearby whilst she raged.

"William spoke with him privately to tell him that in light of the petition for annulment last spring, we had recently married. He expected the lord protector to be favorably disposed toward this news, he having been divorced from an adulterous wife himself afore taking Lady Seymour. But no! He said his power and authority had been thwarted. That no noble may marry without his permission. Never mind that till his sister shared the king's bed he himself was no noble, only gentry." She paused at that, she born the daughter of a noble lord, and looked at me. "Not that I intend to slight those raised to gentry."

"Of course not," I said.

The news only inflamed the queen and Lord Thomas more against Edward, and I felt, to my dismay, that a final point for reconciliation had been met and then quickly passed by as the road diverged.

The queen held a large masque, as promised, in early March, when all were well tired of the ill weather. Yet it was not bright enough to look toward the promise of spring. There were more than two hundred people well-crammed in the queen's beautiful dower estate; all spoke of her homes as the second court. The king was but a boy and Lady Seymour had more talent to pretention than to true hospitality. The tables were laden with jellied eels and baked lampreys with sticky syrup, small pies with whitefish bursting from the crusts, roasted pink salmon, and all other manner of fish as 'twere Lent. My lady did not keep with a somber household for the season, as court did of old, but she did keep with forbearing the eating of meat.

I had taken my rose gown out and let it air; I had worn it but once, when I last met Jamie, and it seemed a shame and a waste not to wear it more than that. But at the last minute, I could not. I sorrowfully put it away and chose a becoming gown of bright red that I knew also showed off my dark brown hair to advantage.

I had danced with many fine young men that night but did not allow any to think that I favored them. When a gentleman about the age of Lord Thomas approached me to dance, I accepted his invitation.

"My lady?" he said. "Sir Richard Hibbart. A dance?"

"I should be glad to," I replied.

He took my hand and graciously led me to dance, and while he allowed me to partner with another, he later came back to ask of me again. I discovered that he was a widower with three children already with tutors of their own, one placed in a noble household and the others remaining with their governess.

"Are you in constant attendance upon the queen?" he asked at the end of the evening.

"I am," I said. "Though I may visit my mother, who resides in Marlborough, or my brother, who is placed in Cecil's household."

He led me to sit, called for a goblet of watered wine, and took one for himself. He broke sweat rather quickly whilst dancing, and his hair was thinning, but he still cut a fine figure in his doublet and jacket. "I shall take my leave for Scotland soon, with the fleet, to defend against the French onslaught. I am supposing that the lord high admiral will accompany us . . . this time."

It was to Thomas's great shame that when last the fleet sailed out against Scotland he had not been at the helm, but rather remained in London pressing his case with the council.

"I will pray for your safety," I said.

"May I call upon you when I return?" he asked.

I nodded. "You may."

Late that night, I helped Kate undress and she asked me if I had met anyone who had captured my interest.

"Sir Richard Hibbart was polite and kindly disposed toward me," I said. "He is a widower with some fine children and I found him to be pleasant company."

"That does not sound very . . . ardent, Juliana," she said.

"Were you ardent with your first husbands, madam?" I asked.

She laughed. "No. But I had no choices. You, unlike many others, do."

" 'Tis possible to build a household with a man and his children already born," I said. "To be a stepmother is noble and worthy, as I have well learnt from you, and I look forward to perhaps doing that with Sir Richard."

She set her brush down and drew me near, taking my hands in her own. "Bearing your own babe is also noble and worthy, as I hope you shall also shortly learn from me." She put her hand upon her abdomen and patted it lightly.

"Kate! You are with child?"

She smiled and then giggled like a girl. "Can you believe it? 'Tis true. And I believe it to be a mark of favor of our Lord upon my marriage with Thomas, as I have never been with child before."

"My lady, I am overcome with gladness for you," I said. "You must rest easy now. No difficult works or harrying situations to discomfort you." I took the brush from her hands and finished the task. "Quietly, calmly, sweetly, till the babe comes."

She nodded her agreement and when I was finished bade me good night. "I shall see you upon the morrow, dear heart."

I curtseyed. "Thank you, Kate. It was a splendid evening. I am overjoyed of your news."

Once in my room, I found Elisabeth already abed; her husband, Sir William, could not attend, though progress was being made with the lord protector toward their reconciliation. I took the red gown off and put it away, but as I did, my hands and eyes and heart lingered upon the rose one.

"Juliana." I felt a hand shake my shoulder. I opened my eyes and found Elisabeth Brooke leaning over me. For a moment I thought I had disturbed her sleep with another prophecy, but no.

"Get dressed," she said. "There is something I want you to see."

I gowned myself quickly and twisted my hair back without a net and followed her down the long gallery, around the turn, and toward the Lady Elizabeth's chambers. Within, I heard high-pitched giggling. Elisabeth pushed the chamber door open slightly and I could see some of the maidens loitering about the back of the room, dismay and discomfort writ on their faces. In the center was the Lady Elizabeth's bed, its drapes pulled back and she cowering, half nervously laughing, half protesting, fully vexed, against the head of it. Lord Thomas drew near to her and, it seemed, he was tickling her leg though she still was in her bed gown.

"He has no leggings on!" I whispered. His long shirt came to mid-thigh but you could see his bare legs and feet. I could not see, nor did I want to see, if his codpiece remained laced.

She nodded. At that moment, Kat Ashley came down the hallway; where she'd been I knew not but she pushed by us and went to rebuke Thomas.

"I have said this to you afore," she said. "My lady will be badly spoken of if you persist!"

"Nay, madam, I will tell my lord protector how it slanders me if others speak evil of this. I will not leave off, for I mean no ill." At that, he reached over and patted the Lady Elizabeth's thigh.

"It is an unseemly sight to come so barelegged to a maiden's chamber. Desist!"

At that, Lord Thomas pulled away, the Lady Elizabeth leapt out of her bed and raced toward the end of the room, to safety, where her maids cowered, and Elisabeth and I made our way to our chambers.

I sat down, heavy in heart and spirit. "How come you to know of this?" I asked.

"Two of my maids, who came with me to Hanworth, share several chambers with the Lady Elizabeth's maids. They told me that this has transpired several mornings, that even with Mistress Ashley remonstrating with Lord Thomas, he persists."

"Someone shall have to inform the queen."

Elisabeth shook her head grimly. "She already knows. She has partaken in the activity once with Lord Thomas."

"Surely not!" I stood, ready to defend her. "I think you misspeak."

"I do not wish to speak ill of the queen any more than you do. When my maidens first told me of this mischief, I could not believe them. I went the first day and saw it for myself, and the queen was tickling her, too, though she did not look happy and put a quick end to it."

"Mayhap she was seeking to temper his behavior with her presence."

She nodded. "I agree. But it has emboldened him rather than stayed his actions. I was"—she paused—"I was hoping you could speak with the queen about it yourself. She trusts you in all matters."

"I am sorry I accused you of speaking out of turn." I paused for a moment. "I shall speak with her. But I must tell you in confidence . . . I have just learned that she is newly with child."

"Oh!" Elisabeth clapped her hand over her mouth. " 'Tis marvelous news."

"Indeed. But I do not want to upset her, nor the babe. So I shall wisely choose when to broach the matter. I suspect Mistress Ashley has shamed Thomas enough to put an end to matters for some time."

She smiled, agreeing with me. Alas, we were both grievously wrong.

May arrived, gowned in a garland of hawthorn, said to be whence our Lord's crown of thorns came. Elisabeth Brooke returned to William Parr, and of a quiet afternoon, I felt a keen and curious desire to wander the gardens. I took nothing with me and went alone. As I made my way through the maze of hedges, as yet untrimmed for the season, I heard loud voices coming from without the hedges and one quiet one from within. I felt dreamlike again.

Who knoweth whether thou art come to the kingdom for such a time as this?

I quietly picked my way down the gravel path, taking care not to noisily crush it with my slippers. Once close, I hid behind the statue of Aphrodite and listened. I could not make out what the voices were saying, but the Lady Elizabeth's voice sounded by turns pleased and then pleading; her laughter scaled from enjoyment to fear. And there it stuck. I looked on in horror as Kate held her fast, as if in a playful tease, but Kate's face looked tense and distressed, near tears, and I had a care for her well-being and for that of her babe. Lord Thomas grinned wickedly and had drawn his dagger and was slashing the Lady Elizabeth's gown into pieces. The Lady Elizabeth held herself upright, never losing her royal posture, but her face looked afraid and vulnerable as I had never before seen it. She protested loudly and was ignored. Pieces of her gown plummeted to the ground, one by one. I felt sickened and fearful of what might come next.

Seymour finally sheathed his dagger and made a

move as if he were going to take the lady in his arms whilst Kate held her. Both the Lady Elizabeth and the queen looked to be filled with woe, forced to drink a cup of bile that neither of them had earned. I felt that he meant to harm her, and that Kate was trapped as a woman drowning, pulling Elizabeth under with her.

Thomas, who had no care that he had asked the king to participate in his treason, was not likely to worry himself for the Lady Elizabeth's or Kate's concern, either. I felt pressed to move, and in spite of the rancor I knew they would cast upon me, I did.

I stepped out from behind the statue, balled my hands into fists, and shouted, "Stop! This is shameful!"

I was out of turn, but my rebuke, as a witness to their doings, shocked them into silence. Thomas stalked back to the manor house. Kate did not meet my gaze but followed him from a distance, while the Lady Elizabeth, who had given me a quiet look of thanksgiving, trailed them both.

There was little time to think upon the matter, though I remained shaken all day, wondering with dismay what kind of household I now lived in. Lady Fitzgerald Browne arrived to stay with us beginning that very evening; she had recently become a widow and came to Kate's household to stay for a time afore moving into her dower estates. Though she were in mourning, Lady Fitzgerald Browne kept our good spirits up with tales of her home in Ireland, which she had left as a child. "My brother, now, he had to disappear back into Ireland to be hidden by our clansmen. He was in hiding for a number of years when King Henry had other plans for him." She did not look at the Lady Elizabeth when she said that. King Henry had, in fact, planned to separate her brother not only from his lands but from his head. Though she did not seem to hold the sins of the father against the daughter, it was not a pleasant memory I was sure.

Lady Fitzgerald Browne continued. "He eventually made his way to the continent without drawing undue attention. Now that good King Edward sits upon his throne, I am supposing that he will come back to claim his lands! It will be good to see him again."

We all heartily agreed with her sentiments, and in her grief about her husband, I was glad to see her looking forward rather than back. Soon, the Lady Elizabeth excused herself, telling the company that she had a headache coming on.

"The babe tires me, as well," Kate said.

"May I assist you this evening, my lady?" I asked, my voice reflecting that I hoped she would agree. She looked wearily and warily in my direction but nodded her agreement.

Lord Thomas was in his own quarters and had

not yet come to join her for the evening so I felt free to speak openly as I took the skirt paneling, undid the laces, and then gathered the rings from her swollen fingers.

"Madam, you know that I love you above all others," I began. "My loyalty to you is unquestionable. And yet it is the very same love and loyalty that compel me to speak."

"The garden," Kate said.

"The garden," I agreed. " 'Tis unseemly."

Her back stiffened at the rebuke. "It was play, Juliana, nothing more."

"And in the Lady Elizabeth's bedchamber? Whilst her governess and maids looked on in horror?"

Kate took the brush from me, set it down, and turned toward me, her face flushing. "I did not begin nor approve of that, and the Lady Elizabeth could have brought her complaints at any time."

My temper flared and I shook my head. "To whom would she speak in your household, madam? To you? When even now you are unwilling to see. To Lord Thomas? Kat Ashley did speak to him, to no avail. The Lady Elizabeth is too loyal to you to write to the lord protector and bring your household under condemnation. And, as a girl is wont to do, she is flattered at the attention of a man, of course. But at her tender age she does not know better. Lord Thomas most certainly does."

And so do you. I let the thought float, and I knew she would discern it though it remained unspoken. My own breaths came quickly and sharp as the situation in its entirety somehow reminded me of John Temple, though I knew things had not gone that far. Once more the girl was held to full account for the wrongs of the man.

"I know. You are right. It has grown beyond the playful to something I do not understand." Kate slouched in a chair. As she did, she ran her hand across her belly. "The little knave grows restless and kicks from within." Lord Thomas had already told all who would listen that he believed the babe to be a boy.

The flock of ravens, the Lady Elizabeth's dress clippings, flying to the Tower in my vision came back insistently. Because I had intervened in one forewarned event did not mean all danger had passed. "We must protect the Lady Elizabeth. And yourself. And your son." I did not mention Thomas. I had no interest in protecting him.

"What shall I do?" she asked quietly.

"You must decrease your household in readiness of your lying in."

She thought for a moment and then said, "Yes, yes, you are right. As I am to shortly depart for Sudeley to bear the babe, perhaps 'twould be a good time for Kat Ashley to visit with her sister Lady Denny and her household in Hertfordshire." A shadow lifted from her face. "The Lady

Elizabeth will benefit of the fresh air and change of circumstances and I shall be well occupied for the next few months. I've also promised Lady Jane Grey she could attend upon me with the household in Sudeley, so mayhap it's better if Elizabeth does not come just now."

I nodded my agreement. I knew the Lady Elizabeth's dismissal would seem to those who knew the situation as if she were to blame, but there was no other alternative. Kate could not dismiss her husband.

Within weeks the queen and Elizabeth had a solemn discussion wherein Elizabeth's departure was confirmed. Elizabeth said little but perhaps she felt some relief and ease too. Within a fortnight after her departure, the queen received a letter from Elizabeth and she asked me to read it to her whilst she rested upon her bed on a warm afternoon.

" 'Although I could not be plentiful in genuine thanks for the manifold kindnesses received at Your Highness's hands at my departure, yet I am something to be borne withal, for truly I was replete with sorrow to depart from Your Highness, especially leaving you undoubtful of health. And albeit I answered little I weighed it deeper when you said you would warn me of all evils that you should hear of me; for if Your Grace had not a good opinion of me, you would not have offered friendship to me that way, that all men judge the contrary. Your Highness's humble daughter, Elizabeth.'"

I closed the paper. "She believes you to be angry with her and hold her accountable," I said. "She wants reassurance of your love."

Kate kept her eyes closed. "Nay, I do not hold her to account," she said softly. "I know whence her fear came. She has my constant love and I shall write and tell her so."

Within the week we took our leave to Sudeley Castle in Gloucester to prepare for the arrival of the little knave. Thomas did not sail to Scotland with the fleet, as Sir Richard Hibbart had hoped. Instead, he went back and forth between Sudeley and the court, pleading and manipulating in public and private for more power and control.

The very night we arrived in Gloucestershire, I dreamt.

It was a cliff, and next to the cliff, a tiny patch of green upon which grew some flowers. They were bright and bold, *flos solis*, sunflowers, with beautiful faces that turned toward the sun as it arced across the lustrous blue sky.

Toward the end of its arc, a seed dropped from one flower's bosom and implanted itself deep within the soil. Within a moment, a tiny shoot sprang forward, unsteady and green.

As it began to grow, the larger flower nodded under the heavy weight. Suddenly Lord Thomas's dagger sliced through the stem right below the head and, thus lopped off, it fell to the ground.

SIXTEEN

Summer and Autumn:
Year of Our Lord 1548
Sudeley Castle, Gloucestershire

We arrived at Sudeley in the flush of summer, when the trees in the gardens budded small, hard fruit and the baby birds pulsed insistently as their parents plucked all manner of bug and worm to satiate them. The household that traveled with us numbered more than one hundred and twenty: servants, attendants, maids of honor such as myself, and the usual ladies and gentlemen. All highborn children required a considerable household in attendance from birth, in accordance with their status, and Kate had arranged for a certain Mrs. Marwick to be employed as the babe's nurse. We spent the summer playing cards, laughing, entertaining our neighbors, and listening to musicians, one by one. It was a season of peace and joy.

Doctor Huicke, who had also accompanied us from London, had instructed Kate to walk often in the gardens in preparation for the birth. None of us dared voice what all of us feared—Kate was, at thirty-six, well beyond the usual age for a first child and the risk of complication to both mother and babe was multiplied.

"Have a seat, Your Grace, do rest," little Lady Jane Grey said to Kate one late August afternoon whilst we walked around the fountain in the garden near the west wing of the castle. I handed the queen a fine linen cloth with which she wiped her brow before reposing on a cool stone bench. Thomas's ward, Lady Jane, was a delightful child of nine who, if given leave, would spend every minute of the day that she was not with her tutors with the queen. Jane's mother, Lady Frances Grey, was especially aware of her royal standing as the daughter of Queen Mary of France, King Henry's younger sister. I knew that connection made Kate attend even more closely to Jane, though the child was so sweet one would care for her even if she were a lost waif—which she oft seemed to be.

The mist of the fountain carried on the breeze and refreshed us; I closed my eyes and enjoyed the moment but then I felt Kate take my arm.

"I feel the lightest of pangs," she said. "Mayhap it be time to find the midwife and Lord Thomas. For precautions."

Lady Jane helped the queen into the castle and I set off to find the others. The midwife was sent for and left immediately to Kate's chambers. I passed

307

the baby's nursery suite—recently done in Kate's favorite colors of crimson and gold with summer light streaming in through the window that overlooked the gardens and the chapel. Fitting, I thought, for Kate's babe. Mrs. Marwick had a room next door to the baby's so that she could attend him in the night and nurse him if need be. There were several other rooms in the suite for the baby, though many of his attendants would be scattered through the house at large. Presently, I came to Thomas's chambers. I knocked upon the door and one of his men appeared almost immediately.

"Yes?"

"I'm here to speak with Lord Thomas," I said. Because I was close to the queen, he nodded, and I was let in immediately.

"Juliana!" Thomas stood from his desk, drew near to me, and took me in his arms for a moment, then held me at arm's length. "How come you to me this afternoon?"

" 'Tis the queen," I said. "Her pains have begun and she sends for you."

His face grew bright with enthusiasm. "I shall take my leave immediately to greet her afore her lying-in," he said. He motioned to some letters he'd left on his table. "Could you please see that my page takes these for delivery?"

I nodded and he departed immediately. I took in hand the letters, which were already sealed. One was to Sir Paget, who Kate had told me had written to Thomas to tell him that the council remonstrated with Edward Seymour's arrogance and unwillingness to take direction or counsel from others. I wondered what mischief Thomas had replied in return. One letter was to one of the king's servants, by whom all knew Thomas sent small bits of spending monies to the king with which he might reward his servants or gamble. King Edward had been given no such funds by his uncle Edward Seymour, the lord protector. The last letter, I saw to my dismay, was addressed to the Lady Elizabeth at Hertford.

After delivering them to the page, who gave them to a messenger, who set out immediately, I returned to my lady's chamber to find her abed. Lady Tyrwhitt, her closest lady in waiting, was at her side.

"Can I assist in any way?" I asked Lady Tyrwhitt.

"You may read aloud, to distract her," she said. "And I've sent for cool drinks to help soothe her."

I read aloud for some hours from Tyndale, from Erasmus, from the queen's own books, and from such other stories and poems as would help her to better pass the time. After some hours the daylight waned and the babe still did not come.

My reading voice sped up with my agitation over her situation, and I had to force myself to speak slowly and steadily. I stopped as the midwife attended Kate.

"Here, now, I'll just massage your belly and tissues and see if that helps the babe along," the midwife said. She reached her hand under the sheets and when she made contact Kate screamed in agony.

The midwife pulled her hand out. "The babe is closer, and he's turned properly. He will come."

Night settled into day and early on the morning of August 30, my lady's child was born with a lusty call from the lungs, upon which we all clapped and laughed with delight. 'Twas a girl and the queen held her to her bosom with delight touching upon ecstasy. I shed not a few tears, thanking God that my lady was safe delivered of the child she'd wished for these many years.

We hurried to get the queen cleaned up whilst she held the babe. The babe was then cleaned, too, and given to Mrs. Marwick to quickly suckle her before she was handed back to Kate.

"She shall be named Mary," the queen dowager declared.

"Mary?" Lady Tyrwhitt inquired. "Are you sure? Not Maud after your mother nor Margery after Thomas's?"

Kate shook her head firmly and insisted, "Her name shall be Mary." It put me in mind of Zechariah, the father of John the Baptist, insisting for mysterious reasons that his child should be named John.

Later, Thomas was brought into the room, and though he had hoped and presumed upon a son, he seemed delighted with both the babe and his wife.

The next day a messenger arrived with a letter from his brother, Edward, congratulating him on the birth of so pretty a daughter and encouraging Thomas that sons would soon follow. He signed the letter, "Your Loving Brother, Edward," which brought Lord Thomas great pleasure as he read it aloud for all to hear.

Perhaps the child would be the soft yarn that knit these hearts together and I had a hope, watching Thomas and the babe and Kate in her birthing chamber, that the worst days were behind us and the best days lay ahead.

The very next day Kate was still abed, not unusual for a new mother, but her face was more flushed than when she'd delivered. I brushed out her hair and noticed that the back of her neck was burning. The day after, it was worse.

"Do you want to sit up or take a walk about the room?" I asked her.

She shook her head. "When I sit up I become faint and weak and must immediately lie down." This worried me. I had seen Kate ill but a few times in the six years I had been in her household.

"Should I call Dr. Huicke?" I asked.

She appeared to contemplate the idea. "No," she finally said. "I am not fully dressed. Mayhap we will wait but a while. You can bring me some cool watered wine."

I left to fetch it and when I returned, Lady Tyrwhitt was attending upon her in my place. I then walked past her chamber and toward the baby's rooms, where Mrs. Marwick rocked Mary and caught my eye as I went past her. She smiled, but wanly. Something was amiss.

Two days later, when I made my way to Kate's chambers to help her dress, she was still in bed and unwilling to get up. "My throat is fair parched and chafed. 'Tis difficult to swallow at all." That evening, the midwife insisted upon Dr. Huicke tending to Kate.

"I think this shall pass, madam, as you take your leisure and allow the body to recover," he said. But when he turned to leave the room his face had a look of stark terror and I saw him turn left down the hallway toward Lord Thomas's chambers and not toward his own.

Kate asked for Mary to be brought to her and so she, with the wet nurse, soon arrived behind Lady Tyrwhitt. Kate cooed to the child and kissed her and held her close, breathing in her powdery newborn perfume afore falling back into her cushions. Lady Tyrwhitt dismissed us all, but the next morning, one of her servants came to knock upon my chamber door. It was September fifth, six days after the birth.

"The queen wishes to see you," she said. "Immediately and alone."

I made my way to her chambers down the long, bright gallery of Sudeley Castle; dawn had brightly broken like an egg yolk tilting out of its shell, but the light did not spill into my lady's chambers, as her draperies were still drawn against disease. One of her menservants stirred up her fire afore leaving the room, making the hot September morning unbearable. When he finished, we were alone.

"Juliana," Kate said weakly. "Come close. I cannot pass my sickness on to you, for it is childbed fever I suffer from."

I drew my chair near to the side of her bed. There was another chair on the other side of her bed, and though I could see no one, I well sensed who sat in it, swinging his legs, abiding his time impatiently. It was the Angel of Death. Therefore, when she next spoke to me, I did not contradict her.

"I will die," she said simply. "Soon." And then she burst out in tears. "I have accomplished so little of what I wanted to. I have been of nearly no use to our Lord above all!"

I drew near and kissed her hot cheeks. "Nay, that is not so. By your sweet temper and remaining

313

clothed with humility, you turned aside the king's wrath, and because of that, King Edward's council is led by reformers who make great strides in all religious manner, which you love. And your books, madam, your books. Many thousands have already partaken of your sweet words of faith, and many thousands more shall do likewise throughout the ages."

She nodded some and then her tears and anguish rekindled. "But there I leave undefended and unloved Mary, my own babe, my own child. After I have mothered so many children I have not borne—my Lord Latimer's children, His Majesty's children, Lady Jane—'tis a folly of injustice to not have time to love mine own child!"

I took her fingers in mine and pressed them to my lips afore speaking. Her hand was aflame. "'The righteous by Christ are never offended at the works of God because they know by faith that God does all things well, and that he cannot err, neither for want of power, nor by ignorance nor malice: for they know him to be almighty, and that he sees all things and is most abundantly good.'"

For the first time that day, I saw a small smile. "My own words return to tutor me."

"As you wrote them, lady, in your most excellent book." I stroked her brow. "They have brought me much comfort in ways you shall never know, and I know they do likewise for others.

Now, what may I do to assist you, Kate, to bring *you* comfort?"

She rolled her head toward me. Her eyes were glassy and still, like the eyes of a newly killed doe. "I have much to tell you, much to ask of you, and little time before Lady Tyrwhitt comes to rejoin us." She kept hold of my hand. "I have a confidence that I must share with you, one that is like to bring you great grief, but I must tell you anyway." She seemed to be gathering what little strength she had. "Although Sir Hugh St. John raised you as his own child, you are not his daughter. Your father is Thomas."

I looked at her strangely. "Thomas . . . whom, lady?"

"Lord Thomas Seymour," she said.

I withdrew my hand. "Nay, lady, you are in a delirium is all. My father was a knight in Marlborough," I reminded her. "And Lord Thomas owed him a favor"—at that I slowed a bit—"for business purposes." My voice grew quiet and I saw that she recognized I was beginning to understand. Dread crawled over and through me.

"Your mother was, indeed, a companion to Jane Seymour, when her own family, though of good standing, fell upon difficult times. Whilst they were both young, and living at Wulf Hall, Thomas and your mother began to keep company. Within a little time it became clear that your mother was with child. That child was you." She took my hand again. "I am sorry, but Thomas's mother did not find the idea of her son marrying your mother to her approval. So the family arranged to have a knight, nearby and of good honor and personal qualities, marry your mother."

"My father," I whispered. "Nay, not my father." My heart rushed between beating so hard that I felt near to fainting and stopping altogether. My lovely, honorable, noble father was not my father at all. Instead, I was the offspring of Lord Thomas, a rogue now chasing a girl much younger than his own daughter! How could this be? I was desperately dismayed and could scarce breathe, and yet I didn't want to unduly upset Kate on her deathbed.

"Who else knows of this?" I whispered.

"Thomas's mother, of course. Edward Seymour and Lady Seymour, I am sure. And my Lady Suffolk, when she had a concern about Lord Thomas's insistence upon placing you in my household, inquired as to the relationship. Because we were dear friends, I told her. But that is all."

I nodded. It was a confidence well kept. I did not have time to dwell upon the implications for myself, though, as Kate pressed on.

"Do not think ill of Lord Thomas," she said. "He has not shared this truth with you these many years so as not to shame your mother. He, too, knew how beloved your father was to you and did not want to turn you from that affection. He sought to prosper your father's business and to undertake to assist you and your brother. He has sometimes ill used King Edward, but he has also sought to bring pleasure and joy into the young king's life. For all his faults—and they be many— Thomas does have finer qualities too."

"He waited to marry you, lady," I said, pointing out one point she had missed.

"Yes," she said. "He did. But now he is blinded and consumed with anger and grief and greed over his brother's position, and I worry for my daughter. If I were here to protect her, she'd be fine. But I will not be." She rolled over, her damp hair falling limply upon her silken cushion. "Juliana, I beg you to remain in charge of my daughter's household, as a highly placed and highly esteemed gentlewoman, mayhap as a governess, though the babe shall not need tutors just yet, until such time as Lord Thomas has remarried and his new . . . wife"—her voice caught like a snagged embroidery thread on that sharp word—"has settled my daughter in her household and provided for her."

"But I am not yet married, madam. May I take such a position? And I have little experience with children."

"Mistress Ashley was not yet married when she became a gentlewoman in the Lady Elizabeth's household. If you have questions, she would be a guide unto you." She smiled at me softly. " 'Tis not your experience with children that will do Mary good. It is your honor, and strength, and spirit."

"Will Lord Thomas agree?" I asked.

"He will," she said. "I shall insist upon it. I shall leave funds for you to use at your disposal in assisting with her household, and you may hire your own servants. Mary's nurse will of course remain with her, unless Sir Thomas's new wife"— she began to sob again—"disagrees."

"I shall ensure she is well placed and much beloved," I promised her. "For this reason you have told me of Lord Thomas?"

She nodded and I began to see her mood whip up again like a squall. "I know you love me well and would endeavor to assist, but now that you know she is your sister—and she has no other but you—there is an especial reason to make sure she is well settled. I have seen the affection and devotion with which you looked after your brother, Hugh. I know you will do right by Mary too. And then, once Thomas has married and my daughter is cared for, you, my dear, should marry too."

"I will do as you say, lady," I said. Tears ran down my own face and I wiped them away with the back of one hand. "I shall love her as you have loved me. And as I love you even now. I shall ensure Lord Thomas's . . . household"—I could not say *new wife*—"treats her gently and well and toward the station that she, as the daughter of a queen, deserves. I will remain with her till that be certain."

She threw off her coverlets and I saw her shivering in her thin bed gown, blood newly staining the sheets. Her eyes grew wild again. "His new household is like to be headed by someone you well know," she said. "If he has his way."

"I do not know of whom you speak," I said, though I did.

"Oh, yes, the Lady Elizabeth would be his choice," she said. " 'Tis all too convenient now, my dying whilst he may have his bidding with her."

I shook my head. "Nay, my lady, that shall not pass."

She reached over to me, her breath hot and fetid. "Do not let him harm her," she said. "You must be aware. Do not let harm come to her through his rash behavior."

At that, she fell back into her bed.

"*Her,* madam? Whom must I guard from him? The Lady Elizabeth? Or your daughter, Mary?"

At that, Kate simply nodded to me and waved her hand. Within a minute Lady Tyrwhitt entered the room and Kate began to rave to her.

"What has taken you so long?" she cried out to her. "I have such feelings in me that I fear I shall not long live!"

"Fetch Lord Thomas," Lady Tyrwhitt said. "Quickly!"

I ran down the hall, praying that I could keep my face steady and my eyes from betraying to him that I now knew that he was my father.

"Lord Thomas!" I insistently knocked at his chamber door without stopping till a page opened up to me. "Lord Thomas, the queen, she needs you now."

He raced down the hallway and I ran after him. When we arrived a number of her household were already present, though mainly tarrying about the edges of the room.

He went directly to her bedside and pulled her to him, taking her full in his arms. I saw the anguish ground into his face, and whatever his other sins were, 'twas clear to all present that he did, indeed, love Kate. She did not seem to recognize for a moment that 'twas Thomas who held her. She directed herself, instead, to Lady Tyrwhitt.

"I fear I am not well handled," Kate said, her voice shrill and still rising. "For those that be about me care not for me, but stand laughing at my grief, and the more good I do for them, the less good they do for me!" She turned her head, her mind seemingly clearing for a moment, and looked directly at Thomas.

"Why, sweetheart, I would not hurt you," he replied, stroking her arm.

"No, my lord, I think so," she said. "You have

given me many shrewd taunts." At that, she began to cry. Many of her household began to cry, too, either silently and remaining, or loudly and leaving the room so as not to disturb my lady.

"Let me lie with you, sweetheart, that I might bring you comfort and cheer," Thomas said. She nodded and he slipped into the bed alongside her.

"I would have seen Dr. Huicke the first day I delivered," she continued. "But I dared not for fear of displeasing you, as you do not care for any man to be with me alone or partially dressed, even my doctor!"

Thomas shook his head and whispered to her, then kissed her gently on the hairline, and within a few moments, she seemed to slump into his arms, her head on his shoulder, and grow quiet.

Within hours, she sent for her chaplain, her almoner, and her doctor, then began to dictate her will aloud, being not well enough to hold the quill and parchment herself.

"I leave all properties, possessions, and wealth to my husband, Thomas, wishing that it were ten thousand times more in value than it be," she said. She gave him complete liberty at how to distribute them, and asked only that the household she had chosen for Lady Mary remain intact until such time as Thomas remarried.

Then my lady was quietly passed from the arms of her husband into the arms of her Lord.

Lady Jane Grey, who had come running down

the hall at the last, slipped onto the floor and began to sob. I picked her up and held her frail body close to my own, sobbing with her.

That night my lady was wrapped in a waxen cloth as we awaited her burial upon the morn. She was not shriven, as that was not her custom. Lady Jane Grey, as the highest-ranking member of Kate's household, would be chief mourner and there would be little fanfare, a simple ceremony, short and in English, with few attending, as the queen would have wished. She was as fully a reformer in death as she had been in life.

I lay abed that night, crying as quietly as I could, though I knew many others within the household, not least Lord Thomas, were likewise racked with grief.

All night I lay abed and not only images of Kate, and her gentle ways and bright laughter, but also thoughts of my father filtered through my heart and mind. He had known that I was not of him, and yet he loved me no less for it. He had never shown preference for Hugh, as my mother had.

It occurred to me that my mother had, indeed, held the sins of the father against the daughter. I would soon find out if Lady Margery Seymour, my grandmother, did as well. I cried until my nose ran, lamenting the loss of both mother and father. I was truly alone in this world now, a world I did not understand, could not command, and which proved more dangerous with each day that passed.

SEVENTEEN

Autumn: Year of Our Lord 1548
Wulf Hall
Brighton Manor
Syon House
Seymour House

The next morning, before we left for Wulf Hall, I packed some of Kate's personal belongings. I recalled how Lady Ogilvy had set aside some of Anne Boleyn's jewelry for the Lady Elizabeth, and to that end, I went through Kate's few remaining pieces and took the best for Mary. I also took a miniature that Kate had done of herself, to show the babe later what her mother looked like, and some of her books, which were her dearest possessions. There was a book of psalms, a book of stories and poems covered in green velvet, and a prayer book covered in her favorite crimson and gold. In the back was a love poem written by Thomas to Kate. I would save this for her too.

Sweet Mrs. Marwick and two servants shared a litter with myself and Mary. Mrs. Marwick fell asleep after nursing her, so I took the child from her and held her, awkwardly at first, as I had no experience with newborns, whilst we made our way, instinctively shielding her from the worst of the jostling with my body. Some few others of Thomas's household rode with him and some others in litters; many of Kate's household would return to London, either to Seymour Place or to other households.

When we arrived we were greeted by one of Lord Seymour's servants, who showed us to the set of rooms that would house Mary and her household whilst we remained. Mrs. Marwick shared a room with the child, and I had a small but richly appointed room of my own. The entire household was welcomed to dinner in a large dining room staffed with a dozen or more servants. As we ate I tried not to glance, repeatedly, at the table where sat my father, my grandfather, and my grandmother.

After the meal I made my way to Lord Thomas, who was in the stone-walled receiving room next to the dining area. His eyes were red rimmed and he had a defeated air about him. "Lord Thomas?" I said softly.

He looked me full in the face, searching, I knew, to see if Kate had made a deathbed confession to me. I steeled my expression and revealed nothing, allowing him to keep the secret he'd so long held. But I treated him with, mayhap, a little more consideration, not only for his grief but for that manner in which he had tried to care for me these years.

"The queen had said that I might hire some

servants for Mary's household, those I know I can trust. I know of some in Marlborough at my . . . mother's home. May I take my leave for a few days and see if they be willing?"

He smiled weakly at me and nodded. "Yes, Mistress St. John, you may do so. And thank you for agreeing to remain with my daughter's household for a little while, till we make our way clear through this thicket."

I nodded politely, not showing how ironic I found his reference to his daughter's household. "'Tis my honor, sir, to serve the queen dowager. And the child. And you." I did not meet his eye. I turned, and as I did, I caught Lady Margery Seymour looking straight at me.

She had a hooked nose and pitiless eyes. I did not flinch from her glance, nor turn my gaze down modestly. In response, she offered me no warmth nor a smile nor any kind gesture at all. But I saw, in her eyes, that she knew who I was and she rejected me as she had my mother.

That night I unwrapped the glass that Kate had given to me and stared at my features—my eyes, brown like Lord Thomas's. My hair, brown like Thomas's, in direct opposition to the rest of my family, all wheaten blonds. My cheekbones, high like those of all the Seymours. My nose was like my mother's, as were my bowed lips. Whose spirit did I have? I had thought it was my father's, Hugh St. John's. Now I knew not.

The next day I took to the stables, with a servant, to ride down to Marlborough.

I had the servant stable the horses and then instructed one of my mother's men to house him whilst we remained.

"Mistress Juliana!" My mother's chamberlain was surprised to see me. "Is your mother expecting you?"

I shook my head.

"But 'tis good of you to come now, whilst you have the chance," he said. "She is abed, ill. But of course you know that."

I did not know my mother was so ill; I had written to her and she had not responded. From time to time Hugh corresponded with me, but letter writing was never one of his better accomplishments and I heard from him less often than I would have liked to.

I made my way to her chamber, and it was as dark as Kate's had been, which was unusual, for my mother was not fond of being shut in. I knocked on her door and Lucy's mother, who also looked drawn, answered it.

"Mistress!" she said. "Your mother will be glad that you have come." She stepped out of the way and let me pass toward my mother's bedside.

"Juliana," my mother said. "'Tis a surprise to see you here."

I spoke forthrightly; my mother would know if I did otherwise, as it was not my habit to dither. "I did not know you were so ill, madam, but I would have come immediately if I had known."

She nodded and did not apologize for not sending for me, but she did not speak unkindly to me either. "I hear that Queen Kateryn has died. It seems she has bested me even in death."

I must have looked shocked, as she smiled faintly and said, "Even here in Marlborough we quickly get gossip through the servants."

"She has died," I said, "of childbed fever. She delivered of a daughter . . . Mary."

My mother held my gaze, looking, I knew, to see if I would disclose in some way that I knew that Mary and I were sisters. I did not flinch. "So what brings you, then?"

"The queen asked me to remain as mistress of Mary's household until such time as Lord Thomas remarries and the baby is thus settled with her new mother," I said, "who will then take charge and choose a governess."

"I shall expect it will not take long for Lord Thomas to remarry," my mother said confidently. "And then . . . what shall you do? Matthias has taken a bride, and they already have a small son. Does your young Irish knight await your release?"

At that, I flinched. "No, madam, he does not."

She sat up a little and looked me straight on. "He did not seem to me to be one who is easily turned away nor one who would take comfortably to defeat."

"Alas," I said, "he has returned to Ireland to find a bride. There is a man, a widower, Sir Richard Hibbart, who is presently fighting the Scots but who has asked to call upon me when he returns."

"And this is your desire?" she asked.

I shrugged and said, "Might I beg a favor, lady?" She nodded.

"The queen left Lord Thomas a wealthy man, and she instructed him to provide her child with the household befitting her standing. She has many servants already, but I should like to ask Lucy and her husband to join the household until I return to Marlborough, or marry. If you agree."

My mother sank back and closed her eyes. "Yes, yes, of course. Until Hugh returns with his bride, we have very little need here." She waved her hand. "If Lucy and Gerald so choose. And then you shall return here?"

"Yes. Unless Sir Richard contacts you or Hugh, I shall return to Marlborough."

I looked upon her as she lay there, so quiet and still. She had lost much of her vitality after the death of my father. "Shall I read to you?" I asked quietly. "For comfort?"

She shook her head and I stood to leave. She reached out and held my arm. "But you may remain beside me whilst I rest."

I sat down and gradually her grip softened and then her arm fell back upon the bed. When it did, I reached my own hand out and rested it upon hers. Her face was younger, smoother, softer as she slept. Even now, she was still captivatingly beautiful. It was not hard to see what Lord Thomas had seen in her, nor my father. To her credit, she had been as gentle to my father as she'd been harsh to me. I understood why now, and whilst it softened it some, that knowledge could never fully heal the bruise of her rejection.

After an hour, I kissed her cheek and then slipped away to find Lucy, who was beside herself with joy at the idea of coming to London for a time. When I inquired as to the nature of my mother's illness, she told me then that the lump in my mother's breast had grown and she might not live to see our return. When I spoke to my mother about remaining with her, she pressed me to leave anyway.

Within a week she had Lucy's mother send news that she was upon her deathbed, but that we were not to return as she would be simply buried at St. Peter's, with the man who remained my father in my heart and mind, Sir Hugh St. John.

One night in early October we were all in the music room of Wulf Hall talking quietly, bathing in the warm firelight, and listening to the delicate pluckings of the virginals. All could overhear Lady Seymour and Lord Thomas talking.

"You cannot stay here forever," she said. "It has been a month now. You have other duties to attend to and so do I. The expense of having your household remain here any longer is more than I care to bear."

He looked taken aback, and mayhap rejected, like a little boy. Then I understood that Lord Thomas and I had something even deeper in common. "Edward has invited us to Syon," he said. "And I mean to take him up on his offer."

Lord Thomas was taking his household to stay with his brother?

"Edward is a good, righteous man," his mother stated bluntly.

"I do not recall you speaking thusly of me, lady mother."

"You lead with your mouth, Thomas, whilst Edward leads with his head." She dismissed him with a flick of her wrist and Lord Thomas stalked from the room as the virginal player strove to play louder still to cover over the exchange.

I looked at Lady Margery Seymour and decided to approach her. It would not have been unexpected for her to have a word for me as I was there with her granddaughter's household. So far she had steadfastly refused, and whenever the situation looked as though we might have to discourse she immediately turned her back and took her leave, as she did now. She would not spare one word of kindness or recognition toward me, and had held the babe but once whilst we were there.

I stopped by Mary's room before going to my own, and looked down upon her still, sleeping body. I could not resist the urge to pick her up, and so I did. She did not wake but, after rustling, fell back into a deep sleep nestled thus in my arms. The moonlight poured in through her cross-paned window, lighting her small face, and I whispered, "What shall become of you?" to her before kissing her and putting her back in her cradle.

We left Wulf Hall two days later, for London.

Syon House was grand, fit for a king, which was only right since Anne Stanhope considered herself nearly royal. I noted with rising bile that she often wore Kate's jewelry. Upon my arrival I sent a letter, via messenger, to Kat Ashley to ask her for some guidance with Mary's household, as Kate had advised.

Within two days came a reply from Kat. "We were sorry to hear of the queen's death," she said, "none more so than the Lady Elizabeth. She loved her dearly and grieves her still, though she were advised not to write to offer condolences to Lord Thomas lest the letter be misinterpreted."

I set the letter down on my desk. Misinterpreted by whom? I then recalled that Lord Thomas had been writing to the Lady Elizabeth the day Mary was born, and mayhap since.

This was brought into sharper focus within a week, when Edward Seymour held a banquet for several hundred and all of the households attended. My brother, Hugh, was there, of course, with Cecil's men, and I sat with him first. His shoulders were broader and his beard fully come in now. "I shan't remain here long," he said. "I expect Cecily to return to London with her father after the New Year. We will then be wed, and return to Marlborough, the simplicity of which I now long for."

"I long for peace and simple joys too," I agreed, wishing I could return with him, knowing I would never feel peace till Mary were settled. "I have Lucy and Gerald with me here. Shall you need them to return?"

He shook his head. "Nay. Cecily will have her own lady maids and I am sure she will prefer them. 'Tis not necessary. And you?"

I explained to him that I was to stay with Mary till Thomas was remarried.

" 'Twill not be long then," Hugh said. "Rumor is that Lord Thomas means to make the Lady Elizabeth his bride, one way or another."

"Will the council give permission?" I asked.

"Nay, never," he said. He finished his glass of mead. "His brother told Lord Thomas that he had better not be thinking upon marrying one of the king's sisters, and Lord Russell told him that it would be his undoing if he did."

"What did Thomas reply?" I asked, nibbling on a cheese wafer.

"He denied having any ideas of it and rebuked them soundly. Then another man came forth and told Lord Thomas that if he did not watch his language the lord protector would have the right to arrest him. Lord Thomas said he wouldn't dare."

Oh, but he would, I thought, *he would more than dare.*

"And what of you, sister?" he asked. "Where will you go when Thomas remarries?"

"Mayhap home, if I am still welcome," I said. He assured me that, as family, I was his responsibility to care for, and a welcome one at that. "Hugh . . . there was a widower who spoke with me some months ago. His name is Sir Richard Hibbart. Could you find out if he has returned from Scotland?"

Hugh raised his eyebrows and grinned. "I shall make discreet inquiries."

After Hugh moved along to speak with a friend, Lady Tyrwhitt, who had remained with Lord Thomas's household for the moment, drew alongside me. She, of course, knew not of my connection to Thomas but well knew my love and loyalty for Kate.

"See there?" Lady Tyrwhitt nodded toward where Thomas had pulled John Dudley, a competitor of Edward Seymour's on the council, to the side. "It has not taken Thomas more than a week to sniff out that his brother has alienated some on the council and, even now, he be seeking support to work his will and marry the Lady Elizabeth."

"Already?" I asked, horrified.

"How long did he wait after His Majesty died to pursue Kate?" Lady Tyrwhitt inquired. She had a point. "He's already promised the Marquess of Dorset that Dorset's daughter, Jane Grey, shall marry King Edward."

I put my hand to my mouth. "He can promise no such thing!"

"He believes he can, so he does. Which is why she remains yet in his household. Wait and watch. The privy councilors have already warned him, strongly, against a marriage consideration with either the Lady Mary or the Lady Elizabeth. But Lord Thomas hears not what he does not want to hear. He draws the net ever closer about his feet till one day it shall spring upward with him in it." She left me then to make small talk with Elisabeth, after which I sought to talk with my dear friend Lady Fitzgerald Browne.

Late that night, after Lucy had helped me ready myself for bed, I lay there and wondered, for the first time, what would happen to the babe if her father did spring the trap. Traitors were attainted, stripped of their lands afore being beheaded, their heirs left without title, shamed and penniless.

'Twas a cliff, and next to the cliff, a tiny patch of green upon which grew some flowers. They were bright and bold, *flos solis*, sunflowers, with beautiful faces that turned toward the sun as it arced across the lustrous blue sky.

Toward the end of its arc, a seed dropped from one flower's bosom and implanted itself deep within the soil. Within a moment, a tiny shoot sprang forward, unsteady and green. As it began to grow, the larger flower nodded under the heavy weight. Suddenly Lord Thomas's dagger sliced through the stem right below the head and, thus lopped off, it fell on top of the tiny shoot, which was crushed to the ground beneath it.

I wakened out of breath and disturbed. I had earlier taken that dream to mean that Kate, after having her child, would die, and she had. But the fact that the dream persisted meant that it warned of something yet to come. I left my room and made my way to Mary's room, opened the door, and went in. Mrs. Marwick stirred, but saw 'twas me and lay back down. I eased the child from her cradle and Mary cooed and woke up and gazed at me without flinching. I felt a rush of love for her and drew her tight to me, feeling her little heart beat against my own. I took her to the rocking chair and held her till she felt a part of me, which she was. I rocked back and forth and kissed the feathery crown of her head, and was overcome with the fierce desire to protect and defend her. I prayed for guidance, wisdom, and help, for little Mary's sake, and, mayhap, for the Lady Elizabeth's.

A week later Lord Thomas came to tell me to ready myself to move the child, and her household, to Seymour Place. I was surprised, as we had not long been there, but agreed to get the household prepared. His steward readied his own household and sent word ahead that we would shortly thereafter arrive. We soon made our way to Seymour Place and settled into a routine. I ordered goods and materials for the Lady Mary's household, managing it for Lord Thomas, and spent time with my friends from Kate's household, many of whom had remained, when I was not otherwise occupied.

One day Thomas Parry, in charge of the Lady Elizabeth's monies as her cofferer, came to visit and sup with us. It was an unusual visit, and during the meal, Lord Thomas asked many questions about the Lady Elizabeth's household, her finances, her estates. He offered the use of his properties whenever she wished it. Thomas Parry indicated that the Lady Elizabeth would be receptive to that, and that application should be made through Kat Ashley.

"I have recently corresponded with Mistress Ashley," I said, "as Her Grace the queen had indicated that Kat was a governess who always looked out for her mistress's best interests and that the household of her own child, Mary, should seek to model itself upon it." I hoped by introducing the queen into the conversation I could shame Lord Thomas from his folly and unseemly pursuit.

But he was not to be turned. Instead, he came later that evening to Mary's quarters. He spent time visiting with her for a moment—which was, I admit, more than many noble fathers did—and then rejoined me in her reception chamber, where we were alone.

"It seems right that you make inquiries upon Mistress Ashley," he said. "She being governess to the Lady Elizabeth, daughter of a king, and my daughter, Mary, being the daughter of a queen. I should like you to make a visit to them at Hatfield, presently."

I nodded. "Certainly."

"And when you go, I should like you to deliver a letter to Kat Ashley and a gift to the Lady Elizabeth, on my behalf."

I nodded faintly but offered no answer. He seemed not to care, or even notice. The next morning he had a litter ready for myself, Lucy, and the packages. I left instructions for Mrs. Marwick, who needed them not, and took my leave.

We arrived at Hatfield, almost a day's journey from London, late in the afternoon. The red bricks of the house looked aflame against the blunt gray winter landscape and dull, clotted clouds. Once shown to our quarters, I met with Kat Ashley, who warmed herself by the fire. She offered me some refreshments that I gladly took.

"I bring a letter from Lord Thomas," I said, and she received the news with pleasure. I handed the document over to her. We talked about her time with Elizabeth—she had joined her household two months after the child's mother was beheaded by her father, when the child was but three. "I do not intend to remain with Mary's household forever, as a permanent member," I said. "But I have promised the queen that I shall remain till Lord Thomas is remarried and the child has a new mother to love and manage her."

"I am sure that there are many who would like to repay the queen's love by mothering such a child," she said. "I know of some, anywise."

I did not inquire further, but 'twas clear to me that she knew Lord Thomas pursued the Lady Elizabeth, and now that Thomas was unmarried, she apparently found no fault in the proposition. I myself found it repulsive. But I knew Lord Thomas better than she did, so I did not find fault with her.

I indicated that I cared to visit with the Lady Elizabeth, and I did so after church the next morning. I was pleased to see that stirring services were still held regularly in the Lady Elizabeth's household, and I felt renewed and refreshed afterward. Lord Thomas had not established such a pattern, though of course there were chaplains about from time to time.

We met in the receiving room, hung with tapestries from her father's collection. In the seven months since I had last seen her she had, indeed, become a woman. I curtseyed slightly and she nodded and indicated that I should sit down.

"You look lovely, my lady," I said.

"Thank you, Mistress St. John. Tell me. Was the queen's death prolonged? I hope she did not suffer."

"She died with difficulty," I admitted. "Childbed fever stalks all women and is no respecter of persons. A queen dies in as much hardship as the lowest born."

Elizabeth shuddered. "I have a horror of that particular death, I shall admit."

"And yet . . . the queen preserved her dignity till the end."

Elizabeth looked at her hands. "I am grieved that I was not with her when this evil overcame her," she said softly.

"She loved you much and well."

Elizabeth did not look up. "As I did her, but I could have loved her better."

"She held you no ill will nor rancor. For anything," I said. "She knew you loved her."

She looked up at me, her eyes slightly moist, but her neck firmly held high. "Thank you, Mistress St. John. Is that all?"

I thought of the package Lord Thomas had given me, the letters, a miniature of him, a piece of jewelry. Should I tell her I had a gift? Or no? I looked at her steadily.

Do not let him harm her.

"That is all," I said. Giving the package to her was likely to harm both the child and Elizabeth.

She stood, and then turned toward me. "You would be welcome in my household anytime, Mistress St. John. You have a way with words, and gowns." She smiled. "And with the heart."

"Thank you, lady," I said, and nodded my head. She nodded back and took her leave.

I hoped that I should not have to find a place in her home and wondered, for a moment, if she meant I might remain as Mary's governess should she marry Lord Thomas, or if she meant as a member of her own household. I had no desire to remain a governess one day longer than required; it limited my freedom to move and act as I might have liked, and kept me at court, which had become tarnished to me.

I returned to Seymour Place and hid Sir Thomas's gifts and letters in my chamber, hoping that he would not find out that I had not delivered them.

EIGHTEEN

Winter: Year of Our Lord 1549
Seymour House, London
Syon House, London
Barbican House, London

L ord Thomas entertained lavishly that winter, well beyond what he'd done whilst the queen was alive, though I was sure that it was her fortune that was paying for the entertainments. One afternoon he held a post-hunting banquet, complete with whole roasted boar, and his guest of honor was Sir William Sharington. After the meal, Sharington came to find me. Though he was long married, he endeavored to hold my attention all evening. He had meat betwixt his teeth and he smelt of spent ale and had not been a familiar during the queen's lifetime, so I did not know why he was there now. In desperation, I threw a look to Lord Thomas, who came and spoke a word into Sharington's ear. Lord Thomas was pulled away by the arrival of a messenger and departed for the receiving chamber. Afore he left me Sharington said, leering, "Thomas keeping you for himself before joining with the Lady Elizabeth, eh? Can't blame him." I pulled myself away, revolted by both the man and his accusation. He dressed beyond his station but spoke and acted beneath it, and I wondered who he was. As I took my leave and went back to Mary's rooms I passed by the receiving chamber, where Sir Thomas spoke loudly to the messenger.

"I care not whether my brother commands my presence. He may ask for it or I shall not respond. I am not his to command." He handed over the document to the messenger and then returned to his guests.

Late that night, Lucy helped Mrs. Marwick bathe Mary whilst I organized the child's clothes and made a note to order some in larger sizes as she was quickly growing. Then Lucy joined me in my chamber an hour later to assist me as I prepared for bed.

"Do ye know of Sharington?" she asked me.

"No," I replied. "And that is a most peculiar question, as I was only today wondering when and how he and Lord Thomas came to be such fast friends."

Lucy shook out my dress. "Gerald was drinkin' ale wi' some of the serving men in tha stables today after tha hunt. After they was in their cups one a them let slip that Sharington is making money for Lord Thomas."

"Making money? Do you mean gathering money?"

She shook her head. "Making it. He's tha treasurer of some sort of a mint outsida London, and Lord Thomas asked a hi' to make enough money ta hire soldiers for a revolt. Sharington readily agreed."

My joints jellied and I sat down in the nearest seat. "Be you sure of this?" I asked. If it were true, he was doomed.

"I be sure it was said," she answered.

On January 17, Lord Thomas was arrested and sent to the Tower along with Sharington.

As soon as Lord Thomas was arrested, the household panicked like a clattering of jackdaws, which, appropriately, nest in ruins. Lady Tyrwhitt, and her husband, who had stayed on only due to Kate's presence and for the sake of Lady Jane Grey, were called to present themselves immediately at Hatfield, where the Lady Elizabeth resided. 'Twas an ominous sign. Lady Jane had been returned to her parents, who had been told by Lord Thomas, wrongly, that his mother was present at Seymour Place and managing the household. Most of the rest of the household scattered, though Mary's stayed intact—for the time being—as they'd been paid through March and I was there to take charge.

We were, however, to take our leave to Syon House, unbelievably as it was the residence of the lord protector, Lord Thomas's chief persecutor, and his wife, Lady Seymour. She was none too glad to see us; she knew I was close to Kate and of course, so was the babe, and she and Kate had not loved one another at all whilst the queen lived. Lady Seymour made room for us in a lesser wing of her sumptuous estate and left word that she would be back to speak with Mary's household staff directly. She did not arrive for days, though we were fed and housed.

Soon after, my brother, Hugh, came to see me. I abandoned the game of peek-fingers I'd been playing with the delighted Mary and greeted him in her reception chamber. Lucy stirred the fire for us, greeted Hugh with warmth and affection, and then took her leave.

"Things go badly," he said. "I remain with Cecil, as you know, and Cecil with the protector, though for how much longer I know not. There is rude murmuring against the lord protector, who continues to alienate friends by his high-handedness. And I have heard of the proceedings against Lord Thomas."

"And?"

He drank of the goblet of wine and took some meat from the cold platter Lucy had delivered before answering.

"The lord protector and the council have found that, during varied and sundry times, Lord Thomas has sought to subvert their will, and the well-being of the realm, for seditious purposes."

Sedition! "What has occurred?" I asked.

"He is accused of arranging a marriage with the Lady Elizabeth without the permission of the council. And it is said that she has agreed. She is being interrogated even now, or will be soon."

"That is all?"

He shook his head. "He has arranged for funds to overthrow the council."

"Sharington," I said.

"Yes, Sharington. And the lord protector owes Sharington a tidy sum of money—a debt that will disappear if Sharington is attainted. Even now, Lady Seymour has taken Lady Sharington's jewelry into her possession and is shamelessly wearing it."

I could not believe it, and yet I could! "Is that all?" I asked.

He looked at me grimly afore finishing off his goblet. "No. Though that is enough, the worst is yet to be shared. He is accused of endangering the king's person."

"Never!" I said.

"But he has," Hugh told me. "Word filtered back to us that Thomas tried to reach the king, in the night, either to speak with him or to take hold of his person for ransom. But then the king's spaniel started to bark. His Majesty awoke and shouted, 'Help! Murder!' alarming the household, which rushed to his side. When they arrived, they found the king safe—for now—but the dog was shot to death to quiet it."

My hand flew to my mouth. "And they caught Lord Thomas?"

"No, he'd be a dead man already if they had. But they questioned the king's household and many of them had been sent on various and sundry errands so they would be dispersed at the time of the offense. Lord Thomas had sent them, and paid for these errands."

"What a fool, an unthinking fool," I said, "who makes mischief where there need be none."

Hugh took my hand. "Juliana, all associated with Sir Thomas scatter. And 'tis for the best, because if, or rather when, he be attainted, he will crush all those who lie close to him as he falls upon them. You must return to Marlborough. I admire your constancy to the queen in continuing on with the babe's household. But we are so lowborn as not to be noticed if we slip away from this mayhem once and for all. I myself will take my leave of Cecil's household soon. And Cecil himself"—he lowered his voice—"intends to leave the lord protector's household for Dudley's as the council grows displeased with the protector, who may follow his brother in short order, as Scotland is a mess and Boulogne all but lost."

I could not, would not, tell Hugh why I must stay with Mary till she was safely placed. That was one relationship I was not going to taint. "If this be true—and Thomas a dead man—I suspect that the Seymours or the Herberts will take guardianship of the child, and when she is well settled I shall return to harry you and your Cecily."

He stood and embraced me. "Do not tarry overlong."

A week later he sent me a letter, via messenger, saying that he had located Sir Richard Hibbart, recently returned for a time from Scotland, and made his introductions. "Alas," Hugh wrote, "when I shared with him that you were yet attached to Lord Thomas's household he declined to pursue further interest. It grieves me to tell you. With deepest love and affections, Hugh."

I now resigned myself to life with Hugh and his Cecily. I prayed in earnest that night for the Lady Elizabeth, that she would be able to withstand during her interrogations and would face friendly questioners, though I deeply doubted that she would.

Whilst Lord Thomas's household was being disassembled—which when done in advance of a trial was always ominous—Mary's household was to be placed with Lady Seymour, Edward's wife. Lady Seymour had a word for me one day.

"Have you made the household as small as possible?" she asked me. It was unbelievable how high-handed she was. In truth, she was my aunt, and the lord protector my uncle—and both knew it. Yet they had not a vial of compassion or affection between them for me.

I coolly shared with her the number of attendants and maids, the amount set aside for clothing, for plate, for horses and litters, and for all other manner of goods.

"Fine," she said curtly. "Sadly, there be no way to do with less for the daughter of a queen."

There was little to do but wait for gossip and reports of Lord Thomas's fall, so it was with enthusiasm that I looked forward to a visitor—Lady Fitzgerald Browne, who had written to say she was coming to stay for a day or two whilst she tended to her dower estates in London. I was not expecting the woman who accompanied her, though.

Dorothy Skipwith Tyrwhitt.

"Elizabeth." I embraced her first, as she led. Dorothy hung back, not knowing, I supposed, how I would receive her.

"Lady Tyrwhitt, I am pleasantly surprised to see you as well," I said, and fully embraced her. Once I did, she smiled back and embraced me with real feeling.

"Lady Tyrwhitt is visiting Hatfield; her husband's aunt is presently the Lady Elizabeth's governess."

I raised my eyebrow and was about to ask after Kat Ashley when Lady Fitzgerald Browne shook her head a little. That would wait for a later time.

"I'm going to rest for a bit," Elizabeth Fitzgerald Browne said. "And I'll leave you two to reacquaint yourselves."

I motioned, awkwardly, toward a richly stuffed chair in the receiving chamber. "Please." A manservant came and stirred the coals, and Lucy brought a tray of wafers and cheese and some watered mead and then took Dorothy's wraps from her.

"How do you fare?" I asked her.

"I fare well," she said. "My daughter grows. And I expect another child, though it does not yet show."

I kept a pleasant smile on my face and hoped I did not let the hurt bleed through.

"I came to see Kate's child," she said. "I hope 'tis meet with you. The queen had been so kind to me."

I stood up. "Of course." I motioned for one of the serving girls to come near. "If Lady Mary is not with Mrs. Marwick, could you please have her brought to me?"

The maid dipped and nodded her head and within a few minutes brought Mary to me. The babe wavered unsteadily in the servant's arms— she was just now able to hold herself erect, and her pretty brown hair was swept into one long curl on the side. She broke into a gummed grin when she saw me and reached both arms out toward me. I stood and grinned back and took her in hand before kissing her cheek. I spun her about a little and then handed her to Dorothy.

Dorothy handled the babe with assurance, as she was an experienced mother. She looked her over and made some quiet trilling noises for a moment and then looked her full on in the face.

"She does look like Kate a bit. But mainly, she looks of Lord Thomas."

I nodded. "I think that too. Same eyes." I took the babe from her and as I did I noticed that Dorothy's eyes went from mine, then to Mary's, and then back again. Some kind of surprise registered, and before she could make another comparison I handed the babe back to the servant girl after quickly kissing Mary's pink and fleshy cheek.

I sat down in the chair and took a cup of mead. It had not occurred to me that as the child grew she might look like me, which would give cause for whispers and speculation. "I am sure Kate would be pleased that you came to visit."

" 'Twas not the only reason for my visit," Dorothy said. "I came, mainly, after I heard from Tristram's aunt that you were here and attached yet to the household."

I looked at her queryingly but said nothing.

"John Temple is dead," she said. "He was run through with a sword in Scotland and died on the field cravenly fleeing the enemy."

I set my cup down. "Be you certain?"

She nodded. "I heard it from his mother herself."

I closed my eyes and let relief overflow my spirit. *"Vengeance is mine; I will repay," saith the Lord. Justice is not the domain of men, John Temple. It is the domain of God.*

"I hoped that hearing this would bring you some peace," she said. " 'Tis why I truly came."

I looked at her, and tears came unbidden, rolling down my face. So much had been taken, so little had been given in return. I had held my back and heart stiff for so long in order to assist Mary as we walked through the evil days that I had allowed myself little emotion. Now some was eagerly spent. "Thank you, Dorothy," I said with great feeling. "It does bring me peace."

"I daily repent that I told Tristram of the attack upon you," she said. "Have you absolved me? Because I have never been able to absolve myself."

I nodded. "I have absolved you, do not dwell upon this matter any longer. And you were right. I was haughty from time to time. You were right about Sir Thomas in many ways, though I would not hear it. I thought I knew much about all, and in fact, I knew little about much. I hope you'll absolve me too."

" 'Tis nothing near the same as my sins, but of course." She reached out and took my hand in hers and we both smiled. I felt, for a moment, that in spite of all that had transpired we were young women again, and great friends. "What came of your Irishman?"

"He left much of the business of his shipping in the hands of his brother and returned to Ireland to marry," I said.

"I'm sorry."

"I too."

We spent the evening talking about old friends, now married, some no longer with us, and of her children, born and not yet born. Before the night came to a close I gave her one of Kate's necklaces, a thin filigree of gold with a carefully wrought Tudor rose, of which Kate had two, for Dorothy's daughter. I would save the other for Mary. Kate, ever generous, would have wanted Dorothy's child to have it.

I found that I wanted her to have it too.

Dorothy left the next day to visit another relative, and whilst Lady Fitzgerald Browne was gone during the day she came back to Syon to spend one more evening with me.

We took our dinner privately, in my chambers, where I inquired as to the Lady Elizabeth's household.

"And now, what of Kat Ashley?" I asked. "Is it true that she and Parry are in the Tower?"

"Yes," Lady Fitzgerald Browne answered. "As I heard it, and I heard it from those who were there, shortly after Lord Thomas's arrest, Lord Denny and William Paulet arrived at Hatfield." She pointed to her plate of food. "After stuffing themselves like geese with the Lady Elizabeth's hospitality, they arrested Kat and Mr. Parry and had them sent to the Tower for questioning! Then they faced the Lady Elizabeth. Sir Tyrwhitt eventually became the inquisitor in chief—after first trying to trick her into believing him to be a friend and disclose all."

"Robert Tyrwhitt? Who was Kate's master of horses?"

She nodded. "The very same. And Lady Tyrwhitt, his wife, was right sharp with the Lady Elizabeth, implying in all manner that she had carnal knowledge of Lord Thomas and the sooner she admitted to it, the easier it would go for her. Sir Robert, of course, reported all back directly to the lord protector."

I set down my knife. "Kate would be horrified to hear that they were treating the Lady Elizabeth thusly."

"Indeed," Lady Fitzgerald Browne said. "And then they soon sent for me—to come and stay with the household and spy upon her."

"Why you?" I asked.

"Mayhap because I remain Catholic they think I am no friend to her, or mayhap because of the way her father ill used my family. But they forget that I was long in the Lady Elizabeth's household afore my marriage to Anthony Browne. I told them, rightfully, that I had never seen her in a compromising position with Lord Thomas, nor with any man."

I sent up a silent prayer of thanksgiving that it had been Elisabeth Brooke and not Elizabeth Fitzgerald Browne who had witnessed Lord Thomas's ill-conceived bedside pranks at Seymour House, though the Lady Elizabeth bore no responsibility for them.

"One night I heard her declare to Tyrwhitt that neither she, nor Parry, nor Kat had ever considered any man, not the admiral or anyone else, for marriage, but that it would have been approved firstly by the king's council. And then she dictated a letter to the lord protector, which her secretary wrote down whilst I was still in the room. In it, she said, 'Master Tyrwhitt and others have told me that there goeth rumors abroad which are greatly both against mine honor and honesty, which above all other things I esteem . . . that I am in the Tower and with child by my lord admiral. My lord, these are shameful slanders, for the which, besides the great desire I have to see the king's majesty, I shall most heartily desire your lordship that I may come to the court after your first determination, that I may show myself there as I am.' "

"And did the lord protector allow her to speak with her brother, the king?"

"Nay, not by any means, and you mark me, he will not allow Thomas to speak with His Majesty, either."

"Is the Lady Elizabeth safe, then?" I asked. "No matter what comes of Lord Thomas?"

She took a piece of manchet, ate it, and considered. "Yes, I believe so. They searched her rooms and found no trace of the lord admiral. And Kat and Parry say exactly as she does. 'They sing the same song,' Tyrwhitt has said, 'and she sets the note.' I believe she will come through safely, though just."

I was fervently glad that I had not left Thomas's miniature with her, nor his letters.

"But this may not be the last of it," she said, selecting a sugared plum. "In some respects, I wish I could smuggle the Lady Elizabeth to Ireland, as we did my brother, for safety."

Especially if, as the Countess of Sussex had predicted, King Edward died in but a few years—according to Sussex, his reign was half-over. The Lady Mary held little affection for the girl she believed to be the daughter of a concubine who had usurped her mother's place.

A few moments passed in comfortable silence as we ate and drank.

"I wonder," I began quietly, not looking at her, but still at my plate, "do you know of the Hart family? I thought perhaps you might, as they're Irish."

"Of course," she said. "I don't see much of Jamie, as he's oft up north in Sligo, I hear, or at sea. But Oliver and his wife, when they come to England, yes, I've seen them a time or two. We keep watch on one another against the English." She looked at me strangely. "Why do you ask after the Harts?"

"Jamie and I were . . . friends," I said. "I wondered how he fared . . . if he'd married." I could not stop the blush upon my cheek so I tried to cover it by quickly cutting another piece of meat.

She grinned knowingly. "I do not know, but I could surely ask. 'Twould not be difficult to get a letter to him. Or to his brother."

I shook my head. "Nay, but thank you." I leaned back in my chair and quickly changed the topic. "I am relieved for the Lady Elizabeth."

"I too," she said. "But I fear that Lord Thomas will not have such an outcome."

On February 25, 26, and 27 the bill of attainder against Thomas Seymour was read out in the House of Lords. On the third day it passed and was sent to the House of Commons. The bill was strongly objected to there, mainly because Seymour had been denied the right to speak for himself and much of the supposed evidence was hearsay; it was not seemly to attaint him without a trial. It was sent to the king for his consideration and on March 4, someone responded in the king's name that he did not think it necessary for Seymour to see the king. In the end, they even accused Lord Thomas of hastening Kate's death.

I wrote to Lady Seymour, on behalf of her granddaughter, Mary, and requested she come to London during this difficult time. I knew a messenger left often from Syon to Wulf Hall and I was surprised she was not already present. She did not respond to me directly, but had her secretary respond that Lady Seymour was too ill to travel and, in any case, had no interest in the present proceedings nor in Lord Thomas's child. It was ambiguous enough that I knew not whether she referred to me or to Mary. I was indignant for us both.

In March, Lord Thomas was found to be guilty of treason and sentenced to death by beheading. The warrant was signed by all of the king's councilors, but the first, and largest, name writ on the document was that of his brother, Edward Seymour. Thomas requested that his execution be delayed, that he have some of his own servants attend to him, and that his daughter, Mary, be left in the care of the Duchess of Suffolk.

His last two requests were granted, but not the first. On March 20, my father, Thomas Seymour, died by the harsh bite of the axe. Gerald later told me that it had taken two arcs of the headsman to fully sever his head and that when it rolled away his jaw was clenched shut with distress, a grim and terrible picture I knew I should not ever banish from my thoughts and dreams.

I dismissed all of Mary's servants that day and kept her to myself. After singing to her, I played quietly with the child and tried to ignore the pressing recollections of the hideous death of Anne Askew, the only execution I'd witnessed, which helped me envision Seymour's all too well.

I'd had, in my lifetime, two fathers and two mothers, and now I had none. Mary had had one of each and yet she was an orphan afore she had lived one year.

"What shall become of you?" I whispered as she slept, her warm neck tipped back into the crook of my arm. For six months earlier Kate had left all her money to Thomas. And Thomas, as a traitor, had been relieved by the council of every shilling. There was nothing left.

NINETEEN

Summer and Autumn: Year of Our Lord 1549
Winter and Spring: Year of Our Lord 1550
Syon House
Barbican House
Grimsthorpe

L ady Seymour, Edward's wife, could not rid herself of Mary's household quickly enough, now she had leave to do so. We were, to her, an infestation to be quickly flushed out. But I was determined to speak with her before we left, as she was Mary's aunt and mine. Her husband had, at best, helped bring this down upon us, if in fact he was not the architect in chief.

I sent one of Mary's servants with a note requesting an interview and, to my surprise, the duchess granted it. I met her in her fine sitting chamber. She had a page usher me in and seat me in the chair across from her. She wore one of Kate's finer diamonds. I looked at it, and then at her, with revulsion, and I saw her acknowledge my recognition of the piece and her pleasure in my so doing.

"Mistress St. John. You asked to speak with me afore you depart for my Lady Suffolk's London property, Barbican House."

"Yes, madam," I said. "I come to speak on

behalf of the child. She is motherless, she is fatherless. She is now, more than ever, in need of family who will champion and protect her. I know not why Lord Thomas chose the Duchess of Suffolk as her guardian, but I am come to ask that you will assist in caring for her. In particular, for her financial needs. Her mother was once rich"—I glanced at the diamond around Lady Seymour's neck—"but now Mary has naught."

She smiled superficially. "You'll be pleased to know that the council has voted to give Mary five hundred pounds per year for the upkeep of her household, as is becoming for the daughter of a queen. I shall ensure that the funds are delivered promptly to the Duchess of Suffolk."

I nearly collapsed with relief. I took her hand in my own and kissed it, not caring that she had been cold to me and sharp with Kate. She would see to it that Mary was taken care of. "Thank you, madam," I said. "I, I had not realized how rich in true Christian charity you are."

She smiled condescendingly. "I shall see to it that Mary's plate is sent along too."

I thanked her profusely and returned to Mary's chambers with hope. Five hundred pounds was a fair sum—enough to run her household with all the requisite tutors and educators, food for all, travel and servant expenses for Mary, and anything else she might need.

It was entirely possible that I would remain with

Mary as governess, now that there would be no new wife for Lord Thomas, as Kate had envisioned, nor any widower come along to marry me, as we'd once imagined. I wished that there was a pleasant prospect for the future, but there wasn't. I felt disheartened and downtrodden at the lack of possibility. I deeply loved the child, and always would, but this was not the life I had hoped for or desired. I would, however, see my vow to Kate through, and take care of Mary as long as need be. My loyalty now was as much or more to the sweet child herself as it had been toward Kate.

We were installed at Barbican House within the month. The duchess did not often eat with or entertain us, as she was oft occupied with flirting with her master of horse. She had a full staff of a hundred or more, many wellborn, and we fit in with her household and passed merry hours. I was surprised, then, that when I went to inquire about the pay for the staff for the month of July she dismissed her staff and closed the door behind them.

"I have not yet received any promised funds from the council," she said. "I have been paying the staff out of my own purse thus far, and, as you can imagine, this is a great expense to me. I am in difficult straits financially, and Mary is yet another burden. This cannot continue."

Difficult straits? She was clearly one of the richest women in the realm. And yet it was true that the five hundred pounds annually required for Mary's household was a sum under which anyone may falter and should have been borne by the king.

"I have written again to Lady Seymour, who had promised me that she would ensure that the funds would come for Mary. She has yet to do so, and she has kept Mary's plate for herself as well. 'Tis clearly an unsustainable position. I will write to Cecil and see if he can assist me in this. You may stay, Mistress St. John, as the letter is composed to see if there be anything in addition you care to add, as governess."

Her secretary came with his quill and paper and she began to speak aloud. "It is said that the best means of remedy to the sick is first plainly to confess and disclose the disease, wherefore, both for remedy and again for that my disease is *so strong* that it will not be hidden, I will disclose myself unto you."

She likened her guardianship of Mary to being slain with disease!

"I am in tight financial circumstances," she continued. "All the world knoweth what a beggar I am, and now most especially if you will understand, because the queen's child hath layen, and still doth lie at my house, with her company about her, wholly at my charges. I have written to Lady Seymour at large, that there be some pension allotted unto her according to my lord grace's promise. And yet, nothing comes despite my pleading."

Of a sudden, I recalled to me Kate's bitter comment that Lady Seymour "promises her friends many comings and performs none."

"Now, good Cecil, help at a pinch all that you may help. Will you plead on behalf of the allowance allocated for the queen's daughter, to be sent to me at once? Additionally Lady Seymour hath promised that certain nursery plate should be provided for Mary. See to it that you attend to this with haste, dear Cecil, as the child's mistress, along with the maid's nurse and others, daily call for their wages, whose voices my ears hardly bear, but my coffers much worse."

She looked at me. "Have you more to say, Mistress St. John?"

I seethed with the implication that I came daily as a lowborn beggar but also felt shamed for all that we were required to beg on Mary's behalf. "I would only respectfully remind the council, which is much bent, and rightly so, upon religious reform, that Saint James reminds us that pure devotion that is undefiled before God is to care for orphans and widows in their distress."

I turned and held her gaze and she mine. She knew I lightly rebuked her as well as them but I did not care. "I should like to visit my Lord and Lady Herbert, if I may, the queen's sister, to plead for their intervention upon this matter. I shall leave the babe in the careful hands of her nurse and other attendants."

" 'Tis a fine idea," she said a little dismissively.

I sent a messenger requesting a meeting with Lady Herbert, the queen's sister, and arranged to see her the following week. She met me in the oak-paneled room of Baynard's Castle, the whole house of which had been given to her as a gift by the queen.

" 'Tis good to see you again, Juliana," she said. Her warmth toward me gave me much hope. "How does my niece?"

I smiled. "She thrives. She can now roll over well on either side, and she has several teeth that harry her nurse. I read to her, often, especially from Kate's work, and she is in all manner a joy. Do come and call upon us and see for yourself."

"I will," she said. There was a silence. I knew she waited for me to broach the subject of our visit.

"You may be aware that the council had voted to allocate five hundred pounds for Mary's care," I said. "And yet, none comes."

She looked genuinely disturbed. "Has the Duchess of Suffolk approached them?"

"Many times."

"I fear I do not see how I can assist in this."

"If, by some evil token, the funds are not

forwarded to the duchess, and she is unable to care for the child, will the babe have a home with you here?"

She sat quietly for some time. "I wish it were, but I do not think that is viable."

"But why not?" My voice raised. "Did not Kate take your young son into her household and care for him out of her own privy purse?"

Lady Herbert nodded. "She did. But his care was not so dear as the care for the daughter of a queen. I am sorry. I wish I could help, but Lord Herbert will not agree to it, of this I am certain. But I will pray for a ready and meet solution."

"Lord Herbert has himself been enriched in all manner by Kate's marriage to the king. Mayhap he could sell one of the manors settled upon him as a result of that bounty and provide the yield to Lady Mary."

"He will not do thusly, Juliana. I am certain."

I stood up and snapped on my riding gloves. "Then there is little more to say, my lady. But I thank you for seeing me."

She smiled sadly and saw me out. I rode home; the serving men who rode with me lathered their horses keeping up.

The next day the duchess asked me what I had learned from the Herberts and when I told her she did not seem surprised.

"I shall write to the queen's brother," I said,

hope rising again. "And see if he might speak with the council on this matter."

"He has a weak back for such a burden," the duchess said. I curtseyed slightly and left.

Within a week I received a letter from William Parr's wife, Elisabeth, saying that, regrettably, they would be unable to assist. The lord protector was still enraged over their marriage and they were in no position to plead a case and might not long have a household together in which to raise a child. Elisabeth suggested the Seymour family.

Late that night I sat in my chamber, braiding and unbraiding my hair whilst I thought, letting the candle burn down to a soft disc. Was there no one interested in this delightful child, whose mother had done so much for them? And after all, Mary was cousin to the king.

As I finally dressed myself for bed, I realized something with a start. *So am I.*

The Duchess of Suffolk sent us to her estate in Lincolnshire, Grimsthorpe. It was less expensive there, she said. She also cut Mary's staff back to her nurse, Mrs. Marwick; myself—who drew no salary; Lucy and Gerald; and a handful of others. "It is temporary," she said, "and not sustainable. The child will soon need tutors, instructors, and expensive gowns and shoes. Cecil will apply to have the taint removed from Mary's name and her titles and funds restored to her. Her household can," she said pointedly, "repay me at that time."

I nodded solemnly, fervently hoping that funds would be forthcoming for such a repayment.

The duchess did not accompany us to Grimsthorpe; instead, she remained in London with most of her household spending time and money with Cecil for Stranger churches. These were being built so that those who were persecuted for their reformed faith on the Continent would have somewhere to worship, and mayhap stay, once they reached England's shores.

As we rode out of London, I remembered the Countess of Sussex's prophetic vision about the king's death. He had been on the throne two and one-half years. If her prophecy was correct—and she had always been true—he was halfway through his reign. I hoped that those building the Stranger churches were themselves prepared to flee to Stranger churches when the Lady Mary became queen. The rest of the way to Lincolnshire I thought about what would become of my sister, Lady Mary Seymour, daughter of absolute reformer families and presently with no money, no title, and no protector who would think to snatch her to safety as he fled the country if need be.

In October, when the leaves progressed from green to gold to russet, I received another visit from Dorothy Tyrwhitt. She and two servants had traveled an achingly long day to come to me.

I embraced her and stoked the fire in the chamber I'd had set aside for her in Mary's rooms.

"It is cheerless here," she said, noting the small staff, the empty hallways, and the distinct lack of furniture and tapestries in many of the rooms. The duchess kept her best pieces with her in London. "This is no place for you nor for a child. I had not imagined you as a governess. You were always so spirited!"

"'Twill be better once the duchess is in residence, assuredly," I said, avoiding her comment about my station, which, I admit, did not seem suitable for my disposition or inclinations. "I'm sorry I cannot offer you much of interest," I said. "But our cook is fine and is particularly good with the venison, which is well aged. Please rest, and then after we sup we shall walk together."

We strolled the autumn gardens, relishing the cold, like ice on a burn, arm in arm, as we had so many years ago at Lady Latimer's, and she shared gossip of London and the court. "Lady Herbert, the queen's sister, is with child again," she said.

"I wish her a safe delivery." I swallowed the grudge I had toward her for Kate and Mary's sake and Dorothy talked on of other tidbits of our friends and acquaintances.

"I was eager to visit with you, of course," she said. "But more importantly, I want you to know what is happening in London because it will affect Mary. I have not forgotten our friendship."

I puffed a breath of steam into the still air and said, "What is happening in London?"

"The lord protector is about to fall," she said.

I stopped dead. "No. How can this be?" And then I recalled that my brother had predicted this very outcome.

"He's alienated everyone with his arrogance and theft. He withdrew, abducting His Majesty to accompany him, to Windsor Castle and issued a proclamation for help. The king wrote that, as far as he were concerned, Edward Seymour had jailed him. 'Methinks I am in prison,' he said."

"Did Seymour not learn from Lord Thomas's attempt to do the very same? What did the council do?" I stepped around an abandoned bird's nest that had fallen from a high branch and broken upon impact.

"They had the lord protector arrested and taken to the Tower."

"On what charges?"

"The king himself said, 'ambition, vainglory, entering into rash wars in mine youth, negligent looking on Newhaven, enriching himself of my treasure, following his own opinion, and doing all by his own authority.'"

"Will the lord protector survive this?" Our situation grew more dire.

"Tristram says yes, but only for a little while. Seymour has been released from the Tower and even now he is fawning on the Lord Dudley, who has taken his place as lead on the council. His wife approached Lady Dudley practically on bent knee whilst the lord protector was in prison. She invited her to sup with her, presented her with a fine diamond, and asked Lady Dudley to speak to her husband on behalf of Edward Seymour. Lady Dudley did so, and Seymour is free. For now. But Tristram is having us leave London because he says this fragile peace will not last long, mayhap not last past the marriage, this coming spring, of the lord protector's daughter and Dudley's son John."

I nodded. I should have liked to have seen Lady Seymour on bent knee.

"As you and the child are so closely aligned with the Seymours, I wanted you to have a care. All who have been their supporters begin to flee now, for Dudley's camp. To be associated with them in any way will truly become, soon, a taint of its own."

I hugged her, grateful for her warning and the time, money, and effort it had taken to deliver it. Like the jackdaws scared up from Seymour Place to roost at Syon, Edward Seymour's home, the courtiers would now take wing from Syon toward Dudley's residence. Dorothy knew nothing of how this further jeopardized the babe, nor me. The Duchess of Suffolk had said she would soon run out of money for Lady Mary, though we were shut away with little left; she had made one final

370

application to the council on Mary's behalf and it would be heard in January. We returned to my rooms and Dorothy told me of the reformist work that her husband was involved in. And then, I knew that if I dared, I could repay her gift to me with a gift of my own.

"Do you hold faith in prophecies?" I asked her.

She nodded. "'Tis in Scripture, so of course."

"I shall share something with you that you must not pass along, excepting to your husband, of course," I said. "This is a confidence you must keep."

I did not say it to shame her for her last indiscretion—and she knew that—but rather to protect the countess.

"The Countess of Sussex told me, and Kate, of a vision she'd had that foretold Anne Askew's racking and death. Exactly as it later happened."

Dorothy leaned closer. "This be truth?"

I nodded and lowered my voice further, though there were none around that I knew of and we were well away from the manor. "But shortly afore she left the queen's household she shared another prophecy with me. She had foreseen that the king would not reign for more than five years."

Dorothy grimaced. "And then . . . Queen Mary."

"And then Queen Mary," I said, "who has no love lost for the reform or its champions. Have a care. Tristram is well-known."

She nodded solemnly. "Mayhap because of this prophecy, evil has fallen upon the Countess of Sussex."

"What evil?"

"She was questioned by a commission for errors in Scripture."

"Never! She held completely to the text."

Dorothy nodded. " 'Tis possible some have heard of her prophesying, and did not find it agreeable or understand it. Wriothesley convinced Sussex that his wife had been adulterous and bigamous. The countess claimed innocence, and of course she is innocent, but her husband threw her out. She lives in poverty, even now, in a foul, miserable corner of London. She has some friends and supporters—including my Lady Suffolk's sons, at Eton—but 'tis a difficult time, a difficult place. So now you know why I will be especially careful."

Wriothesley had played the lyre whilst Anne Askew burned and then helped Gardiner chase down the queen to near death. Now he incited against the Countess of Sussex. "I grow chilled, of a sudden," I said as I tucked her arm in mine and we made our way back to the house in silence. Inside, though, I was in turmoil over what had befallen the countess, who had foreseen the king's death, considered treasonous, and yet was compelled to speak. She had no protector. Neither did I. I had to determine what next to do.

• • •

Late in January, after celebrating the New Year in London at court, the Duchess of Suffolk returned with a small retinue to Grimsthorpe. She did not intend to stay but came to check on her property and the handful of servants tending it, and apprise me of unwelcome tidings. She called me into her receiving chamber, which had been warmed with tapestries she'd brought for her visit.

"Cecil applied to the council on behalf of Lady Mary," she began, "at my instigation. The council removed the taint from her and made her eligible to inherit all of her properties that had not been returned to the crown or otherwise assigned."

"This is marvelous, my lady," I said, flooded with joy to the point where I felt light-headed. But her countenance was not enthusiastic and I quickly became grounded again.

"It would be," she said, "if there were any properties or money left. Alas, others have already carved up her properties, incomes, and purse. Mary has nothing left to inherit, as it has all been given to or taken by them who will not gladly return it."

I sat down without being asked to, and she did not correct me. "But she is the king's cousin; surely he will insist."

"The king has no power in this, Mistress St. John. Power lies with those who received the bounty. Nor does His Majesty, I am sorry to say, seem to have sundry warmth for family, and has even, of late, taken to spurning his own sisters."

I nodded glumly. "So Mary is . . ."

"Penniless. And I cannot afford her upkeep in London, assuredly. Mayhap Grimsthorpe for a while. But I cannot keep her in this style, and as there is no money for her, I am sore vexed."

Within the week I dismissed Mrs. Marwick, whose milk had begun to dry up in any case, and hired a local girl to help with the child, who was beginning to prefer bits from the plate to milk. I did not ask for pay for myself, using instead money I'd saved from that earned whilst in Kate's service, which would last a little longer. My Lady Suffolk agreed to pay Lucy and Gerald, for some meager clothing and some shoes as Mary was now toddling about, and for a handful of other servants. It was an unreasonable expense, I know, for her to have taken on an entire household on her own, and yet none stepped forward to help. It was not sustainable, and truly, she, too, had tried. I did note, though, that her Christian charity was more concentrated upon large buildings for strangers and not the helpless child of a friend.

"Mayhap I can plead with Lady Seymour, the child's grandmother?" I asked.

"She's been asked," she said. "And refused. I think her cares now all be focused on her favored son, who is besieged."

"I have a certain . . . personal interest from which I might plead with her," I said.

The duchess looked up at me. "Yes, yes, now I do recall that Lord Thomas Seymour was, well . . . I see your point. Quite. Yes, mistress, if you desire to plead your case to her, do write. And send one of my messengers, if you like."

I spent the next weeks rehearsing how I might best appeal to a woman who loved me and my mother not, and who had already bluntly refused help to her own grandchildren. As far as I could see, this was Mary's last hope.

In late May a messenger came from Barbican House, the duchess's London residence. I had asked her for funds for Mary's clothing and an increase in the money required to feed her small staff. She replied that the clothing would have to do, for now, and that I should not expect her to return to Grimsthorpe until after the June wedding of Lady Anne Seymour, the daughter of the tottering lord protector, to John Dudley, son of the Seymours' rival and enemy. All of London would be present for the festivities.

"Will there be a response, mistress?" the messenger asked me.

"Yes," I said. "I shall have it to you tomorrow." I did not have any idea what I was going to say. I prayed for direction but, I admit, worried that there would not be an answer forthcoming as we had been left on our own for so long. I dressed

Mary in a slightly too-short gown and hose and took her hand.

"Walk, Am?" she asked me, her face delighted, as it always was when we took our daily stroll. Lucy had done up her hair in some small curls anchored by ribbons at the base of her scalp and she looked angelic.

"Yes, dearest, we'll go for a walk." She called me Am, not being able to say Juliana, and I took her first to the stable as she loved the horses best. When we got there, one of the stable boys waved us away.

"Do not bring the child here," he said, a worn look upon his own face, "nor come yourself. Jemmy's got tha plague and he was here just yesterday. It arrives right regularly in the summer now."

I hurriedly backed away from the stables, picking Mary up and clutching her close to me, quickly making my way to my own room, not to her chambers. Jemmy's wife was her new nurse. I called Lucy to me.

"Did you know Jemmy is suspected of having plague?"

"No!" Her eyes looked toward the stable, where Gerald sometimes worked.

"Gerald is in the house," I said. "But we must dismiss Mrs. Tiller, his wife, till we know she does not have it." I hurriedly scribbled out a note and put some money with it. By evening, the little household thrummed with fear, scattered among Grimsthorpe's many long corridors. There was not enough kitchen staff to light the hearth so we ate cold platters.

The messenger came to find me. "I be leaving in the morning, miss, no later, seeing as . . ."

I nodded. "I will have my response ready."

That night I stayed in Mary's room watching for any sign of the shivering or hot flesh that predicted the onset of disease. Who would have whisked this child to safety if I had not remained? There were truly none, save I, who loved this child, whose mother had so readily loved so many. They had divided the carcass of her inheritance, devouring it shamelessly for themselves. The king, whom Kate had loved so gently till the end, had not a word on behalf of his cousin. Gardiner, the wolf, would be set free when the Lady Mary came to power as queen and then the lambs the duchess spoke of so easily would not be merry.

I read to Mary in her room after her servants had been dismissed and she was quiet in her cradle. I often told childish stories to her, and tickled her and laughed at silly antics, but this night I chose her mother's book once more so she could know something of Kate. I began at the place where I had last left my own reading. Within ten minutes I began to tire and had almost closed the book when I arrived at a passage that startled me anew.

"But our Moses, and most godly, wise governor

and King, hath delivered us out of this captivity and bondage of Pharaoh. I mean by this Moses, King Henry the eighth, my most sovereign favorable lord and husband . . ."

I then closed my eyes. *Did you really think the king to be Moses, lady? Moses noble, leading his people, or Moses ill tempered, striking out to murder?*

Of a sudden, I was pricked with the desire to read of the account of Moses for myself. I reached into the cupboard in which I kept Mary's books and pulled out a copy of holy writ. I opened it to the second book of Moses, called Exodus, and read with opening eyes. Though pharaoh had commanded the children be slain, the midwives had cunningly hid them whilst claiming they were dead so they would not perish. And for their good works, they were promised by God households of their own. I closed my eyes in a rapture of certainty as I realized who was sent, in particular, to look after the child Moses, floating on the river.

His older sister.

Who knoweth whether thou art come to the kingdom for such a time as this?

My heart quivered with excitement and would not be stilled. I would not have to wait about any longer, allowing time and chance to overcome us. I stirred from the torpor that the mannerisms of court had lulled me into and determined to take action. I set Mary down and made my way to

Lucy's chamber. She was already abed in her knitted cap but she came to the door anyway.

"I have something to ask of you," I said. I told her of my plan and asked if she, and Gerald, too, would be willing to assist me.

"Ooh, I'm certain of it," she said. Her face gleamed. "Who can ye get ta help us, then?"

"I need someone who knows how to smuggle."

"The child's father is dead," Lucy reminded me.

"Someone of good character who knows how to smuggle," I said, amending it.

"*Your* father is dead too," she said. "God rest him."

My eyes opened wide. "You knew my father smuggled?"

She nodded. "We all did. He did ri' by it, though, not for profit, only for others."

I shook my head and pressed on. "There is one other."

"Tha man wi' the strawberries," she said, grinning widely. "I knew you'd come back ta him. You don't lose lightly."

I grinned back. "But I don't know if he will help. And he is like to be married already."

"He will help anyway," she said. "I told ya, he be a man."

The next morning I sent the messenger off to London with a letter for the duchess saying that, as plague had hit Grimsthorpe, I was taking Mary with me to Wulf Hall to plead with her grandmother in person. Then I handed him a second envelope.

"If you promise to get this letter to Lady Fitzgerald Browne at Horsley within a day, I shall pay you a month's wages in advance."

He took the letter, and the money.

"You must keep this to yourself," I said. "Or I shall find some way to come back and reclaim the moneys."

"I will do as you say, mistress." He left quickly, spurred on not only by money but by fear of contagion.

I watched him as he rode away, the horse's hooves sponging heavily in the mossy green, the horse's meaty flanks flexing as they made speed out of the property. I sank to my knees in the damp field and prayed, but with hope now, not caring if I ruined my gown.

Whom have we now but You?

TWENTY

Summary: Year of Our Lord 1550

We made our way in a litter with the drapes pulled, though it was summer and hot. We left Lincolnshire and then made our way to Rutland, whence we would then aim for Northamptonshire, Oxfordshire, and finally Wiltshire on the journey of one hundred fifty miles toward Marlborough. I made a great display of stopping at an ancient, mighty, and imposing cathedral headed by priests likewise described. I loudly asked one, "Where do you bury children who die of plague, if they are baptized? In consecrated ground? And whom shall I speak to about this if I have such a child who died on a journey?"

He indicated a lesser clergyman and could not remove himself from my presence quickly enough when I waved my perhaps contagious garments in his direction. I claimed to grow chilled and hot at the same time and asked if he could get me a drink, which he declined to do. He tripped on his robes upon his retreat. Should anyone come and ask after a child said to be buried quickly, due to plague, he would surely remember this encounter.

I headed back to the litter, in which Mary mostly slept or played with the leather straps that held down the draperies. Gerald drove the horses on, and soon enough we reached Brighton. It was nighttime, for which I was glad, as the cover of darkness allowed me to slip quietly into the house with Mary, up to my old room, and hope that no one had taken up residence there in my absence. Within minutes my brother's steward came to greet me.

"Oh, it be you, Mistress Juliana. Does your brother know you're here? Did any let you in?"

He seemed befuddled at my quick and strange arrival.

"He does not, but will you let him know that I am here?"

"He is with his lady, Cecily," he said. "But I shall call upon them."

I left Lucy and Mary in my room, instructing them to be quiet. " 'Tis a game," I told Mary, and she clapped her fat hands softly, played with Lucy, and obeyed. I went down to meet my brother, who soon came to me, hastily dressed.

"Juliana! Why are you sneaking into the house like a thief in the night?" He clasped me in a great embrace and called for food and drink, and my heart lurched because he looked so like our father. I told him that Gerald would need some of the same, that he was in the stables, and that I needed to bring some to Lucy, who was upstairs too.

"I have a child upstairs as well," I said quietly. "Though I wish that none should know of her."

"Your child?" He looked concerned. "Not that he wouldn't be welcome," he hastily added. Dear Hugh. He would welcome my child even it was baseborn.

"No," I said. " 'Tis Lady Mary Seymour."

I spent the next hour explaining the situation to him—from Edward Seymour's likely fall, which did not surprise him, to the refusal of all of Kate's friends and relations to help Mary, which did not surprise him, either.

"I may have been at court but for a few years," he said. "But 'twas long enough for me to take the measure of those men who betray their brothers with pleasure and little cause. There is nothing to be gained in caring for a child with no wardship, title, or potential. So what will you do?"

"I mean to raise her myself." I steadied myself to appear more confident on the outside than I did on the inside.

"Surely all will recognize her, if not you," he said. "We are of no account and like as forgotten already. But Mary Seymour?"

"I mean to take her to Ireland," I said, emboldened now. "I have friends who have told me that 'tis easy to be lost among the Irish. I plan to sail to Father Gregory and ask for his assistance. I can present myself as a widow and live on the money that would have been my dowry, if you agree. He will settle me in his village, I know, and give merit to my account."

I did not tell him that Thomas Seymour had prospered our family's income through his protection and trade connections, though it were true, and therefore some help toward Mary would be just. Hugh would give me the money for my own sake, I knew.

"And not marry? Nor bear children of your own? Even now, my Cecily is with child."

"Already?" I teased him and he adjusted his shirt in embarrassment. "I am so pleased, Hugh."

I kept my voice quiet. "I was once, whilst at court, attacked by a man who harmed me in such a way that 'tis unlikely I shall bear children."

"Who was it? I shall direct myself to him immediately!" Hugh stood up.

"He's dead."

"If he weren't already, he would be shortly," Hugh said. He grabbed me and pulled me close. I held him tight, then he brought me to arm's length before speaking. "You are welcome here."

"I know it, dearest." I reached up and wiped away his spilled tears, and then wiped away some of my own. "But Mary is my child now, and I must attend to her. It cannot be safely done in Wiltshire so close to the Seymours."

"None will miss her?"

"I shall have you send a letter from me, if you are willing, in which I tell the duchess that Mary died of plague on the way to her grandmother's, and that will be the end of it. All will be relieved not to have to fund her keep. None will make an effort to inquire lest they be held financially accountable for her should she be found."

He nodded. "I can arrange for passage to Ireland if you need it. On one of our ships. I shall have to tell Cecily of this matter but I shan't have to tell anyone else—not Matthias. Nobody. And of course you may keep your dowry funds."

I nodded. "I may need your help with the ships," I said. "I am hoping, though, that help is coming from someone who can better assist me to navigate Ireland once there. If I do not hear from him within two weeks, you shall have to find us passage. We cannot keep this secret longer."

We spent the days quietly, with Mary playing softly in my chambers; Hugh's lovely wife Cecily suggested allowing the dogs into the house—something our mother would never have done—to help Mary pass the time. I spent the day in nervous prayer, wishing I had the certainty of faith that all would be well. I had near given up hope when one night I heard a commotion between the manor and the stable. Hugh's man went down to see what it was, as 'twas past the time when visitors would politely call.

Lucy came racing up to my chamber. " 'Tis him! He's come, as I knew he would."

I will never leave thee, nor forsake thee.

I closed my eyes for a moment in rapture and then opened them with a small laugh. I knew he would come too. I hurriedly brushed my hair, but did not have time to slip from the simple gown I wore. I made my way down the stairway and as I did Jamie strode through the door.

I moved softly forward to greet him politely, but he brooked no polite compunction, and instead, he picked me up in his arms and spun me around afore kissing my forehead and then both of my cheeks. He did not kiss my lips, though I greatly wanted him to. I wondered if he were perhaps married but this was not the time nor place for such a conversation . . . yet.

"You came," I said, unable to hold back my tears.

"Of course I came, love," he said, and drew me to him, and then under his arm, whence I felt safe for the first time in years. I absorbed the feel of him, his arms tight about me, the scent of him, the spice of soap mixed with the lather of a hard ride, the look of him, a bit older but mayhap even a bit stronger. After some minutes those about us were stirring in curiosity, so Jamie took my hand and I led him to the receiving chamber, where my brother and his wife soon met us. His wife called for her servants to prepare a meal for the guest, and we all ate together.

Jamie's eyes rarely left me, nor my eyes him. I hungrily took in the curve of his chin, the sound of his laugh, and his attention toward me. After dinner, I stopped him. "Shall we talk?"

He shook his head and took my hand. "Not tonight. I and my men are right weary, and we must leave early tomorrow. The ship we have used to come and fetch you and Mary will shortly be required for commerce, and I expect you must pack to prepare to leave early." He must have seen my disappointment at losing his company, however temporarily. "Tomorrow we shall speak freely. I promise."

I reluctantly agreed, and my brother had his

steward show Jamie and his few men to their rooms. I remained with Cecily.

"How do you know . . . Sir James?" Cecily asked politely. She was sweet and interested but not rude or pressing, and I wanted to share some of the truth as I knew it might be the last time I could talk with my new sister.

"We were friends and, well, perhaps desired to be more, whilst at court," I said. "But our lives took us in different directions. I knew that he was honorable and hoped that he would come to help me and Mary now, in our hour of need."

"Will you marry?" she asked bluntly. 'Twas clear Hugh had not shared my predicament with her.

"I think not," I said.

"Be he already married?"

"I do not know," I said.

She pressed no more but kissed me softly and bade me come to her if I had any need before we left or even after.

The next day, while the rest of the realm was busily preparing for the Seymour-Dudley wedding, we prepared to make our way to the port at Liverpool.

As Hugh and I clung to one another and said our good-byes, he insisted I take the tapestry of St. George for Mary's chamber. "I do not want her to forget that she is English," he said.

I slipped off a rose-colored ring that had been a prized possession for many years and placed it on Cecily's finger. "Sisters," I whispered, and kissed her cheek. We took our leave, and I did not look behind me for fear of wanting to turn back, but I felt Hugh's desolate gaze upon me and I shared his misery.

Jamie and Gerald rode whilst Lucy, Mary, and I shared a litter that Jamie would pay to have returned to Brighton Manor. As he was the ship's owner, none questioned who his guests were. He showed Lucy and Gerald to a small, private room for the quick crossing and then installed Mary and me in his own stateroom.

There, over a small dinner of cold fowl and a goblet of wine, I shared Mary's sad story with him and reminded him that I planned to ask Father Gregory to assist me as I lived as a widow with the babe somewhere deep in an Irish thicket. "Elizabeth Fitzgerald assured me that I could be lost and not found if I chose not to be," I said.

He nodded. "She is correct. Few English bother with Ireland outside of the Pale, where most English live. We Irish help one another, and as soon as they accept you as their own they will close ranks around you."

"So you think my asking Father Gregory for help is a good idea?" I asked a bit wistfully, wishing, I suppose, that he would help me himself. His care of and affection toward me did not seem to be that of a man already married, but mayhap he had done as he'd said he would and married a woman not of his choosing.

I cast my eyes down and resolved not to allow myself further affection with him, in case he belonged to another.

"I think it be an excellent idea," he said. "As soon as I received your letter, I set some men to locate him and I'll take you there presently."

We set foot in Ireland and I was immediately charmed by the open, friendly manner of all who spoke to us, low- and highborn. Jamie had arranged for us to be taken some miles inland to the village where Father Gregory ministered.

We arrived at his small church midafternoon. Jamie held my hand as I got out of the litter and I held on to his hand longer than I needed to steady myself because I did not know when or if I would hold it again. Lucy and Gerald attended to Mary, who ran around in circles, happy to let her dimpled little legs regain their strength and her lungs fill with air to shout. I grinned and chased her for a moment, happy, too, to be carefree.

Father Gregory had heard the commotion and came rushing out of the church, taking me in his arms. His face was wrinkled with the age that the past eight years had bequeathed, but he looked happier than I'd ever seen him.

"Mistress Juliana," he said to me. Then he saw the babe in the background. "Or . . . lady?"

James stood forward. "Sir James Hart, Father. We're here to have you marry us, if you will."

My knees nearly collapsed and Father Gregory reached out his arm on one side and Jamie on the other to steady me. "Oh, no, no, we cannot," I said, though I could think of nothing I yearned for more.

James looked at me sternly. "And why, Juliana, can we not? Did I misunderstand you yet again?"

I looked at him quietly, begging him for patience, but I would have understood if he had none left. "Jamie, will you please let me speak with Father Gregory alone?"

Jamie excused himself and there, in the back of Father Gregory's lovely, tiny church, I poured out the whole story to him, including the visions, Mary's rejection by her family and friends, and John Temple's attack.

"Now you see, Father, why I cannot marry Jamie. I do not wish him to think ill of me, and I don't wish him to choose between having a family and having me."

Father Gregory took my smooth hand in his spotted one. "Do you want to marry him?"

I nodded.

"If he be man enough to fetch you after you rejected him, don't you think he be man enough to hear the truth and make his mind up for himself?

You were required to be strong and independent to master the years that now lie behind you, for Mary, and for yourself. But you don't need to make all the decisions on your own anymore. James must know the truth and then you must let him decide."

"Tell him *all?*" I asked.

"The truth will set you free, daughter," he said. "You have passed through many evil days. But now, perhaps, you have someone you can lean upon and don't need to stand alone anymore."

I held his gaze and knew that, though I was unwilling, I had always trusted Father Gregory and could trust him still. A tiny shoot of hope sprang up within me.

"Now, bring the child to me, and I'll feed your man and servant, and you set about telling your knight your tale."

I sat with Jamie in the gardens, the grasses whispering softly with a lilt of their own in the afternoon wind, and told him all. When I came to the part about my rape he stood up and marched away, running his hand through his hair.

"Who was it? Who did this? I will revenge you upon him and ensure he is unable to . . . harm another woman thusly."

I let him pace for a moment and when he returned to me I told him, "He's dead. He was run through with a sword in Scotland fleeing the enemy."

"Glad I am of it," he said. "The coward. I shall repay the Scots in favor somehow."

"Jamie," I whispered. "Do not think ill of me for bringing this upon myself. I was young and did not understand that if I spoke intemperately or wore a becoming gown I might engender such a response."

He drew near and took my chin in his hand. "Juliana. Love. You have not been thinking that you were to blame?"

I shook my head and let my gaze drop, unable to contain my sobs. "Perhaps. Perhaps partly if not in whole."

He came near to me and lifted my chin with his finger. "You, love, did not bring this upon yourself no matter what you said, no matter what you did, no matter what you wore. He was a knave and a criminal. You were, and are, innocent and strong. Be this why you rejected me?"

I nodded. "The midwife who attended me said I would like as not never bear a child due to the scarring. You love children, I know. I will never bear a son."

"*Mayhap* never bear a son," he said.

"Yes. I don't want to deceive you." I looked away.

He sat still for a moment. "It would be a sore disappointment, I admit, not to have my own sons to train and to inherit my estates. But there is no other woman I want to marry. As you see I am, these years later, still unmarried because I am besotted with you, have always been besotted with you. The topic is one I have let no one raise with me. You and me, and Mary, we can make our hearth merry. Is that not so?"

He lifted my face to his and the tears came again, spilling over my lashes, and he kissed the tears away.

"And, in my pride," I continued, "I didn't want you to think less of me for not being a maid. I wanted you to keep me in your heart and mind as pure and lovely."

"You *are* pure and lovely. I do not want to keep you merely in my heart and mind, love, but in my arms." He drew me close to him and as he did, I felt the truth of his words, truth that I had known, somewhere inside me, but that needed to be liberated by the affirmations of another. The hard nub of shame was replaced by the bright star of belovedness.

I am my beloved's, and my beloved is mine.

We stood before Father Gregory that very afternoon, Lucy and Gerald as witness, Mary napping in the nave, and were married. My heart sang with the birdsong that accompanied our simple wedding; my traveling gown was dusty with the journey, and perhaps that was apt, as man and woman were joined together for whatever life may hold.

I heard again the gentle whisper in my heart.

Who knoweth whether thou art come to the kingdom for such a time as this?

Yes, Lord, you have wrought all things together for good. Thank You.

Father Gregory kindly arranged for us to take over a nearby cottage inn for the night whilst Lucy, Gerald, and Mary remained at his parish house.

The servant laid out some cold ham and cheese along with fresh bread and some ale. She started the fire and turned back the finely wrought Irish linens on the soft bed. I dressed myself in a thin white gown edged with lace; I had not thought to bring anything to wear for a wedding night. And then I sat on the edge of the bed.

"I should have preferred to wear a lovelier gown," I said.

"No gown at all is required or, indeed, desired," Jamie teased, and when I blushed he laughed aloud. "You shall have to get used to the forthright speech of the Irish, madam, but I suspect you will fit in well. Soon you will meet my mother, and see what I mean."

"I am a bit afraid," I said.

"To meet my mother? You are English, so I can well understand that."

I opened my eyes wide. "Will she not take to me because I am English?"

"Nay," he said. "I but jest with you. What do you fear?"

"My introduction to the . . . intimate matters was not, as you know, pleasurable, but fearsome."

He stroked my hair. "Do not vex yourself, Juliana. 'Twill be different with a man who loves you, who would chase across the sea for you with a day's notice, who would forgo children of his own and love the one you bring. Who would die for you. We will take hours or weeks or months, if need be, till you are comfortable."

He kissed my eyelids again, and then my cheekbones, and then traced his way down my face till he nuzzled and kissed my neck, which commissioned a legion of chills to race over my skin. I warmed with desire and as I leaned into him and kissed him back again and again with more eagerness than I realized I felt, I was certain that all would be well.

Later, when we lay listening to the quiet call and response of insects tangled in the marsh grasses, he said to me, "Mayhap God hath sent me to bind up the brokenhearted."

I turned on my elbow to face him. "I thought you did not read holy writ."

"I have of late become convinced that it's better to be familiar with that which I transport," he teased, and then sobered. "I began reading it after you said you would not have me. For solace. I found it to offer that, and more."

I slipped as close to him as I could go. " 'Tis the truth, you alone bind my broken heart. In

His goodness, He has sent you. You are right."

"I'll be right about my mother taking to you too," he said. "Wait and see."

Although Jamie had his own estate that was deeper in Ireland, we stopped, on our journey, at his mother's home, which was nearby his brother Oliver's. I rode pillion behind him on his horse whilst the others followed nearby.

"Will you tell her that we are just married?" I asked. I nervously patted my hair and sought to brush any dust from my gown. "And how will you explain Mary?"

"I will tell her that you are my wife, and are now free to join me in Ireland, and that Mary is our child," he answered. "More will not be required. All knew I had set my heart upon you and might expect that we married afore I set out to sea. They can wonder and answer their own questions as they may."

I smiled and took his hand, glad to have married a bold man. "I do not wish to deceive her."

"We shall not," he said. "My mother is clever and kind, a secret keeper like my love." He slowed the horse, turned around, and kissed me afore we continued.

His mother received us in her sitting room; she was a quail of a woman bustling about her rich reception room.

Mary, exuberant, ran in first and giggled as we tried to chase her down for a more respectable entry. She bumped into Jamie's mother, marring Lady Hart's gown with her face, red-stained from the wild strawberries we had enjoyed along the way.

"And who is this wee beauty?" Lady Hart reached down and took Mary by the hand.

"I Mary," she said, and curtseyed unsteadily as she'd been taught.

His mother looked up at Jamie. "Mary! She's named for me!" She took the child in her arms and I thought how different a grandmother she was from cold Lady Seymour.

Then Lady Hart smiled at me as Jamie drew me closer.

"This is my wife, Mother. Her name is Juliana."

She took my hand and squeezed it before enveloping me in her warm, motherly embrace. After a moment, she looked at me kindly, but quizzically. "Juliana. 'Tis not a particularly English name."

I grinned. We would get on just fine.

Finis

AUTHOR'S NOTE

What ever happened to Lady Mary Seymour? This is an enduring mystery. The last known facts about the child include that Thomas Seymour did ask, as a dying wish, that Mary be entrusted to Katherine Willoughby, Duchess of Suffolk, and that desire was granted. Willoughby, although a great friend of Kateryn Parr, viewed this wardship as a burden, as evidenced by her own letters. According to biographer Linda Porter,

> On 22 January, 1550, less than a year after her father's death, application was made in the House of Commons for the restitution of Lady Mary Seymour . . . she was made eligible by this act to inherit any remaining property that had not been returned to the Crown at the time of her father's attainder. But, in truth, Mary's prospects were less optimistic than this might suggest. Much of her parents' lands and goods had already passed into the hands of others.

The five hundred pounds required for Mary's household would amount to approximately one hundred thousand British pounds, or $150,000 U.S., today, so you can see that Willoughby had reason to shrink from such a duty. And yet the daughter of a queen must be kept in commensurate style. Many people had greatly benefited from Parr's generosity. None of them stepped forward to assist baby Mary.

Biographer Elizabeth Norton says, "The council granted money to Mary for household wages, servants' uniforms, and food on 13 March, 1550. This is the last evidence of Mary's continued survival." Susan James says Mary is "probably buried somewhere in the parish church at Edenham."

Most of Parr's biographers assume that Mary died young of a childhood disease. But this, by necessity, is speculative because there is no record of Mary's death anywhere: no gravestone, no bill of death, no mention of it in anyone's extant personal or official correspondence. Parr's biographer during the Victorian age, Agnes Strickland, claimed that Mary lived on to marry Edward Bushel and become a member of the household of Queen Anne, the wife of King James I of England. Various family biographers claimed descent from Mary, including those who came down from the Irish shipping family of Hart. This family also claimed to have had Thomas Seymour's ring that was inscribed *What I Have, I Hold* till early in the twentieth century. I have no idea if that is true or not, but it's a good detail and certainly possible.

According to a recent article in *History Today* by biographer Linda Porter, Kateryn Parr's chaplain, John Parkhurst, published a book in 1573 titled *Ludicra sive Epigrammata juvenilia.* Within it is a poem that speaks of someone with a "queenly mother" who died in childbirth, the child of whom now lies beneath marble after a brief life. But there is no mention of the child's name, and 1573 is twenty-five years after Mary's birth. It may hint at Mary, but certainly does not insist, which is odd if it was Mary Seymour. Why not simply come out and say it, as was done for dozens, or hundreds, of other children of lower birth, if indeed it was a queen's daughter?

Fiction is a rather more generous mistress than biography, and I was therefore free to wonder. Why would the daughter of a queen and the cousin of the king not have warranted even a tiny remark upon her death? In an era when family descent meant everything, it seemed unlikely that Mary's death would be nowhere noted. Far less important people, even young children, had their deaths documented during these years; my research turned up dozens of them. Edward Seymour requested a state funeral for his mother, as she was grandmother to the king (which was refused). Would then the death of the cousin of a king, and the only child of the most recent queen, not even be mentioned? The differences seem irreconcilable. Then, too, it would have been to Willoughby's advantage to show that she was no longer responsible for the child if she were dead.

The turmoil of the time, in which Mary's uncle the lord protector was about to fall; the fact that her grandmother Lady Seymour died months after Juliana would have taken the child to Ireland; and the lack of motivation any would have had to seek the child out lest they then be required to pay for her upkeep all added up to a potentially different ending for me. The lack of solid facts allowed me to give Mary a happy ending, one I feel is entirely possible given Mary's cold trail, and one I feel both Kate and Mary deserved.

Parr's sister, Anne Herbert, was a true courtier, having served in every one of King Henry's wives' households; in 1552, only two years after the disappearance of Mary Seymour, Anne Herbert died too. At that time she was attached to the household of the Lady Mary, who would soon become queen.

William Parr, the queen's brother, was forced to set aside his wife, Elisabeth Brooke, during Mary Tudor's reign and return to his first wife, who was one of Queen Mary's friends. Parr had his titles and lands removed and Brooke was required to live by the kindness of her friends. When Elizabeth I became queen she restored to Parr his titles and parliament, his wife; Brooke became a close friend of the queen until Brooke died of breast cancer in 1565. Parr had a taste for witty, beautiful, highborn women and later married Helena Snakenborg.

Katherine Willoughby lost her two sons, then at Cambridge, within an hour of each other, most likely by plague, about a year after this book ends. I like to imagine that the deaths of her own sons would have given her a different, softer perspective on the orphaned daughter of her friend Kateryn Parr. Willoughby married again, for love, and had two more children.

Alas, the dynastic marriage lord protector arranged between his daughter Anne and Dudley's son John did not bring about the protection he himself needed, nor a lasting détente between the two families. Edward Seymour was beheaded in January 1552, just eighteen months after this book ends. His rival Dudley followed him to the block in 1553. But the Dudley family would famously live on through yet another son, Robert, the great love of Queen Elizabeth's life.

Of Kateryn Parr, Paul F. M. Zahl says, "Fortunately, providentially, a sheet of paper with the coming accusations scrawled on it somehow fell out of the pocket of one of the orchestrators. This paper was picked up by a Protestant—we have no idea by whom—and passed to Katherine. Katherine turned white, grasping the whole picture in exactly five seconds." I believe that the warning that document offered gave her the opportunity to save her own life as well as turn Henry away from Gardiner and his faction during the last months of the king's life. Like Zahl, I believe that was not coincidental, which is why I've written it within the context of a vision sent to assist her.

Historians, readers, and others throughout the ages have taken different positions on whether or not Thomas Seymour sexually assaulted the Lady Elizabeth or whether she was a willing participant. I firmly believe she was not. It's my own belief that he did not have intercourse with her, but I believe his sexualized teasings, ticklings, and other intimidations did add up to harassment, and it affected her the rest of her life. Seymour wielded great power in his household and Elizabeth had no power to stop him when she tried to. That, in essence, is at the core of all abuse, isn't it? In various circles, she's still sharing blame as people continue to ask to what extent she complied with or encouraged him. This, sadly, is so often repeated in modern-day society for those who suffer sexual violence that innocent victims often wrongly question themselves. This is why I wrote Juliana's thread thusly, and had Jamie rebuke that wrongheaded thought.

Upon Thomas Seymour's death the Lady Elizabeth remarked, "Today died a man of much wit and very little judgment." She was already precociously astute. Perhaps the questioning she underwent in this situation, no matter how uncomfortable, gave her the practice she needed to help her prevail during the much more important questioning that was to follow during her sister's reign.

The story of Anne Askew written herein is largely true, except for her contact with Juliana, of course. However, Kateryn Parr's friends and ladies most certainly did support Anne Askew, which was one fact that Gardiner's faction tried to use to trip them up and perhaps have them arrested. John Knox recounts that someone provided gunpowder so Askew would die more quickly.

The Countess of Sussex's account is also largely true, though I have fictionalized her much more than Askew for story's sake. Like the fictional Juliana, Anne Calthorpe, the Countess of Sussex, was supposed to have a gift of prophecy and was examined by a commission "for errors in scripture," and, toward the end of Edward's reign, was arrested for "dabbling in treasonous prophecies (sorcery)" and sent to the Tower. It was, of course, treasonous to imagine or speak of the king's death, so I tied those two things together in my story. Sorcery and prophecy were often confused during the age and the word *prophesyings* took on yet another meaning altogether during the Elizabethan years. Anne Calthorpe fled to the Continent when Mary Tudor became queen.

Those with the spiritual gift of prophetic visions

share that it is not like being a fortune-teller or seeing the future, and it is not at the person's beck and call. It may seem like the prophets of old heard a word from the Lord every day, but on closer inspection that is not so. The biblical account of the prophet Hosea covers a period of fifty to eighty years. During all that time Hosea may have had only five to ten prophetic visions or words from God. The prophetic gift is given to the prophet, but the visions are given when God chooses and normally for the benefit of others, often during times of danger or transition, and are not usually for the benefit of the person with the gift but for the body overall.

Prophecies may come in dreams, visions, or "hearing" from God in a person's spirit and can be either symbolic or exact representations of events. True prophetic visions never contradict other parts of the Bible and come to fulfillment 100 percent of the time. It may seem like a strange or unusual gift, but it's not. There are over 1,800 prophecies recorded in Scripture and many people, very often women, are actively using their gift of prophecy today.

I have taken a fictional liberty with Juliana as lector. During those years, the actual position of lector went to clergy-in-training, which meant men. However, the king specifically disallowed women teaching and reading Scripture in public during his 1542 Act, so it seemed to me that it was possibly happening or could possibly happen—Askew proves that to some extent.

I wanted to demonstrate that the real women in Parr's household were actively using all of their spiritual and intellectual gifts. Parr wrote and taught; Askew reasoned and boldly spoke out, eventually being martyred; Calthorpe had the gift of the word of knowledge and prophecy and was courageous enough to speak when called to; Willoughby used her financial resources to benefit reformed causes. There were steel frames beneath those soft and marvelous gowns.

Spelling was not standardized during the Tudor years; I have chosen to spell Kateryn's name as such because it is how she signed her own documents and because we know that Henry called her "Kate." Because Parr was a writer, much of what we know of her, in her own words, comes from her books and her letters. I have quoted some of them as books and letters, but there are other places where I have taken her own words and put them in dialogue, for the sake of getting the reader on the scene. Sometimes I have used her exact words, and sometimes I have retained the concepts but modernized the language to match her dialogue throughout the rest of the book.

I have sometimes made accommodations for titles: for example, I continue to refer to Lady Seymour as Lady Seymour even after her husband is made an earl and a duke simply so the reader will be able to better follow the story line and characters and not confuse her with the Countess of Sussex. Similarly, I refer to Elizabeth Fitzgerald Browne as Lady Fitzgerald Browne rather than simply Lady Browne or Elizabeth, because there are many people named Elizabeth in the book and I wanted to retain her Irish heritage. The genealogy charts are accurate, but I do leave off a few connections because they are placed at the front of the book, before the story. Some readers will not have known, for example, that Kateryn Parr and Thomas Seymour did marry and have a child before reading this book, and all will not know how Jamie and Juliana's story plays out. I did not want to spoil the surprise.

My deep desire is to add to the effort to rescue Kateryn from the only thing she is popularly known to have done: survived. She did much more than that. She was a warm and loving wife and stepmother, a generous emotional and financial benefactress, a learned and devout woman whose extraordinary books sold tens of thousands of copies and went back for many printings; they still resonate with today's readers. She was also a beautiful woman who had a blind spot for a bad boy, had a wry sense of humor, and was known to make mistakes and lose her temper a time or two. In short, Kateryn Parr was a woman many of us would have liked as a friend.

ACKNOWLEDGMENTS

Oh, how happy I am to write in the age of the long arm of the Internet, rare-book dealers, and out-of-print books magically reappearing in PDF. I have read parts of dozens, if not hundreds, of these while writing this book and yet one feels that there is always more to be uncovered. I have done my best to be as accurate as possible with the information available, but new information is being found and sifted through every year, so perhaps even more will be discovered about Parr and her household in the years to come.

This book would have been more difficult to write, less accurate, and less period-specific if not for the spectacular talents of Lauren Mackay, historical research assistant. Among other things, she expanded my list of good resources, corrected unlikely speculations and awkward period verbiage, edited the manuscript, helped brainstorm sixteenth-century solutions, and assisted in verifying sources and finding facts. She is an all-around genius.

Thank you, too, to those brilliant and kind author friends who read the book in its earliest stages and offered timely, pointed, and immeasurably helpful advice as well as life-giving encouragement: Liz Curtis Higgs, Debbie Austin, and Ginger Garrett. I truly appreciate Danielle

Egan-Miller and Joanna MacKenzie, simply the best and brightest agents in the world; my confidence is bolstered knowing that they are in my corner. Thanks, too, to the team at Howard Books that helps bring these books to life. Sylvia Croft, a humble woman with a gift of prophecy who instructed me and vetted the manuscript, was a God-given resource. Strongest thanks and home-cooked meals are immediately due my wonderful husband and children, who love me through the hand-wringing and late nights each book inevitably brings.

PRINCIPAL WORKS
OF REFERENCE

Elaine Beilin, editor. *The Examinations of Anne Askew.* 1996.

Nicolas Canny. *From Reformation to Restoration: Ireland. 1534–1660.* 1988.

John Foxe. *Foxe's Book of Martyrs.* Various editions.

Christopher Gidlow. *Life in a Tudor Palace.* 2008.

Maria Hayward. *Dress at the Court of King Henry the Eighth.* 2007.

Susan E. James. *Catherine Parr: Henry the VIII's Last Love.* 2009.

Colm Lennon. *Sixteenth-Century Ireland: The Incomplete Conquest.* 2005.

John Maclean. *The Life of Sir Thomas Seymour, Knight: Lord High Admiral of England and Master of the Ordnance.* 1869.

Natasha Narayan. *The Timetraveller's Guide to Tudor London.* 2004.

Elizabeth Norton. *Catherine Parr.* 2010.

Clare Phillips. *Jewels and Jewelry.* 2008.

Linda Porter. *Katherine the Queen: The Remarkable Life of Katherine Parr, the Last Wife of King Henry VIII.* 2010.

Evelyn Read. *My Lady Suffolk: A Portrait of Catherine Willoughby, Duchess of Suffolk.* 1962.

Alison Sim. *Masters and Servants in Tudor England*. 2006.

Chris Skidmore. *Edward VI: Lost King of England*. 2009.

David Starkey. *Elizabeth: The Struggle for the Throne*. 2007.

William Tyndale. *Tyndale's New Testament*. Translated by William Tyndale. A Modern-Spelling Edition of the 1534 Translation with an Introduction by David Daniell. 1989.

Brandon G. Withrow. *Katherine Parr: A Guided Tour of the Life and Thought of a Reformation Queen*. 2009.

DISCUSSION QUESTIONS

1. People sometimes say that, with historical fiction, we insert twenty-first-century values like "girl power" into the world of sixteenth-century women. But could that be a bit dismissive? How were women such as Kateryn Parr, Anne Askew, and Juliana St. John empowered in ways similar to and also different from contemporary women?

2. Two of the charges against both Askew and Calthorpe is that they were unnatural and unkind, mainly because they continued to use their given names in some capacity and for their forthright speech, especially where the exercise of their spiritual gifts was involved. Has that changed with, for example, women such as Anne Graham Lotz, or is there still a sense of that today?

3. Juliana felt social pressure to remain quiet about her sexual abuse, as there were messages, both overt and subtle, that she was "damaged goods" after having been assaulted and that those in power could twist the

circumstances to harm her reputation as well as bring trouble to those she loved. Are today's women equally pressured to "keep quiet" due to the shaming of society, with messages that the way they act, dress, or speak encourages rape? Or are young women today likely to speak up?

4. Why do you think most women are drawn to "bad boys" at one time or another?

5. Have you ever learned a secret that changed your life or the life of someone you know? What was it?

6. Although we come to understand why Frances St. John acted so dismissively toward her daughter, it did not undo the longing Juliana had felt her entire life. Kateryn Parr stepped in, as she did with so many others, as mother and mentor. Do you have a female mentor, or have you had a good mentor? What role did she/does she play in your life that is different from or the same as that of a mother?

7. When Kateryn Parr was mothering Juliana, she had no idea she was teaching her how to be a mother. That kindness was repaid in a way Kate could never have imagined, as Juliana then mothered Kate's daughter, Mary.

Have you known of a circumstance in which you or someone you know has given to another only to be rewarded unexpectedly in kind?

8. Juliana let her pride—her concern that Jamie would view her as unlovely if he knew the circumstances of her life—play a role in her silence. Are there issues today that women are reluctant to be forthcoming about, worried that others would view them badly, when in fact, the truth would set them free? What are some of those common issues?

9. Do you believe that prophecy is an active spiritual gift in today's world? Why or why not?

10. In the end, the haughty Lady Seymour was reduced, herself, to begging on bended knee for the life of her husband. In the end, Juliana got the man she loved and her own child, though perhaps not the way she expected it to happen. Do you believe that people eventually "get what they deserve"?

The Secret Keeper
Author Q&A

A CONVERSATION
WITH SANDRA BYRD

1. In the opening of the novel, we learn that Juliana occasionally has prophetic dreams, and her mother suspects of her being a witch. Indeed, many meaningful dreams end up coming into play in the novel. Why did you choose to use these as a medium?

I had a few reasons, all of which fused in the novel. "Seers" often appear in the Tudor genre, perhaps because spirituality was such an overt part of many peoples' lives then, or they more readily recognized it. I like keeping some traditional elements of a genre in the books I write, as long as I can do them a little differently. I hadn't seen it utilized and explained as a gift of the Spirit as explained in the Bible's book of 1 Corinthians, and so I decided to do that.

Much of this book is about women overcoming the roadblocks they faced, partly in the expression of their spirituality. Various women in the book have the gifts of teaching, of preaching, of giving, of prophecy, and one is called to martyrdom. I wanted to show women publicly exercising their spiritual gifts in an era which did not readily accept anything outside the norm—therefore, dangerous. And then there is that document that historian Zahl says was dropped and then found, warning Parr that accusations which would threaten her life were coming. I believe that was no accident, but was providentially arranged. My plot illustrates one way that could have happened.

2. Both *The Secret Keeper* and *To Die For* tell a story from the perspective of a friend. Do you think it is easier or more difficult to write from this perspective? How would you write differently if you were writing in the voice of Kateryn Parr?

I think it's easier to write from the position of a friend, because a friend sees things a bit more objectively than we might see ourselves and is able to report thusly. A friend sees our good moments, and our bad moments, and loves us anyway. Telling the story from the position of a friend gives access that, for example, telling it from the position of a servant would not allow. I don't know that it is easier to write this way; I think it depends on what you want to put across. In this series, I'm seeking an insight into the queens' hearts.

I never considered writing as Parr, because it

417

was important to me to tell a projection of Mary Seymour's story too. If I had written as Parr, I would not have had the relative outsider's viewpoint. Juliana was less protected, less studied in the ways of court, and less noticeable, with more freedom. It gives a different point of view than had it been from someone of great power. It was important to me to show the vulnerability of those at court.

3. Is there a reason you chose this particular moment in the Reformation as your background? What kind of research did you do for this novel? What was it like to write a fictional account of this monumental moment in British history?

I've always been enamored of Tudor England, so setting the books during that era was bliss. The English Reformation was transforming the nation during those years; religion played a major role in every sixteenth-century English reign and even those which closely followed thereafter. It is an angle which I felt was underexplored in historical fiction, but was a huge part of the everyday lives of Tudor-era women. Kateryn Parr was an on-fire reformer, perhaps much stronger than I've even put across in the novel.

To research, I read her biographies, I read her own written works, I researched what was happening in the world around her, and I read how she'd influenced others. I did a study of the rise of gentry during these years and also of the development of the Church of England. So much has been written, and will yet be written, about this amazing era; I simply hope that whatever books I contribute bring a new shading or nuance to the genre.

4. Juliana is raped by a man at court, John. Some of John's excuses seemed all too familiar to the modern reader. Was this a difficult scene for you to write?

Sadly, I believe the self-justification and excuses for rape are as old as humanity, and they haven't changed. It was a terribly difficult scene to write, and I didn't add it to the story line gratuitously. I wanted to show the real dangers women faced, and face, because of the lack of access to power and protection. Women then and now face significant emotional, physical, and social repercussions from rape. Wrongly ascribed shame and the physical damage persist long after the attack. Women today are still shamed into silence, though, thankfully, there are now legal consequences and help available in many countries. But it hasn't changed the numbers.

Up to half of all women still suffer sexual trauma of some kind during their lives. I wanted to acknowledge that, while also encouraging them that they, too, can still have a happily ever after, and to remind them that God sees all and promises to repay.

5. Anne Askew is another woman to face a horrible fate. As she burns at the stake, her religious convictions remain strong. Do you think that same level of conviction remains today? Or has it faded? What role does faith play in your life?

My Christian faith is central to my life, though as in any long-lasting relationship, there are times when God and I are close, times when I feel distant from Him, questions I wrestle with that aren't quickly or even ever answered, times I feel like I'm deeply in love, and times when I am angry with Him. When I work through things with God honestly (He's said, "Come, let us reason together," right?) our relationship grows deeper and more intimate. I don't feel the need to have a tidy, easily boxed-up relationship.

I think Askew's convictions remained strong because she had that certainty, that intimacy with the Lord, conviction, and the courage to stand. There are definitely people today with that kind of strength, but I don't think you'll find many where the living is easy! And if you do, once they begin to stand apart, the living won't be easy anymore.

What it will be though, is deeply rewarding in a way that an easy faith, or an easy life, is not.

6. How you imagine the fate of Lady Mary Seymour is a lovely answer to the long-standing mystery. Did you think of the ending before you wrote the novel? During? After?

I knew before I began the novel that I wanted Mary to live. There is no record that Mary Seymour died, and even the hints are ambiguous. I admire Kateryn Parr, I feel deep affection for her, if I may, and I wanted to give her daughter a life. The book is, at its heart, about mothering: the mothers we are born to, the ones we choose, the people we mother unofficially, and how important good mothering is. How we crave it. There is no doubt that Kateryn Parr mothered the Tudor children well. I think she had a gift for mothering. She mothered Juliana. And in a way she could not have expected, she reaped what she'd sown, in teaching Juliana how to mother Mary.

7. On your website, www.sandrabryd.com, the first line of your biography states: "After earning her first rejection at the age of thirteen, bestselling author Sandra Byrd persevered and has now published more than three dozen books." Was this the first story you ever wrote? What was it about?

Actually, it was a poem. And in my innocent naïeveté, I sent it off to a publisher and thought, well that is that, now I'll be published. I am forever grateful to the intern who took the time to send a rejection postcard to me. I think the first full story I ever wrote, as a teen, was about star-crossed lovers who were magnetically, tragically, melodramatically, attracted to one another, although they were from opposite poles, North and South. You can see why that didn't get published, either. But writers learn by writing and reading, and by being edited, so I expect it helped somewhere along the line, because here I am, published!

8. You offer your services as a writing coach on your website. If you had one piece of advice to give to an aspiring writer, what would it be?

I'd echo author Jane Kirkpatrick, whose work I admire:

> My best advice is to silence the harpies, those negative voices that say "who told you that you could write?" or "what makes you think your book will get published?" Just write the story of your heart and put duct tape on those harpies.

Sometimes the harpies are inside your head, sometimes they're other people. Find people who will nurture both you and your story, who help you protect your talent all the while insisting that you grow in your craft. And trust yourself.

Center Point Large Print
600 Brooks Road / PO Box 1
Thorndike ME 04986-0001 USA

(207) 568-3717

US & Canada:
1 800 929-9108
www.centerpointlargeprint.com

DATE DUE

DEC 1 0 2013			
AUG − 4			
OCT 1 5 2016			

LP
Byrd, Sandra
The Secret Keeper